Nelson's Cave

A. Isobel Sutcliffe

Whenever a doctor cannot do good, he must be kept from doing harm. Hippocrates

JaCol Publishing Inc.

Table of Contents

Acknowledgement

This book is dedicated to my sister, Jean Burey-Porter, RN, Midwife, BNP (surg). She called me one day and said, "What if…" and Nelson's Cave began. Her professional knowledge and tireless research helped Penrose's dream become fiction. Thank you, Jeanie.

As always, thank you, Randall Andrews and JaCol Publishing. Thank you, Karen Brosinsky Edwards for the cover.

Foreward

A. Isobel has been a joy to work with. Her enthusiasm at writing, and writing as many genres as she can concoct is only surpassed by her drive to produce. She has been a huge reason for the success to JaCol publishing, and hopefully the returns will be worth her time and effort, because her work is well worth the read.

randall 'Jay' andrews

1978. The boy smiled at the flutter of wings inside the shoebox tucked under his arm and checked the garden path for his father; the shed door closed on the bright afternoon sun. He set the box on the bench alongside a steel mouse cage. A quick inspection of his theatre; kitchen knife, scissors, cutthroat razor, cardboard tube from a toilet roll and threaded needle. He nodded, slipped his hand inside the shoebox and seized the bird. It made terrified sounds as he encased it in the tube with its head protruding. The cutthroat razor gleamed, his nostrils whitened and his heart soared as the feathery head fell away. He opened the mouse cage and grabbed the tiny rodent by the skin of its back, one slash severed its head—blood warmed his fingers. Taking up the bird head, he carefully joined the spinal column to that of the mouse and sewed the tiny mismatched muscles together. Halfway through joining the bird's head to the mouse's neck the shed door flung open.

"Penrose, what are you doing?"

Penrose tucked his patient under his shirt. "Nothing, father, I'm just playing."

Three steps and his father towered over him. His eyes flicked over the bloodied workbench and returned to his son. His voice quivered with rage. "Show me your hands, boy."

The boy scowled. His father, a professor of clinical medicine had little interest in his son's surgical obsession. Penrose made a dash for the door but his father grabbed the back of his collar.

"Show me what you have under your shirt, Penrose. Now!"

Penrose's lip curled as he presented the bird-headed mouse, and his father blanched.

"Put that down and go wash your hands. Then you can go to your room while I talk to your mother."

The boy's eyes tightened. "I hate you, Father. I hate you! All you care about is what little Kenzie does."

"Do as I say, boy! Now."

"Kenzie this—Kenzie that—Kenzie's such a—"

"Go!"

Penrose bared his teeth. "One day I'll show you all how clever I am. One day the whole world will know my name. One day—"

"Penrose! Do as I say!"

"One day, Father," Fury swelled in Penrose's breast and spilled from his tongue. "One day I'll make you proud or I will make you weep!"

His father's lip trembled out the words, "Go!"

Penrose sneaked from his room, pressed a glass to his ear and listened through the closed door to his parent's voices.

"Oh Elliot, what on earth did I do wrong with my son?"

"I don't think either of us did anything wrong, Poppy." His father's voice sounded muffled. "I believe he has a personality disorder."

"Do you think he's mad?"

"In the old days they called such disorders mad—even criminally insane."

"What do you suggest I do?"

"We, Poppy. I'm his parent too. Perhaps we should take my Aunt Dorothea up on her offer and send him to live with her."

"That would make life so much easier for little Mackenzie. Penrose seems to get some kind of thrill from inflicting violence. That scar on Kenzie's back will take years to fade."

It wasn't that his parent's sent him to Aunt Dorothea that upset Penrose, it was how. They bundled him into a Yellow Cab with his belongings and gave the cabbie Aunt Dorothea's address. From that day Penrose lived with his spinster, great-aunt. Dorothea Nelson was a biologist and a loner. The only person she had ever wanted to have around was Penrose; she adored her nephew's oldest son. She had inherited half of the family fortune but had little interest in money and all the joys it could bring. She had deposited it in a trust account and collected an annual dividend to live on, but she spent a fortune on Penrose's education. She encouraged him to perfect his surgical technique and guided him along the cutting edge of medical technology.

"But don't be just a surgeon, Penrose. Look deeper into the human body. Look inside the cells. I feel this is where we will find the secret of creation. I believe it is inside those cells where you" she tapped his chest with her forefinger, "will find your path to greatness."

The years and unchecked fanaticism rolled on, no idea seen as impossible; no concept seen as too monstrous or unethical. Each of them slightly unhinged, Penrose and Dorothea feasted on one another's genius

"Look Penrose, they have isolated the infectious protein, which causes scrapie in sheep and goats and Creutzfeldt-Jakob disease in people." Aunt Dorothea traced her grubby nail down the column in the scientific journal. "This could be the key—these transmissible and degenerative diseases of the nervous system occasioned by misfolded proteins might actually point you in the right direction."

2

2008. Penrose stopped centre stage and waited for the hum of voices in the auditorium to abate.

"Ye shall be as Gods!"

The veterinary students' chatter muted at his words. Professor of Molecular Biology, he loved to challenge his students to think divergently—nay—climb right out of the box.

"How?"

"Why?"

"More to the point, when?"

"Genesis!" Penrose Nelson eyed the youthful faces, bobbed his head and pushed his spectacles higher. "You are wondering why I am quoting the bible?" He aimed the remote control and switched on the overhead projector. "Molecular biology is moving so fast now that in the not-too-distant future, you—" he probed the room with the point of a pen, "—will have technology and know-how that we, even ten years ago, could only dream about.

"As you are aware, the genotype is the set of genes in the DNA that are responsible for a particular trait. The phenotype is the actual physical expression of that trait. Now..." Penrose strode back and forth; he licked bubbles

5

from the corner of his mouth and pontificated. "...the genotype that produces the phenotype in mega bats—in example—" he arrowed down the PowerPoint display, "—wings. With Darwin's natural selection in play, the superior or stronger phenotypes have the advantage, as it were, to get to breed more but—" he tongued a fleck of foam from his lip and turned from the screen. "I believe there is another factor at play here, partly because of the pace at which a fast breeding species can change. It is not just down to the rapid regeneration of the numbers in these species—and I feel, in time, research will tell us it takes such a miniscule alteration to the genome phenotype—that this could also be down to another at presently unknown factor in the equation. Not to disregard Darwin's law of natural selection, but it appears to me that with these miniscule differences there may be a factor in play here that could be used as a switch. If that factor could be uncovered then it would be more than possible to turn this back on in humans thus to clone an animal human hybrid..."

"What?" The voice reached Penrose from the higher seats in the auditorium. "You can't be serious!"

"Indeed, I am very serious." Penrose searched for the challenger. "Genetic engineering has given parents the ability to choose the sex of their child, why shouldn't they be able, in the future, to choose other enhancements?"

"Enhancements? But that's unethical!"

"Unethical by what standard? The bible? Hippocrates?"

"How about human morality?"

"We humans crawled out of the primordial swamp and evolved into the highest life form on earth. In a few years' time we may well have god-like powers to shape the direction of our future evolution. We will have the wherewithal to hasten evolution and take our species down any road we choose. Indeed, we may come to a fork in the road of evolution. Crossroads perhaps. Evolution in the traditional sense is over, how we evolve going forward is entirely in our hands."

"Are you suggesting we should mix our genetics with those of an animal?"

"We shouldn't rule it out. Take something another animal has that we don't—the ability to fly for instance. If we could keep our human traits of intelligence, language, and—and culture but add the ability to fly—wouldn't that not make for a superior human?"

Penrose scanned their faces and drank in their silence. A textbook clunked to the floor. Some heads nodded. Many batted away the suggestion.

"Imagine, if you will, a human who could—say—run at sixty or more kilometres per hour—can you imagine? Statistics prove that taller people tend to be more successful—can you imagine what that might mean for the future?"

"Yeah, mate." His heckler recovered his voice. "I can imagine a city full of ten-foot-tall people who eat twice as much as present-day people do. Use twice the amount of resources."

Another joined him. "Imagine if China produced an army of ten-foot-tall soldiers, what would the USA produce? Twelve—fifteen—nah fuck that, make them twenty feet tall."

"It's immoral—it's evil!"

"There's no good and evil knowledge, that's just a religious point of view. One man's actions can be seen as either moral or immoral, yes, but knowledge should not be labelled in that manner. To a scientist, to any intelligent person, all knowledge is morally neutral."

Voices hummed as the students spoke among themselves, eyes shone; hands gesticulated and framed hushed debate.

"Applying knowledge is part of the process of scientific discovery. In the laboratory, the scientist applies his or her findings to where each application leads. The ethicality rests with those who take the technology out of the lab and use it for corrupt purposes."

"No!" The interjector's voice quivered. "This goes against everything we have been taught about ethics."

"I think this bloke needs reporting—"

"Yes, yes, indeed—the science will pose many questions for debate, and it is a debate we should—must—have." Penrose pushed his glasses up the length of his nose and flicked another fleck from his lip. "Now we have much to cover so we will move on."

3

Agnetha was a fourth year student of veterinary science. Professor Penrose Nelson intrigued her. He wasn't attractive but neither was Agnetha. His lecture series on zoonotic diseases had been inspirational but today his talk on genetic engineering and subsequent debate with the students, turned Agnetha's curiosity into avid devotion.

As she left the auditorium, one of her friends whispered, "Jesus, old Penrose went the full Alphonse Mephesto today, eh?"

Agnetha didn't stop to argue, she hurried to catch sight of her favourite professor. She knew it was wrong but she followed him to his car.

"Can I buy you a drink, Professor Nelson?"

He looked her over and raised an admonitory finger. "Do you realise, alcohol can result in the build-up of liver fat, a condition most closely associated with cirrhosis and alcoholism. Heavy use can also result in diminished cognitive function and is implicated as a probable cause of several types of cancer."

Agnetha blinked, unsure if he had just rebuffed her advance.

"However, it also has many benefits such as lowering your risk of cardiovascular disease. It can promote longevity, improve your libido and it is thought to help prevent the common cold. It also decreases the chance of developing dementia. It can reduce the risk of gallstones and lowers your chances of developing diabetes. So of course you may buy me a drink." The thick lenses of his glasses shrunk his irises to pea size and his intense gaze made Agnetha blush.

"I can?"

"Certainly—yes. I am in need of the calming effect of alcohol."

He accompanied her to a pub full of drunken students. As he sipped a scotch, he gave her and a glazed-eyed group of fellow students a lengthy history of distilling, brewing, and fermentation.

"…and so you see, this is why people with European genetics have such remarkable tolerance for a substance that can poison people of other ethnicities.

Agnetha frowned as a Chinese-Australian student hiccoughed and raise his glass. "Cheers, mate."

"That is fascinating, Dr Nelson."

Penrose Nelson smiled; he had small teeth and large ears. His brown eyes fixed on Agnetha and her heart gambolled in her chest.

This man must surely be my soul mate.

She had done her research; he was twenty years her senior and worked for a private medical research company attached to the university. In a fun-facts file she had found in the faculty webpage, he enjoyed reading, had Asperger's Syndrome, and loved fruit bats.

Agnetha began dating Professor Nelson, the first was a trip to a prawn farm in the grip of a white-spot disease outbreak. On their second date Penrose took her to visit a flying fox colony. Agnetha had never had a steady boyfriend; most of them dated her once and fled. With her parents' encouragement, she took Penrose home to meet them and her sister, Annifrid. While Penrose talked at her glaze-eyed parents, Agnetha could contain herself no more. She broke the good news to her sister.

"He asked me to marry him."

"You're kidding!"

"I can hardly believe it myself but it's true."

"But he's weird!"

"No, he just has Asperger's, that's all. I thought as a psychology student, you'd have recognised that in him."

"A psychological textbook would need a special chapter to accommodate that weirdo! What do you see in him? He's not even good looking!"

"I'm not interested in physical appearance; it's the man inside I care about."

"I fear the man inside might be uglier and weirder than he appears on the outside."

"I think you're jealous, Annifrid."

"I think you're being taken for a ride, Agnetha. I know the symptoms of Asperger's; that's not Penrose Nelson's problem. I can see signs that he is some kind of sociopath. You need to be careful."

"So you don't like him."

"I hate him."

"I should've known you'd be like this." Agnetha turned her back. She had found her place in the universe and that was by Penrose's side.

4

Penrose squinted at the people sitting opposite. Three of the faculty heads sat in various poses of censure.

"I have been teaching here for ten years, you've never had cause to doubt my methods before."

"As I said, we've had several students complain. Did you, or did you not, advocate unethical cloning?"

"I raised the subject of genetic engineering as a technology that will—might be available to them in the future. I suggested they think about the direction of molecular biology and what it might mean for humanity going forward."

"Did you, or did you not, suggest mixing animal genes with those of a human?"

"No—well—yes! But it was meant to inspire them to think of the possibilities." Penrose laughed and a rivulet of sweat meandered down his spine. "I wasn't suggesting they try it—I mean—heaven forbid!"

"Mr Nelson, we're going to insist the recordings of your lectures are reviewed in future. You are advised to stick to your field of zoonotic diseases. Your email account will be closely monitored too." The department boss's head panned left and right to her colleagues. "Does anyone have anything else to add?"

"Only this, keep within the guidelines, Penrose. I like your work but if you bring this institution into disrepute again, I will withdraw my endorsement."

"Do you want to raise any further points, Penrose?"

There were many points Penrose wanted to raise.

You're a rabble of narrow-minded imbeciles. Stupid, jumped-up public servants who wouldn't know good science if it fell in your lap and laid an egg. And don't fucking-well call me mister, you moron!

"No, I don't."

Penrose hissed between clenched teeth as the door closed behind him. He mumbled his way along the corridor and hissed again as the lift doors opened.

5

2009. One year later. The lab might have been empty. The triple row of fluorescent lights glared above the stainless steel benches, white walls, and bacteriostatic floor. A Spartan white clock ticked on the wall, the minute hand nudged seventeen minutes past eleven. The man hunched before the screen of an electron microscope, his soul quivered on the brink of epiphany. The hum and whir of electronics the only sound until he cried, "Eureka!" and smacked the desk with a surgical-gloved hand. Penrose Nelson leapt to his feet and cavorted in a circle, the stool twirled across the room in a drunken waltz but revelry held little place in Penrose's nature; he straddled the stool and trundled back to the console to continue his task. Meticulous by nature, he often fogged glass beakers as he held them eye-level, to measure the water for his coffee. He trembled with excitement as he worked on through the night, oblivious to the pain in his shoulders and back. He gathered his data and formed a plan.

Before he left the building, he stopped to check on little Blossom and Myrtle, the fruit bats he and his colleagues had used in their efforts to find a cure for the new zoonotic pathogen they called Hendra virus. A code among scientists dictates they never name the animals they experiment on, but Penrose loved his fruit bats.

His voice pitched up to falsetto. "Good morning, my lovelies! I have a special treat for your breakfast." From the refrigerator he produced a two bowls of sliced mangoes with drizzled warm honey on them. "There you go. Ooh, Myrtle, you're a hungry girl this morning." Years hunched over his work had given Penrose bottle shoulders; his large head jutted forward vulture-like on his skinny neck. "Big things are coming to our world, girls. The future belongs to the Pteropus poliocephalus. Eh?" A bubble gleamed on his lip as he pouted, "We'll show those nasty old humans."

On his way home, Penrose pulled in at a seven-eleven and bought a carton of milk and a bunch of flowers.

At home, he shook his young wife, Agnetha, awake.

"I bought you some flowers, Agnetha. They are Lilieae hybrids, commonly called Lilliums. I notice the florist has used Gypsophila or baby's breath as a visual enhancement."

"Oh! Thank you, Penrose. Flowers for me—how considerate you are."

"You should put them in water to extend their serviceability." Penrose's tongue swiped a bubble from the corner of his mouth. "I believe they use a little bleach to stop the water from becoming rancid. One point two-five millilitres to a litre is recommended."

Agnetha hurried to the kitchen to find a vase, Penrose watched her go then fetched his thermometer. He returned to find his wife in the living room, shifting the flowers to the exact centre of the coffee table.

"Penrose, they are so pretty." She inched them a little further left.

"Come here, Agnetha. Stand still."

"Yes, Penrose."

Agnetha stood without question as Penrose lifted her hair and held the thermometer to her ear. "Perfect." He laid the thermometer on the coffee table beside the flowers, grasped the hem of Agnetha's nightdress and pulled it over her head.

"Penrose!" She gasped as he threw the garment aside and twiddled both her nipples between finger and thumb as if adjusting the volume.

"I believe you may be ovulating, Agnetha. I need to make a human embryo. Come, I have work to do."

****

The stirrups pinched Agnetha's ankles but she daren't complain. Her husband's lab was no place for such whiny behaviour and she would never distract him from his world-changing work.

"Are you sure this is going to work, Penrose?"

"I'm quite confident. I've had to review my own work and I have found myself correct in each of my expectations."

"What were those expectations again, Penrose?"

"That there is so much of our DNA that appears unused you might say. Almost as if nature, nurture, accident, God—call it what you may—has experimented with particular traits and then discarded or at least set them aside when they proved not useful for the conditions being faced by that particular organism. It appears to have discarded the trait but not the actual genotype."

Agnetha gasped as Penrose probed a little too hard.

"I believe that this has been kept in our DNA as junk. Mother Nature's reserve if you will—set aside for some future contingency. I, after years of painstaking research, have found a way to switch certain, selected factors back on. Mother Nature is rather blasé with the fate of her miracles. For instance, take the millions of sperm used and discarded in the race to fertilise an ovum. Only one makes it and the ovum shuts the others out and thus millions are wasted. The fall and rise of millions of species does not appear to faze the lady at all and yet she saves a lot of what would appear to be junk. In fact, Agnetha, she's something of a hoarder."

"It's a little like a Facebook account, Penrose. You can delete it but it just stays—" Agnetha bit her tongue. Penrose's blank stare exhorted her silent. Likening Mother Nature's DNA collection to a social media account was unworthy of a Veterinary Science undergraduate.

"Now, keep perfectly still, Agnetha." Penrose pushed his spectacles higher with the back of his wrist and inserted the speculum.

Agnetha lay immobile with teeth clenched.

Close your eyes and think of England.

Her thoughts meandered to Penrose's younger brother whose work she had known of long before she met Penrose. She had only met him in person one week before. Mackenzie Nelson was a star in the world of natural science. Handsome and extroverted, the golden haired boy of the Nelson family; all the world knew of Kenzie Nelson and his nature documentaries, his books sold in their millions. Few people even knew the famous biologist had an older brother. Agnetha shared her husband's contempt for Kenzie and his shallow portrayal of the natural world. Kenzie had never taken part in an animal rights rally as Agnetha and Penrose often did. Instead, Kenzie Nelson sought a camera and a microphone and asserted his coveted opinion.

Penrose withdrew the speculum. "Now, you need to lie there until morning and then I will take you home before my colleagues arrive. You must spend the coming weeks doing as little as possible. I will do the cooking and cleaning."

"Penrose, can I take my feet out of the stirrups now?"

"Of course and I will get you something to keep you warm. I must not allow anything to cause you distress."

6

Penrose watched his wife closely over the coming months. The floral dresses she always wore grew tight and she often plucked at her yellow Doc Martin boots. Her feet and face swelled in hot weather but otherwise she remained healthy. A less clinical man might have appreciated the glow of pregnancy hormones, he might have even crossed his fingers that all went well. Instead, he injected T Cells to prevent her body rejecting the foetus. Pregnancy induced hypertension set in with the second trimester and Penrose took her to an Obstetrician. He and Agnetha, though both atheists, refused an ultrasound scan, citing religious beliefs.

Week twenty-two arrived and all seemed well. Penrose arrived at work and went about his duties, chatting to his colleagues, Robert and Mandeep, while he watched the centrifuge spinning vials of blood.

Their conversation came to an abrupt halt when Agnetha burst through the door.

"Penrose! I think—" She stopped and clutched her skirt to her crotch. Amniotic fluid gush down her legs and into her Doc Martins, a pool of bloody slush spread across the bacteriostatic floor. With a squelch and a viscid thwack, the foetus fell to hang by the umbilical cord. It writhed and swung like a pendulum between her ankles.

Mandeep's eyes bulged. "Jesus! Mary—mother of fucking God! What the fuck am I seeing?"

Robert, Penrose's boss, gaped at the tiny creature that quivered and slowly sank towards the floor. Nature, wilful and indelicate, saved the worst for last; the placenta delivered itself with a sickening splat on the floor beside the foetus. The tiny creature's mouth opened to emit a faint whine.

"Oh, Penrose—" Agnetha sobbed. "I've ruined it for you."

Mandeep circled and tilted his head. "What the fuck am I seeing?

"No—no, it's too early." Penrose fell to his knees and gathered his experiment. A monster—premature and tiny. He pressed a finger under its wing stub, searching for a pulse.

Agnetha's chest heaved. "Can't you do something?"

Penrose squeezed the tiny chest, working air in and out of its lungs. The heartbeat faded beneath his fingers.

"It's no use, it's too early."

"What is that fucking thing?" Mandeep's voice gained pitch but lost strength.

Penrose jumped to his feet and hurried to the store cupboard.

"Are you going to explain what the hell that is, Penrose?"

"What the fuck—?"

Robert cut off Mandeep's question with one similar. "What the fuck have you been doing, Nelson? Speak, damn you!"

Penrose shouldered aside his colleagues as he ran back to the lab with a canister of liquid nitrogen. He set it on the floor next to Agnetha as she sobbed, frozen to the spot in her soggy and bloodstained boots. He eased the bat-child—placenta and all into the basket, lowered it into the vapour and twisted the cap tight. He straightened to face his white-faced colleagues.

"Can't you see? I have created the greatest miracle—the most important breakthrough of medical science in history! I have mixed the genetics of humans and megabats. I have made a new species!"

"You made a fucking monster! And you broke every law of ethical medicine!"

"Why—but, a—aren't you thrilled?"

"Thrilled? I'm bloody horrified."

"But I—"

"I always knew there was something badly wrong with you, Mate. You're a fucking madman."

"Please don't call the police! Please—they will stop my experiment! The government will take it away from me!" A fleck of foam landed on Robert's shirtfront as Penrose pleaded.

"Police! Why would I call the police? Fuck that—Jesus! I'd never hear the end of it. As far as I'm concerned, this ends here—it didn't happen. You're fired. Take that fucking freak and get out!" Robert raked a shaking hand through his hair. "What the fuck am I going to tell the faculty?"

****

That night, Mandeep Singh paced the floor, the scene in the lab played on a continuous loop in his mind. He worried he may have developed some mind-altering, bat-born disease. He measured his temperature but found nothing out of the ordinary. Strewn across the coffee table, spilling onto the floor were books and journals, and every PDF file he could printout on genetic engineering. Gradually the horrible truth busted through and gushed contention over everything he had learned about genetics. Somehow, Penrose Nelson had defied the laws of nature and created a human-bat hybrid. That tiny creature writhing in the hands of its father—creator—refused to leave Mandeep's thoughts. A ding startled him and with a shaking hand, he snatched up his phone. A text from his girlfriend, Deanna, *'Meet me and the gang for cocktails in the city.'*

He replied, *'A boozy night on the town is exactly what I need.'*

'Sweet, see you there.'

7

Alice Barnes wandered into the lounge to set a plate of roast chicken and vegetables on the coffee table.

"There you go, Darl. Chicken and veggies."

"Thanks, Alice. Can you get me another beer before you sit down?"

"Sure, Darl."

"Hurry back, Alice, the news is coming on."

Eating dinner in the lounge while watching TV had become routine in the Barnes household since Barry had retired. Their children had left home years ago and they could be a slovenly as they wished. Their years of setting a good example were over.

"Jesus, Barry, did you hear that?"

"Huh?" Barry set his can of beer on the coffee table, belched, and forked up a spoonful of pea-freckled mashed potato.

"Shh, listen."

'*...University is tonight denying any knowledge of a failed attempt to genetically engineer a human with wings.*"

"What the fuck?" A couple of peas rolled down Barry's front and disappeared between his legs. "They did what?"

"Shh, listen!"

'...the Queensland Premier tonight stated that no such thing had taken place.'

The footage switched to the hard-hat, Day-Glo vest-wearing Premier at a sod turning ceremony. *'I don't know where such a nonsensical story came from but there has been no genetic engineering at any of our universities. Now, if any of you have questions to ask about the government's infrastructure projects I'm here to answer—'*

A persistent journalist threw another question at the group of politicians. *'A story has surfaced today on social media that a scientist at a government funded university has been sacked after he attempted to mix human DNA with that of a fruit bat. What have you got to say about that, Premier?'*

The premier laughed. *'That is the silliest thing I have heard since the leader of the opposition said he could balance the budget in his first three years in office.'*

A claque of nodders chortled.

"She batted that one back at them eh, Alice?"

"Sure did, Barry."

"If that scientist wants to experiment on fruit bats he should come up here to Warby Creek. Every week there seems to be a few hundred more of the stinking mongrels."

"Sure is, Darl."

"A man'll have to give this up." Roy muttered and dragged on his cigarette. "Stupid nanny state won't let me smoke in the pub anymore and standing out here might just kill me."

The years of smoking had charred his olfactory nerves, but not enough to deaden the stench of flying foxes. The midsummer heat had seared Warby Creek for three days and hundreds of flying foxes had dropped from the trees and died in the streets. Roy scowled as he watched a team of council workers bagging the dead animals.

"Gidday, Rapid Roy," the team leader called. "Ya want some lunch?" He waved a dead bat a Roy and grinned.

Roy gave him a sour glance, dropped his cigarette butt into the sand tray and retreated into the bar of the Warby Creek Hotel.

"The stink got too much for you, Roy?" Dave the barman filled a glass and set it on the bar.

"Yeah, fuck it, Dave. I reckon them greenies all want us to move to the city where they can control us."

"Hm." Dave grinned and picked up his tea towel. "Something like that, Roy."

8

People often said Penrose Nelson's insanity equalled his intellect but Penrose was medically sane, though few psychologists would disagree with a verdict of dangerously psychopathic. Caustic and offensive one minute, perfectly charming the next. He channelled the absent-minded professor when it suited his purposes and feigned Asperger's Syndrome when expediency demanded. He charmed, bullied, manipulated, and lied his way through life. He'd taken Agnetha for a wife because he had anticipated in the near future, he'd need her ovum. Now disaster struck; Agnetha's womb had proven ill equipped to birthing a variant offspring, and he'd lost his job. He paced, hissed, and ranted, bemoaning his former employers' lack of foresight. Just as he thought things hit rock bottom, Agnetha had to be hospitalised with severe blood loss requiring surgical intervention to save her life. The resulting hysterectomy with complicating infection ended Penrose's ambitions for her womb. All his hopes lay dashed with the sight of Agnetha's reproductive organs flaccid and spent in the plastic kidney dish Penrose insisted the surgeon show him. He spent three days worrying about the future but then good fortune befell when all seemed lost.

Right on cue, great-aunt Dorothea died and left him her vast estate. The cresting wave of Penrose's madness rolled on, the crash would break over the rocks of mankind somewhere in the future.

Comfortably unemployed, he ventured north to look at a run-down farm near the rural town of Warby Creek where a small flying-fox colony had taken up residence. The weatherboard house was old and creaky with no hot water and a frog infested septic toilet attached to the back. Blackwattle Hollow, the last item of a deceased estate. On Grinder's Gully Road, the real estate agent had pointed to the house just visible among the trees.

"There's the place, it needs an awful lot of work. I can show you much better properties around the area."

"I'll take a look at this one first."

"Okay." The real estate agent checked his watch.

Later that day, Penrose returned alone, he wanted a closer look; he had noticed something that piqued his interest but the agent had seemed keen to get back to town. Hidden some seventy metres behind the house was an entrance to an enormous limestone cave. When he ventured in, Penrose saw its potential. The previous owner had concreted the floor for about twenty metres into the cave as if he had contemplated converting it into living quarters. Where the concrete floor ended, the cave continued, winding deeper, into the mountain. Penrose listened to the distant dripping of a subterranean spring. He returned to town and paid the bemused real estate agent a deposit for Blackwattle Hollow.

He and Agnetha spared no expense when they built their sanctuary close behind the house and began taking in orphaned and injured wildlife. Penrose outfitted a modest surgery for his wife in the back room of the house. For his experimental purposes, Penrose transported in a pre-fabricated laboratory. Situated in the wattle scrub behind the house, the ordinary building revealed nothing of the sophisticated interior. He kept the liquid nitrogen canister stored in a cupboard in the lab. Inside the cave, he assembled cages and prepared for his new venture. The smaller cages in the lab housed four black-market mandrills—one male and three females. His other experiment he kept in a more comfortable cage with warm bedding and toys.

As they unpacked their belongings, Agnetha watched the news. The story of a missing two-year-old boy led the bulletin, Agnetha clucked her tongue at the sight of the distraught parents, pleading for the public's assistance.

"He's your child; you should have taken better care of him."

9

Warby Creek got its name from the waterway that ran through the town. One hundred and fifty years old with a population of around two thousand people, the town had become a Mecca for tourists who visited to snap photos of its beautiful heritage buildings and old country charm. They drank coffee and enjoyed the relaxed lifestyle. For one hundred years, the Warby Creek Hotel had been the social hub of the town. Along the street, a variety of shops thrived. In the year after the Nelsons bought Blackwattle Hollow, the flying foxes' numbers began to increase. There had always been a small colony along the creek. Then one week, around fifty took up roost in a fig tree near the town hall. A month later, their numbers had swollen to fifty thousand; another month passed and the town played host to an estimated three-hundred thousand, defecating over everything and urinating in the town's water supply. Wildlife experts told residents to be patient—the bats would move on in a few months. Two years passed and they remained. The acidic excrement peeled the paint from buildings and cars; many families fled the stench and relocated to a bat free area. The stink and noise of the bats

33

halted the steady stream of tourists to the once lively rural town.

Two notable events happened that year in Warby Creek.

Stressed beyond endurance after an expert chiropterologist told him the flying foxes' rights outweighed those of the people, the publican, Jack Nolan, dropped dead as he hosed bat faeces off the front of the Warby Creek Hotel.

A month later, the ADF decorated and discharged Major Tom McPherson, SAS Regiment and wounded war-hero. After twenty years serving his country, he came home to stay. He bought Sunnyview Farm on Grinder's Gully Road, one kilometre from the edge of town. It shared a boundary with Blackwattle Hollow. The town's progress association held a welcome home party at the Warby Creek Hotel. Invitations found their way into every letterbox across the district.

Agnetha Nelson's face contorted as she read about the war hero and screamed, "Murderer!" She crumpled the invitation and threw it into the corner of the living room where it would remain for another two years. "And they gave him a medal for gallantry. Filthy murderer!"

Tom McPherson didn't attend his welcome home party and nobody dared ask why. At an intimidating six

and a half feet tall, limping about with a walking stick—
surly and reclusive; the people backed off and left him
alone. Locals whispered he wasn't the same good-natured
boy who had left home all those years ago.

10

Tom limped around the kitchen and made a lonely breakfast. He smiled as he gazed out the window across a brown paddock, he liked Sunnyview Farm. The house was a little too big for a single man but comfortable and modern. Later, a truck would deliver a load of Hereford cows, all guaranteed in calf. He looked down the length of hairy leg protruding from his boxer shorts. The scars healed well. Those on the middle of his knee and either side of his ankle looked much less dire than when they removed the cast. The spot scars where they inserted the rods into his femur and tibia would diminish in time. The worst, where the blast ripped into his calf muscle would take years to fade.

After breakfast, he sat down to watch TV. He'd take it easy; when his new herd arrived there'd be plenty of work to do. A car approached, sunlight reflected off the windscreen and through his window. The temptation to pretend he wasn't home circled in his thoughts but he dismissed it. The front door stood wide open. Well, if they were here to tell him about God, they would get the short shrift; he'd already banged on heaven's door and found it wanting. He waited. The click of heels on the concrete path made him sit up.

"Hello?" A woman's voice.

"Come in." Tom frowned at his boxers and hoped she had a broad mind. A vision of vivid green eyes and red, spiralling curls stepped into the room.

"Hello. I'm Celina—I came to say welcome to Warby Creek." Celina was all dimples, plump lips, boobs and pretty legs; silver heels wove a strappy web around her delicate feet. Tom swallowed the jibe poised on the tip of his tongue.

"Uh—thanks." He checked her out, his heartbeat accelerated and the stalk in his shorts stiffened. "Does Warby Creek always send you to welcome newcomers?"

Her cheeks grew pink. "No—I saw you in town the other day and thought you looked lonely."

"Desperately lonely now that you're here."

A smirk played about her lips. The breeze through the window carried her scent to him—expensive perfume and lust. Such a woman on such a golden morning.

"Are you a hooker?"

"Of course not! Is it such a crime to be attracted to someone?"

"Not in the least." As Tom rose, her eyes widened— women often reacted that way. One of the perks of being tall. He drew her against him and her arms slid around his neck. "You're not going to cry rape, are you?"

"I've never wanted a man as much as I want you."

His cock throbbed against her softness, He lifted her leg, and his mouth devoured hers, biting and sucking. Along her thigh, he groped his way to the elastic of her knickers. His probing fingers brought forth a whimper; her hands slipped into his shorts and pushed them down. He found the zipper on her dress and eased it open; she wriggled it to the floor. Her eyes held his as she slipped out of the black lacy underwear and stood before him, naked and inviting.

"Come on, you big hunk." She bulldozed him back onto the couch and straddled his lap. He cupped her breasts as she slid onto him.

"You don't waste any time, do you?"

"No need for foreplay when I've done nothing but think about you for days." She rocked her hips, taking him deep inside her. "I knew you'd be huge."

"How about that? And I didn't know you existed."

"Are you glad I'm here?" her breath was ragged on his neck, her lips nibbled, her tongue flicked.

"Immensely. A pleasant surprise, for sure."

"Would you like me to come back?"

"Every day if you like."

"I wish I could, but I have to work." Her lips devoured his, their tongues entwined. He kissed her savagely; his hand encircled her waist, her breasts bounced and swayed with each thrust. He strained, mind and body to fight the rush building inside him. The need to explode a rising crescendo—he growled with pleasure as she cried, "Oh God!" and his pulsing cock gushed deep inside her.

The months rolled on and Celina visited several time a week. Tom found himself eagerly anticipating her visits. Her perfect little body with slightly oversized boobs never failed to electrify him. His feelings for her became deeper, he wanted to know more about her but she evaded his questions. On Anzac day, he arrived at the cenotaph to pay respect for the fallen soldiers of years gone by and saw her standing in the crowd with a man who looked close to fifty. On his hip, he carried a little red-haired girl and he held Celina's hand. Celina had played him for a fool. She looked every bit the happy wife and mother. Tom scowled as Celina's husband took the stage to make a speech. *Sweet!* The mayor, Peter Edwards, obviously didn't know his wife had a lover and he, her lover, never knew she had a husband and a child.

"Hello, Tom." She appeared beside him and touched his hand.

Tom folded his arms and looked at the mayor. "You're married."

"Yes, I guess I should have told you."

"You guess."

"I'm sorry."

"You took off your wedding ring so I wouldn't know."

"I'm sorry—"

"It doesn't matter, forget it."

"You don't mind?"

"I do mind. A lot. Stay away from me."

As Peter Edwards finished speaking, the crowd applauded. Tom walked away without looking back.

11

The new mother bared her teeth and clutched her baby to her breast. Her head jerked about, the big yellow eyes darted from Penrose to Agnetha.

"I'm going to have to tranquilise her while I examine the baby."

"What's wrong with it, Penrose? It seems to have flippers instead of feet."

"Yes, I fear I may have, once again, switched on some of the more primitive parts of DNA."

"You'd have to go a long way back to find a mandrill with flippers."

"Don't make light of my work, Agnetha."

"But can't you see, Penrose. It is funny."

"I said don't laugh!"

"That last one had a beak-like thing on its face. This will be another to add to the freak show in the cave."

"And the next will succeed."

"Wings are what you're aiming for, Penrose. Try to give the next one wings, not gills. Or flippers. Or feathers."

Penrose's fury reared. He hissed and swung a stinging slap to his wife's face. "I said don't laugh, Agnetha!' Drool flew from his mouth. "I am negotiating a path no man before me has treaded—there is bound to be a few small missteps. I will succeed in the end—I always do."

Agnetha picked herself off the floor. "Yes, Penrose."

"I am creating new life, new species to add to the earth's ever shrinking menagerie. I will not have you making light of my work, Agnetha!"

"Yes, Penrose."

"Now get me the tranquiliser gun."

"Yes, Penrose."

12

Barry Barnes had had enough. Outside a beautiful sunset beckoned and he glowered at the distorted picture through the kitchen window. The sun sank behind the Ranges and turned the clouds from golden to pink to red. As he watched, a splatter of green muck hit the glass and slid down in three separate rivulets, each vying to reach the silky-oak frame first. The one with the chunk of undigested substance had its nose in front. All his life, Barry had loved his peaceful little town of Warby Creek, nestled in a wide valley in the ranges, its people had maintained the heritage buildings in mint condition. The town had spiralled into ruin since the colony of grey-headed, fruit bats had taken up residence in the trees that provided shade in the heat of summer and shelter from winter winds. As the fruit bat population grew, they destroyed the trees and covered the streets and houses with their acidic excrement. Their screeches and squabbles filled the air from dawn until dusk. As night fell, they blackened the sky overhead as they set off to forage. Their stink lingered heavy in the country air.

"Fuck it!" Barry's false teeth shot from his mouth but with reflexes born from years of loose dentures, he snatched them mid-air and rammed them back in place.

"Alice! Those fucking flying foxes have destroyed this fucking town."

"Yair, I know." Alice shook her perm. She'd grown used to her husband's foul mouth, exacerbated by the aches and pains of age, and the arrival of the fruit bats. She prodded the shredded cabbage; another ten minutes on the boil should render a translucent slush. She turned back to the enamelled bowl of mashed potato and recommenced the attack; pounding and whipping the roots to slurry. "Sausage and mash for dinner, Darl," Alice announced. "Onion gravy too."

Barry watched some locals dash along the street with boxes, newspaper, and umbrellas aloft as they headed for the pub. He straightened and eased the cricks from his spine. "I'm just gonna nip up to the pub for a few minutes, Alice."

Alice sighed. "Okay, Darl. There's some cash in my purse."

Barry flicked open a camouflage umbrella that leaned outside the front door. It had originally been white but several years of flying fox shit had turned it kaki and brown. Some strange little native bees had found it ideal for their hive and gummed it with splotches of wax where they had built into the folds of fabric. The bees had abandoned it when the umbrella's usage increased but their wax remained in chunks over the canopy. Barry held his breath as he emerged from his house, trying to avoid breathing the rancid stench of a quarter million fruit bats. In the street, the volume of their squabbling increased to ear splitting. Splatters of excrement rained upon Warby Creek.

As he approached the batwing doors of the Warby Creek Hotel, the shit-eating grin of the mayor raised Barry's hackles. A couple of years on the right side of fifty, his rakishly unkempt hair had a textbook smatter of grey at the temples. Peter—the Poser—Edwards bared his almost but not too perfect teeth at Barry.

"Gidday Barry! How are you going, Mate?"

"I'd be better if I didn't have to carry this fucking umbrella every time I wanted to go outside."

"Well, you know how it is, Mate. The bloody greenies won't let us do anything about the bats."

"Tell the fuckin' greenies to take a hike and do something yourself—there's plenty of men in town with shotguns who are willing to blast the bloody things to kingdom come. But you won't let them will you? Cause you want to run for parliament and if you piss off the greenies too much the city politicians will think you're a redneck."

"No, no—it's not like that at all, Barry."

"Not fuckin' much." Barry partially closed the umbrella then let it flick open again, hoping to dislodge some of the shit and send it flying onto the mayor's face. "Oops, sorry."

Not.

He slid in, "Arthritis you know."

I might have known, shit doesn't stick to Peter the Poser.

Barry pushed past the mayor and let the batwing doors spring back—once again, his effort to land an accidental blow on the mayor failed.

A group of young people sat around sipping beer and eating chips. Nearby a game of darts drew raucous cheers and guffaws. Balls clicked on the stained felt of the pool table. The noise of the public bar almost drowned the screeches of flying foxes. Barry inhaled; since the state-wide ban on smoking inside public buildings, the pub's smell had changed. Now only beer and perfume—female and male—filled the air. He breasted the bar and ordered his usual starter kit. A nip of OP Rum and a ten-ounce beer chaser. He threw the rum past the back of his tongue, swallowed and coughed. The warming effect had immediacy more akin to an anticipated physical reaction than reality. Still, it warmed his limbs and numbed his senses.

"Ay Baz, in for your nightly heart starter?"

Barry lifted his eyes from the foam of his beer to Dave, the publican's father, working his evening shift behind the bar, while his daughter spent some time with her kids. Sara Nolan had tried to sell, but since Warby Creek had become a colony of filthy flying foxes, the real estate market had collapsed. Her father's arrival had eased the burden.

"Gidday, Dave. How's it going for you this evening?"

"Can't complain, mate." Dave glanced at the mayor further along the bar. "Well I can. Cleaning flying fox shit off the beer garden took me all morning. It has to be done even though nobody uses it. I no sooner get it cleaned and the bastards cover it with a fresh layer.'

"Must be a pain in the arse, Dave."

"Mate, I swear, this town is screwed if we don't get rid of those filthy animals."

"Try telling that to the politicians. Did you go to that town meeting last month? Those bastard politicians sat there and smiled. Just because we live in the bush, they take us for idiots. They told us to put up with it—they're endangered you know."

"Endangered?" Dave's eyebrows disappeared into his hairline.

"Endangered my arse! There must be a million of them living in this area and they weren't here until a couple of years ago."

"They're being pushed out here because of urban development on the coast."

"Yeah." Barry threw a scowl at the mayor. "Old Poser won't do anything. If he can get himself elected to State Parliament he'll leave us here to fend for ourselves."

"We're already doing that." Dave straightened as the batwings creaked and the hubbub of the barroom dwindled. Barry followed his gaze; Tom McPherson limped through the batwings and advanced on the bar, ignoring the drinkers either side of him.

"Tom, Mate! How are you?" Peter the Poser sidled up to the newcomer with outstretched hand. "I see you've stopped using the walking stick—good to be on the mend, eh?"

Everyone watched, eager to see if McPherson treated the mayor differently to themselves.

He greeted Peter with a non-committal grunt and ignored the hand as he pulled a handful of notes from his jeans. "A bottle of Scotch please, Dave."

"How's the farming and roo-shooting business, Tom?" Peter swung the unshaken hand back and forth past his thigh, undeterred by the ex-soldier's surly response. As

Barry looked on, he recalled the day when Tom McPherson had returned to Warby Creek eighteen months before, after years of active service. A former Major in the SAS Regiment, he'd retired after injuries received when a roadside bomb had exploded. He had never told anyone what his injuries were, but since he walked with a limp, speculation settled on a broken leg. Tom ran cattle but shot kangaroos as a sideline and helped Roo-box Ruth McPherson, his elderly aunt who ran the local game-meat abattoir.

"It's alright."

"Guess you like to shoot things, eh?" Peter laughed.

McPherson's lip curled as he stuffed his change in his pocket, snatched up the bottle, pushed past Peter and made his way out the door.

Rapid Roy, the local barfly seated at the end of the bar, came to life. "I don't think 'e likes you, Peter."

"No—Tom's okay. He has a few issues."

"Ya wanna watch 'im, he's barkin' mad."

"Don't be silly, of course he's not."

"I wouldn't be so sure. I heard 'e was discharged as non-compost mantis." Roy raised his hand and drew a circle in the air around his ear. "Off 'is rocker from too much killin'." Roy's moniker came from his ability to down a beer, not from his mental or physical athleticism.

"You shouldn't say things like that, Roy. He's a war hero."

"Hero or no, I reckon 'e's dangerous."

"Well, thanks for the drink, Dave. I'd better be getting home." Peter drained his drink, set the glass on the bar and retreated.

"That Peter's a dodgy bastard." Roy's malice switched focus as the batwings stilled. There simply wasn't enough available information on Tom McPherson for a lengthy assault; the mayor, however, was a veritable goldmine. "I reckon he's ticklin' the till down there in the White House."

"Can you prove that, Roy?" Dave's eyes flicked from Roy to Barry and back.

"Nah, but I've heard rumours."

Barry lifted his drink to his lips and paused. "Rumours from where?"

Rapid Roy shrugged. "You know how people gossip."

"Yeah. We sure do, Roy."

"They reckon 'e's rootin' his secretary, too."

"Here, drink this and shut your mouth." Dave thrust a glass of beer at Roy, as a mother would stuff a pacifier in the mouth of a squawking baby. He extracted payment from Roy's cash pile on the bar.

At the pool table, a local began singing, "Flying fox frolic, flying fox frolic, screeching all night in the mango trees—" His mates joined him. "Flying fox frolic, flying fox frolic, mister flying fox fly away please."

"Boys!" Dave bellowed across the room.

A local lad potted the eight ball and flourished the song's ending. "Fly away please!"

"Boys! Stop now, you know I banned that song, now shuddup!"

The old John Ashe song faded into giggles and snorts. "You're a killjoy, Dave, that's what you are."

"Sing it again and you're barred for a month."

Barry drained his drink. "Well, I better get home, Dave. I'll see you tomorrow."

"Goodnight, Barry."

13

Tom McPherson held the umbrella over his head and climbed into his Landcruiser; night fell over the town but high above the sun's dying rays illuminated the endless flight of fruit bats. He tucked the bottle of Scotch into the glove box and hit the ignition. Another night of shooting kangaroos and staying as far from people as he could. It wasn't that he especially disliked the company of his fellow humans; just their stupid questions pissed him off. *'How many people did you shoot?' 'What's it like to be shot at?' 'Did you really get blown sky-high by a bomb?'* And from one local lad—*'Did you get much Afghan pussy?'*

As Tom pulled away from the kerb, Peter Edwards exited the pub.

Just another politician with a mouthful of words. Why, Celina?

The local mayor had never stopped trying to befriend him. Even without his stupid remarks, Tom would still keep his distance. His little affair with Celina had left its mark on him. Tom wasn't entirely convinced he wouldn't go back for seconds. For that reason, he kept his acquaintance with Peter at arm's length. There were no single women of suitable age in town except the new schoolteacher, and Tom hadn't had a chance to evaluate her. He wasn't ready for a permanent relationship; too angry, too depressed, and too hard to please; after Celina, he put his love-life in the too-hard basket.

He drove out of town to the chatter of his thoughts and memories. He'd spent most of his childhood here, and like many country kids, left school and migrated to the city lights to live and work. He signed up for the army in a time of peace and trained as an SAS *chicken strangler.* He saw the world's lesions at their festering worst through peacekeeping missions and invasions. He and his comrades had moved across war-torn lands, marking enemy locations and structures for annihilation. *'Who dares, wins.'* The motto by which he had lived and nearly died. The motto tattooed over his heart. He gave in to the lingering nightmare of two years before and pulled to the roadside as the memory paralysed him. *World shatters. A trickle of awareness. A freeze-frame of smoke, dust, and a crater; a twisted Land Rover. Whining in his ears like a jet engine. Where is everyone? Hop—fall—crawl. Ignore the pain, don't look at it! Enemies are approaching—move—find a rifle. Can't see for dust. Shoot. Again. Again. Faint screaming. Marty. Can't see him—can't see anyone. Too much dust. Where is everyone? Someone is there; it's a Kalashnikov—shoot—blow his head off! There's another;*

shoot. Blood soaked robes thrash with the dying throes of an insurgent. Poor bastard! Bone, blood, and guts are everywhere. The rhythmic throb of a Blackhawk is vibrating in his chest—help is coming…

"Stop!" Tom gasped in air and shook his head.

Get a grip, McPherson!

He cracked the seal on the scotch and swigged a gulp. As he lifted it to take another, a car pulled alongside.

Fuck! Trust Mark Fitzgibbon to turn up right when I've got the heeby-jeebies, and a bottle of booze in my mouth.

"You okay there, Tom?" The local police sergeant shone a torch with the power of a white dwarf into his eyes. Tom threw up a hand and wondered how Mark would like it if he turned his roo spotter on him.

"Yeah, Mate—just got a phone call. All good."

Who are you kidding, McPherson? Nobody calls you.

Mark shone the neutron beam over Tom's Landcruiser as if the caller might be that close. "Okay, Tom. Have a good night."

"Chee—good night."

Shit McPherson, don't say cheers to a cop when you've got a choke-hold on a bottle of Johnny Walker.

He drove away remembering the day they gave him the Cross of Valour. "Your country is grateful and proud." The Prime Minister had said.

He fared better than his father had; drafted and sent to Vietnam, he had served his country and returned with no physical injuries but his mind in shreds. The perception of rejection, fuelled by the rat-bag anti-war, anti-conscription, anti-government and anti-anything crowd played on his fragile mind and sent James McPherson into a self-destructive spiral of alcohol, drugs, and violence. He killed his wife in a drug-induced rage and put his son in hospital with concussion. Devastated and confused, Tom came to live in Warby Creek with his aunt, Roo-box Ruth McPherson. His father died in prison one week after Tom's fifteenth birthday. His Aunt Ruth decried his decision to enlist, but for Tom it was a way to make something of himself. Spend his life labouring for a living or join the army and see the world. He'd been discharged with a full pension, maimed but with his mind intact. He grieved for the loss of his comrades; courage hadn't made him stand and face the oncoming enemy. It was the knowledge that his mates would have done the same for him that made him face the enemy.

Who dares wins?

"No. That had nothing to do with it." The only lesson he remembered from Sunday school went something like, *'All things whatsoever ye would that men should do to you, do ye even so to them.'* That was what motivated Tom McPherson.

14

Inside the cave, Penrose moved from cage to cage. After three years, his work with the mandrills proved an outstanding success; the small municipal zoo had bemoaned the loss of their valuable troop, but Penrose had put them to good use. The recombinant DNA therapy, gene splicing and editing he used might see him condemned, sent to prison, but Penrose brushed aside the laws of his country and the ethics of modern medicine. He had done what scientists considered at best, impossible. At worst; highly unethical and dangerous. He'd prove why the law shouldn't apply to Doctor Penrose Nelson. His fellow scientists who cast him adrift, the students who ridiculed and reported him to the dean, the faculty who'd denounced him, and his father who sent him from the family home. His brother—the famous Kenzie Nelson had been nothing but kind and considerate. Try as he might, Penrose could not tease out a thread of ill will from the spindle of Kenzie's compassion. Contempt would have been easier to endure in return for the cruelty he'd inflicted on his sibling.

All of them will see how wrong they were.

Soon he would release his pride and joy—his magnificent creation, a new species, Pteropus-mandrillus

Penrosia into the wild. He had already written a one-hundred and eighty-thousand-word paper documenting his work. He granted them a common name, the hyacinth bat, though he referred to all his creations as 'my variants.' Agnetha named them death on wings. The last part of his experiment had yet to happen, would they mate and breed? Would they be fertile and produce fertile offspring? Would the offspring revert to one or the other of their grandparents' species? He observed the eldest of the young males rubbing a wingtip along his penis.

A good sign. Not long now, Penrose.

Penrose turned out the lights on the hyacinth bats and went back to the laboratory. The other experiment had taken much more work and most had died. He noted his observations as he moved from table to table and nodded with satisfaction—they were in varying stages of growth and exhibited varying levels of success. He stopped at the last of the creatures strapped to the bed. This was his favourite of the menagerie and probably the finest. He hadn't gained any height but rather a lot of upper-body muscle, a deepening of his ribcage, and a coat of fine auburn hair. Penrose hoped the elongation of the fingers would continue to provide an adequate frame for the wing membranes which grew at an astonishing rate. The creature whined as he smoothed and stretched the leathery skin.

"Now, now—beautiful fellow, I just want to measure your wings." He held his calliper across the width of the membranes; their rate of growth had slowed over the past week. "Excellent! We just need to keep those bones strong. Now Agnetha, just put the drip into our baby's arm. Careful, careful—be gentle!"

"Yes—sorry, Penrose."

"Good. Good. Now for their weekly shot of Denosumab. They're getting a little thin; I'm going to have to reintroduce some animal proteins."

"But you said they'd survive on a vegan diet."

"Indeed, I thought that possible, but I think with all the skeletal changes they are undergoing, they need a more substantial diet. We mustn't forget us humans evolved as omnivores." Penrose lifted his head at his wife's disapproving hiss and licked foam from the corner of his mouth. "As distasteful as that may be for you and me, Agnetha, we cannot dismiss proven science. We'll start them on raw eggs. Blended with milk and honey would be best."

"Yes, Penrose."

15

Alice Barnes carried the dinner tray into the lounge where Barry sat, watching the late news, the volume high to compensate for his dodgy hearing.

"Jesus, Alice, there's been another kid gone missing, this time down on the central coast."

"How can they just disappear? Somebody must be taking them, but how come nobody ever sees it happening?"

"I think it's probably someone that no one would expect."

"A little old lady or maybe another kid?"

"Everyone expects the guilty party will be a man. Maybe in this case, it's not a man."

"You might be onto something there, Darl."

First light saw Tom McPherson choked down in a paddock, feet out the window and eighteen roo carcasses hanging on his ute. A crow landed on his spotlight and rattled it. Tom woke with a snort, sat up and tried to clear an over-dry throat. The crow squawked and flew into a nearby tree to join its companions. The Scotch bottle lay empty on the dash.

"Oh fucksake, McPherson! You've done it again. Ah, Jesus!" His patched up leg throbbed when steel met bone; the hours spent resting on the windowsill had wreaked havoc. The sky glowed apricot in the east as he stepped out, groaned, and urinated into the grass. His stomach gurgled as he jumped in and started the engine. Thirty minutes back to town and another hour hanging the roos for Ruth. He hoped he'd make it back before the other shooters arrived. They liked to deliver the roos, collect their money, and get home; some of them forgot to mind their manners when dealing with his elderly aunt.

On Grinder's Gully Road, just past Nelson's Wildlife Sanctuary, Tom slammed on the brakes and the carcasses on his ute swung violently. Agnetha Nelson stood in the middle of the road in her floral op-shop frock, hand-made straw hat and badly stained Doc Martins. Her mouth moved; Tom couldn't hear her words but her expression would curdle milk. He rolled down the window and stuck his head out.

"What's up, Mrs Nelson?"

"Murderer!"

"Oh fucksake!" Tom's head began to throb. He massaged his temples and cast a recriminating glance at the Scotch bottle gleaming in the sunrise. A fug of alcohol fumes clouded the glass. "Are you attacking my war record or is this about the roos?"

Agnetha crunched around to stand beside the ute. "You're a murderer! Why don't you think of all those poor little joeys whose mothers you kill?"

"Lady, take a look. Every last carcass on there has a set of testicles. I don't shoot does. We're not allowed to shoot does."

"How can you tell the difference?"

"Testicles."

She waved a hand at the roadside. "In long grass?"

"I'm kidding. Their faces are different."

"How can you tell from a distance?"

"Spotlights and telescopic sights." Tom ground first gear and drove away before she could hurl any more accusations. He'd heard them all before.

Only one shooter beat him to Roo-box Ruth's and unfortunately, for Tom's delicate condition, it was Sid Walker. When Tom had begun high school, Sid had been the class bully, and Tom his favourite punching bag. It was after a puberty driven growth spurt he finally took Sid down in an epic schoolyard brawl that ended in a two-week suspension for both boys.

Sid leaned against his ute and folded his arms across his bulky chest. "Well, fuck my arse if it ain't G I Joe."

Tom climbed out of his ute. "Good morning, Sid."

"Ya lookin' a bit worse for wear, McPherson. Stayed up past your bed time?"

"Hm, yeah that would be it."

Tom limped to where Ruth fiddled with the lock on the cold room. "Hello, Tom. We'll have to store them in the cold truck for a few hours; some mongrel has sabotaged the cold room."

"Again?"

"I'm afraid so."

Sid joined them and extracted his tobacco pouch. "Probably that pair of greenie freaks that run the possum sanctuary, they—"

"When?"

"Must have been only a few hours ago because the temperature hasn't risen a lot yet but it's running like mad and definitely not getting any colder." Ruth pointed a frail hand at the temperature gauge. "Bastards! They did the same thing as last time, poked a sharp instrument through the suction pipes on the compressor. Darth Vader is on his way."

Tom's mouth twitched. Darby Jones , the local electrician and refrigeration technician had a breathing problem. "Have you called Sergeant Mark, yet?"

"That useless cunt—" Sid ran his tongue along his cigarette and secured the seam of rice paper with his fingers.

"Do you think it's worth it?" Ruth's head pivoted from Sid to Tom. "He couldn't find a culprit last time."

Sid's sausage fingers fished in his top pocket and withdrew a lighter. "Fitzy couldn't catch a cold in Alaska."

Tom shrugged. "Still, he's gotta know."

Sid struck the flint, trying to coax the lighter to life. His hands were big and clumsy with scabs of toil on the knuckles. "What you need is a big savage dog." He plied the flame to his rollie and sucked life into it.

The combination of a big savage dog and a tiny old lady worried Tom. "You'd be better to install security cameras and lights."

Worry crumpled Ruth's old face.

"I'll sort it for you, Aunty Ruth." Tom patted her shoulder.

"Thanks, Tom. You're a good boy."

"Boy? He's big enough to hold a bull out to piss and then shake off the drips." Sid coughed and smoke streamed from his face. He spat a sliver of tobacco. "McPherson must be forty in the shade if I'm a day—are you forty yet, G I Joe?"

"Not quite, Sid. Not quite."

Thirty-eight going on sixty.

"Go put the kettle on, Ruth. Me and Sid will stuff these roos in the fridge van."

Ruth smiled. "Thanks, Tom. I couldn't run this business without you."

Roo-box Ruth marched to her office, reassured in the presence of brawn. Tom and Sid transferred the kangaroo carcasses into the back of Ruth's truck. As they unloaded the last of Sid's harvest, Tom spotted something that set alarm bells ringing.

"Sid, what's this?"

"It's a roo. What's it look like?"

"It's got a pouch, Sid."

"Yeah? Well fuck my arse, so it has."

"It doesn't have a tag, either."

"Lay off, Tom. It's meat for me dog—old bitch has got pups."

"Do you need glasses? Can't you tell a doe from a buck?"

"So, I might a have shot one by accident—couldn't see its face."

"It's a doe, Sid. Cover it up and go collect your cheque from Ruth."

"You're not gonna dob me in are ya?"

"Not this time, Sid, but don't do it again. You'll fuck things up for the rest of us who follow the rules. Now get out of here."

"Speaking of pups, here. This little fella is gonna be a good working dog; both parents are good cattle dogs."

Tom hauled back from the little blue heeler. "I don't want a pup."

"You don't want it, mate, but you need it. Take him. He's a present from me and Trudy." He thrust the wriggling pup into Tom's arms and stumped away. Tom looked down at the pup and copped a wet tongue across his mouth.

"Looks like I'm stuck with you."

<h1 style="text-align:center">17</h1>

Penrose stood in the clearing and congratulated himself. His torch beam fixed on his experiment. His outstanding experiment.

"These don't look like fruit bats, Penrose."

"Nor should they."

"They don't look like boys and girls anymore, either."

"Of course not, they are a new species, Homo-pteropus Penrosia. This is what I have worked so hard for, Agnetha. If you judge them on either branch the genome, of course they aren't perfect. There is no precedent on which to judge them. They are the first of their species and my creation. The second version of my Variants."

"Yes, Penrose. You have achieved what scientists the world over said was impossible."

"Oh, they suspect it's possible, Agnetha. None of them have had the courage to try, nor the know-how." Penrose snapped a photo as the Homo-pteropus unfurled his wings. "Magnificent!"

The smallest male flapped and wafted leaves across the grass; he lifted off the ground then crashed face first into the dirt.

"Dear, dear!" Penrose clucked and hurried to set him back on his feet. "A little more exercise and then we'll put you to bed, eh—er—Jake?"

"I have my eye on another prime specimen, Penrose."

"You have? Excellent!"

"A female, around four years old just like you asked."

"Excellent. That will make three of each."

"When are you going to release the death-on-wings?"

"Hyacinth bats, Agnetha."

"Yes, hyacinth bats."

"Not until my observations are finished and fully documented."

"How long will that take? I'm getting a little tired of feeding them all."

"Patience, Agnetha. You cannot hurry such important work."

"They eat so much! I'm having trouble sourcing enough meat for them all."

"Persistence is what I require of you, Agnetha, and patience."

"I fear they might break out of the cages, they're so strong and aggressive."

He turned his icy gaze on her. "I said patience, Agnetha."

"Yes, Penrose."

18

Peter Edwards twiddled with his onyx pen and stared at the people across his desk. His secretary had told them Peter was busy but the president, secretary and publicity officer of the Warby Creek Progress Association had just invaded his office. Now they stood, one tall and cadaverous, one small and unremarkable, the other on the tubby side of cherubic.

"Pee—ter," said the cadaver, "You are going to listen to us."

"Well, good morning, people. What can I do for you?"

"You can arrange a meeting with the State Government about the flying foxes."

"Well—I'd like to help, but—"

"No buts, Pee—ter, we will take no answer but yes."

"Here—look at this, Peter." The cherub passed a sheaf of paper across the desk. "This is a legal petition, signed by ninety percent of the district's voters. If you don't do something to help us, we will drum you out of office, for good."

"For good." Unremarkable nodded.

Peter wet his lips and picked up the petition. His eyes travelled down the list of names and fell upon the name,

Celina Edwards. His wife had signed a partition against him.

Damn! Is there nothing sacred?

"Okay, people. Leave it with me."

"We want a report from you by the end of the week, Pee-ter, or the campaign will begin."

Unremarkable uttered his third and fourth words. "It will."

****

Barry watched Alice through the screen door as she slipped off her gumboots and set the bag of groceries on the floor. She folded the camouflage umbrella and leaned it against the wall.

"Barry, where are you, Darl?" The screen door squeaked and the string of tiny bells jingled.

"Here, Alice."

"Barry, guess what?"

"What?"

"There's a meeting on Wensdee night in the pub, the progress association are going to demand that the government allow us to get rid of the flying foxes."

"About bloody time."

"That naturalist bloke that gets on TV, he's coming to talk to us."

"Fuckin' David Attenborough?"

"No. This chap is a Queenslander—remember? Kenzie Somebody-or-other. We watched his show last week; it was about how girl kangaroos behave differently to boy kangaroos."

"Ah yeah—him. Wonder what the fuck he knows about bats?"

"Dunno. All them naturalist people reckon the bats have rights."

Barry snorted. "What about human rights?"

"Yeah, that's a question we should ask him."

"Yeah, where do human rights and animal rights begin and end?"

"I'll write that down, Darl, so we don't forget."

****

Freezing Antarctic wind ruffled Kenzie Nelson's hair as he clutched the struggling Tasmanian devil and fixed his eyes on the camera lens.

"With an effective vaccine for Facial Tumour Disease just around the corner, the next step for a little female like this one might be to act as a surrogate mother to a cloned thylacine." The marsupial growled and bared its teeth. "Isn't she beautiful? Now I'll just set her free before she gets annoyed." Kenzie winked at the camera. The devil vibrated in his hand as a growl rumbled in its tiny chest.

"Cut!" Andy, the director raised a dramatic hand. "Good work, Kenzie."

Kenzie got to his feet, still clutching the snarling animal.

Andy gave the devil's teeth a wide berth. "Okay, over there by the log, Kenzie."

"Let's hurry up, any minute now this little bugger's gonna go off like a frog in a sock."

Mickie, the cameraman, lugged his camera to the log and spent a moment experimenting with angles and focus. Tim, the sound recordist, swung his boom above Kenzie's head and Chris, the gaffer, shifted his beam.

"We're ready—go on Kenzie." The director clicked his clapperboard.

Like previously rehearsed, Kenzie strode into view and knelt; he held the devil with the log in the background.

"There you go, sweetie!" he released the Devil; as they had hoped, she turned and snarled at the humans who held her captive for the past hour. Sensing her ordeal had ended, she hurtled into the ferns. Kenzie sat on the log and finished his spiel on what it might mean to Tasmania should scientists clone a thylacine.

"And that's a wrap." Andy shivered in the frigid wind. "Jesus, let's get out of here before we freeze."

"What time does that plane leave?"

"Three. Bugger that wind—it's freezing."

Kenzie grinned at his crew. "Smile guys! We'll be back in Queensland tonight."

"Can't wait to catch a bit of sunshine."

19

In the Warby Creek Hotel lounge, Sara Nolan oversaw the setup for the meeting. The town hall was out of the question; at that end of the main street, the stench of flying foxes predominated. Sara's father, Dave Master's, and her son, Justin, arranged chairs in rows facing the official tables. The aroma of baking wafted through the big pub and into the street to mingle with the odour of the flying foxes as they took to the sky. Cars arrived, and people dashed from the street to the shelter of the pub veranda then into the public bar to stand shoulder to shoulder. They left a forest of umbrellas leaning against the weatherboards on the veranda.

When the room half filled, Sara and her daughter, Gracie, carried trays of finger food into the pub lounge and set them on a long table against the wall. As the food disappeared down voracious throats, they hurried back to the kitchen for more. When the chairman called the meeting to order, Sara took the end chair in the back row. As she settled down to listen, she became aware of the man seated beside her. Tom McPherson. She knew who he was but had never spoken to him. His gaze set her face alight;

she resisted for a full minute before she lost the battle and met his eyes.

"Hello," he whispered, "I'm Tom. How come I've never seen you before?"

"Poor timing, I guess." She suppressed her smile. "I'm Sara Nolan, I own this pub."

His voice rumbled in his chest. "Really? Well Sara, you're my kind of girl."

From the row in front of them, Alice Barnes turned to hiss, "Shh! Kenzie is about to speak."

Sara wondered how long Alice had known who Kenzie Nelson was and how long would it be before she would condemn him. Fair-haired and handsome, the famous naturalist got to his feet and flashed his boyish smile. As he spoke, Sara tried to rein in her scepticism. Like every other big city expert, he'd be sure to tell the town they would just have to put up with the vulnerable species and their noise and stink.

"...flying foxes are a vital part of our eco system and they should not be wiped out, but here in Warby Creek, they are proving to be a nuisance..."

"No shit, Sherlock." Barry Barnes took an elbow from his wife.

"...even a danger to the people and clearly need better management..."

"We ain't got no dinosaurs," came an opinion from the front, "and we shouldn't 'ave no bats neither"

A voice from the middle of the room declared, "I say we get in and start shooting until they're all gone!"

Kenzie Nelson raised a placatory hand. "Please, hear me out! We don't have to kill—"

"It's alright for you; you don't have to live in the town!"

"We have a right to a clean town!"

"Please—there is a solution, just—"

Sara's head swivelled to the back of the room as voices began a straggly chant. Penrose Nelson, his wife, and schoolteacher, Eden Tate stood with a group of sign-toting activists against the back wall. "Every creature needs a home; leave the fruit bats well alone. Every creature..."

"Ah shuddup!"

"...leave the fruit bats..."

From the middle of the room, a half-eaten sausage roll flew and hit the schoolteacher. She and the protesters continued their chant.

"Oh fucksake!" The big man beside Sara muttered as Sid Walker got to his feet and faced the activists.

"Shuddup ya bunch of wankers!"

"Sid! Sit down!"

"I'll sit down when they shut up!"

Barry Barnes added his advice. "Shuddup, ya bloody galahs!"

The mayor, Peter Edwards, called over the noise. "Doctor Nelson, we will have to ask you to leave if you keep disrupting the meeting."

The chants faded and died. Sara turned back in time to see Kenzie Nelson staring.

I wonder if Doctor Nelson is related to Kenzie?

She could see no family resemblance.

When the noise faded to a soft hubbub, the naturalist picked up his thread. "The—er—flying fox is a—er—remarkable creature. Unique. They help regenerate forests and keep our ecosystems healthy…"

"Not too healthy 'round here, mate!"

"…through pollination and seed dispersal. Please, here me out!"

Disaffection swelled again.

"Please, listen. They are a keystone species. A species that plants, and other animals rely on for their survival…"

"Bah!"

"Greenie bastard!"

"…flying foxes, like bees, help drive biodiversity, and with the threat of climate change, land clearing, and other ecological pressures, we need them more than ever."

"I don't need 'em."

"Sir," Kenzie Nelson pointed to Sid Walker. "Sir, what do you do for a living?"

Sid sat legs akimbo and arms folded across his belly. "I shoot roos."

"Murderer!" Agnetha Nelson's eye shone.

"You—oh. I see."

Sara heard the man beside her snort. His shoulders shook with silent mirth and he whispered, "I love this town."

Kenzie Nelson cleared his throat and squared his shoulders. "My suggestion is this: over a period of two weeks we lop the trees, starting at this end of town where there are fewer bats, each night cut back the trees to just three to four metres high—"

"Murderer!"

"Every creature needs a home; leave the fruit bats well alone…"

Tom McPherson slumped in his chair and clasped a big hand over his face.

Kenzie Nelson's face darkened. "If we progressively remove all the tall trees from the town, the bats will move on…"

"…needs a home; leave the fruit bats well…"

Sid Walker's chair tipped over as he lumbered to his feet, trampling across people's toes he barged from the row of seats and with an ominous cracking of knuckles, advanced on the group at the back of the room.

"Oh fucksake!" Tom McPherson rose and cast Sara a hunted smile. "Excuse me while I put Sid back on his leash." His hand touched her shoulder as he passed, limped across the room and cut off Sid's progress. "Sit down, Sid."

"Out of the way, McPherson—"

"Murderer!"

"Sid, calm down."

"Piss off!"

"Murderer!"

"You're not helping anyone—"

"Shift your carcass, McPherson, or I'll rip your throat out!"

"Murderer!"

"If there's any throat ripping tonight it'll be by me. Now sit down—fuck!"

Sid's scabrous fist connected with his cheek and Tom seized the roo shooter's wrist. Wiry muscles in his forearm bulged as he twisted Sid's arm; the old pub shuddered as he rammed him against the wall.

"Fuck off, McPherson!"

People seated nearby retreated to a safe distance.

Agnetha Nelson repeated her verdict. "Murderer!"

Eden Tate resumed the chant. "Every creature needs a home; leave the fruit bats well alone!"

"Murderer!"

The besieged soldier propelled Sid in the direction of his seat with a shove and a kick to his plump buttock then rounded on the protesters. "Will you just shut your mouths?"

"Murderer! Murderer! Mur—"

"I said, 'shut up!'" The Nelson's and their claque shrunk from the towering Tom McPherson as his voice fill the room.

Silence reigned as he checked behind him for further incursions from Sid. "Now, we're all going to listen to the nice man at the front and we are all going to be quiet. Aren't we? Aren't we!"

Scattered agreement murmured from the crowd, a few hands clapped, and they turned to face Kenzie Nelson. McPherson limped back to his seat.

He grimaced as Sara smiled. "I haven't had to shout at anyone like that since I left the ADF."

"Well, I think it worked. You need an icepack on your cheek."

"I need a drink."

"Right!" Peter Edwards buffed his palms. "Let's take a vote; all those in favour of Kenzie's proposal raise your hands and say aye."

Hands rose across the room and a hubbub of voices said, "Aye."

"Good, good! The ayes have it. When do you recommend we start, Kenzie?"

"Naturally, we will need to get approval from the authorities and I don't think that will pose a problem." Kenzie turned to the lone Member of Parliament who had attended the meeting and received a nod. "As soon as we get the go-ahead, we'll begin."

Sara groaned. "That should take what? Twelve months?"

The chairman got to his feet. "I'll call this meeting to a close then. We will keep you posted on our progress. Thank you all for coming."

Sara stood; Tom McPherson laid his hand on her arm.

"Can I buy you a drink?"

"Only if you allow me to put an icepack on your cheek. Is it painful?"

"No." His fingers groped the welt on his cheek. "Ouch—now that you mention it. I owe Sid a shiner."

****

The meeting over, people drifted into the street outside the Warby Creek Hotel. Though the stench persisted, the sky above was bat free but many of the locals, out of habit, opened their umbrellas. Parting voices sounded between the heritage buildings. Car doors slammed, engines revved and exhaust fumes made a pleasant change from the stink of flying foxes. The people both hopeful and annoyed made their way home. Penrose Nelson accompanied his wife to their little ecofriendly car.

"Pen! Wait." Kenzie Nelson left Peter Edwards midsentence and ran to catch up. "Pen! So this is where you got to. Mum and Dad haven't heard from you in years. You should get in touch with them, Mum hasn't been well, Pen."

"It's Penrose."

Kenzie ignored his sister-in-law's rebuke. "So—er— what are you doing with yourself these days?"

Resentment passed across Penrose's face like the track of a bitter memory moving beneath the skin. "Important work." The little car sank lower as Penrose climbed into the front seat and slammed the door. With a whir and a ping of gravel from under the tyres, it rolled away. Kenzie gazed after his brother's taillights as the little car disappeared around the corner.

"You know Doctor Nelson, do you?"

Kenzie turned as the Warby Creek Mayor came to a halt beside him. "Yes, he's my older brother."

The kids' school lunches took shape on the kitchen bench. Sandwiches for Justin and salad for Gracie. Sara held the apples under the tap, and once again, her thoughts turned to Tom McPherson. Since the evening before he'd proven a pleasant distraction. Two years had passed since Jack dropped dead as he hosed the veranda, and since then, the endless struggle to survive besieged her mind. Maintaining an operational pub while mothering her kids had left little time for outside diversions—that is except the flying foxes. The discomfort the bats had imposed on Warby Creek had taken its toll; a portion of the population had packed up and moved. Sara would have joined the exodus but the Warby Creek Hotel kept her chained to the town. Sara never considered herself lonely until the night before when she applied the ice pack to Tom McPherson's face. A thrill had tingled her skin as his work-roughened hand lightly grasped her arm, and she saw the same sadness in his eyes that she saw each morning in the mirror. Haunted, homeless eyes, hardened by the world and its wars.

Sara wiped the water off the apples and added them to the lunch boxes. Her fingers touched her lips and a thrill twirled in her stomach—McPherson had toyed with his keys as he thanked her, then stepped so close his body heat radiated onto her face. For a brief moment his lips covered hers and drew her sensuality from its slumber. Then he was gone.

****

Tom spent the morning tending the cattle. As they crowded around the lick blocks, he examined them for parasites and signs of ill health. Egrets gave him and the pup a wide berth as they stalked around waiting for the cows to frighten breakfast out of the grass. The pup stayed close to Tom's heels and evaded the protective mothers' horns. The calves lowed and licked their shiny noses; their eyes rolled and legs propped as they watched the pup pass by.

As he worked, Tom's mind kept drifting to Sara. He should give her a little space, time to decide if she wanted him around, but even as the thought turned in his mind, he searched for an excuse to drive into town. He had chores to attend that afternoon but he wanted to see that lovely face again, lest he forget a single detail. The hair that shone golden brown. Her eyes—were they green or brown? She had made the lonely man sit up and bask in her sunshine. Given hope where none abided. Was she the woman who would bring him back across the void to re-join the human race?

Lunch at the pub sounds good, McPherson.

21

Celina had been a little irritated when Peter said the TV naturalist would spend the night with them. She had seen his documentaries, he was handsome in a cheeky, boyish way, but his on-screen exuberance and restlessness exasperated her, there was something unsexy about a man who scrabbled around in the dirt, chasing reptiles and rodents. She preferred men who presented a calm and dignified presence. Then last night, Peter had opened a bottle of wine and as they talked and laughed, Kenzie's boyish charm and intelligent humour drew her in. Celina's one flaw was an addiction to men, and forbidden men were the sweetest of all.

In the morning, lusty warmth stole over Celina as Peter slipped his arm around her and addressed Kenzie. "I hope you won't mind if I leave you for an hour or so. I have a quick meeting to attend at the office with the honourable member and then I'll return to drive you to the airport."

"I don't mind at all. I have emails and my Facebook presence in need of attention. I can take care of those while I wait."

Peter pecked Celina's cheek and hurried out the door.

Celina flicked a smile at Kenzie and went to check on her daughter, Madelyn, who rode her new trike up and down the garden path.

****

Kenzie's eyes followed Celina out the door, his wilful imagination pictured her naked and brazen before him. His breath caught in his throat as his eyes travelled down her legs to the kitten heels. They alone set a fire in his jeans but her curves were as dangerous as the Incas trails of the Andes. Even as he told himself to back away, he knew he would have her. Just as soon as her husband's car drove away and she returned from checking on her daughter, he would possess this diamond of a woman he'd found out here in a little one-horse plus a quarter-million fruit-bat town. Kenzie had reached forty-two and had never married. He hadn't found anyone he wanted in his life every day, but Celina Edwards would have fit the bill.

Too bad, Kenzie. Old Peter found her first.

He contemplated various ways he might seduce her, but when she returned, she seized him by his belt buckle and led him upstairs. The rush of blood to his loins left his legs barely able to negotiate the stairs. She kicked the bedroom door closed and slipped her arms around his neck.

89

"Quickly—we don't have much time; my husband never takes very long to complete any task."

He cupped her head, fingers entwined in her fiery curls and her perfume filled his lungs. Her lips were warm and welcoming; her body trembled against him as he glided the zipper down the length of her spine and pushed her dress to the floor. She eased his T-shirt up his torso, her mouth followed, kissing and licking. With unnerving expertise, she undressed him and pushed him onto the bed. He rolled her onto her back, parted her thighs and dived, drowning in her taste. Her face flushed pink as he moved over her; he paused, standing at the pearly gates, waiting to slip through behind St Peter's back. She guided him in and Kenzie feared he might beat her husband's personal best. He panted for control as she nibbled his neck and declared orgasm number one. He held out for another then joined her for the third. He allowed himself to bask in a few moments of her luxurious body. She entwined herself around him, smooth and inviting. Reluctantly, he rose and dressed. It wouldn't do to fall asleep with exhaustion in the arms of the mayor's wife.

****

Madelyn sped along the garden path, across the lawn and laughed as she crashed into the hedge. As she got to her feet, movement caught her eye. A Furry face and big brown eyes—long ears flicked. The animal called. Madelyn climbed over the fence and the animal struggled, pulled by a string, across the park and into the bushes. The little girl followed. Sweaty hands grasped her neck and squeezed.

"Mummy!" The word fell into blackness and something stung her arm.

****

Celina watched Peter drive away with Kenzie and smiled. That had been a little too close but it had been worth it. Kenzie Nelson had some exceptional qualities and that she'd probably never see him again was a bonus, she didn't need the awkward glances across a crowded room which happened more often than she deemed comfortable. She sighed. The street was quiet. Too quiet.

Madelyn!

She hurried into the back yard, Madelyn wasn't there. Celina found her trike on its side near the back fence but no sign of her daughter.

I wonder if she has gone across to Edna's place.

As Tom stepped out of the pub, a woman's voice split with terror reached his ears. Celina Edward ran towards him, fitful words swallowed by sobs. Tom's face turned from passive to serious.

"Celina, what's happened?"

"Madelyn! I can't find her! She's gone!"

Tom thought a moment—Madelyn was Peter and Celina Edwards's only child. Four years old, beautiful with red curls and big blue eyes. "Gone—where—when did you last see her?"

"She was playing in the back yard, riding her trike. She must have gone out the gate. I can't find her! Please help me, Tom—I—I know something bad has happened. I know it!"

People gathered; curiosity turned to concern. Everyone knew little Madelyn. Sergeant Mark Fitzgibbon arrived and organised a search party.

Celina was incoherent when her husband returned from driving Kenzie Nelson to the airport; for once, Peter Edwards' face carried no smile. His eyes reflected his wife's terror.

"We'll find her, Celina. We'll find her."

The people searched all afternoon, wider they spread, into the surrounding bushland, in the park, in the creek.

The sun sank lower and the cool breeze grew colder. Night fell and the search continued until the defeated citizens of Warby Creek returned; exhausted in the dawn's light. The little girl had vanished. A nationwide red alert went out and Madelyn's picture, which should only reside in her loved ones' homes, graced newspapers, social media, and billboards. Beautiful, red curls—an image of innocence. Where had Madelyn gone?

Tom regretted his tryst with Celina; she and Peter losing their little girl woke him to the perfidy of his actions—he should have asked about her background before their affair. He had blundered into a family—there was a child involved. The expensive car, designer clothing, and diamonds—the well-cared-for façade should have warned him—this was no single, nine-to-five working girl. Loneliness was never excuse enough to take advantage of the fallout of a failing relationship. He'd never married and had never experienced parenthood, but observation of parents in the various war zones he'd served had shown him the power of the love they held for their offspring. Many had proved braver than the toughest soldier.

****

Each night, as darkness fell over Warby Creek, a sad figure haunted the streets, the parks, and surrounding bushland. Celina Edwards wandered in the night, calling for her daughter. The purity of moonlight could never overcome the despair of a mother's empty arms or her guilt. For just ten minutes of madness, lust driven by boredom, Celina had paid a parent's highest price. The object of her lust had left town, oblivious to the devastation in his wake. Peter never asked why. Instead, he'd disengaged and threw himself into his passion. Politics. Celina's self-loathing drove her into the night—searching and failing. Dying in increments and searching.

23

The first crop of calves continued to arrive. Tom's cows dropped their offspring at rate of two or three a day. He kept them in the house paddock, the better to monitor the new arrivals. In the twilight, a bull-calf gained his feet and made the miraculous navigation along his mother's side. He nuzzled the teat, his tail wagged furiously as he bumped the udder, seeking colostrum. Tom leaned on the rails and watched. The pup ventured through and planted his rump in the dirt beside him; his head tilted and his tail wagged. The new mother rolled an eye at the dog and mooed a warning to keep his distance.

Emptiness descended on Tom as it often had since his discharge. Major Tom McPherson. He'd had a place and a purpose with the SAS. Why was he now here raising cattle? What was he hoping to achieve? A normal life? He'd like to be one of the locals, but he couldn't. He'd like to subscribe to their truth but he couldn't. All his youthful bridges burned; his warrior years had depleted him—he could not, after so long, open up and say, *'Here I am—I'm one of you.'* He could either turn his back on those who had seen his youth or else admit to its nakedness—the boy whose family imploded and left him homeless. He shook off his desolation. Sara. Because of her, Tom had cut back on his drinking and that in turn had given the depression an added foothold. He hadn't been roo-shooting for over a week. The only way Tom could shoot anything these days was from behind a veil of alcohol.

The blue heeler pup yelped in terror and shot under the rails. The air shifted, Tom's heart lurched as a shadow darkened the sky and the swish of leathery wings slapped his face. A creature snarled and lunged at the newborn calf, the cow bellowed and swung her head. Tom's fist glanced off the creature, it kicked at him and Tom fell against the cow's ribs. The pup bristled, bayed and wailed but he stayed outside the fence. The creature shrieked, it's strange pale face a blur as it retreated into the night; sensing a win, the pup gave a frantic chase. The cow shook her horns; Tom recoiled, stumbled on his maimed leg and sprawled on the ground. The new mother stamped about, lowered her head and mooed.

"Whoa there, old girl. It wasn't me!" He scrambled to his feet and vaulted the rail. He gave the cow space to inspect her precious baby. She lowed and scrubbed the calf's face with her tongue as if to remove the danger. Tom searched the sky. "What the fuck was that?" His heart bounded against his ribs. The moment had spanned only seconds, however, he'd caught a glimpse of a pale face, sharp teeth and enormous wings.

A flying fox. No. Too big. An eagle? Eagles don't hunt a night. An owl? No. Too big—and it kicked like a—it had wings, dammit! Jesus, McPherson, you've really lost your marbles this time.

The pup returned, all growls and bristles, to cower behind his master.

"You nearly got him, Dog." Tom stooped and rubbed the dog's head with a shaking hand. "And fuck sobriety, I need a drink."

24

The sight of a helicopter on the helipad at the hospital unleashed a dam burst of gossip rushing through Warby Creek. News of the student vet's Hendra Virus diagnosis spread like a pandemic and alarm bells rang in the fear. Late that afternoon, the helicopter returned and evacuated the chief vet. The next morning, the TV news announced the student vet had died.

The Warby Creek Times' lone reporter, Blake Rush, just made his deadline to head office. His report on the Hendra outbreak would set events in train that would shake the town to its foundations. *'BAT-BORN VIRUS KILLS VET. AQIS ORDERS SLAUGHTER OF HORSES. The flying foxes of Warby creek have claimed another victim. The death of a young veterinary student is the latest casualty of Warby Creek's flying fox infestation. He died after treating a horse that had contracted the virus from bat faeces in its fodder. His employer has also fallen ill to the bat-born virus and has been evacuated to Brisbane in critical condition. Previous to this incident, at least two people died from stress related causes brought on by the presence of the bats. How many more people must die? When is the government going to stand up to the activists and say no more? Will the people of Warby Creek finally say "enough?" The time has come to stop procrastinating and move the bats on.'*

In the public bar of the Warby Creek Hotel, an impromptu meeting opened at ten a.m., and a half hour later a unanimous decision brought cheers and a scurry of preparations.

In a shady paddock on the edge of town, a child sobbed in her father's arms as a quarantine officer's bullet ripped through the skull of her pony.

****

The screen door creaked open and slammed; the little bells tinkled. Alice looked up from her long-stitch as Barry strode through the lounge and into the spare room. She frowned at the gleam of fanaticism shining in his eyes. Only the promise of a nip of OP rum and a beer chaser could normally elicit such fervour therein.

"You're in a bit of a hurry, Darl?"

"This is it, Alice. We've all agreed—we're going to chase these bats away, once and for all."

"Has the government approved it at long last?"

"Fuck the government, we're gonna do it ourselves."

Alice rose and hurried after Barry. "But Darl—how are you going—Barry! What are you doing?"

"I told you, Alice—we're getting rid of the bats."

"Darl—no—you'll be arrested!"

"They'll have to arrest half the town."

Alice's mouth fell open as Barry cracked his duck-hunting shotgun and thumbed cartridges into the chamber.

"Barry Barnes—I've never seen such—"

"Stand aside, Alice." Barry straightened his creaky spine, and tightened his belt to prevent his trousers slipping down under the weight of his cartridge stuffed pockets. "This has been a long time coming and we've all agreed, today we rid the town of the bats."

Alice gaped as her husband of fifty-three years squared his shoulders and strode out the door. He left the camouflage umbrella leaning against the wall.

****

Sergeant Mark Fitzgibbon was about to have the most remarkable day of his career. He and his officers gathered for their own meeting. How best to manage the people's panic in the wake of the Hendra outbreak?

"…and I've sent a request for a few extra officers to be assigned to this station. We need to be out there, show that we're not worried about contracting this virus ourselves—"

"But I am worried, Sarg."

"Don't be. It doesn't spread from person to person or even bat to person, if you don't go near a horse, you'll be safe. Read that fact sheet and memorise it. Take a handful of the flyers and hand them out. Okay, finish your coffee, boys and girls and then it's—what was that?"

"Sounded like a gunshot."

The officers rushed to the front door of the Police Station to gape in disbelief. Pops and bangs broke out down the street. The screeches of flying foxes multiplied to ear splitting as they took to the sky in a storm of wings and a shower of excrement. Shouts rang—some angry—some gleeful. The occasional whoop, "Got 'im!" A two-stroke motor snarled to life. Then another. Civil disobedience marched along Baker Street in the form of gun-toting men and women, young and old, shooting at screaming flying foxes. As they advanced, a cherry picker fell in behind, stopping at each tree. Council workers with chainsaws lopped the branches and let them fall to the street.

A young constable retreated from the window. "Wow! I wonder how many of those guns are unlicensed."

Senior constable Riley pushed the door open and stepped outside. "Okay, Sergeant Fitzgibbon, how do you plan to arrest this lot? One at a time or en masse?"

Mark brushed aside the senior constable, hurried into the street and stared; he moved to take shelter under the awning of the pie shop. Blake Rush, the local newspaper journalist stumbled about among the shooters, video camera in one hand and an umbrella in the other, frantically describing the action.

Constable Riley ran to join Mark, a splatter of green muck dribbled down his shirt. "Perhaps we better call for backup."

"—Um yeah." Mark watched as pensioner Barry Barnes, equipped with earmuffs, blasted a flying fox with his shotgun. "Not that they're going to arrive in time with the next big station over an hour away."

"But it will cover our arses, Sarg. Jeez! Heads are going to roll over this."

Mark groaned as the Senior Constable hurried back into the station. "Yeah. Probably mine."

****

An amused voice came from behind Mark. "Well, we saw this coming, didn't we, Mark?" Tom McPherson stopped beside Mark and belched, an open bottle of Johnny Walker in one hand and a pie in the other. "Good to see Sid brought his pea rifle and not that cannon of his."

"I thought you'd be in there with Sid, shooting bats, Tom."

"Nah, I'll just stand here undercover, eat my lunch and watch. I don't like guns much."

"You—" Mark's eyes scanned the big ex-soldier and settled on the bottle. "Tom, what are you doing?"

He gestured at the street with his pie. "Admiring Sid's shooting skills, what does it look like?"

"I'm talking about the bottle—you're drinking in a public place. You can—I should arrest you for that."

"Ah come on, Mark, instead of harassing a man having a social drink, why don't you arrest them?" He poked the neck of the bottle towards the street then flinched as an out-of-control flying fox swooped low; a green stream of excrement splattered Marks boots.

"Ah shit!"

McPherson took a swig and grinned. "Yep."

Out of a side street, farmer Wayne 'Woolley' Lambe rode on his flamethrower-equipped four-wheeler, as he drove past the pie shop he aimed the nozzle at a tree and blasted a jet of flame. Mark feared Woolley might accidently turn the flamethrower on him if he tried to interfere but interfere he must; a flamethrower in a town of valuable, timber heritage buildings was hazardous to say the least.

Tom McPherson had no such reservations as he raised his bottle. "Way to go, Woolley!"

Black smoke rose from the tree and a bat shot out. Woolley flicked his wrist and flames engulfed the bat and the pie shop awning. The bat crashed to the street in an agony of writhing, burning wings. Gunpowder, diesel fumes, burning leaves, and singed fur fouled the aired and competed with the flying foxes' stink; gunshots and the angry buzz of chainsaws competed with their screeches.

McPherson tilted his head after Wooley. "You better chase him down, Mark, before he burns the whole town. I'll tend to the fire." For a man who had already drunk half a bottle of scotch, McPherson proved himself a quick thinker. He hobbled into the police station foyer and seconds later emerged with a fire extinguisher.

"Good thinking!" Mark ran after Wooley's four-wheeler.

****

The receptionist at the police station was having an interesting day. She had cowered behind her desk when

Armageddon broke out in the streets of Warby Creek. Then Tom McPherson limped through the doors and asked her to mind his pie and half-empty bottle of Scotch. He unclipped the fire extinguisher from the wall and hop-ran outside.

Minutes later, he returned and placed the extinguisher on the floor beside her desk.

"That'll be empty." He grinned, took up his pie and bottle and jerked his head in the direction of the street. "S'all happenin' out there, you should take a look. You're missing the action sitting in here."

Several hours later, seventy-eight men and women arrived to turn themselves in. The magistrate was in for a busy day, the next time he visited Warby Creek.

25

In the empty streets, the roar of chainsaws and the whining chatter of the council's tree shredder replaced two and a half years of flying fox squabbles. Hundreds of bats lay dead and the survivors had fled to where nobody cared. Warby Creek was no longer an ideal flying fox habitat; council workers had defied the chief executive officer and the mayor, they lopped every tall tree in the town to a height undesirable to bats. Now they moved along the street to tidy the mess and wood-chip the fallen branches.

****

Penrose walked along Baker Street in the late afternoon light, tears fell on his cheeks. National Parks and Wildlife rangers had already euthanized any bats that the shooters hadn't finished. His heart hurt to see a female bat, her still moist eyes reflected his face. Flies buzzed around her wounded chest. Her head flopped as he scooped her up, her tongue lolled and her wings unfurled like a brown umbrella.

"Poor little girl. What have they done? What have—"

"Doctor Nelson, I strongly advise you to not handle the carcasses. I'm sure you've heard there's been a Hendra outbreak."

****

Constable Riley approached Penrose Nelson as he got to his feet, cradling a dead flying fox.

"Have you arrested those responsible for this carnage?" His thin lips shivered and his eyes fluttered behind his spectacles. "Those murderers?"

"Whether you like it or not, Doctor Nelson, it is not murder to kill an animal, it—Mrs Nelson! Stop!" Riley hurried to where Agnetha and the schoolteacher, Eden Tate, gathered the carcasses in a wheelbarrow. In the distance, the tree shredder corroded the peace of the cool evening with its grinding whine.

Constable Riley had only seen Agnetha Nelson from a distance. As he stepped closer, her mad eyes made him take a backward step.

"I will not!"

"Mrs Nelson, please—the department will be here at first light to collect the carcasses, so leave them alone."

Blood and muck coated Agnetha Nelson's hands and she shook a dead bat at the constable. "The department—

the government is responsible for this carnage. They should have been here to protect these innocent fruit bats from those vile, murderous humans."

The constable had never imagined uttering the words: "Put the bat down, Mrs Nelson or I'll have to arrest you."

26

The little red-haired batgirl whined in her cage. Penrose rubbed the backs of his fingers against his jaw. He had miscalculated something in his experiment—the differences in the life span and age of sexual maturity between (bats) and modern humans likely the problem. Was the genetic gap between the two species too wide after all? His first batboy had become stronger than Penrose imagined he would and he frequently needed a tranquilizer to control him. The other boys progressed along a similar trajectory. The batgirls had reached sexual maturity much earlier than the boys had. Penrose had planned to put them together and see if they would produce offspring. Now the batgirl's urine sample had indicated menopause; the boy's thinning body hair and drooping testicles showed he too approached old age.

Penrose shook his head. "Such a waste."

"What is, Penrose?"

Penrose shifted away from his wife, the more his stooped posture advanced, the more his wife now towered over him.

"This experiment has not panned out as I expected. They're aging too fast. The hyacinth bats have been an outstanding success, but they're not as intelligent as the homopterous, the human hybrid. But this premature aging problem—I will try adding a cocktail of amino acids to their intravenous infusion; perhaps that will help." Foam bubbled at the corner of his mouth. "I fear my only option is to concentrate on cloning. Altering the genome of a human embryo."

Agnetha's face darkened. "Well, I can't help you there, can I?"

"No-no. I shall have to look elsewhere."

"I can't even offer you a womb."

"No—"

"You should have thought of that before you allowed them to perform a radical hysterectomy."

"Now—now, Agnetha. You know the damage and ensuing infection was too extensive. You must not allow bitterness to cloud your thinking, must you, Agnetha?"

"No, Penrose. I mustn't."

"I am thinking that Eden Tate is an ideal host."

"She won't agree to—"

"There are several cages spare. The school term ends soon. Invite her to dinner on the last Friday."

"But what if she doesn't want—"

"Do you want me to get angry?"

"But you'll need her consent; otherwise you're breaking the law. It's considered immoral."

"My work is important, Agnetha, it might be distasteful but I need her for my research—I can't be concerned with what is moral and what is not. Now, do I have you're ongoing loyalty?"

"Yes, Penrose."

"You know what you have to do?"

"Yes, Penrose."

Intuition of Tom's mended bones and the wind's direction predicted a storm. The cumulus clouds gathered from midday; they floated in like sailing ships and dropped anchor. By mid-afternoon, the first rumble of thunder sounded from the nearby ranges. Tom checked his cows and their offspring. Two remained to give birth and they both showed signs of labour.

Hope had woken with him and he rose with the morning sun—Sara was coming for dinner. Years in the ADF had taught him cleanliness but he still straightened the house and changed the sheets on his bed. He told himself it needed doing anyway, but if he was honest, he hoped Sara might share it that night. He took a shower and shaved his whiskers. Back in the kitchen, he checked the oven—Roo-box Ruth's lasagne looked good and smelt better. Tempting as it was, his preferred painkiller wouldn't be alcohol; he threw down some Panadol and lay on the couch with his impaired leg resting on a cushion.

When Sara's car approached along the gravel road, Tom had a moment of self-doubt. Apart from his brief fling with Celina, he hadn't had a steady girlfriend since the SAS Regiment had proved him a different breed of human. The strength he'd summoned to make it through the physical and psychological torture of the selection process changed him. Would Sara see that side of him? If she did, would she reject it?

Relax McPherson; that part of your life has ended.

Really?

Really.

"Go and sit down." He pushed the dog with his foot.

Sara stepped from her car, and in her eyes, the same doubts that punctured his esteem bounced back. Her hand in his was warm and soft and trembled like a dove.

Her eyes met his and then roamed to the white-faced cattle in the field next to his house. "So many of your cows have calves."

Tom smiled; glad it wasn't he who had broken the tension with such an awkward statement. "Want to take a look?"

Now who's being awkward?

Thunder rumbled—a storm approached.

She lifted her eyes to the roiling dark clouds. "We might get wet."

"Yes, we might—maybe we shouldn't"

"No, I want to see them."

"We'll be quick."

Through the gate and into the calving paddock, Tom led Sara. Curious cows loped towards them, their ears pricked and tails swished.

"They won't run over the top of us will they?"

"No—they're just coming to have a look at you, they haven't met you before."

"The calves are so sweet."

"Hmm, yes they are kind of cute."

The wind began to blow and a flash of lightening brightened the late afternoon. A cacophony of clinks and screeches filled the air as a flock of galahs zoomed past, excited by the storm's approach. Fat marbles of rain pelted down and petrichor rose from the dry soil.

"Quick! If we run we might—"

Sara pulled him back. "No—let's enjoy the storm."

"You want to get wet?"

"Yes, why not? It's been so long since I could enjoy the outdoors without the stink of flying foxes."

"We've got the stink of cows instead."

"Much nicer than flying foxes." She shrugged her shoulders against the icy rain.

"Come here." Tom drew her close as the storm burst and rain sluiced over them, the wind tore at their clothes. Her laughter blended with the hiss of rain in the trees. Sheets of water, pricked and dimpled by raindrops, covered the ground. His mouth sought hers, rain soaked hair clung to their faces and channelled streams of water to where their lips met.

"Come on—we'll get washed away out here."

Through yellow eddies and rivulets, they splashed back to the shelter of the house. Sara shivered and looked at the pelting rain.

Tom drew her aside as the dog became a whirl of flapping ears and jowls. Once again, he shoved him with his foot. "Go and sit down, Dog."

"It's a little cold."

"And I don't have a dry dress that I can loan you either."

Her laugh tingled down his spine.

"I'll put your clothes in the dryer."

Sara's eyes widened. "Er—"

"You were the one who wanted to get wet."

"Yes. Silly me."

"I'm sure I have a towelling robe you can wear."

"Oh. Good. Thanks."

Tom caught a glimpse of a lacy bra rolling with her dress in the dryer and tortured himself wondering if she wore anything at all under his bathrobe. She dried her hair as he set the table and listened to the rain drumming on the tin roof. Her cheeks were pink as he pulled out a chair for her.

"Are you warm enough?"

"Yes, thank you."

"That robe is a bit big on you."

"It's very cosy."

Dinner over, they moved to the veranda to sip wine and watch the storm as it passed to the east. Words slowly pulled and wove the threads of two diverse lives. Her life so simple, school, work, marriage, children, and then widowhood. His story, he stretched over gaps of the life he had yet to grapple with; ghosts of his childhood and unutterable secrets of his years in the Special Air Service Regiment. Across the world, the lives of his former comrades might depend on his silence.

A big platinum moon pushed above the flashes of the retreating clouds, illuminating drops of water that hung from the gutters.

"That moon is blinding."

Sara's body heat warmed his arm where it lay across the back of the seat. His eyes scanned the empty sky. "And no flying foxes to ruin the view."

"I can't help but feel sorry for them. I wonder where the survivors went."

"I don't much care as long as they stay away from here."

"You didn't take part in the shoot."

"No. I need my gun license."

"Sid Walker accused you of being a wuss."

"Ah well. Sid likes to say his piece."

"You didn't think of getting involved."

"Sure, but decided it wasn't a good idea. I feared someone would get hurt—it's a miracle there were no injuries. Apart from the trees, there was very little damage."

"I suppose you've seen a lot worse."

"I have, but—"

"You don't want to talk about it?"

He allowed his fingers to touch her shoulder. "I can't. Even if I wanted to, I'm not allowed."

"I'm told you weren't an ordinary soldier."

Tom shook his head and before she could ask more questions, he pulled her against him and kissed her.

"Sorry, I asked too many questions."

"And some other time, I will answer the ones I'm allowed to answer, but tonight there's a full moon and I have you alone at last."

His lips covered hers again and he fumbled with the bathrobe.

"Tom," she whispered. "Let's go inside."

"Let's." he nibbled her throat.

****

Sara trembled as she watched Tom throw back the bed covers. It had been more than two years since she had been with a man. Since Jack had died, Tom McPherson was the first man to whom she wanted to give herself. He pushed off the bathrobe; the reassuring strength of his arms around her reconciled her doubts. Desire sweltered through her core and tingled over her body. She inhaled as he lowered her to the bed and opened her lips to his kisses. His breathing ragged as he mouthed his way down her neck, kissing and nibbling the hard tips of her breasts. Her blood surged and breath quickened as his mouth moved lower, across her stomach and nuzzled her inners thighs. She cried out as he roused her, hot and ready; wet and eager. He teased her open, questing and conquering. Her back arched as waves of pleasure washed over her body. Tom rose and removed his shirt and jeans; the front of his boxers bulged. Sara grasped the waistband and pulled them off his hips. He grew harder in her hands, as he filled her mouth a drop of salty fluid spilled onto her tongue. His fingers entwined themselves into her hair as he pushed deeper. His voice

118

husked her name as he withdrew and pushed her back on the pillows. He parted her thighs and slipped inside her. Sara clung to him as he thrust deeper and faster, her hands stroked his back. She whimpered as the pleasure deepened and screamed as another orgasm rippled through her loins. He grasped her hips for the final thrusts, his thighs trembled, his body hard. He spilled into her—pushing and pulsing. He collapsed over her, panting; lips sought hers, warm and hard.

"Jesus, Sara. That was incredible."

****

The bawling of a cow woke Tom in the middle of the night. Sara slept beside him and his first impulse was to wake her for round two.

No, that cow sounded distressed.

"Tom? What is it?"

"Just the cows kicking up a ruckus. I'm going to take a look."

Other cows called and calves bawled. Tom pulled on his jeans, hurried to the kitchen and snatched up his torch. He limped down the steps and across the yard. The rough gravel jabbed into his bare feet. The torchlight found the rumps of cows and shining eyes, their tails swished as they huddled in a group. Except one who remained separate to the herd; she stamped around with her head down, butting at something, her tail lashed and she threw up clods of mud with her hooves. As Tom approached, something flew into the air.

"Tom, what is it?" Sara's voice shook as she halted at his side. "What is that?"

In the beam of the torch, a pair of black leathery wings flapped away in the moonlit night, it carried a newborn calf clamped between its feet and in its jaws.

His heart pounded and his skin crawled. "Did—did you see that?"

"Yes. What—was that a bird?"

Tom shook his head and swallowed. "No. Whatever it is, I'm sure it's not a bird."

"It kind of looked—"

"Like a flying fox only bigger. I saw it a couple of weeks ago. Its face is strangely human—but it had wings."

"Tom, that's impossible."

"I know. I swear I'm not lying, Sara—I'm not mad."

"How could it be a human with wings?"

"I don't know—maybe I am mad."

"But I saw it too."

"Yes, you did. Did you see its face?"

"No." Sara shook her head. "Should we report it?"

Tom laughed. "Do you really want to tell Mark we saw a real-life bat man?"

"Yeah—no."

"Me either. The locals already suspect I've stripped a gear. I don't want to fuel their rumours."

"What are you going to do?"

"At first light, I'm going to try and follow where it went." His face turned to the ranges at the southern end of his farm.

"Tom, that might be dangerous."

"It's big, Sara but I'm bigger, and I own a gun."

****

In the early morning light, Tom kissed Sara and watched her drive away. Once again, gloom settled over him. The night with her had been his happiest for too many years. As always, misery lurked in the darkest corners of his mind—memories of the mother he knew briefly, his father who could only view life through the bottom of a bottle. Roo-box Ruth remained the only relative who wanted to know about Tom McPherson.

Dog yipped as Tom walked away, leaving him tied to the veranda post. The blood trail from the calf began to peter out after several hundred metres and Tom continued in a straight line towards the hillside. The warm sun on damp leaves and loam released a heady scent. Up the hillside he trekked and found a wallaby path to follow. His stiff leg troubled him as he climbed over logs—trees of yesteryear fallen in storms long forgotten. He passed from his own land onto Penrose Nelson's land. No fences crossed the steep hillside; only wallabies used this path. As he climbed, Tom contemplated giving up; he hadn't seen any drops of blood for some time. He stopped, on the ground several paces downhill from the path lay a clump of russet calf hide, still fresh—large ants stood around it as though discussing how best to take it home. Tom searched the terrain, looking for further signs his quarry had passed this way. Uphill from the path another splash of blood in the grass. His leg protested but Tom left the path and began the steeper climb, taking his time, searching for signs of life. Or death. When he came face to face with a boulder plastered with blood and muck—some fresh, some dried, he slipped the rifle from his shoulder. As he climbed around the boulder, his stomach churned. At his feet a hole, dark and around three metres wide, penetrated vertically into the hillside. Shadowed by the trees, he couldn't see the bottom. The lichen and ferns that grew from the crevices in the rocky throat showed signs of damage; something had crushed them. He shivered at the dark smears on the rocks;

this was where the creature took its prey. He kicked a stone into the hole, it clattered and smacked its way deep into the earth. Tom's heart leapt to his throat, below in the darkness, something moved and hissed. A demon? The pale, human-bat face stared up at him with large obsidian eyes, it ears pricked and then flattened; it bared its fangs, snarled, and by the time Tom raised and cocked his rifle, it vanished. Tom immediately doubted himself.

Okay, I must be going mad.

He took one last looked at the blood-smeared boulder and skittered away down the slope.

28

Tom didn't want to be alone. He breasted the bar of the Warby Creek Hotel and ordered a drink. The day's events played endlessly on his mind and annoyed him; he wished only to spend his time thinking of Sara. Each time he tried, his mind dragged back to the thing in the hole. The thing that reminded him of a horror film.

What the hell is it?

He knew what he saw but it wasn't possible. Demons are mere imaginings of a fevered human brain. This creature was the size of a human child with a humanoid face, sharp teeth and wings. He looked around. Dave Masters tended the bar along with a young barkeep. As much as he wanted to see her and hold her, he hoped Sara would stay upstairs with her kids. He'd rather she didn't see him here, drinking in the bar. He ordered another scotch and returned to brooding about the bat-creature—the only description he could think of. If he were an artist, he could draw it.

No! It's impossible. There's no such thing on earth.

So far, since his discharge, he had scraped by without the aid of a counsellor; they always managed to make him doubt his sanity. Now he couldn't rule it out.

124

"Another one, Tom?"

Tom's eyes fell surprised to his empty glass. "Yes—please, Dave. Just another one and I better get home." A mouthful of wooden words.

Another ten and then I might think about going home.

Tom stiffened at movement beside him.

"Well fuck my arse if it ain't G I Joe."

"Bugger off, Sid."

Rapid Roy raised his head as he sensed the possibility of conflict.

Sid splayed his arms. "Aw come on, McPherson. Surely you don't like to drink alone."

"I do, Sid. I do."

Roy grinned. "He's mad, Sid—watch 'im."

"Shut up, Roy. So, what's bugging you, Tom? Joining the army sure made you a cranky cunt."

Tom threw back his drink and got to his feet. Sid grabbed at his arm and Tom shook him off.

Rapid Roy's head swivelled from Tom to Sid. "Watch 'im, Sid. He could be dangerous."

"Fuck off, Roy. Tom's not dangerous—he's depressed—aren't you, Tom?"

Tom's fist clenched, his knuckles itched. "You're an expert, are you?"

"Nah! But when you first came to this town as a snotty nosed kid, your mother had just died and your father was in jail and you had a shaved patch on your head where he hit you."

"Shut it, Sid."

"I'm not trying to be a nark, Tom—you should talk about it. Talking helps to—"

"Talking is what's gonna get your head busted, Sid."

Sid lifted a beefy arm to Tom's shoulder, "Come on, let's buy a bottle of Scotch and go sit on the veranda. We'll talk about old times."

Tom's discipline deserted him; it did him good to twist Sid's arm, spin him around and kick him towards the door. Sid stumbled and as his head centred between the batwings, Tom hauled him back for a second pounding. He planned to kick Sid's arse again but instead, broke the batwings.

"Now look what ya done, Tom." Blood poured from Sid's ear.

"Oh fucksake!" Tom scowled at the batwings then at Sid.

Dave Master's stopped beside him. "I hope you're going to pay for that, Tom."

"Don't worry, Dave." Sid mopped at his bleeding ear. "Me and Tom'll fix it tomorrow. Won't we, Tom?"

"I'll fix it, Dave." Tom pulled a handful of money from his pocket. "In the meantime, give me a bottle of Scotch. I should have stayed home."

Tom took the bottle, jostled past the broken batwings, and with a slur of boots on the boards, he rambled across the veranda.

Sid's voice caught him on the sidewalk. "You right to drive, Tom?"

"Fuck off."

"Old Fitzy might get you for DUI."

"Thought you said Fitzy couldn't catch a cold in Alaska."

"Ah-hah! McPherson does listen to me after all. See you tomorrow, Tom."

"Not if I can help it."

29

Tall and gaunt, Magistrate Murray Boyle was hungry. In all the years he'd been conducting hearings in the Warby Creek District Court, he had never seen so many defendants. Tempers among the legal fraternity frayed, they had all missed lunch. Afternoon tea time rolled past and there were still twenty people to process. Since they all pleaded guilty, it was a case of tick and flick. Apart from a few who needed their gun licenses to make a living, he revoked them and served a twelve-month good behaviour bond. A group of activists arrived when the bailiff called for defendant number seventy-eight. Wayne 'Wooley' Lambe sauntered in wearing a too-tight brown suit, the reek of moth-balls reached across the courtroom and assailed Murray's olfactory nerves. A journalist and a sketch artist sat in the front row and scratched the proceedings in their note pads. Murray had a few moments' distraction as Wooley Lambe stated his case. The noise from the activists rose to an intolerable level and he quelled them with a downward motion from his bushy eyebrows before returning his attention to Wooley Lambe.

"...we had to do something about the bats, your honour. People were dying and nobody outside Warby

Creek cared—we truly felt like we'd been left to fend for ourselves. I mean, hell—I couldn't even take the missus to the pub for tea, and we had always enjoyed eating at the pub once a week. The beer garden was covered in shit—err—ex—excrew—excrur—"

"Excrement." Murray nodded.

"He should be jailed!"

"Silence!" Murray searched for the voice that interjected. "I allowed you people in on the condition you stayed completely silent. One more sound from any of you and I'll clear the court."

Murray nodded and Wooley cleared his throat. "The people have rights—get on your 'puter there, your honour and gargle it. People have a right to live without—"

Murray threw up a hand. "Okay, enough Mr Lambe—we understand your position." Murray laid aside his gavel and straightened the papers on his desk. "Now, I have heard it said many times today that people should have the right to a clean and safe environment. One of you stated that if the bats had taken up residence in Queen Street they'd have been moved on immediately. It is a fact that people in the country pay the same rate of tax as those who live in the city and therefore, they are entitled to the same rights as their city counterparts."

"What about the trees?"

Magistrate Boyle's eyes seared the activists one at a time. His lingering gaze elicited squirms and fidgets from each. Only the sound of a blowfly buzzing against a window disturbed the silence. He took up his gavel by the head.

"I would throw the lot of you out but of all the people in this courtroom, you—" he poked his gavel handle at the activists. "—need to hear what I have to say.

"The trees have not—I repeat—not been destroyed. They were lopped as they would have been anyway had the bats not been occupying them. It is standard practice throughout towns and cities all over this country to lop trees to prevent them becoming too tall and the trees of Warby Creek were well overdue for lopping, please do not tell me they were harmed. Indeed, a number of those trees died during the years of infestation due to the bats stripping off the bark and leaves. As for the bats themselves, it is sad that so many died, I'm told around three hundred were destroyed. When you consider that there were an estimated three hundred thousand of them roosting in the town, I don't think losing three hundred is cause for excessive grief.

"It is the people of Warby Creek we should save our sympathy for. They have been subjected to intolerable conditions for far too long and I will risk my career to declare the politicians of this state grossly negligent in their failure to help this town. Far be it from me, a humble magistrate to make recommendations but we need a 'Warby Creek Law' that dictates if a fruit bat colony in an urban area reaches more than five thousand animals then they should be immediately moved on. Mr Lambe, as a protest to the government, I dismiss all charges against you. This session has ended."

30

As Tom removed the last screw from the batwings, heavy footsteps behind him turned his head.

"What do you want?"

Sid grinned and splayed his hands. "I came to help you fix the batwings we broke last night."

"I broke them—I'll fix them."

Sid planted his arse on the top step and pulled out his tobacco pouch. "Alright then. I'll just sit here and watch."

Tom sighed. "Why—"

"Why am I looking out for you? I always look out for my mates. The army turned you out on the street to fend for yourself and I don't think that's fair."

"No they didn't, Sid. I can get help if I need it."

"But you won't, will you?"

"I don't need help."

"But you could use someone to talk to, right?"

"What makes you think I need someone to talk to."

"I've watched you, mate. You arrived back in this town all stiff in one leg, prising yourself around on a walking stick, grim-faced and pissed off. People whisper and back away—you're pretty fucking scary, Tom."

"I don't use the walking stick anymore and my leg isn't as stiff—why the fuck am I even—go away, Sid."

"So what exactly happen to your leg?"

"It got busted."

"How bad."

"Every last fucking bone in it got busted."

"Bet that hurt."

"Surprisingly little."

"You shot up a bunch of ragheads while you dragged it around behind you."

"Sid, don't. Just stop."

"How come they didn't just lop it off above your balls?"

The laugh bubbled up without warning. "I guess the nurses liked my balls."

Sid shuddered. "Nah—don't want to talk about that. So how did they fix it?"

"A brace and bit, pliers and a screwdriver."

Sid's mouth opened and closed. "Ah—what? Are you a fucking bionic man?"

"They implanted some steel rods, screws and wire."

Another shudder and Sid's face paled. "Nah—don't want to talk about that either."

"So much for my needing someone to talk to."

"Yeah. Stupid idea."

"And there ended Sid's illustrious career as a shrink."

Sid went quiet and watched Tom pull the broken door apart. He spat out a sliver of tobacco and squinted. "I know what you do need help with, McPherson."

"What?"

"That." He nodded at the broken batwing and lumbered to his feet. "As a joiner, you'd make a fucking good soldier. Here, give me that."

"I can do it."

"Bullshit. Sit over there and watch."

****

Sara sat a glass of beer before Rapid Roy and extracted payment from the pile of coins and notes on the bar. On the veranda, she could hear Tom and Sid, they traded insults and occasionally they laughed. Men.

They don't do relationships with each other very well.

As she worked, she mentally rehearsed the words she had to say to Tom as soon as a chance presented itself.

I really enjoyed our night together but—

Almost two years had passed since Jack had died and she still hadn't sorted through her emotions. The evening before he died, they had quarrelled over what she couldn't remember. She had spent a sleepless night stewing over his stubbornness. She had even entertained a reckless fantasy of packing herself and the kids in the car and leaving. She wouldn't have. She had loved him. She would never have left him to run this place alone. The following morning before they had a chance to make up, he collapsed and died from a heart attack. Thirty-seven years old. She had dated him through high school, and they married when Sara was twenty. All those years and they never knew about the congenital defect—his heart had been a ticking time bomb. Too much stress and he dropped dead. The kids still mourned their father. She frequently slept with one or the other—sometimes both—in her bed. Night terrors still plagued Justin. Here she was now ready to move on but how could she? What would her children say if they knew she had spent the night with Tom while they both had sleepovers with their friends? She badly wanted to be with him but her kids had to come first. She would have to raise the subject with them. She needed time and distance to think. She needed to talk to Tom.

I hope he understands.

Agnetha made a song and dance about attending an anti-dam protest in North Queensland and basked in her activist friends' praise. She drove her little car to her parent's place on the Sunshine Coast and parked it behind the house. They were away on a month-long trip to Europe, her own trip would be over long before they returned. She took a taxi to the next suburb, used the false ID Penrose had acquired for just this purpose and hired a van. She drove north on the Bruce Highway and took a back road to avoid Rockhampton. She headed west on the Capricorn highway. For three days she drove, sleeping in the van and eating from the supplies she brought with her. Along the Landsborough Highway, she pulled onto a remote road out of sight of passing traffic and changed the registration plates to one of several sets Penrose had acquired for this purpose. Back on the highway, she continued on to Mount Isa. Practice had made her an expert at this. Hang about and watch for a non-diligent parent. This time she snatched a boy of around three years old, a ten-second squeeze of his carotid arteries to knock him out and then a shot of Midazolam. Agnetha was out of town before the boy's mother noticed him missing. Two nights later, exhausted from long hours of driving, she delivered Penrose another specimen.

Another child became a household name: Tyler McLennan. Across the country, newspapers, billboards and social media pled for his safe return.

32

The gun lay there on the table. His exit.

Walk over there and pick it up, McPherson. You know how to use it. It's your way out of all this shit. But Sara promised she would call.

That promise had given hope where none had survived. Even as she asked for his understanding. Even as she told him she couldn't see him for a while, her eyes betrayed her feelings for him.

Don't kid yourself, McPherson.

Tom smiled and swigged another mouthful.

She said she would call.

"She'll call, Tom. You've got to believe that."

The dog startled him as it growled and barked. His claws slipped on the smooth floor as he charged onto the veranda. Tom followed, fearing another visit from the bat creatures.

Sid Walker grinned as he stepped from the car with a plastic shopping bag. "Gidday, Tom. Trudy made too much chutney, she told me to bring you some."

Tom sighed, Sid's unsolicited friendship would take some getting used to, but a friend was a friend and sometimes they arrive like a stray dog to endear themselves to the hardest heart.

"Chutney? I haven't had that for years. Thanks, Sid."

"The cows look like they're doing well, Tom."

"Come and take a closer look."

"Then we'll have a few snorts of this." Glass clinked as Sid pulled a large bottle of Scotch from among the jars of chutney.

Sitting at the veranda table hours and many drinks later Sid's eyes lit as he remembered something.

"I almost forgot! Just stay there, Tom. I have a present for you." The wooden floor shook and Sid stumbled across the veranda. Out into the dark he fumbled the door of his Landcruiser open and carefully removed a supermarket cold-bag. A glow of pleasure spread over Sid's whiskery countenance as he returned.

"Got you a surprise, Tom." He puffed up the steps set the bag gently on the table.

"Why do I fear your surprises more than a Halloween gift from an Afghani warlord, Sid?"

Sid hiccoughed, reached into the bag and withdrew a large green egg. "Whaddya think of that, Tom?"

"An emu egg—what the—where did you get that?"

"I got three of the buggers."

"It's illegal to steal emu eggs, Sid."

"Nah—there's millions of those bloody birds wandering in the bush." He waved a meaty hand. "Won't hurt to remove a few."

"I know, but they're a protected species."

"Well yeah—you can't have everyone stealing their eggs, then they would be endangered. But that old man emu had about fifteen eggs, I reckon he'd be glad to be rid of three of them."

"How did you manage to get past him?"

"I took me boy shooting with me last night. We shot a roo and while we were dragging it back to the ute we disturbed that bird from his nest. While he was busy chasing my son across the paddock I grabbed three of his eggs and tucked them in my shirt and legged it back to the ute."

Tom snorted despite his disapproval. "So why are you giving them to me? They're a bit big for one man to make scrambled eggs out of."

"I remembered that carved egg you brought to school when you were a kid. It was really good, I thought you might like to make another one."

"But you didn't like it. You told me I was a poofter."

"Yeah, but you know—I was hardly going to tell you I was impressed."

"No, you would never have done that. So now you want me to do another one?"

"Why not? All you gotta do is tap a hole in each end and blow all the yoke—well you know how it's done. Give it a go. Might be a good hobby for you."

"Sid, I don't need a hobby."

"Well, I'll leave them here and you can think about it."

"Gee thanks, Sid."

It was after midnight when Sid agreed that he had better not drive home and collapsed on the couch. Tom cast a despairing glance at the bag of emu eggs and staggered off to bed.

A strange whistling woke him. Tom rolled onto his back and stretched. The previous night filtered back.

"Sid? Do you have to do that?"

No reply. The whistling continued and a scrabble of claws on the polished floor brought him to his feet.

"Dog?" Certain he had locked the dog in the garage the night before, Tom pulled on a pair of jeans and went to investigate. Three striped emu chicks mingled beside the couch where Sid slept, they cheeped and watched Sid with expectant eyes.

"Sid, you cunt! Wake up!"

"Huh, what's up, Trude?" Sid lurched upright and coughed. "Ah Tom, what are you yelling about?"

"Those fucking things!"

"What fucking—holy shit! Where did they come from?"

"Out of those fucking eggs, where do you think?"

Confusion turned to comprehension. "Whoa, I didn't think those eggs had chicks in them."

"What did you expect? Smarties? Did you think that bird was sitting on them because he liked the feel of them under his arse?"

"Oh! That's not ideal, hey?" Sid wiped a patch of stale drool from his cheek.

"Not ideal at all, Sid."

"We could take 'em to the Nelsons."

"You do it. Every time I go near old Agnetha she calls me a murderer or a baby killer." Tom shuddered.

"She calls me a murderer too. Nah, put them in your chook pen and feed them lettuce. They eat anything you would feed to a chook, except meat. When they get big enough put them in with the cows." Sid prodded a sausage finger at the chicks. "Hewy, Dewy, and Lewy—there you go, I named them for ya."

Tom sighed. "I'll make some coffee."

"While you're there, feed your pet emus, I think they're hungry."

"Why is it whenever you come near me, Sid, I end up in some kind of shit?"

"Speaking of shit, you'll also need a mop."

Tom laughed. Yesterday's troubles faded as he mopped a hatchling's excreta off his floor.

33

Barry came back from the pub a little late for the six o'clock news. Alice shook her head as he entered the lounge room.

"Sorry I'm late, Alice. Me and Dave got talking."

"Nah, it's alright, Darl. I was just listening to them talking about that little boy—Tyler McLennan, that went missing from out west—what's that place—Mt Isa. They're trying to work out if it's connected to all those others that have gone missing over the past years."

"Poor little boy. I sure hope they find him. Unharmed."

"Yeah, Darl. And I'm glad our kids grew up safe and healthy."

"Yeah, we didn't think nothing of them roaming around with their friends."

"The world's becoming a scary place, Darl."

"Sure is, Alice."

34

In the dawn's light, Tom turned off Grinder's Gully road and took the shortcut around the town to Roo-box Ruth's. The night before he had crawled out of his pit of despair and went shooting. The load of kangaroos on the back was his first for some weeks. Through the trees, Tom saw the taillights of a vehicle stopped on the edge of the dirt road. As he drew near recognition dawned. It was Sid's rig, jacked up; the back wheel lay in the middle of the road. He pulled in behind the ute and climbed out.

"Sid?" Only the sound of an alarm pierced the air. Sid's ute warned him he had left his headlights on. "Sid, where are you—don't you try and sneak up on me or I'll kick your arse. Again."

No sound.

Away in the long grass, a glow caught his eye. "Sid?" Tom turned his roo-spotter on and aimed it. Something moved on the edge of the beam, dark wings flapped away into the trees, an eerie cry like fingernails scraped across his soul.

Shit, is it that demon-bat-thing again? Maybe it was a crow.

145

His eyes returned to where he'd seen the glow in the grass and hurried over.

"Sid?" A man lay on the ground, as Tom drew closer he froze. "Sid!"

During his years of active service, Tom had seen countless dead bodies in varying states of dismemberment and decay. The sight of a mutilated friend he would never come to terms with. Sid Walker lay on his back, his eyes wide and a frozen scream had left his mouth agape. Beside him, his torch shone on a clump of grass. Sid's blood, a lot of it, had sprayed the surrounding ground and painted the grass crimson. A gaping wound in Sid's neck splayed open, pink bones and white sinews, naked and obscene in the tranquil countryside.

Tom covered his face. How many flat tyres had Sid stopped to change in his lifetime of moonlighting as a kangaroo shooter?

"What the fucking hell are you?" He shouted into the trees where the dark shadow had flown. "You bastard! You evil—I'm coming for you!"

Tom hurried back to his ute and took his phone from the glove box. He called triple-O and made a somewhat incoherent request for the police.

Mark Fitzgibbon and two of his constables arrived followed by the ambulance.

"What's the problem, Tom?"

"It's Sid."

"What? Where is he?" Mark stepped back and cast his eye over Sid's rig.

"He's over there. He's dead."

Tom stayed leaning on his vehicle and pointed to where Sid's body was visible in the growing daylight.

The junior constable picked his way through the grass and fired a question over his shoulder. "How do you know he's dead?"

Intuition.

"He's dead."

"How long ago did you find him, Tom?"

"Dunno—must be a half hour. You guys were a long time coming."

"Oh Jesus Christ!" The younger constable stumbled away and vomited into the grass.

"What the hell happened to him—a dog attack?" Mark's shoulders drooped as he gazed at the carnage.

Tom hadn't thought a dog might be responsible. "Search the ground. Are there any tracks?"

"This looks fresh. You must have disturbed whatever it was. Did you see anything running away?"

"No." Tom shook his head. How could he explain what he thought had killed Sid? But explain he must. Marks face clouded as Tom told him what he thought he had seen. He told him of the creature he had encountered three times before, and that Sara Nolan had also caught a glimpse of it.

"You must have seen an eagle."

"Do you think an eagle did that?" He jabbed a finger in the direction of Sid's corpse.

"I don't know. There are no dog tracks, only claw marks on the ground near the victim."

"Sid. His name is Sid."

Mark didn't respond to Tom's rebuke. "Tom, have you been assessed?"

The surge of anger died as quickly as it formed. "I know you think I'm crazy—half the town thinks I am."

"Tom I have to ask these questions."

"Yeah. I'm sorry I can't give you a clear description of what I saw. How do you describe something that your mind knows is impossible? The biggest flying carnivore in Australia is a wedgetail eagle. This creature is bigger—heavier, and I'm fairly sure it doesn't have feathers."

Mark agitated his scalp with frustrated fingers. "Look—Tom—for now we'll have your statement say you saw something dark fly into the trees. The forensics will take a swab from around the wound to see if they can find some DNA."

Tom fixed the sergeant with a thoughtful gaze. DNA would be the thing that might prove what he saw—or maybe it would prove him completely mad. "How long will that take?"

"A few days—a week. Not sure, we're getting better at this stuff every day."

"Mark, can you let me know the result of that test? I've got to know what it is I saw."

"Okay, unless the case becomes a murder investigation. If that happens, well I'm sure you get the picture."

"Yeah—I'll be hauled in."

Mark opened and closed his mouth. A feeble smiled hiked the corner of his mouth. "In the meantime, don't leave the country."

"I plan never to leave this country again." Tom yanked the door of his ute open. "For what it's worth, Mark. I didn't do that." He tilted his head in the direction of the corpse. "Me and Sid liked to hit each other, but we were mates."

****

Later that day, Tom swigged the mug of coffee his Aunt Ruth had sat on the desk, rubbed his eyes and continued to stare at the screen. Seven days of CCTV footage was a lot to get through. Much of it he played at high speed. He snickered at the footage of himself and Sid penguin trotting back and forth across the yard, lugging roo carcasses. He leaned in and slowed the footage. Darkness fell, the occasional moth fluttered across the screen. He straightened in his seat as an image of a woman in a floral frock and blucher boots halted like a kangaroo in the spotlight as the motion sensor saturated the screen with light. Agnetha Nelson's eyes glinted white then she hurried away.

"Yes, Mrs Nelson. Roo-box Ruth has security lights now. Fuck off and take your sharp instrument with you."

Sid's voice in his head said, *What did I fuckin' tell ya?*

Daylight rolled around again and Tom once again accelerated the video. Night came and he slowed it.

"Right. This is last night's footage. Eyes peeled, McPherson."

He'd found Sid's body around eight-hundred metres from the roo-box and accepted this might prove a fruitless exercise but the creature had been in this vicinity—maybe it had flown past Ruth's camera. He lifted the cup to his lips and fumbled it back onto the desk, dark brown liquid slopped across the wood. He stopped the footage and wound it back. As it rolled again, a grainy image of something dark flickered and disappeared just as the motion sensor flooded the scene with light. He rewound and rolled—rewound and rolled. Too grainy and too dark but compared to the size of the moths in the foreground, the thing he strained to see seemed much bigger—big enough for the motion sensor to pick it up from a distance. Satisfied he'd find nothing more, he cut the three second long scene from seven days of footage and copied it to a separate clip.

Mandeep peered at the screen and muttered, "What the fuck am I seeing?"

Since he had begun working in criminal pathology, he had routinely analysed the DNA samples supplied and gave his verdict. Many times, he had helped convict a suspect and many times, he had freed one. A week before he had sipped his tea and cast a bored eye over the forensic officer's notes. *'Saliva sample taken from wound on deceased's neck. Likely animal DNA. Most likely a dog or possibly a wild pig.'*

Mandeep had sniffed. "Let me be the judge of that, Mate."

He pressed enter and blinked at the electropherogram; he'd known to expect animal DNA but the image before him set his heart racing. As he rubbed his eyes and refreshed the screen, his mind flew to that morning in the university lab when Penrose Nelson's wife miscarried a monster right before his eyes. He and his boss had cleaned up the mess and promised one another they would never mention it again. Several years on, the incident still played and replayed in his mind but he kept it inside. In the field of biology, scientists universally agreed what he and Robert had witnessed was impossible. Penrose had removed the foetus before Mandeep could take a closer look, which he told himself was a good thing. The lack of photographic evidence gave plausible deniability—even to himself.

The screen pulled up the same image and Mandeep shook his head. He would have to repeat the whole exercise.

"Ah bloody hell!"

Forty-eight hours later the same image greeted him.

"No! Jesus Mary mother of God! This is impossible!"

I wonder where Penrose is living these days.

His eyes flicked to the phone on his desk and he rose, went to the staff room to make a mug of strong coffee. Back at his desk, he came to a decision, picked up the phone and called Kenzie Nelson. For once, Kenzie answered his call on the first try. A couple of long, nervous hours later, he met the naturalist at a street café in the city and steered him to a table where traffic noise roared loudest—this conversation could not be overheard.

"It's good to catch up, Mandeep—where are you working these days?"

"I am working in police forensics doing the DNA profiling."

"Sounds interesting."

"Not as interesting as your job, I'm sure." Mandeep's smile kept falling off his face.

Kenzie Nelson frowned. "So, what can I do for you?"

Mandeep sipped his coffee and waited until a truck roared away from the nearby traffic lights. "Your big brother, Penrose. Where is he these days?"

"Funny you should ask. If you had asked me that a couple of months ago, I couldn't have told you. I saw him recently; he's living just outside a little town, inland from Bundaberg called Warby Creek."

Oh fuck no!

"Ah, I see."

"Why, what has my big brother been up to? Is he in trouble with the police?"

"No. But I suspect he is behind some very odd DNA that I identified this past week."

"How?"

"Well, let me tell you a very strange story. One morning we were in the lab…"

****

Kenzie gazed at Mandeep, doubt and disquiet chased each other around in his mind.

Is Penrose that smart?

"Is that possible?"

"Cloning is possible and genetic engineering—or editing—is possible. As far as we know, combining the two like that has never been done before."

"Then how?"

"Penrose is very dedicated to his work. He often worked long hours, I'm certain he sometimes stayed in the lab all night. Went home for breakfast and came back for work."

"But—"

"Robert and I went through the computers with a fine toothed comb and could find none of Penrose's work. We think he was saving it all to an external hard-drive. There was no evidence of internet searches. We even got a nerd to search his metadata—there was nothing incriminating."

"But how could he—"

"We think he must have found a trait on the genome that was switched off in humans and switched it back on. Possibly a trait that is switched on in bats but off in humans. He took a human embryo and had a fiddle and reimplanted it. Just because it hasn't been done before, doesn't mean it's impossible." Mandeep sipped his coffee and grimaced, "We've known for many years that at least seventy-five percent of human DNA is just junk. In fact, only a quarter of our DNA appears to be of any use.

Mutations happen—from radiation or just mistakes made with replication—the majority of mutations have no effect and those that have a bad effect usually result in the death of the offspring who inherit it. I suspect Penrose found a way to switch redundant traits back on. The year before he gave a lecture and the Dean got complaints—he was raving on about mixing the genetics of animals with humans and growing super humans. Some of the students really took offence."

Kenzie snorted. "I can imagine."

"And now, this hybrid DNA turns up in the very place that Penrose is living. Maybe it's a mistake—I don't know how. I double checked."

"The implications are horrendous, not just for the human race but for bats as well. Jesus, Mandeep, if what you're thinking turns out to be true—are you going to alert the government?"

Mandeep cast a worried glance at the street. "I don't know. For now I'm going to have to show this DNA evidence to the forensics—Jesus—I'm going to be the laughing stock. I'm supposed to be a molecular biologist not a comedian."

36

The cage door clanged shut and Tyler McLennan crawled to the far corner and pulled the grubby blanket over himself.

"What's the problem with him, Penrose."

"I suspect he carries a divergence in his DNA and my treatment, which has worked so well on the others is not working for this one."

"I don't understand."

"Of course you don't—only I would understand—but well—I err it seems, Agnetha, that Mother Nature never saved everything in all humans after all. Or perhaps some humans never had the trait to begin with. I wonder why that would be, Agnetha? Do you know that some three percent of European Caucasian shows some Neanderthal genes on their DNA? Perhaps something like that may account for the differences."

"What are we going to do with him then?"

"Put some food in for him and let me think about it."

"I'm not driving all the way back to Mt Isa."

"No—of course not. We could just leave him outside a hospital or something."

"So I'll have to risk capture to dispose of him then. You haven't seen the social media comments—what they would do to the person who took little Tyler. Flaying—hanging—castration. The McLennans and their supporters are threatening all manner of horrors. Why do I have to put myself in danger? Why don't you deal with it?"

"You know I'm too busy, Agnetha."

"You're busy? What about me, I have to feed all these infernal animals that people keep bringing as well as your freak show."

Penrose fixed a wintry gaze on his wife. "Don't make me angry, Agnetha."

"No, Penrose."

"Now go and find some food for this specimen."

"Yes, Penrose."

37

Peter Edwards smiled as the branch president toasted his preselection. This was his lifelong dream; all he needed now was to gain the support of the electorate. Losing his only daughter had given him an unexpected public platform, his campaign on child safety was going great guns. His marriage was another thing. Celina spent most of her days sleeping; when she woke she stumbled about the house in a substance-induced daze, rarely getting out of her filthy nightdress. She had refused to front the media with him. Each day she sank deeper into the pit of depression. What could he do but continue his career? Many on social media said he was a cold bastard; how could he just carry on when his beautiful little girl had vanished? He had to carry on. If he stopped to dwell on it too long, he'd simply lose his mind. He would head home in the morning and begin preparations for his election campaign. The Premier had called a snap election and Peter's moment to prove himself arrived.

"Thank you." He waited for the applause to die down. "Thank you for your confidence in me. I am humbled…"

****

Agnetha's face in the mirror greeted her with surprise. Her blond hair, moulded to her head by her straw hat had become brittle. Not yet thirty, her face had aged, eroded by the muddy currents of time and ill-use. Her moods swung in chaotic rhythm to her body temperature—today in a coinciding surge, the two peaked together. Agnetha needed to kill something.

"Agnetha."

"What!"

"Are you angry, Agnetha?"

"What if I am?"

"Anger is unhealthy, Agnetha. You know that."

"I can't help it—I'm sick of these hot flushes."

"There are drugs and natural remedies to treat your condition. I'll jump online and order some for you."

"Yes, Penrose. Thank you."

The same promise you made last week, Penrose.

"Now, you have work to do. It's feeding time."

"Yes, Penrose." Agnetha bunched her fists and went to perform her twice-daily ritual. Under her mask of devotion she battled an urge to defy her husband, take his precious animals and drop kick them into the fence. She wandered through the animal enclosures feeding the various injured and orphaned wildlife.

"Feed the animals, Agnetha—feed the bat kids, Agnetha—invite Eden to dinner, Agnetha." Anger hissed between her teeth. "Commit unpardonable crimes, Agnetha."

Past Penrose's lab and up the hill she trudged, the hot flush had burned itself out but her anger redoubled. Through the trees, up the narrow path, through the boulders and into Nelson's cave.

Penrose's dungeon of horror more like it.

Into the cold room to fetch chunks of meat. Penrose had instructed her to microwave it to medium rare but this afternoon she couldn't be bothered. She carried the big lumps in a bucket and pushed them through the bars. At the last cage, Agnetha tossed the meat and it fell into the filth on the floor. The youngest of the bat kids let out a high-pitched shriek and sprang at the bars. Agnetha's heart leapt, her skin tingled, and her anger exploded.

"That's it! You can go back to your capitalist pig parents!" She flung open the cage, seized the screaming batchild by the wing and dragged her to the front of the cavern. "Get out! Out!" Agnetha broke into a flood of sweat, her face burned and her anger seethed. She swung a kick at the red haired bat child and sent her on her way. The batchild blew leaves across the cave entrance as she took to the sky. Penrose came running out of his laboratory, a stethoscope swinging wildly around his neck.

"Agnetha! What have you done? You set her free—oh dear God! I must find her."

Agnetha stormed away to the house, shut herself in the bathroom and soothed her rage under a cold shower.

****

Edna Wilcox shot out of her bed faster than her eighty-five year old body had moved in years. A great whomp and screeching of claws on the tin roof set her teeth on edge. She hurried across her darkened bedroom and reefed the curtains open to peer at the street. As she watched, sparks showered from the power lines and a bang at the other end of the street made her trembling legs wobble under her. The streetlights went out. Edna felt her way to the door and clicked the switch. No electricity. She fumbled in her bedside drawer and found a torch; the batteries were flat. She opened the front door and peered into the street, shuffled down the steps and across the yard. Only five metres away a dark figure twitched in the gutter. Across the street, someone hurried with a torch. Peter Edwards hurried from his front yard and across the bitumen. The torch beam fell on the face of the creature, smoke rose from its wings, its beautiful red hair vivid in the light. Edna clapped her hand to her mouth to stifle a scream that threatened. Peter fell to his knees and sobbed.

"Oh god! Maddy? No, it can't be—"

Was it Madelyn? Edna could see the face clearly but her eyes refused to believe. The creature had auburn hair over its body; around its head and face was Madelyn's beautiful red hair—curls still evident. Voices echoed from three blocks away. Startled residents shone torches at the transformer smoking at the top of a pole. Edna couldn't speak. As she stood frozen in the shadows, lights washed over Peter Edwards. A small car pulled silently to the kerb. The headlights extinguished and the driver climbed from the car.

"Hello, Peter."

"Doctor Nelson." Peter got to his feet and rubbed his hands over his wet cheeks.

"Is she dead?"

"Yes—" Peter dissolved into pitiful sobs.

"I'm sorry."

Edna didn't think Penrose sounded at all sorry.

"I can remove her for you, Peter."

Edna clamped her hands harder across her mouth, the tears spilled over her fingers.

"Remove her?" Peter's eyes widened.

"Are you seriously going to show your wife what has happened to her little girl?"

"What has happened to our little girl?"

"It's tragic, Peter. Those bats that you allowed to plague this town for so long—well, you're not a scientist, you wouldn't understand even if I could find the words to explain. This is biology at its enigmatic best—or worst as it is in this case. It's best for your political career and for your wife if you just let me remove her and then you can get back to living your life, remembering your little darling as she was." Penrose Nelson moved to Peter's side and laid a comforting arm across his shoulder. "You couldn't have known what would happen. Let me remove her for you and you'll hear no more about it."

"I don't know, I—"

"How are you going to explain this to the police? To the voting public? Do you think they'll believe you?"

Peter gaped at Penrose.

"Is it worth sacrificing your political career to have people believe you're mad? Perhaps they will hold you responsible." Penrose removed his arm from Peter's shoulder and looked along the street. "You'd better hurry and make a decision, Peter. There are people up the street, they'll call the linesmen. They will want to know why the transformer blew. The linesmen will check."

"What can I do?"

"Let me take her away. You'll never hear anything more about it, I promise. Come on, Peter, make a decision or I will get in my car and drive away. I'll leave you to sort it out all by yourself."

Peter nodded and hurried back to his house. Edna held in the cry of despair with both hands. Penrose Nelson gathered up the body and laid it in the boot of his car. As the little car performed a U-turn and sped silently away, Edna fell to her knees in the garden, her hands clasped before her face.

"Our Father, who art in heaven…"

Sara wrestled with an elusive and formless dream. Somewhere a rooster tore at the last rags of her slumber. She bolted awake as a door along the hallway slammed and Justin hurtled into her room.

"Mum! He dived onto her bed, the safest place in the world.

"Justin—what's going on?"

"There was a thing climbing in my window—I think it's still in my room."

Her chest heaved with fright and shattered sleep, Sara climbed from the bed.

"Are you sure it's not one of your nightmares?"

"No, Mum—I was wide awake—I saw it."

"Let's take a look." A glance at her bedside clock showed just after four a.m.

The hallway flooded with light; Sara's father stood in his pyjamas and squinted in the sudden glare. "What's going on?"

"Justin said someone was trying to get in his window." Sara pushed open the door to her son's room and froze. A snarl, the slither of leathery wings. The hallway light cast a narrow ray on teeth bared in warning. A strange humanoid face with obsidian eyes glared at her from the bed, a foul odour filled the air and its head shifted in rapid jerks from Sara to Justin and to the window. Sara fumbled with the light switch as the creature dived for the open window. As the fluorescent bulb fashioned a sluggish light over the room, Sara glimpsed a leathery wing and a stumpy leg covered with dark hair. The creature disappeared through the torn fly-screen. A chilling, alien cry rippled across Warby Creek.

"Mum!" Justin huddled against her back. "What is that thing?"

"I don't know, Justin."

"Who was it? Where did he go?" Dave pushed past Justin.

"It went out the window, Dad."

"It?"

"It wasn't a person, Dad, it was some kind of animal—didn't you see it properly?"

"No, those stupid greenie bulbs take too long to light up." Dave stepped to the window and stuck his head out. "It's a long way down to the ground, how did it get up here?"

"Dad, don't. Come away from there." Sara pulled him back and closed the window.

"Sara? What—"

"Dad, I'll talk to you about it in a minute." She glanced at Justin, his eyes wide in his bloodless face.

"Mum—what was that thing?"

Gracie burst in the door. "What's all the noise?" Her gaze flew to Justin's bed. "Ew! Justin—what happened to your bed?"

Blood and foul green muck smeared Justin's sheets.

"Gracie, and you, Justin. Go and get into my bed." Her children surveyed her with suspicion. "Just do as I say, come on."

Sara ushered her children to her bedroom, locked the window and drew the curtains. "Stay away from the window, I'll be right back—I just need a word with Grandad. Leave the door open, I'll be in the hallway."

Gracie's eyes shifted from Sara, to the window and back. She shrugged and pulled back the covers.

"Go on, Justin. You're safe now."

Sara joined her father where he waited, bewildered. "Sara, what just happened in there?"

"I'm not sure I know how to tell you what happened, Dad."

"Have a stab."

Sara leaned on the wall and whispered. "Well, you know that night I spent at Tom McPherson's place? You knew I spent a night out there, didn't you?"

Dave Masters smiled. "Of course I knew. I was waiting to see if you were going to tell me. You haven't gone back—why?"

Sara shrugged. "I need time to sort things out, find a way to tell the kids. But Dad, that night something very strange happened…" The story poured from her on quivering lips. She told her father what she had seen and what Tom had told her. Incredulity clouded Dave's face and Sara worried he suspected she had lost her mind.

"What on earth could it be?"

Sara shook her head, her mind full of dread. "It didn't seem to have a human's intelligence but its body—what I've managed to catch a glimpse of—looks a bit human."

"But with wings?"

"That's one thing I'm sure of."

"It must be a flying fox."

"It's far too big, Dad."

****

Tom woke with his maimed leg throbbing where steel met bone. He shifted position and contemplated swallowing a handful of painkillers. Instead, he lay there and thought about Sara.

She said she'd call.

A boner had begun to throb when the phone on his bedside table lit and trilled softly. Sara.

"Hello, pretty lady."

"Tom, I'm sorry to wake you."

"It's okay. I was awake and thinking about you."

"Oh." Her soft breath whispered in his ear.

"Sara?"

"Tom, that thing we saw, it was here. It climbed in my son's window."

Tom leapt to his feet; the erection yielded the blood it had pilfered to his limbs where need was greatest. "I'll be right there."

****

The arms of wattle scent enveloped Tom as he got in his car. The dog whined at being locked in the garage but with current events, it was the safest place for him. Driving to town, he wondered if Mark Fitzgibbon had received the DNA result and decided he would front him in the morning. He badly needed to know what that creature was. His Glock rubbed against his ribs, going armed in public could land him in all kinds of shit but that creature was growing bolder by the day. Tom carried his gun at all times and he would kill the creature at the first opportunity.

Tom pulled up in front of the darkened pub, hurried around the side of the building, through the beer garden, to the door marked 'Private' and knocked Sara opened the door and ushered him in.

"Tom, I'm so glad you came." She snapped the door shut. "I feel guilty dragging you here but—"

"Hey, it's okay. I don't mind in the least."

Sara led him up a long flight of stairs to her living quarters on the upper floor. "I'm sorry about the stairs."

"I can get used to them—I mean—my leg is getting better every day."

Her cheeks darkened in the dim light of the stairwell but she smiled and took his hand. Upstairs she showed him Justin's room and the mess the creature had left on the bed.

"I'll talk to Mark in the morning and see if he can get his forensic people to examine those sheets and find out what this blood is from." He stepped over, pushed the window open and took out his iPhone. Until the sun came up, the best way for him to study the windowsill for scratches was photograph it using a flash.

"Do you think Mark can do anything? I wasn't going to bother."

"I think the more the police know, the better they can manage this thing. As it is, I'm sure Mark didn't believe me when I told him what I thought had killed Sid. Do you have a laptop I can upload these photos to?"

"Sure, come with me."

Seated beside Sara on the lounge, Tom took a moment to steer his brain away from the warmth of her body and concentrate on the photos. His camera had revealed only one clear set of claw marks but they appeared the same as those on the ground in the calving paddock, and those near Sid's body. The danger this thing posed grew direr by the day.

"Right. I think I'm going to have to go after this thing before it kills someone else."

"Do you think the police will like you doing that?"

"Well, if they won't do something, someone will have to. But I'll give them every chance; I'll even offer to help."

Tom closed the computer and laid it on the coffee table. Sara remained beside him, thoughtful and still.

"So, am I still on hold?"

"Tom, I'm sorry. Just give me a while. I've got to talk to my kids—I haven't found the right moment. I'm worried how they will react."

"In the meantime." Tom pulled her onto his lap and held her to his chest, tilted her head to receive his lips and his hand squeezed the warm skin of her thigh. It would have been a never-ending kiss but he needed to take a breath and let his heart rate slow to a pace less likely to kill him. "I can't stop thinking of you."

"Nor I of you."

"Tell me again, why are we wasting time?"

39

Tom had hoped sergeant Fitzgibbon would be on duty, but instead he encountered Senior Constable Riley who greeted him like an old sour with a new litter of piglets.

"Why didn't Mrs Nolan call us if she had an attempted break in?"

"I guess she wanted me to be there. The DNA they found on Sid's neck, what was it?"

"I can't comment."

"Sid was a mate; I want to know what killed him."

"You're not family, McPherson. I cannot tell you what they found. Now if Mrs Nolan wants to report a crime, she should call me."

"I'm reporting the crime, are you going to attend or are you going to sit there bitching?"

Riley's mouth open and closed; he fumbled the pen in his fingers and dropped it onto the desk.

"She's waiting."

"Alright—but there is no need for you to be there."

Tom had intended to go home and feed his dog but dug in his heels at Riley's attitude. He would be there.

****

Tom battled the urge to tear his hair out.

"Fucks sake, Mark, you need to warn the people to stay indoors at night and keep their windows closed."

"What am I going to tell them? There is some half man, half bat out there waiting to rip their throats out?"

Tom winced. A vision of Sid, lying there with his throat torn open assailed his mind.

Mark's eyelids fluttered. "Sorry—poor choice of words."

"Those DNA results prove what I told you, Mark. Sara saw it too and now, so has her boy."

"But dammit, Tom—it's not possible. I think that forensic guy must have mixed up the samples."

I've seen the bloody thing, enough times to know it exists."

"But you said you only ever caught a glimpse of it."

"Well, if you're not going to warn the town, then I will."

"Okay, okay! And if they laugh at me, I'll tell them you're the one behind all this crap."

"And are you going to try and catch the critter?"

"I don't have the resources to send a SERT team after a figment of someone's imagination."

"Well, if you're not going to go after that thing, I'm going to."

"Don't break the law, McPherson—I've been more than lenient with you, push me too far and I'll have you banged up."

"Right. Fair enough. Now are you going to put out that public alert?"

"Yes."

"And you'll let me know what is on that bed sheet?"

Mark filled the room with his sigh. "Yeah, yeah. I will."

"Good."

****

The screen door creaked and the bells tinkled.

"Darl?"

"I'm here, Alice." Barry sat on the back porch with his feet on the rail. The Courier Mail in his lap.

"Look at this. It's a leaflet I found in the letterbox. The police are telling us not to go out after dark and to keep our windows closed."

The newspaper slid to the floor. "What for?"

"An undisclosed danger it says. What undisclosed danger would there be roaming the streets of Warby Creek at night?"

Barry read the leaflet. "This probably has something to do with Sid Walker's death—I heard a rumour that he had his throat ripped open by some animal."

"Marge at the post office said her hubby was talking to Rapid Roy and Roy reckoned that big returned soldier with the hoppy leg dunnit. Roy reckons him and Sid were always fighting and threatening each other."

"I don't think—"

"Well, you saw them at it on the night of the public meeting at the pub. You heard what McPherson said—I'll rip your throat out."

Barry shook his head. "No, Sid said that to him."

"I don't know—Roy reckons that soldier bloke lost his mind in the war."

"Alice, Rapid Roy lost his mind in the bottom of a bottle. Don't believe anything he says, he's full of shit—always has been."

"Well, you'll have to stay home at night—no more going to the pub."

"I can still go before dark."

Alice sighed. "Well, I'm gonna go and cook dinner."

40

Hannah, Kirsty, Nic, and Ben, ecology students from Brisbane arrived in Warby Creek for a weekend break and booked into a motel. They ignored the manager's warning to stay indoors at night. The torreliana trees on the edge of town were in full bloom and the little redheaded flying foxes came each night in search of nectar. The students intended to spend a week studying them.

The nights were clear, ideal for observing the flying foxes' behaviour. On their second night, a half moon lit the bushland around them. Stars shivered through the leaves and branches.

"Come on, Ben. Let the rest of us have a turn with the goggles." Hannah crunched over the twigs under the trees to where Ben stood, gazing into the canopy. One set of night vision goggles between the four of them caused a few arguments.

"Yeah, here. Man, they're awesome!"

"Here, have a turn at this." Hannah passed Ben her reefer and took the goggles.

"Jesus, you two—get a room!" Ben turned his attention to Nic and Kirsty where they lay on a blanket in a tangle of passion.

178

"Don't look if you don't like it."

Hannah's voice piped from the tree's shadow. "Aw, they're so cute!"

Ben wandered to the esky and took out a beer, twisted the top off and dropped it into the ice. He poured a draught down his throat, belched, and lifted the reefer to his lips. "This is good shit, Nic—where did you get it?"

"I never reveal the sources of my brilliance. You know that."

"Your brilliance? Dude, You're just a dumbshit!"

"But I supply good weed."

In the branches above, the squabbles of the flying foxes escalated to screeches, the alarmed animals fluttered and took to the sky.

"Oh darn!" Hannah stumbled about, searching among the leaves for any stragglers. "Something scared them—they're all gone."

The canopy of a nearby tree shook, branches cracked and a shower of twigs and leaves fell.

"Wow, something big just landed in that tree. Gimmie a look—"

"Wait your turn!" Hannah hit Ben across the chest and trotted towards the shaking tree. Something jumped from branch to branch.

"It looks like some kind of monkey—"

"You're a monkey—come on let me have a look."

From the blanket on the ground, Kirsty screamed and shoved Nic off her. She clambered to her feet and backed away.

"What's up, Babe!"

"It's a monster!"

Nic guffawed. "Don't be stupid—what kind of monster?"

The tree trembled and a branch broke. A dark creature spread its wings and fell on Hannah. She hit the ground screaming and rolling, the creature flapped and snarled. Blood sprayed. Teeth gnashed. Ben charged in kicking and shouting. The coppery scent of blood and the animal's stench saturated the air.

"Fuck! Help! Nic! It's killing her!"

Nic picked up a camera tripod and swung it at the ball of wings, teeth, and claws. It shrieked and fell away from the girl.

"Go on! Git!" He lifted the tripod over his head for a second assault and the creature leapt away, its wings flapped and lifted it into the air. The alien shrieks faded as it flew into the night.

Ben fell to his knees beside the girl thrashing on the ground. "Hannah!"

"Jesus! What did it do to her?"

Ben fumbled, trying to staunch the flow of blood. "Call triple-O, quick! She's bleeding badly—oh shit, Nic—shit!" Warm blood flowed through his fingers and soaked into the dirt. Hannah's limbs weakened, slowed and stopped. Her wide eyes reflected the moon and stars—the straps of the night vision goggles tangled in her hair.

"What's wrong? Is she—" Kirsty approached, visibly shaking.

"I think she's dead—I can't find a pulse." Ben held his blood soaked hands in front of his eyes.

"Is that blood?" Kirsty came closer. Ben nodded and Kirsty began screaming.

"Call triple-O." Dazed, Ben remained kneeling beside Hannah, he lifted her lifeless hand and rubbed it between his. "How am I going to tell her Mum what happened?"

****

The keyboard rattled under Blake Rush's fingers. With minutes to the deadline, he cobbled together a new headline article. If this didn't earn him a Walkley Award, nothing would. His phone rang unanswered. His mobile pinged with messages he ignored. Messenger boxes popped up in the corner of his screen; it seemed everyone wanted to talk to Warby Creek's lone journalist this morning but he typed on—notoriety beckoned.

'GIRL DIES IN MYSTERIOUS CIRCUMSTANCES. Police are refusing to comment on what killed student, Hannah Pearson, but her companions reported a flying monkey set upon her from the branches of a gum tree...'

One hour later, Blake cringed at his head office editor's scathing voice. "...fucking ridiculous! This is a serious newspaper, not one of those crazy tabloids! We pay you to report the truth—not the ramblings of some drunken student..."

He lifted his head at a tap on the door and smiled. He waved Marina Slade into the seat across his desk, clamped his hand over the mouthpiece and whispered. "I'll be right with you."

The ten minute tirade from his editor ended and Blake hung up.

Marina grinned. "He didn't like it, eh?"

"Hated it."

"Well, my bosses are very interested so, let's begin with 'once upon a time in a little town far from the city...'"

41

Mandeep had spent the past week trawling through the university and the state libraries searching for references to bat-like creatures, certain he would find nothing. Finally, at home late one night, he found his way to an online cryptozoology site and found an article about the mythological aswang of the Philippines, also known as berbalangs. *Could this be what happens when you mix the genes of the Pteropus poliocephalus—the grey-headed flying fox with those of humans? No, don't be stupid.*

"But how?" Mandeep raked his scalp with trembling fingers. "How the fuck did you do it, Penrose?"

More to the point, why?

"Fiddling with genetics in this way could cause a major pandemic, especially with a new bat-born disease already doing the rounds. Penrose specialises in zoonotic diseases; he must know the risks. For a smart man, Penrose, you sure are a bloody fool."

The only hope was to go up there and find a way to contain the aswang and kill it before it destroyed humanity and possibly several species of native bats as well. A plan formed in his head and he shuddered; it would take a lot of organising.

183

Deanna appeared in the door, dishevelled, her pyjamas rumpled and askew. "Mandeep, are you coming to bed any time soon?"

Mandeep exited the website and stretched. "Yes. Right now. But I don't know if I'm going to sleep."

"Don't you think it is time you trusted me with what is bothering you?" Deanna massaged his shoulders, "And don't say nothing is bothering you. You've been like a cat on hot bricks for the past week. Come on, tell me about it."

He closed his eyes as her fingers unknotted his muscles. "Oh, that feels wonderful."

"Don't try to change the subject, Mandeep—I know you. Now tell me what is bothering you."

"First you must promise you won't have me sectioned."

"It's that bad?"

"It's worse."

****

Kenzie chewed the inside of his cheek and his eyes scanned his crew.

"This isn't going to be an ordinary shoot, guys."

"Then what is it?" Andy, his director usually made all the decisions about an upcoming expedition but today,

Kenzie had taken control. He needed to investigate Mandeep's bizarre story. The implications raised by the DNA evidence before them tantalised Kenzie. The possibility he might be the one to break the news of this ground-breaking science set his stomach a-flutter. Their father long ago opined that Penrose didn't have the level of intellect required for his chosen branch of science but should this evidence withstand scrutiny, Kenzie wondered if his father, Professor Elliot Nelson, had misjudged his eldest son.

"It's more of a fact finding mission, but I want to film it as I go."

"How can I film you conducting research?"

"Just follow me with a camera."

"Can I take my handy cam? I don't fancy lugging the big one about the countryside."

"As long as you can get a reasonable quality—fine."

"I'll take the big one, just in case."

"Good. Now boys, we're going to rough it a bit, so if you're not up for a week or maybe more of camping out, say so now."

None of the crew spoke. A camping trip with Kenzie Nelson promised a lot of fun and adventure. Nobody wanted to miss this opportunity.

"So where are we going?" Mickie glanced at Mandeep Singh.

"We're going up to Warby Creek but we won't be staying in the town. Mandeep is coming with us—he is a molecular biologist."

"What are we looking for?"

"Don't know yet. Steve, Jared, and Brett I want you to lay in provisions for a week—maybe more. We'll need to feed and house nine people."

"Okay, when are we leaving?"

"Tomorrow morning, so chop-chop. Go prepare."

42

The creature had a name. Sometime the man called him
Jake. Jake wasn't it. No human tongue could utter his name.
No human mind could bear his mores. No human heart
could embrace his being. The alpha male, first of his kind,
ruled his species. What remained of his humanity gave him
pre-eminence—he used his intelligence to bluff the blue-
faced ones. Behind their yellow eyes lay a primitive mind.
The man had given him freedom to roam the cave, but the
man didn't know the creature had found a back entrance
and spent the hours of darkness roaming free, flying with
pure joy of life, delighting in the cool night air—eating
fresh meat, relishing fresh blood spraying into his maw,
growing stronger of body and wilier of mind. By day he
had used his freedom to wander from cage to cage,
intimidating his fellows, rearing, grimacing, and staring
into their eyes until they cowered; they dipped their gaze
whenever he approached. Human intelligence combined
with primal instinct, inherited memory, and an animal's
physical prowess made him formidable. Now he dug deep,
drawing on the human child to liberate his subordinates. As
darkness fell, he moved from cage to cage, sliding the bolts.
One by one, the cages opened and the creatures stepped

out, yawning and grimacing; their wings rustled and their claws scratched the cave floor. They followed the alpha's silent communication of movement and pheromones, their eyes watchful and alert, each body a coil of tension. They bypassed the cage where the human child slept and sometimes wept—he was not one of them. The alpha led his troop deeper into the earth; they followed, hissing as icy water dripped onto their skin. Through a cool spring that gurgled across their path and vanished into the bowels of the earth. The tube of limestone narrowed and climbed, weaving a jagged path through the mountain. Up and up, from rock to boulder disturbing and snapping at the tiny bats that dwelled there; the alpha both feared and hated those primitive, subsistent little vagabonds. On up, until a twilit sky beckoned, starry and still. They followed where he led, clambering over stones and tree roots and into the chill evening air.

The alpha feared the one who emerged last. Evan, the newest. Bigger and stronger, crafted out of curiosity by the creator. Timid and restive with his new form, he skulked over the boulders, whining and scratching; the alpha snarled at the lingering humanity; snapping and grimacing, he held him in his bluff. The maker's experiment was flawed, this latest creation's skin itched and wept; the growing nerve ends tingled and prickled. The alpha waited as his troop tried their wings without the impedance of iron bars. On his signal, they took to the air, dark wings rustled into the night. Evan shrieked as he lifted his wings but they lacked the power to bear his weight. The troop left him on the mountainside to whine and scratch.

43

Jayden Pearson had just finished his Bachelor of Criminology degree when his younger sister, Hannah died in horrendous circumstances. Between the police department, journalists, and politicians, the vague explanations had left him angry, frustrated, and curious. Her boyfriend, Ben, had sobbed throughout his explanation of what had happened; his tears were as genuine as his story implausible—a bat the size of a monkey had killed Hannah, he told Jayden.

"Come on, Ben—you must have been drunk."

"I had one stubby and two puffs of a joint—I know what happened. I kicked it—Nic hit it with the tripod. It had wings. It—"

"Okay. I'm going up there; I'm going to do some digging."

Jayden arrived in Warby Creek to a town in lock down. The streets empty, a police patrol car drove past as he pulled up in front of the pub. The only business that seemed to be trading.

As he stepped onto the pub veranda, a police sergeant hurried to intercept him.

"Excuse me, Sir. You shouldn't be on the street at night, it is dangerous."

Jayden squinted at the man. "Dangerous—why, what could be dangerous."

"Please, read the poster there on the wall and stay indoors."

"Is this to do with the death of Hannah Pearson? The university student who was killed last week?"

"I cannot answer your questions except to say you must stay indoors."

"Why can't you answer my question? Hannah was my sister; I have the right to know what happened."

"And you will get an explanation but it's not my place to give it."

"Then who is going to give it?"

The sergeant turned and paused; he opened his mouth but closed it and shook his head. "Just stay indoors."

Jayden watched him hurry back to his car and drive away.

Inside, the lone barman looked up from his book. His only customer snoozed, forehead on his arm and a half-empty beer glass before him.

"A schooner of light please, mate?"

The sleeper lifted his head and fixed Jayden with a bleary gaze. "Are ya brave or are ya mad?"

"Neither." Jayden sipped his drink and turned his eyes to the barman. "Why am I not meant to be outdoors? What's going on?"

"Trust me, mate, you don't want to be out there."

"One of them bat creatures'll get ya."

"Shutup, Rapid."

"Bat creatures?"

"Mate there is something out there, we don't know what it is and it's dangerous."

"I reckon it's that big soldier bloke."

"Bullshit, Roy—I know it's not Tom." The barman gestured with his head and moved to the far end of the bar. Jayden followed and the barman introduced himself.

"So, Dave, what is this thing—bat creature?"

"Mate, I saw it with my own eyes, it looked a bit human, only about yay-high." He held a flat hand above the bar top. Jayden snorted and Dave shook his head. "Mate, I don't want to believe it either—but I saw from only six feet away and I wasn't drunk."

As Jayden listened to Dave's story, a flicker ignited in his memory. A story about a molecular biologist who had attempted to clone a human-bat hybrid. It was legend among medical, law, and journalism students, though the story remained undocumented.

In the morning, in his motel room he began to make phone calls. Two hours later, he had just one name. Jayden pulled out the local phone directory and opened it to N. Nelson, Dr P. "Penrose Nelson, Blackwattle Farm, Grinder's Gully Road. So that's where he got to." He stuffed the phonebook back in the drawer. "This cannot be real. It just cannot."

****

Peter arrived home late from a last minute meeting with his polling booth attendants. The sight of Celina passed out on the couch restored the heartache. The next day would be the highlight of Peter's life. The polls predicted he would take the seat in a landslide. His will to win had floundered in the past week. Since he'd relinquished his daughter's transformed and grotesque body to Penrose Nelson, Peter could find no joy in the prospect of proving to his schoolyard tormenters that little Peter Edwards was a somebody—a man of wealth and influence. Tomorrow's win would not bring back the happiness he'd found when he married Celina and watched as she gave birth to his daughter. Madelyn was the reason he strove for greatness; all he had desired was to give her a rich and comfortable life. Where had it gone wrong? What had sent Celina into the arms of those other men? He hadn't wanted to admit it, but it was his fault—he had spent so much time trying to prove his childhood detractors wrong, so much time making money and making a name for himself that he had neglected his young and beautiful wife. He had put on a brave face and continued.

A bottle of scotch sat on the floor beside Celina, a dark stain show she had spilt more of it than she had drunk.

He shook her gently. "Celina, honey. Are you okay?"

She mumbled and rolled onto her side. She still wore her shoes; they were caked in mud, the bottom of her jeans muddy and wet.

"Celina—you're not supposed to go out after dark, it's dangerous."

The loss of their daughter had torn away the moorings that bound her to life—to the world of the living. His wife snored softly; Peter sat beside her and smoothed her curls. His lip trembled, tears filled his eyes and sobs shook them loose. As he cried for his family, the tears turned to fury. He picked up Celina's bottle and took a long drink, the raw scotch seared his throat. Penrose Nelson had blamed Peter for what had happened to Madelyn, but with Sergeant Fitzgibbon's explanation of the imposed curfew, he was now certain that Penrose was to blame. He had intended to leave it until after the election and then quietly take care of the mad scientist who lived on Grinder's Gully Road. Peter tipped the rest of the scotch down his throat, strode to the kitchen and removed the biggest, sharpest knife from the knife block.

****

Penrose awoke to a banging on the door. Agnetha was already awake, staring at the ceiling.

He sat up. "Who could that be at this hour?"

"I'll go and see, shall I?" Agnetha's voice dripped sarcasm. She pulled on her filthy night coat and strode to the door. Penrose scrambled out of bed and followed.

He recognised the man swaying in the door, clutching a knife. "Mr Edwards—Peter, what brings you here at this early hour."

"You miserable arsehole, I should have killed you in the street and not let you take my little girl."

"Agnetha took her—"

"Don't blame your wife, you slimy little creep." Peter Edwards advanced on Penrose.

****

As Agnetha watched her husband back away, she picked up the poker from beside the woodstove. Peter Edwards closed on Penrose, tears poured down his face—Agnetha's lip curled. "Capitalist pig!"

She mustered her strength and swung the poker. A piece of Peter's scalp came away and he dropped to his knees. Another swing felled him. She struck again to finish him then knelt to check his pulse.

"Agnetha—you saved my life." Penrose pulled her to her feet, his arms closed about her for the first time in ten years. "You'll have to dispose of the body."

"Of course, Penrose."

"But where?"

"I already have a plan, Penrose. Remember I said Peter's wife had an illicit affair with the baby-killer?"

"You did? Ah—yes—you did."

You don't remember.

"I'll dump him near his farm gate. The police will immediately suspect he killed him in a jealous rage."

"Brilliant! I married you for your intelligence, Agnetha."

You married me for my womb.

"Yes Penrose."

"Quickly, before it gets light. I'll help you load him into the car. Then I have important work to do."

44

Election Day. 5 a.m. The dog woke Tom in the hour before dawn. The frantic barks and scratching from inside the garage did not bode well. He leapt from his bed and pulled on a pair of jeans. Gun in one hand and a torch in the other he ran from the house. Cows bawled in panic, Tom swung the torch towards the sound of galloping hooves. A pair of black wings swooped over the heads of the cattle, then another.

"Jesus Christ! How many of these fucking things are there?"

He sprinted toward the besieged cattle huddled in the corner where the fence joined his hayshed. Above them, enormous wings swooped and knocked a cow off her feet, she bellowed and thrashed, her attacker growled and snapped, the big wings unfurled over her like a leather umbrella. Tom halted and fired a shot. The creature screamed and took to the air; it swerved at his second shot. Something hit the back of his head and knocked him against the railings and onto the ground. He rolled; the torch beam showed a glimpse of wings, teeth and a dark, furry body. He fired again. The creature snarled but flew on. Tom stumbled to his feet and fired more shots at the dark forms in the sky. One of the creatures shrieked and the rest followed, they flew away towards the ranges. A warm trickle tracked through Tom's hair and down his back as he vaulted the fence and hurried to the cow. Her thrashing legs slowed and stopped as he halted beside her. Her calf lay torn in two. The creature had carried the back half away.

"How fucking big are these things? They can attack and kill a grown cow."

He ran back to the house, blood trickled down his back. A quick shower to wash the wound. Once the bleeding slowed, he tied a granny knot in his hair over the wound. That would have to do until he could get it properly stitched. He bolted down some breakfast, reloaded his handgun and stuffed a box of rounds in his pocket. As an afterthought, he strapped his hunting knife to his belt. He grabbed the bowl of vegetable scraps and lettuce and tipped it into the chook pen. The baby emus cast him confused glances. He normally let them out for their morning feed after which they spent the day following him and Dog around the farm.

"Not today, little fellas. Come on, Dog." The creatures had yet to attack during daylight hours so Tom deemed it safe to let the dog come along. His powerful olfactory system might come in handy.

The eastern sky lightened as Tom set off towards the ranges, the dog walked ahead, sniffing the ground, his tail waved happily over his back. In the timbered country at the base of the range, Tom caught a whiff of wood smoke, and Dog growled.

"What is it, boy?"

The dog pricked his ears and padded silently into the trees.

"Can't be too bad if Dog isn't holding back."

6.30 a.m. Ahead, a white object caught Tom's eye, and as he drew closer, he noticed an all-terrain bus parked among the trees. Pitched around it was a group of tents. In the middle, the embers of a campfire. The dog barked and returned to Tom's side, growling. The temptation to fire a shot passed quickly, Tom turned to walk away when a man emerged from the tent nearest.

"Hello there, can I help you."

The dog bayed at the man and Tom shoved him with his boot. "Shut up, Dog. Good morning, sorry to wake you at such an hour but I didn't realise I was playing host to a tour group."

"Is this your land? My apologies, we drove in here from the main road." The fair-haired man nodded towards Grinder's Gully road. "We'll move if you like."

"No it's okay. Kenzie Nelson I presume?"

"Yes. You're the returned soldier who kept the peace at the town meeting a few months ago."

"Yes, Tom McPherson." Tom shook the naturalist's hand and looked around; tall trees and dense wattle scrub surrounded the tents. "Did you guys see anything unusual last night?"

Kenzie Nelson's face grew serious, his eyes narrowed. "No. What kind of unusual?"

"Very unusual. Something you would never have seen before."

From a smaller tent beside Nelson's, another man appeared. "Are we talking some kind of mutant by any chance?"

"Tom, this is Mandeep Singh, he is a molecular biologist—the police forensic officer who ran the DNA test on the saliva taken from Sid Walker's body."

"The DNA on Mr Walker was most unusual, Mr McPherson."

Tom straightened and lowered his voice. "I was the one who found Sid's body; I know what it was that attacked him."

"Can you describe it?"

"A monstrous bat that looks strangely human."

"In the Philippines they call them aswangs."

"Aswangs are a mythical creature, these things are no myth."

"Mr McPherson, you've no idea how much I didn't want to hear that."

"I'm sorry. I wish I could say 'go home, it's a load of bullshit.' But I can't, I've seen the thing—things—too many times to doubt my eyes or may sanity. They are real, don't ask me how, but they're real."

Kenzie Nelson's gaze bounced from Mandeep to Tom. "Mandeep has a fair idea how. Can I offer you a coffee while he tells you about it?"

Tom glanced at the range above them, still shrouded in shadow. He knew where to look for the aswangs, and he had all day to look. "Sure. Thanks." He made to scratch his head but desisted as his fingers found the knotted hank of hair.

As Tom listened to Mandeep's theory his skin prickled. "Old Penrose is a dweeb—do you really think he is behind this?"

"I know what I saw in the lab, Tom. His wife miscarried a baby right before my eyes—and the fucking thing had wings."

"I haven't seen his wife look pregnant, so how do you think he has produced a whole colony of them. At least ten of them—probably more, attacked my cows last night. One of them was the size of a ten-year-old. How? How has he managed to produce them? I'd accept he could probably come up with one—but—no, I saw the bloody things. I swear I'm not delusional."

"He must have found a way to switch on dormant DNA in a living creature—not by cloning, which is how he would have created the one I saw on the lab floor."

Kenzie tossed the dregs of his coffee into the fire, a puff of steam hissed into the air. "How the hell can you take a person already born, even a small child, and alter its genes to make it grow wings? It's impossible."

"Impossible—I keep telling myself—holy shit!" Tom sat up straight; his gaze flew away in the direction of Warby Creek. "Little Maddy Edwards! No—no! That is just too evil."

"Peter and Celina's little girl?" Kenzie's shoulders sagged.

"There have been so many child disappearances in Queensland and in Northern New South Wales." Mandeep stared at Kenzie then at Tom. "Maybe that is where they have gone."

"This has just become way too big for us."

45

The baby possum trembled in the chill of morning. The sun had not yet reached the paving stones in the beer garden. Sara watched it unwilling to handle the little marsupial for fear it might bite her. Gracie hurried from the storeroom with an empty beer carton.

"He doesn't appear to be wounded so I guess taking him to the vet is pointless."

"We should take him to the Nelson's Sanctuary; they'll take care of him."

Sara shivered; she didn't like the Nelsons. "Why don't we take it to Miss Tate?"

"I thought of that, but it's a school holiday—she will be out of town."

"Oh yes, that's right." Sara stooped to help Gracie usher the tiny marsupial into the beer carton. "Okay, the Nelsons it is."

As Sara drove along Grinder's Gully Road she thought of the last time she had been out this way. She had seen the hope in Tom's eyes when he left her house two days before. Her stomach ached with fear; he said he was going after the creature. He hadn't been in contact; in fact she hadn't seen him since he showed Sergeant Fitzgibbon where the creature had climbed in the window. She missed him; she wanted to see him again. Soon. On Monday, when the kids went back to school, she would go and find him. At the turnoff to Nelson's sanctuary, she could see Tom's mailbox in the distance.

First thing Monday, Tom. I hope you haven't made other plans.

"Mum, look. That looks like Miss Tate's car. I thought she was going to Brisbane for the holidays."

"Maybe she left her car here; she seems to be good friends with the Nelsons."

Sara pressed the buzzer and waited. She could hear voices inside the old house, the minutes ticked by and she buzzed again. Maybe they hadn't heard it. After a five minute wait, Agnetha Nelson answered the door. Her mad eyes flicked over Sara and Grace then on the box.

"What's in there?" She poked a curious finger at the box.

"It's an orphaned possum." Gracie opened the box and tilted it in Agnetha's direction. "We hope you can take care of it."

Agnetha folded her arms and stepped back. "Bring it through to the surgery."

It alarmed Sara to see the filth of the Nelson's surgery; it wasn't at all what she had expected. Gracie set the box on the examination table and extracted the tiny possum. A scrape of a foot on the gritty floor startled Sara and a hand slammed a rag in her face. The room swayed and rippled and Sara saw Agnetha Nelson pick up the baby possum and wring its neck. It didn't make sense, the room spun and oblivion took her.

****

Her early morning visitors taken care of, Agnetha yawned. She wanted only to sleep but knew it was pointless—the minute she lay down she would start itching and sweating. That aside, she had her early morning chores. She stumbled into the cave for the seven a.m. feed and found empty cages. Her shrieks of laughter brought Penrose running; his head swivelled left and right.

"Where are my babies?"

Her husband's shout halted her mirth. She wiped a tear and inhaled. "What did you say, Penrose?"

"What's happened," he strode towards her, "to my creation?"

"They're gone! Every last one of them gone!" A wild cackle rang in the cavern; Agnetha laughed herself breathless. "The death on wings are loose! They're all g—"

Penrose silenced her with a head-ringing slap and she sprawled onto the cave floor. "You have disappointed me, Agnetha."

Agnetha sat up and rubbed her ear.

"What have you done with my variants—my creation?"

"I never did anything, the front gates were locked, they can't have gone out that way—but they're gone. Someone has opened all the cages."

Penroses's nostrils flared, his face purpled. "You had better find them! Now!" His voice cracked and flecks of foam sprayed from his mouth. "Now!"

"Yes, Penrose."

46

Blake Rush climbed into the helicopter and greeted Marina.

Her eyes shone with excitement. "Okay, let's go after the story of the century. Do you know where to go?"

"Yes—they are apparently going to quarantine Penrose Nelson's wildlife sanctuary. They're waiting; it's either the army or the feds. If we can get up on the hill above it and fly a drone over the top, we might get some good footage."

"Footage? Of the wildlife sanctuary? I want better than that, I want to get right in there and get some footage of the monster."

"Fuck that—I've seen what that thing did to Sid Walker and to that uni student." Blake shivered. "I'm not going near it."

"Well, you can play with your drone, I'm going to get in close and have a look."

"It's your life, Marina. I'm staying right back away from it."

"I can't help wondering if it's just small-minded redneck hysteria—what else could it be? But if I can sell the story to the highest bidder, I don't much care—photos can be enhanced."

The helicopter's shadow ran ahead as it flew away from the morning sun over Grinder's Gully road. Blake pointed at the boulder and tree strewn slope to their right.

Marina's voice crackled in the headphones. "Drop us down there, we can hike up. We'll call you when we want you to pick us up."

Blake and Marina shouldered their packs, gave the pilot the thumbs up and set off into the trees.

"The wildlife sanctuary is just over there and I know by the chatter on police radio that they suspect this creature comes from somewhere near there—don't know how they know that and I don't dare ask. If Mark Fitzgibbon finds out I'm listening to their conversations, he might arrest me."

The two climbed the slope, their eyes searching for signs of unusual lifeforms. Red sap oozed from the lumpy trunk of a tree, down the bark to form a clot between the roots. Marina snapped a photo as she passed.

"They call those bloodwood trees." Blake tried not to sound like a schoolboy trying to impress the new girl but trees had become his thing. He had learned a lot about trees since moving to Warby Creek. He had watched as flying foxes destroyed many of the trees along the creek and in town, and also watched the council workers in a fit of rebellion, lop every tree in town.

"Hm—I wonder why." Marina eyed the red streak that coursed down the trunk.

They pushed through thick undergrowth, slowly climbing the steep hillside. Marina snapped another photo, this time of a sarsaparilla vine spilling its purple flowers over a rock. A gargaloo vine wound rope-like, strangling a small eucalypt. They came to an animal pad that led up the hill.

"Fooie! Something sure does stink." Blake covered his mouth.

"Oh my god! Would you look at this?" Marina circled a boulder. "That looks like blood."

"Ah yuk—that has to be animal intestines." A torn tube of stomach tissue lay beside the boulder. Blowflies swarmed over it.

Marina picked her way around the boulder; her camera snapped every angle.

"Look out!" Blake grabbed her arm. "You'll fall into that hole."

"It looks like something has been going in there."

"Yeah, and coming out." Blake gagged, his stomach churned at the stench. A cloud of flies buzzed around them. Blake set up his drone and switched it on. The tiny blades cut through the blowflies as it lifted above the trees. He pulled his eyes away from the screen.

Marina set her backpack on the ground and took out a coil of rope.

"What are you doing?"

"I'm going to rappel into that hole and see what's down there."

"Don't be stupid, that bat thing is most likely down there."

"And boy, won't I get the snapshot of the century?" She secured the rope to an ironbark sapling and slipped into the harness. The camera swung as she leaned over the edge of the hole. "Wish me luck."

"Marina, don't. It might be dangerous."

"You said yourself, this thing only hunts at night, don't be such a wuss."

"Marina—"

"Ciao! See you in a bit." The belay device whirred and Marina disappeared over the edge of the hole.

Blake sighed, shrugged and move away from the hole. He guided the drone around the hillside, and over Nelson's Wildlife Sanctuary, keeping the camera pointed at the ground. He brought it back around to film himself standing among the trees. A scream from inside the hole sent his heart into his mouth and he scrambled back up the hill. The rope juddered across the rim of the hole, stones clattered down. Blake halted the drone and peered into the hole.

"Marina!" His legs shook and his heart hammered. A fire burned in his throat. The rope heaved, stretched and shook violently—a twang and it slackened. Throaty growls and shrieks sounded in the darkness below. A scuffle and the screeches of claws on rock. "Marina!" Sweat poured down his face as Blake leaned as far as he dared over the hole, trying to see his fellow journalist. The sight of a pink and blue demon face, big yellow eyes and dark wings sent Blake running, tumbling down the hill. Dry branches tore his skin and clothes as he ran. A nerve-shredding shriek. Wings swirled the air around him as a creature swooped and swooped again. Claws stung as they raked his flesh, the creature's hot breath gusted in his ear. Blood, decay, sweat and animal funk filled his nostrils. Scream. Steel-trap jaws closed. Sharp teeth sank into his throat. Hot blood on his tongue. Choking. The morning sunshine flared and died.

47

Celina Edwards sat and stared at the black television screen. Watching TV was her past; she could no longer listen to laughter or music. Just the weather report could bring her to her knees. She couldn't bear to listen to the news—she had no part in the normality of the world around her. The all-pervading guilt. It was her fault. She shouldn't have taken her eyes off Madelyn. She shouldn't have seduced Kenzie Nelson. The game she played had seemed harmless. She only had to give a man that look and she owned him. She had relished the power, small and fragile; she wielded her femininity like a weapon—big, powerful men melted like jelly in her radiance.

Losing your daughter was punishment, Celina.

The only reason she survived was the dregs of hope inside; maybe one day, Maddy would come home.

Knuckles rapped on her door and startled her.

"Celina!" She knew that voice. Edna Wilcox from across the street.

She rose and went to the door.

"Celina, I came to see how you're going, dear."

"I'm fine, Edna."

"No, you're not—you poor girl." The old arms around her gave her comfort. Edna had always been grandmotherly to her.

"I miss her so much, Edna. Why? Where did she go?"

"That man took her."

"Man! What man? Edna—"

"Didn't Peter tell you, dear?"

"Tell me what?"

"About your beautiful winged Madelyn."

Celina stared; Edna was getting confused again. "Oh no, my Maddy has not gone to heaven! She can't—I have to believe she is alive. I have to."

"No, no, Celina. Not an angel, she had real wings—not feathers. Wings just like those flying foxes. That man told Peter he would take her away—she was quite still and burnt by the powerlines!"

"Edna, what are you talking about? Please stop it—please—"

"Celina, you have been medicating with the bottle too much. You must have been very passed out—she made a fearful noise when she fell on my roof, then she hit the powerlines. That man was truly evil—he threatened Peter—he blamed Peter. I think your Peter was very afraid."

Celina shook her head. She held her throbbing heart in her folded arms. "Edna, tell me everything—I—I don't understand what you're saying."

"Yes, I can see you haven't a clue. It happened that night—remember when the power went out in our street? I woke to a whomp on my roof…"

Celina shivered and clutched her stomach as she listened to Edna's story; bile stung her throat and a weight crushed her chest.

"…I have been afraid to say anything, but now I see Peter has obviously not told you since I know you are still searching every night. You must stop wandering in the night; the police are saying it's dangerous. Rumours around town say the bat people are out at night. You are in danger…"

Sobs shook Celina as she gazed into Edna's faded blue eyes.

"…of course your Madelyn would have never been a threat to you. I believe she would have known her mother. I believe she was trying to come home to you"

"Man? Which man? Who is the man who threatened Peter?"

"That mad scientist from the wildlife sanctuary."

48

The rest of Kenzie Nelson's crew emerged from their tents and joined them for coffee. The camera crew filmed the camp and those seated around the fire. As an hour passed, the dog continued to growl, Tom put it down to inexperience. He was a pup and not used to strangers.

"Fucksake, Dog. Shutup."

Kenzie cocked his head. "Did you hear that?"

"No—what? I'm still half deaf from being blown up." Tom shoved the barking dog away. "Shutup, Dog!"

"I heard it." Mandeep jumped to his feet. "Sounded like somebody screaming."

The dog barked frantically, his hackles erect. Tom jumped to his feet and drew his gun. "We've got company, get inside that van! All of you!"

Sable wings appeared above the trees.

"Aswangs!" Mandeep pointed skyward. "They're real!"

The cameraman aimed his lens into the canopy.

"Fucksake you people, take cover!" Tom fired as one of the aswangs alit in the branches of a tree. "Take cover!" Another shot. The creature swooped, snarling. It flew at Kenzie. Tom fired and hit its leg.

"Get down, dammit!" He feared he might shoot one of Kenzie's men. Another creature swooped at the microphone boom and Tom fired again. It flew, snarling into a nearby tree. Tom stepped forward to get a better shot but the dog ran under his feet and the shot went wide. The creature screamed and took to the air. Tom aimed—fired; the creature swerved, snarled, and flew away towards the range, the rest followed. Tom fired shots after them and their shrieks faded.

Kenzie raised shaking hands to the sky. "That was incredible!"

White to his lips, Mandeep squeaked. "That was fucking scary!"

"Incredible!"

"Is everybody okay?" Tom looked around at their ashen faces—he could see no blood.

"It's a good thing you were here, Tom. Thank you." Kenzie's hand shook as he wiped the sweat from his face.

"Pack up your camp and move down to my house— hurry. The country there is open; it might be safer. My house is unlocked, go inside and keep watch. I'm going to investigate what that screaming was about."

Tom reloaded his gun then left Kenzie's party and set off up the hillside, he went slowly, watching the sky and searching the ground for footprints. The dog crowded his heels, alternately whining and growling; the hair along his spine raised and his tail tucked. "You and me both, Dog."

Past a bloodwood tree that bled down its trunk, Tom found a footprint. Then another. Two people had walked this way; their tracks rambled ahead of him, one wore joggers; the other hiking boots. He scanned the hillside and his scalp prickled—he already feared their fate. The dog rumbled his inner doubts and terrors as Tom moved on.

"You'll be right, Dog. You can run a lot faster than I can." Tom drew his gun.

The sun gained altitude—Tom checked his watch. 8.05 a.m. The dog stopped puffing and loosed a deep growl.

"Shut up." The footprints led to exactly where Tom had hoped they wouldn't. The blood splattered boulder and its attendant flyblown stench. He picked his way around the boulder, the dog snarled—his canines showing. A rope, tied to an ironbark sapling, hung limp into the hole, it had dragged and cut into the rim. He pulled it up; the end was frayed and bloody. "How fucking stupid could they be?"

The boulder should have given them ample warning to stay out of the hole.

He searched the ground, the hiking boots had gone into the hole but the joggers had lingered. Something white caught his eye. A drone lay on its side next to a log. He picked it up, a pilot light winked.

"So where the hell is your owner?" Then he saw where the joggers had run away, at an angle to their original approach. The tracks skidded; a handprint showed the person had fallen. "Well here's the drone's controller."

He went slowly down the slope, keeping to the side of the desperate retreat—a backpack lay discarded in a cycad. The dog bayed savagely, and backed up the hill. Tom followed the direction of the dog's gaze and met a pair of fierce yellow eyes. A blue and pink face jerked from Tom to the dog and back to the object it crouched over. It bared huge canine teeth and hissed.

"Oh fuck, you got him then."

Animals fear a bigger animal; as Tom advanced on the aswang, its ears flattened and it slunk backwards. As it lifted its wings, he fired a shot; the piercing scream punctured his soul. The dog charged away down the hill, yelping. Tom fired again, the aswang flapped and rolled down the hill; blood spurted into the grass. Tom came to a stop at the man's body, a horror of torn flesh and naked bones. An alarm on his smartwatch twittered a reminder to its dead owner; it remained attached to the arm that lay nearby, torn from the shoulder. Down the slope the creature trembled—its life fading. "And I thought I had seen the worst of the world."

Tom climbed down for a closer look. The cut on his scalp stung as he examined the monster; the big yellow eyes stared vacantly at the sky. The part of its face that wasn't covered in blood, carried the colours of a mandrill. The other one he'd glimpsed resembled a human and had black eyes—a different species. "How many different kinds of these things are there?"

He looked around; the dog had gone. He hoped he'd find his way home. Tom looked at his phone; there was no signal up here.

49

Senior Constable Chris Riley had the day off. Voting day. He woke late and took a walk along Grinder's Gully Road. Since the departure of the flying foxes, one positive thing about Warby Creek emerged and that was the clean country air. Grinder's Gully Road was an ill-kempt strip of bitumen road, which meandered through the ranges and onto a state highway. He passed Blackwattle Farm and glimpsed Penrose Nelson's house through the scrub. Crows squawked ahead of him, and as he approached, a flock of them flew into the trees. Something blue lay in the grass and Chris turned up Tom McPherson's drive to investigate; his heart rate increased as he ran into the long grass.

"Oh shit! Peter?"

Chris pulled out his phone and called the station.

****

As Mark Fitzgibbon raced along Grinder's Gully Road the radio crackled to life.

Sam, the weekend receptionist's voice greeted him. "Mark?"

"Go ahead, Sam."

"I've just had another call from out where you're headed. Tom McPherson has reported finding a body up the hill somewhere behind his place. He says he shot one of those creatures, like the one that attacked Sid Walker."

"Jesus—I thought today was going to be a quiet one."

"And Sarg?"

"Yes?"

There's been a young man here called Jayden, he's been asking about those creatures and about Penrose Nelson."

"What did you tell him?"

"Nothing. I told him to come back later."

"Good. Alright, send Brandon and Carla to attend Chris' callout? I'll deal with Tom.

"Okay. Will do."

50

Celina sped along Grinder's Gully Road; she didn't know where Peter was but guessed he would be doing the rounds of the polling booths. The wheels of her Mercedes skidded as she turned into Nelson's Wildlife Sanctuary drive. Murder. She would kill those who had taken her daughter. The wheels shuddered on the gravel as she braked sharply in front of the run-down farmhouse. She marched up the steps and bashed on the front door, shoved it open and reeled at the pissy stench. Through the empty house to a filthy vet's surgery and out the back door. Celina saw Agnetha Nelson's floral frock in the distance, running into the wattle scrub.

Celina hurried after her. "I'm coming for you, bitch! You and your pansy husband!"

****

Agnetha waited, hiding in the shadow; she had seen Celina Edwards' Mercedes pull up and she bolted for the cave. She gathered the net that Penrose kept as an emergency control for the hyacinth bats. Celina Edwards ran in the door and stopped as her eyes adjusted to the gloom.

"Oh, God—no!"

Agnetha smiled at her distress.

Celina Edwards fell to her knees before Penrose's specimen tanks. Agnetha had little love of beautiful objects, even the roof over her head only served to provide a dry place to sleep. Her house had no adornments; in the ten years they had live there, she hadn't cleaned it. However, she truly admired the specimens Penrose had preserved in alcohol. The missteps on his way to triumph. The square fish tank, one metre high and filled with a solution of alcohol and formalin was Agnetha's favourite. The corpse of Madelyn Edwards floated in the tank, her head bowed; a red curl fell over her closed eyes. Her ethereal beauty altered by the hand of unethical science. Long fingers splayed, unfurled wings glowed in the tank's backlight, bubbles boiled up as a pump circulated the liquid around the body. The little girl hung naked, like a grotesque sculpture hewn with a clumsy chisel that hadn't yet learned the dishonesty of art.

Agnetha raised the net and crept forward.

****

Celina's blood froze at the beloved face of her daughter, preserved and lifeless; floating in a glass tank. The world bent out of shape and lurched. Awareness returned in a haze of dull colours, tangled in a web of filthy ropes—someone dragged her. At eye level in the half-dark, Agnetha Nelson's dilapidated Doc Martins marched ahead, the frayed hem of her floral dress swung about her unkempt legs. She gathered the net and grunted as she hauled Celina into a cage and kicked out. A sharp pain pierced Celina's ribs; the ropes burned her face. Agnetha clanged the cage shut, dragged chains through the mesh, and snapped the padlock.

Celina fought to untangle herself from the net. "Let me go!"

Agnetha Nelson's laughter chilled her marrow.

"Your rich husband—your cash-cow is dead."

"Dead—what? How."

"I killed him."

"I don't believe you."

"The baby killer has been taken in for his murder. I saw the police car take him away." Agnetha screeched with laughter. "You thought nobody knew but I watch his place all the time. Every Tuesday morning you used to visit him."

"Stop it—"

"You'll be next. I'm going to kill you—I might feed you to the hyacinth bats. No more pretty Celina—no more of the Edwards family. Such a shame. And tell me, did you enjoy your little tryst with my famous brother-in-law? Was Kenzie worth it?"

Celina gazed, her mind numb—her lips shivered.

"I suppose you're wondering how I knew you'd fucked Kenzie Nelson after your husband left for work?"

Bile choked Celina's words.

A yellow grin gashed Agnetha's face. "By the looks of you, I'd say the guilt at what you did that day has just about destroyed you. You're a slut, Mrs Edwards—you're no better than a prostitute! Your little Madelyn would have been the same only I took her away and gave her a higher purpose. You've worked it out haven't you? While you were screwing the great Kenzie Nelson, I was making off with your daughter." Agnetha picked up a steel bucket and swung it at the glass. Celina screamed as the alcohol solution burst free and Madelyn's body fell onto the concrete floor; Agnetha's face reddened, her eyes bright. "There she is! Dead!"

"No!"

"A freak!"

"No!"

Laughter gurgled around the word. "Baaat!"

"Please stop." Celina sobbed; Agnetha's words lashed like whips and ripped her soul apart. "Stop! What kind of monster are you?"

"I'm a scientist. My husband is a scientist. We collect specimens from all over the country. Neglectful parents—they don't deserve their children. We needed your daughter for our project. My husband transformed her into a homo-pteropus—a human-bat hybrid…"

"God no! Stop." Celina curled in pain. "Stop, please."

"…your child had a poor temperament—she was ill-suited for our experiment and I set her free. She flew away home." A chuckle bubbled in her throat. "Too bad she didn't have the sense to stay away from the power lines." Agnetha unleashed a burst of deranged laughter. "Too bad! Little Maddy-bat fried herself in the powerlines and blacked out the neighbourhood." She inhaled loudly and ruptured with another mad cackle.

Towering despair crushed Celina, her muscles paralysed; Agnetha Nelson's voice faded behind the throbbing roar in her ears. An endless torrent of grief hollowed her soul to a lifeless shell, sobbing in a tangle of ropes, caged by steel. Imprisoned in anguish. Tormented sobs poured from Celina's heart until the agony deadened and exhaustion drained the energy from her grief. Celina stirred and opened her eyes. Silence. Agnetha Nelson had vanished. Sunlight shone in the cave's entrance. Celina's hands trembled as she untangled the net and slowly extricated herself. Calmer now, she picked over her life, facing her past—drawing the poison from her soul and facing her demons. She had always looked up to well-educated people. Celina found herself out of her depth among Peter's friends and associates. When the women weren't ignoring her, they whispered about her—Peter's little piece of fluff. The gold digger. When Madelyn arrived, Celina had an excuse to distance herself from Peter's social and political life but there was more to her than motherhood. Boredom and loneliness crept in and Celina took a lover, then another. She loved Peter but needed more than he could give. Here she was, alone in the world, none of the men she had given herself to were there to rescue her. She believed Agnetha Nelson's claim that Peter was dead. She believed that mad woman meant to kill her too.

A hiss made her look around. Celina gazed dispassionately at the black eyes peering from the shadows; nothing could scare her now. The creature stared motionless, its human-bat face jerked to Madelyn's body. It shuffled forward propped on leathery wings; its stumpy legs waddled. It sniffed the body on the floor, raised its head taking snapshot looks around the cave, and then sniffed the body again. Celina inhaled as the creature screeched, spread its wings and zoomed out into the sunlight.

Her tears returned as she gazed at her daughter's motionless body.

You have to get out of this cage. You have to take your daughter and bury her alongside her father. But first you are going to kill Agnetha Nelson, before she destroys any more lives.

She sat locked in a steel cage with nothing but her expensive clothes and jewellery. Diamonds would not help her to escape. She pushed on the cage door and it moved. A gap opened. As a mischievous twelve-year-old, she had asked her wayward uncle how he picked a lock—his stock in trade until the police caught and sent him to prison. He showed her. If only she had a paperclip or a piece of fine wire. She covered her face and moaned in despair. Her teardrop diamond earring tapped on her jaw.

"Wire!" She removed her earring and reached through the mesh.

The cheap lock sprung open and Celina slipped the earring into her pocket.

51

Agnetha woke from her nap in a lather of sweat and torment. She had made no effort to recover Penrose's creations. They could fly wild forever, she didn't care a jot. She looked at the bedside clock that ticked away the endless hours of her life as Penrose Nelson's slave.

Why do I wind it once a day so it can continue to taunt me?

A slave to her husband and slave to a 1970s alarm clock. She should have been working in some big city veterinary clinic, not stuck up there in the scrub, feeding her husband's creatures—committing murders and kidnappings. Her life was over at thirty-five.

Get real, Agnetha—you miserable swamp donkey, your life ended the day you met Penrose Nelson.

Penrose. An expert at displaying the symptoms of Asperger's Syndrome and garnering people's empathy. *'Oh look at dear old Penrose, the Aspie.'* It had taken a couple of years for Agnetha to conclude he was no such thing. Penrose Nelson was a completely sane sociopath.

Though Agnetha spoke aloud, only the spiders on the ceiling heard. "All you've done, Penrose, is create a headache for me and for humanity."

What use to the world were flying mandrills?

Natural mandrills are bad enough, why would anyone give them wings?

She rose, went to the kitchen and made herself a strong coffee.

52

When Tom arrived back at his house, the dog writhed and grinned but his tail stayed fixed in its tucked position.

"Yeah, Dog—I survived, no thanks to you, you bloody coward." He stooped to pat the speckled hide and triggered a joyous paroxysm.

The voices of Kenzie Nelson's crew reached him where they made camp around the other side of the house. Tom strode through the back door, straight to the bar and cracked the seal on a bottle of Scotch. He had just grown comfortable when the sound of tyres on the gravel compelled him to his feet. He swigged the scotch, picked up Blake Rush's backpack and greeted Mark Fitzgibbon as he climbed from the patrol car.

"I hope you're not planning on leaving the district today, McPherson."

"Why?"

"There is a dead body back there beside your mailbox."

"What? Another—who?"

"Have you had contact with Peter Edwards last night or early this morning?"

Tom shook his head and studied the sergeant's face. "Peter Edwards? I haven't seen him in weeks."

"Where were you at around daybreak?"

"I walked up there and just got back now. I went after a bunch of those creatures that are causing all the mischief. They attacked my cows again and one of them killed a cow and then flew off with a half of her calf." Tom passed Blake Rush's backpack to the police sergeant. "I found this up on the hill. It belongs to Blake Rush, the young reporter."

"Yeah, I know who he is. It was him you found?"

Tom nodded. "Whoever was with him is missing too. Do you remember I told you about a hole in the hillside? His friend went down that hole and now there is no sign of them—just some abseiling gear."

"And you shot one of those things?"

"Yeah. Fuck, Mark—this one looked different to the one I saw previously. This one looks like a flying baboon."

Mark peered into the backpack but lifted his eyes at Tom's revelation. "Yeah?"

"I think young Rush was using this drone to film the area, it might have something useful on it. There is a phone still attached to the controller. Sorry, I probably should have left them where I found them, I wasn't thinking."

"Okay. I think I'd better contact a higher authority. Will you be able to lead us to the body?"

"Sure. I hope you're armed because those things were flying around up there earlier this morning."

"Did you see them?"

"Kenzie Nelson and his crew did too." Tom pointed to the white, all-terrain bus beside the shed.

"Kenzie Nelson?"

"They were camped up there. Lucky I found them shortly before those bat things did. They attacked but flew away when I started shooting. Nelson has decided to camp down here instead."

Mark licked his lips and turned to towards the hills that formed Tom's back boundary. "How far is it up there?"

"About a kilometre. We can drive to the base of the hill. I don't want to walk the whole distance again; my leg is giving me hell as it is." The sound of a car caught Tom's attention. Another police car pulled up. "Are they here about Peter? Jesus Christ—it's Election Day—has anyone call the Electoral Commission?"

Senior Constable Riley climbed out of the squad car and approached.

"I'd like you to accompany us to the station, McPherson. We'd like to ask you some questions."

Mark Fitzgibbon shook his head. "First he is going to show us to the other body, Chris."

Tom swigged his scotch, lowered the bottle and frowned. "Do you think I killed Peter?"

Mark sighed. "We have to cover all angles, Tom."

Chris Riley's eyes narrowed. "I believe you had an affair with Peter's wife, McPherson."

"Which ended the minute I discovered she had a husband."

"That's what you—"

"Chris, stop. I want you to go home and get into your uniform. Go to the station and call AQIS. Tell them to get as many of their people as they can to Warby Creek, as soon as possible. Then you can file your report. Tell Brandon to stay with Edwards' body until forensics gets there. Carla can accompany me and Tom up the hill." Chris Riley inhaled and opened his mouth but Mark cut him off. "Don't worry, Chris, Tom is not going anywhere, except to accompany me up the hill."

"There is a police forensic man with Kenzie." Tom waved his bottle towards Kenzie Nelson's crew.

"There is?" Fitzgibbon followed his direction. "He might be useful, but for now we'll play it by the book."

"Whatever." Tom took another mouthful. The alcohol was beginning to round off the edge of his nerves.

53

It was after midday when Mark brought McPherson and Mandeep Singh into the police station.

The young man he'd spoken to the night before accosted him in the front office.

"Sergeant Fitzgibbon, I'm Jayden Pearson. We spoke last night."

"Hello, Jayden. What can I do for you?"

"What are you doing about Penrose Nelson?"

"What do you know about Penrose Nelson?"

"Enough to know he's a maniac."

"Look, unless you have some hard evidence, you should leave. I'm busy."

Pearson's gaze dropped. "I don't have any evidence, only suspicions."

"Well, leave it for me to be suspicious, Mr Pearson, it's what I do. Now please go home and let me get on with my job." Mark hurried away to join Tom and Mandeep in his office. "First thing I'm going to do is order in some lunch. You guys want a sandwich?"

"Yeah—sure. Another bottle of Scotch might go down well too." McPherson held the bottle against the light from the window and squinted "This one's got a fly in it."

Mark lifted his chin; the bottle tested his tolerance. "Will a coffee do instead?"

McPherson grunted. "Nuh. I'll make do with this."

The big man carefully lifted the bottle and with one eye on the fly allowed the liquor to siphon into his mouth. Mark watched, fascinated as the insect drifted down, swirling and twirling. As it approached McPherson's mouth, he loosened his lips' seal around the neck and allowed a stream of bubbles to carry the fly up and away from his mouth. He let another swig trickle into his mouth, lowered the bottle and belched.

Mark shook his head. "Okay, sandwiches for three, coffee for two."

After he sent a junior constable out to buy their lunch, Mark opened Blake Rush's backpack and took out the drone controller.

"Okay, let's see if this thing can show us anything useful."

****

Tom continued to swill the flyblown whisky as he watched Mandeep patching the drone into Mark's computer to get a look at the footage. His mobile rang; a call from an unknown number. Dave Masters, Sara's father came on the line.

"Tom, sorry to bother you, but have you seen Sara and Gracie?"

"No."

"They should have been home hours ago. Sara's phone is switched off and so is Gracie's."

A tendril of fear crept up Tom's spine.

"They took a baby possum to the wildlife sanctuary early this morning. I called; Mrs Nelson said they left hours ago. I'm getting worried, it's not like Sara to just go off and not tell anyone where she's going."

What has that creepy little twerp done with Sara and Gracie?

Disquiet passed like a shadow in Tom's mind. "I'm going out there for a look. I'll call you back." Tom jumped to his feet. "I've gotta go, Mark" He poked a finger at the computer. "Let me know what you find."

"You haven't got a car."

"Gimmie your keys."

Mark hesitated. "But you're drunk."

"No I'm not."

"You wanna put it to the test?"

"Where's your Alcolmeter?"

Mark looked at the gadget on his desk. McPherson snatched it up and blew in a lungful of air.

"Whadaya reckon 'bout that?"

Mark tried to hide his astonishment. "You're under. But I don't think I—"

"Come on, Mark—I'm not going to leave the country. Sara Nolan and her daughter are missing. This has to be seen as exceptional circumstances."

Mark reached into his desk drawer. "Blue Camry, parked out the back. If you crash it, you'll pay for it. I'm only allowing this because of your military background, McPherson, break the law and you're on your own."

"Of course, and if Constable Riley gets in my way, I'll deck him."

"Assaulting a police officer is breaking the law but I believe he's at the morgue so he shouldn't get in your way."

A distant rumble of a helicopter reached them and grew louder.

"What's with the chopper?"

"That'll be the cavalry."

"You called for outside help?"

"I got on to the deputy commissioner; he said he'd send help."

"That's not a police helicopter. I'm a bit deaf but I know a Blackhawk when I hear one." Tom shook his head. "Whatever. I'm out of here."

54

Penrose left Agnetha with instructions to dispose of Peter Edwards' body, then find his Pteropus-mandrillus Penrosias and homo-pteropus Penrosias.

"Find them, Agnetha," he had said, "and coax them home."

Confident Agnetha would obey, Penrose shut the door of his lab and busied himself with his latest study. Three women writhed, strapped to the tables, each with a piece of cotton wadding taped firmly over their mouths. He spent an hour readying his equipment and carefully documenting each procedure that was destined to prove him the greatest molecular biologist of all time. He had done what no scientist had done before and Penrose revelled in his brilliance. He had never forgiven the university faculty for treating him like a naughty schoolboy. He had never forgiven the lab for sacking him like a common assistant. When he unleashed his creation on the world, they would learn what happens to those who treat a genius such as him with contempt. He snapped on clean latex gloves and arched his nose over his instrument trolley. A white crumb of excitement crusted the corner of his mouth.

"Now, Eden, you first. Now calm down. You know you're going to be at the forefront of scientific history. You see, Eden, I am nothing more than a visionary with a dream, and that dream is to improve the human race. I have produced wondrous creatures that no man before dared dream of. But sadly, they lack intellect. No, I, with my superior brainpower, must father these new clones; mix my DNA with the natural wonder that is the Megachiroptera." Eden Tate's bare foot trembled in its tether. Penrose stroked and bent to kiss it. "Such fair beauty." His breathing grew ragged and heat flooded his loins. "Natural loveliness." He grasped her foot in both hands and rubbed his erection against it. "Warm and lovely human flesh. Ripe for conception." He tore open his lab coat and freed his penis.

Eden's eyes expanded; she made frightened sounds behind the gag.

"Penrose! What are you doing?"

Penrose's neck cracked as his head swivelled to his wife standing in the doorway. "I'm in the middle of a procedure, Agnetha, you cannot come in."

****

Agnetha pulled down her mouth and blew air out her nose; her face grew hot. "I can see that, Penrose! You forget that I am your wife, your science has my approval but fucking a lab-rat's foot does not!"

"Get out, Agnetha! You don't want me to get angry!"

"Fuck your anger, Penrose Nelson. I'll show you what anger is." Agnetha swung an oxygen cylinder against his temple and Penrose crashed to the floor, his erection slunk back into his lab coat. "Right, you sluts! Agnetha pulled Peter Edward's kitchen knife from her boot and approached Gracie Nolan.

****

Celina fell to her knees and kissed her daughter's forehead; fumes of alcohol and formalin stung her eyes. From a nearby bench she picked up a greasy, bloodstained hatchet. Before she could bury her husband and child, she had to destroy those who took their lives. As she left the cave, she heard shouts, Agnetha Nelson's voice raised in anger.

Who is she tormenting now?

Celina ran towards the cobweb-encrusted laboratory. Air conditioners whirred along the back wall. Celina stopped and listened through the open door, her anger mounted as jagged words laced with venom, spilled from the door.

"Now you sluts are going to die too." A sound of tape ripping and a girl screamed. "The youngest can go first!"

Celina's wave of fury crested. The girl screamed again as Celina charged up the steps, across the tiny laboratory.

"Right you bitch!"

Agnetha was much taller and heavier than Celina and as she entered the laboratory, the woman spun and drove her elbow into Celina's throat. Celina toppled backwards down the steps and sprawled in the dirt, coughing.

"How did you get loose?" Agnetha raised the knife and dived at her. Celina rolled, gained her feet and swung the little axe into the top of Agnetha's head. The knife slipped from Agnetha's hand and she slumped into the dirt.

Celina left the axe buried in the dirty blonde hair and sprinted back to the cave to where she had left her daughter's body.

55

Tom jumped into Fitzgibbon's Camry and racked the seat back to accommodate his long legs. As he sped out of town and onto Grinder's Gully Road, a Blackhawk landed on the high school oval. He hoped the commissioner had sent his best men and not a bunch of public servant wannabe-warriors. Thick scrub wove a leafy wall on either side of the track into Blackwattle Farm. Parked in front of a shabby old weatherboard house was Sara's car, Tom pulled in beside it and drained the bottle of scotch. He spat the fly on the ground as he hopped out of Fitzgibbon's car and drew his gun. The sound of the Blackhawk fluttered in the distance. He checked the sky; there were no aswangs. He kicked open the front door of Nelson's house and searched room to empty room. Something metallic clanked under his foot, a stove poker lay in a pool of blood. Tom's face tingled, his heart rate accelerated.

"If you bastards have hurt Sara and Gracie, I'm going to kill you both."

A baby possum lay dead beside a rubbish bin in the filthy veterinary surgery at the back of the house, its head turned backwards. As he left by the back door, he heard a vehicle approach, he peered around the side of the house,

Kenzie stepped from his bus; his film crew followed with camera rolling.

"Visiting your big brother, Kenzie?"

Kenzie flinched. "Tom!" He cast a worried glance at the house. "Do you think we should wait for the chopper? Mandeep called, he and the local cop are coming with them."

"Who's them?"

"A half-dozen soldiers from Amberley, I—Celina?"

A small figure emerged from the scrub behind Penrose's house; she carried a child.

Or is it a bat?

Tom shoved Kenzie's cameraman aside as he set off towards Celina. "Celina!"

Celina moved trancelike. Her red curls ruffled in the breeze, her pretty face dirty and bruised.

Kenzie and Tom stopped as one, gazing at the lifeless figure in Celina's arms.

Kenzie whispered. "Oh Jesus! What has my brother done?"

Celina stopped. Her deadened eyes streamed tears. "I killed her. I killed Agnetha Nelson. She's back there. She took my little girl so I killed her."

"Celina, did you happen to see Sara and Gracie Nolan?"

Celina's gaze lifted to his. "No."

Tom cast a worried glance around.

Celina drew a sharp breath. "Agnetha was shouting at someone in that building back there, I didn't go inside."

Tom ran, his aching leg shot agonizing signals to his brain.

He stepped over Agnetha Nelson's body; face down in the dust, flies buzzed around the burial site of the tomahawk and limped up the stairs. Penrose Nelson lay on the floor, Tom didn't check to see if he was alive. Sara, Grace and Eden Tate were strapped and gagged on the beds. He released the buckles that bound them.

Eden Tate jumped to her feet. "Thank you." She sobbed hysterically and ran for the door.

Gracie swung her legs off the bed and staggered to her mother. "Mum!"

Sara seemed asleep. Tom felt for a pulse and blew out his relief at the gentle rhythm in her wrist.

"She's alive."

"I think he drugged her because she told him what she thought of him." Gracie sobbed. "Please help me get her out of here."

"I'll get her. Walk beside me, where I can see you. " Tom gathered Sara into a fireman's hold and hurried down the steps. "Quickly, make for the white bus over there but stay close to me." He held his breath as he watched Eden Tate dive into Mark's Camry and drive it away. Kenzie and Celina waited where he'd left them.

The roar of the Blackhawk increased as it crested the hill; an otherworldly shriek rang out and the air above them filled with leathery wings.

****

The sun warmed Mandeep's face as he pressed it against the Blackhawk's window. He caught a glimpse of Nelson's farmhouse and dropped his gaze to the hastily scrawled map in his hand. From the journalist's drone footage, he had drawn the position of the house and the animal rescue cages nearby. Some forty metres behind the house an air-conditioned building that must be a lab stood among the trees. Further on, he'd marked the wire-gated entrance to a cave in the hillside, almost hidden by thick wattle scrub.

Mandeep had never been a religious man, but he whispered a little prayer: "Please God, if it's the last thing I do, let me destroy what Penrose's madness has created?"

56

Jayden drove along Grinder's Gully Road, keeping an eye on the Blackhawk. He braked and backed up as the helicopter stopped and descended into the trees. The sign said Blackwattle Farm Wildlife Refuge. The car fishtailed as he tore up the gravel driveway and pulled up near a white bus. As he stepped from the car, black wings and gnashing teeth descended on him, Jayden ducked back into the car and slammed the door.

****

"Take cover!" Tom held Sara tight over his shoulder, aimed and fired as an aswang swooped; he caught its animal scent. Gracie screamed. Kenzie gathered Celina and the dead child in his arms and ran for the bus.

"Quick, this way!" He threw his gun arm around Gracie's shoulder and ran after Kenzie. "Stay close!" Tom pushed the girl behind him and fired again. A mandrill-bat crashed to the ground, it rolled snarling and spurting blood. Gracie screamed again, she halted at the sight of the creature on the ground.

"Keep moving!" Tom pushed her ahead of him still shouldering his burden he made it to the back of the van. Kenzie pulled Gracie inside and helped Tom lower Sara.

"Behind you!" One of the crew dived in.

Tom turned and fired as a bat swooped.

"Close that door and don't come out until all these things are dead."

"Tom! What are you doing?"

Tom ignored Kenzie's shout and hurried to draw the aswangs away from the van. The Blackhawk landed and the soldiers spilled from the open door, their guns blazing. The wounded aswang scrabbled upright, its great wings lifted it off the ground and Tom fired again. The bullet struck the blue face just above the eye. It dropped dead in the dirt.

As Tom turned away, the air around him shifted and the hot stench of a bat enveloped him. He dropped and rolled as the sting of claws tore his shoulder. His bullet hit the furry chest point-blank and blood sprayed on his face. His leg protested as he leapt to his feet and fired again. Ahead, a soldier screamed as a creature wrapped itself around his head and shoulders, blood spurted and his assault rifle dropped from lifeless fingers.

"Ah fuck sake!" The aswangs descended on the soldiers, Tom fired until his gun was empty. He charged in, rolled, and grabbed the dropped weapon.

"Get back in the chopper!" He yelled at Fitzgibbon, frozen, clutching his service pistol. Behind Tom, a human death scream made his stomach clench. He ran at Fitzgibbon and shoved him towards the Blackhawk. "Get in!"

He looked over his shoulder; Mandeep Singh carried a hefty backpack and sprinted past Penrose Nelson's house. Penrose Nelson staggered from the wattle scrub, he faltered and shook his fist, Tom couldn't hear his shouts over the noise of the bats, gunfire, and the whistle of the Blackhawk's turbines.

****

Mandeep stopped at the lab. Agnetha Nelson lay on the ground, blood oozed around the tomahawk blade imbedded in her skull. He placed a finger on her neck. Dead. He ran up the steps and went inside.

"So this is where you've created your monsters, Penrose."

His shaking hands removed the smaller device from his backpack, placed it in the middle of the room, and set the timer for three minutes. He turned on Penrose's gas taps, closed the door and hurried away.

"Pull out!" Tom yelled at the three soldiers still standing. "Pull out!"

Kenzie's cameraman crawled under the van and poked his camera out.

Tom's shout went unheard. "Fuck sake, turn it off!"

A short burst from the assault rifle and an aswang fell at his feet, its wing twitched against his leg. The soldiers clambered back into the Blackhawk and Tom followed. "Shut that door!" The cockpit was empty. "Where's the pilot?"

"Out there." The soldier jerked his head towards the window. "Dead."

"Fuck sake." Tom jumped in the pilot's seat and started the rotors. The turbines whined.

"Hey! What are you doing?" A soldier put a hand on Tom's shoulder.

"Flying you guys out of here before you're all killed."

"Who are you? What—do you know how to fly this?"

"It's been a few years but I'll manage." As he lifted off, huge wings slapped against the glass in front of him. "Get on that mini-gun and shoot that fucking thing!"

"Ah, shit!" Mark Fitzgibbon shouted. "Doctor Nelson is under attack."

"Good, that means I won't have to shoot the bastard."

"I'll pretend I didn't hear that, McPherson."

****

The alpha panted as he flew wildly through his troop and at the one who attacked the creator. Claws and teeth slashed and bit—he drove him back and screamed as another swooped over the creator, snapping and growling. The alpha swerved and something invisible ripped through his chest and he fell to the ground. Blood spilled from his mouth.

****

The young soldier loosed a war whoop as he shot two of the bats out of the air. "Jeez, those two looked like they were fighting each other."

"Vicious bastards." His companion eased the door open and poked his weapon through.

"Ah fuck sake!" The Blackhawk rocked as a bat flew into the rotor. Only a metre from the ground, the Blackhawk thumped down. Tom sped the rotors, checking for signs of damage.

Penrose Nelson swayed against the draft, dust and debris, his fists flailed and he mouthed words and foam.

"We better pick him up." Fitzgibbon bellowed over the noise.

"I'm not sending anyone back out there."

The gunner loosed a new burst and another bat fell. Satisfied the craft was undamaged, Tom lifted off again but hovered, distracted by the sight unfolding on the ground. An aswang attacked its creator; great jaws clamped across the back of Penrose's skinny neck and shook hard. It flew into the air, lifting the thrashing, bleeding man. It whipped again and Dr Nelson's head tore from his neck. The bat dived and snapped at the falling pieces. It seized the severed head and rose; the savage yellow eyes glared into Tom's. Its teeth held Penrose's scalp, pulling wide his eyes and mouth—frozen in a startled, silent scream. Blood dribbled from ragged skin of his severed neck, the spinal column protruded—obscene, and jagged, a fragment of flesh fell to the ground.

"Oh, Christ!" Mark Fitzgibbon howled and covered his face.

The moment dragged; Tom's eyes fastened to the horror. He inhaled and dropped his gaze. Penrose Nelson's headless body thrashed and sprayed blood in the dust below.

"Shoot the fucking thing." He looked back, the gunner stared, transfixed at the spectacle. "Shoot it!"

The gunner shuddered, aimed and fired a volley into the creature. The bullet riddled carcass dropped to the ground, Penrose's head found a resting spot among the carnage. The dirt-caked face sat still; wide-eyed and open mouthed.

"Can you see any more of them?"

"I think we got 'em all."

Tom set the Blackhawk back on the ground and disengaged the rotors. "Check your weapons, boys. There might be more of those monsters."

"Who are you?" The gunner repeated his earlier enquiry.

"I'm Major Tom McPherson, SAS Regiment, retired. Let's go check on the wounded."

Both soldiers snapped to attention and saluted.

"No need for that, boys—around these parts I'm Tom the roo shooter."

"You're the guy who won the CV or was it the VC?"

Tom scowled. "Who cares what I won. I lost a couple of good mates in that debacle. Now watch above and watch each other's backs. We have to check for survivors. Fitzgibbon, call for backup and an ambulance."

****

Into the cave, Mandeep ran and stopped to allow his eyes to adjust to the dark. The interior of the cave was cool but the screeching aswangs, gunfire, and the Blackhawk didn't allow the silence he might have expected. The reek of alcohol and formic acid burned his nostrils. The offending chemicals dripped from a smashed fish tank. Mandeep moved further into the cave and gaped at the row of creatures preserved in jars of alcohol all collecting dust on a shelf. Penrose's failures. Further on stood two rows of filthy cages—all empty save one.

"Jesus Mary, mother of fucking god! Penrose, you evil bastard."

A little boy, filthy and dead eyed sat up, his thumb in his mouth. Naked, his rib bones stark against his skin.

"Hello, who are you?" Mandeep moved closer; he recognised Tyler McLennan from Mt Isa. The little boy who had become famous when he disappeared without trace.

Mandeep pulled the cage open and held out his hand. The little boy leaned away, his eyes limpid pools of mistrust. Mandeep inhaled, remembering the timer on the lab bomb. He hastened to set the backpack on the floor and removed the largest explosive device. He set the timer for one minute, snatched up the boy and turned to leave. Movement and a whimpering sound stopped him in his tracks. Between him and the exit crouched an adolescent boy. No, not a boy. Yes a boy, with wings. A human-animal hybrid. He snarled and coughed blood.

"Hello?"

The creature propped himself on his wing and scratched. Its skin showed patches of red, bleeding irritation. He whined and moved towards Mandeep. Muscles bunched ready to fight, his skin gooseflesh at the horror before him. His mind screamed panic; the little boy in his arms struggled. He had less than forty seconds to get out. The bat-boy continued towards him, eyes averted. The human-animal odour filled his nostrils as it shuffled around him and proceeded into one of the cages. The little boy Mandeep held whimpered.

The bat-boy bared his teeth, grimaced and coughed. "G—go." A rattling wheeze trailed the word.

Mandeep was unsure if it spoke or if he'd heard a random noise.

"I'm sorry. I'm so sorry." Time ticked rapidly, he clutched the little boy tighter and dashed for the cave entrance and down the slope. The creature had the look of death in its eyes; its continuing existence flew in the face of all he'd learned about life and humanity. Mandeep ran towards Kenzie's van in the distance. As he drew level with Nelson's house, the lab exploded and knocked him off his feet. He rolled upright, renewed his grip on the child, and continued towards the Blackhawk—the second explosion might kill them all.

****

As he checked for survivors, Tom sighted Mandeep Singh pelting towards them with a child clutched under his arm. He waved and shouted words Tom couldn't hear over the turbines. A great mushroom of red flames exploded and Mandeep fell, rolled and regained his feet. The explosion threw Tom and Fitzgibbon backwards in a rush of leaves and dust. A bigger explosion shook the ground under them and blew Mandeep through the air to land amid a pile of dead bats. The child found his feet first and wailed in terror. The hillside collapsed in a cloud of dust and rubble—rumbling and crashing—boulders rolled through the flames. As the thunder faded, loud crackles erupted from the dust cloud. The wattle scrub had caught fire. Birds rose into the air shrieking and squawking.

Tom lumbered to his feet and probed a finger in his ear. "Nice work, Mandeep. Fitzgibbon, call the fire brigade as well."

57

Jayden Pearson ranged from happy he hadn't had the foresight to take photos of the battle at Blackwattle Farm and kicking himself for not doing so. As it happened, a crew from ASIO descended and sanitised the scene; they took Jayden's phone and bagged it. Kenzie Nelson's crew had all their footage confiscated. During the debriefing, an ASIO official ordered them never to mention it again. Jayden did not intend to utter a word of what he saw. What had killed his sister would remain a secret. He'd let his mother believe her daughter had died from a dog attack.

****

Mandeep poured over the rubble as soon as the dust cleared. He wanted to be certain he had destroyed all of Penrose's equipment and records. He had a shouting match with an ASIO official who ordered him to stand down.

"I know more about this fucking disaster than any of you and I won't stand down!"

"Very well, continue but you'll be taken in for a debriefing when we have finished."

"Really? Mate, it's you who is going to need debriefing, trust me."

"Why did you destroy all the evidence?"

"For the good of humanity."

"We need to know what happened here."

"Supply me with a good bottle of Grange and I'll tell you all about it."

The parents of Tyler McLennan arrived in Warby Creek the next morning, tearfully joyous to see their son again and thanked Mandeep repeatedly. It was only a little surprising when ASIO recruited Mandeep rather than send him to prison. With what he knew and what he'd seen they deemed it wise to keep him where they could watch him. Mandeep accepted the position in Canberra with gratitude—he needed a change of scenery.

****

Tom and Sara dropped roses into the graves and moved on. They waited as people filed silently past, paying their last respects to little Madelyn and her father. Peter Edwards had won the seat in a landslide; a by-election would run in three weeks' time.

Celina cast a sad figure as she stood motionless by the graves of her husband and child. Tom waited until the crowd left the cemetery.

"Celina?"

She looked up, her face bloodless, her eyes tear swollen.

"Thank you for coming, Tom."

"Are you going to be okay, Celina?"

"Yes." She looked towards the cemetery gate, Tom tracked her gaze. Kenzie Nelson waited alone. "Kenzie has offered me a job with his crew."

"Is that what you want?"

"Yes, I need to get away from Warby Creek for a while. I need to make myself a new life—keep busy."

Tom stepped forward and took her in his arms. "I hope the world will treat you more kindly from now on, Celina."

She nodded and eased out of his arms. "Goodbye, Tom." She flicked a glance at Sara. "And good luck."

Her eyes held his for a moment before she turned and walked towards the gates. Tom slipped his arm around Sara.

"Let's go."

58

Barry Barnes slammed the window. "I've just about had enough of this shit, Alice."

"Me too, Darl."

"Whose fucking idea was it?"

"Dunno, Darl but it's a bloody awful noise."

"There'll be another twelve hours of it yet, Alice."

"Yeah, but we've got the earplugs the Progress Association supplied so we'll be able to sleep tonight."

"I'm going to the pub, Alice."

"I think I'll come with you, Barry."

Barry and Alice made their way to the pub, fingers in their ears to shut out the god-awful racket that blasted from speakers on every corner in town. A small group of grey-headed flying foxes had taken up residence in the regrown fig tree near the town hall and the progress association voted unanimously to drive them away with 24 hours of the rankest death metal available.

The bats had already fled.

Epilogue

Thirty years later. Tyler McLennan held his wife's hand. "Not long now, Honey. We'll have our family."

"Keep still now Averil." The anaesthetist fiddled with the syringe, "You must be completely still."

Averil clenched her teeth as the anaesthetist inserted the needle into her back. "I just wish it didn't have to be this early."

"The doctor said it's nothing to worry about, twins usually come early and with the new eWomb technology they will be in no danger."

Tyler watched as the surgeon prepared his instruments. As a doctor himself, he had performed many caesareans sections; with modern technology, complications rarely occurred.

The surgeon prodded Averil's leg. "Now, Averil, can you feel that?"

"Feel what?"

"Good, we're ready to begin. You're about to be a proud mother of two healthy babies."

"I'm so excited." Averil clutched Tyler's hand tighter.

He grinned. "Me too."

Tyler held his breath as the surgeon cut a neat incision and the nurse applied the suction tube to the wound. Deeper into the swollen belly and through to the uterus—a textbook procedure. A gentle poke with a scalpel ruptured the amniotic membrane and the midwife hovered with a sterile drape, waiting the catch baby number one. Latex gloved fingers groped, seized a head and eased it into the world. The surgeon reeled back and let the baby fall onto the operating table. It loosed a shriek, flapped it's wings and sprayed the theatre with amniotic fluid.

The midwife stumbled backwards. "What the fuck?"

Tyler lurched to his feet for a closer look, his daughter whined. Her baby blue eyes fixed on his. Behind the wound's bloody lips, something stirred…

THE END

BIOGRAPHY

A. Isobel Sutcliffe lives in Western Queensland, Australia with her husband, two dogs and two cats. She has an adult son and daughter. A child of grazier parents, she grew up in remote rural Queensland. She spent thirty-three years as a working musician. A visual artist she turned to writing in 2015.

Ms. Sutcliffe's other works can be found on Amazon and at www.Jacolpublishing.com

GOSPEL

A novel by
Stephanie Vichinski
and randall 'Jay' andrews

Acknowledgement

Stephanie Vichinsky

For you, Mom. It's all been for you.

randall 'Jay' andrews

To all the usual suspects who have kept me engaged and busy. I write every day because it's what I do. This book needs the acknowledgement of Stephanie Vichinsky who wrote a little story that needed a push. To Writers World, bootcamp, and my family, the family of writers who are my dearest friends, I thank you.

Foreward

Stephanie wrote this story in a bootcamp I offer to authors to sharpen their skills. When she handed me this manuscript and said she just couldn't find the purpose in it, I requested she let me make some changes to it, because I felt then and feel now that her writing is compelling. This story is, first and foremost, written in HER style. I mimicked it as I made plot changes, developed some of the nuances, and tightened a few screws. Other than that, her name belongs as the first billing. I merely gave her story a little clearer direction.

randall 'Jay' andrews

Contents

Chapter 1

The phone rings, another soulless sucker jingling pennies in his pocket because he's got the itch. His cousin's stepson's girlfriend found a pamphlet in a mini-mart outside the city, and now he wants to be infinite. He wants to look better to impress the girl of his dreams, to land a better job, to like the face in the mirror, and none of it matters.

It's the modern-day Emerald City I tell him—not like there's anyone left who hasn't heard of Gospel—lying to him, lying to myself, and it's usually a bad comparison because no one cares about the wizard's forgettable town of Oz.

They want the glamour. They want the prestige, the status only a solid gold Bugatti filled with washboard stomachs and 6-inch stilettos can bring. They want the penthouse apartment, the sex, the money, the respect, everlasting life, everlasting youth, beauty, beauty, beauty. They want my life, a life that isn't what it seems, and they want everyone to know about it.

The doctors can't give me an answer. Hell, I'm a doctor and can't give myself an answer. I remember yesterday and the day before, but the further I look into my memories, the muddier it gets. The specialists call it amnesia. All that really means is I don't know who I am, not all of me anyway; none of us do, and the only thing more rampant than the amnesia is the reluctance to talk about it.

I remember the early years, some better than others, some I'm sure never happened, some I'd rather not remember. The details come and go, and most mornings I spend my time jotting them down in a journal, creating a timeline of events that might explain what I'm doing here, rather than poring over the addicts in my waiting rooms. There's something wrong with the people in this city, with me, and the answer is in those memories.

At least I'm in good company today—a bottle of elixir on my desk, forcing me awake in the dim office light, helping me sift through patient notes before I open the clinic doors.

I'm not sure why I still look through their files. I can't help them. I give them what they want, and for a short time, it satiates them, but they all come back. I could poison them, cut them, gut them, leave them for dead, and they'd still be on my doorstep, ready to hand me their paychecks. Everyone wants to be happy.

That's what it's all about, isn't it? Happiness. We're programmed to follow it to the ends of the earth like sharks after blood. Most of us spend a lifetime searching, but let's face it, if any of us knew a thing about happiness, we wouldn't be stuck in this shit hole.

I'll go as far as saying we'd be better off dead, but I've been told that's the epitome of a poor bedside manner. The locals say a lot of things about me, but none of them give a damn whether the stuff is true, good, or bad, and neither do I. They want to be someone else, anyone else it seems, and they know I'm the only guy in town who can make it happen, the guy who has everything except that one-way ticket to paradise.

Maybe I'm jaded. Maybe I've given up. Maybe I'm sick of pouring myself into bullshit and having my investments come up empty. Maybe I'm tired, and the people here can't see it because no one gives a fuck about anyone else anymore. Maybe I'm one of them.

The screens loop their messages in the background of the office, televisions with beautiful faces and bodies speaking directly to me, day and night, night and day, bribing me with gold-plated insanity.

I changed my life for those screens, the way young people do. I dove into a dream, desperate to belong to something, desperate to be someone else, to believe in something, to live with passion, whether it was right or wrong, whether I believed in it or not. I gave them everything, but they're static now. Everything's static.

I don't think about it much anymore. I don't think about much in general. I lube my robot parts with chemically-engineered nutrition, paint a smile on my face, and go about my day like the machine I am. That's the beauty of being a plastic surgeon; I can make myself look like anything, even happy.

Grace, my assistant, stands at the front door of the clinic while the computer system scans her face and opens the door, her sweet voice mumbling along with the screens as she totes her bags through the doorway. Some days I wish I could reach out and tell her what she means to me, but despite the static in my head, I'm smart enough to hold my tongue.

I know how to make money. I know how to double and triple that money. I know the difference between a quality suit and a cheap knock-off. I know fine wine and luxury hotels. I know fast cars, hot women, and flawless cosmetic products. I know how to swindle innocent people, and most of all, I know Grace is too good for me. I keep my distance.

"You're early." I close the files on the computer and help her with her things.

"We have a lot scheduled today." She takes her place behind the reception desk, her heels clicking along the floor, breaking apart the sounds of the screens.

People file one by one outside the doors until there's a crowd spreading into the street, a web of cancer.

"We better get started." She opens the files I stared through this morning and hands me the patient list for the day. I stand in front of the door, entranced with the crowds blending and morphing and raging like a beast from hell. Eight o'clock strikes and the system unlocks the doors.

"We better get started."

A new client names her price. She's come with the city ordinance of residency, the waiting period of confirmation, and I cut her open. She's like all the others; they come to my office in brown paper sacks, vomit their life stories, and expect me to fall on my ass in disbelief at their dedication. We exercise. We eat right. We moisturize. We, we, we....

M-O-N-E-Y, I spell it for every birth mark, sun spot, love handle, and set of A-cup boobs desperate to be someone else. Money puts you on my operating table, but at the end of the day, even money falls short.

I used to believe in standards. Everyone should look their best, whether they're leaving their house or our office, but here we are, day after day, filling molds like steel machines in a factory, prepping, creating, and shipping perfect models off a cliff's edge and into oblivion, no purpose, no direction, endless globs of clay drowning in debt and dissatisfaction.

"She's awake." Grace hands me the paperwork. If physical perfection exists, Grace is it. Perfect breasts, eyes the changing color of the ocean, and legs up to her throat. She's the first thing clients see when they arrive and the last thing when they walk out. That's brilliant advertising.

"Just give her the usual pain meds, and tell her to leave the stitches alone. I can only pad those breasts so much before they split down the middle." A screen rises from my desk, and with a few swipes of my finger, I pull up a mold. It's a simple design, but revolutionary in its possibilities. I brighten the backlight and straighten each strand of hair until it matches the faceless image on the screen. Suit smoothed, shoes buffed, cuff-links shined, and the screen flashes red. It used to anger me, knowing I still couldn't access the elusive green screen, but I don't worry about it now.

"You're leaving already?" She glows in the light of a lipstick advertisement, fidgeting with the rings on her hand. As much as she's beautiful, she's persistent. She wants the things she deserves out of life, the things I can't give her.

"I leave at this time every day, Grace." My bag hangs on the chair behind her, and I know she planned it that way.

"I thought we could look over the new fashion lines, play around with Botox, talk."

She uses that word a lot, talk. I tell her it's unbecoming, but I forget Grace wasn't always beautiful. I made promises; I'd give her a life she only dreamed of, my first patient. Everything since then blurs in my head.

"I can't." I reach around her waist and pull the bag's strap up my shoulder while a single line of mascara runs down her cheek. I grab a tissue from my pocket to wipe her face. "Don't do that. It's bad for business."

She steps into the front lobby, screens chatter around her, and she follows me to the door. I step out, the hum of screens offering forever-beauty adorn every corner, every high rise, every waking moment. I race to my parked car, wondering if I'll ever tell her who I am.

People from the streets crowd me, offering gifts, money, human organs, anything to get their next fix. "It's the famous Dr. Jax Mason," they say. Most of them with a dozen surgeries under their belt, hoping to buy their way to a baker's dozen, schmoozing me like con-artists. You can't con a con.

I rush to open the car door, and the screens come to life. Cars began with two televisions, until they introduced the autopilots. Now the whole interior is a screen flashing beautiful faces and bodies wherever we go.

I toss my bag on the seat, linger in the crowd long enough to hear them hiss at some passersby, spit misting over cuss words and sexist remarks, and I know its four o'clock on the dot. They're here.

A woman—old, ugly, and heartless toward any good-looking suit like me—parks her filth outside my office every day at four o'clock and waits. She's part of the people living on the mountain outside the city. Call them whatever you want—gutter punks, gypsies, drifters. They're not like us and wish they were.

She sets up a chair at the bottom of my steps and sits with a black-eyed kid on her lap to stop the people who belong here from spilling her insides all over the city streets. She stares through my office windows, and I'm sick in my gut.

"Move." I push through the crowd and walk toward the woman.

She looks at me—not at my body or my smile—at me. I remove the cufflinks from my shirt; you never know what these people are looking to steal. I offer her my hand in broad daylight.

The kid looks down my arm and cries before the woman can cover his face with her hands. She rocks him back and forth like a mother coddling a newborn, and I pull my hand away before they decide to do away with it altogether.

"Welcome to Gospel," I say under my breath. The crowd sucks me in their shield when I walk away, cursing her like a fashion model past her prime, and I settle into my car.

It turns the corner, and I lie across the back seat, holding my bag close to my chest. Reflections of beautiful bodies dance over my face and animate the familiar static in my head. A burning, empty static.

Chapter 2

Cancer. That word stands out. The doctor removed his gloves and handed my mother some pamphlets to explain the various treatments available. I saw, tasted, smelled, heard, and felt the silence in that room, smoke choking our lungs before we had time to process the end of the world.

"What happens now?" She held my hand under the table, the last person in her life.

"It's somewhat advanced, but we should be able to fight it, and hopefully you'll make a full recovery."

"What's the first step?"

"We'll start with surgery to remove as many small tumors behind your eyes as we can, but due to the sensitive area, we may not be able to safely remove them all. We'll follow up with radiation and chemotherapy either way."

"And you've seen this before? I mean, you've seen people overcome this type of cancer?" She squeezed my hand, probably wishing she hadn't asked.

"Yes, a few times, but there's no telling with cancer. The good thing is we caught it before it progressed any further."

He shook our hands and sent us on our way, two soldiers carrying a death sentence back to the trailer park. She wept in the car, deep sobs from her chest, and there was nothing I could do. The sounds drilled holes into my head and made it their home. I ate with them, bathed with them, walked with them, talked with them, slept with them.

She parked the car in front of our trailer and watched the sun go down on the fields, on the life we'd never know again. I helped her through the front door and to her bedroom where she stayed for days, crying and sleeping and worrying what would happen to me.

Most nights I slept outside to let her cry without feeling self-conscious, without worrying what I thought, if I was eating, if I was sleeping. I stared through the stars, wondering if things really became any better with time.

One night, an egg hit the bottom of the porch and splattered onto my sleeping bag.

"You'll always be a loser, Doug Mason." A local girl and her friends found their shits and giggles in terrorizing the park at night.

"Please don't wake my mom." I wiped the egg from the porch with my sweater.

"Haven't seen you in school. Really think you're going to graduate on Saturday?" They threw more eggs and laughed.

"It's just a piece of paper. It doesn't mean anything."

"To you, yes. It wouldn't matter if you graduated a hundred times. You're going nowhere, Doug." She made a career of belittling people to get the prized homecoming crown. They crowned her a few months back, and she never let anyone forget it.

"Your future doesn't look so bright either. We live in the same shitty park, go to the same shitty school in the middle of nowhere."

"And sometimes there's a diamond hidden in all that shit."

"What are you talking about?"

"I got a scholarship. To Westridge." She pointed to some of the other kids. "Actually, most of us got into great schools."

"How? Your grades are no better than mine."

"It's not always about grades. Sometimes it's about who you are." She ran her hands down her hips and thighs, a perfect body. "And sometimes it's about talent. Of which, you have none. We can be anything we want."

I didn't answer because she was right. I wasn't good at anything. I never took the time to be good at anything.

"That's what I thought." She threw another egg and walked into the night with her posse, another reminder I didn't stand a chance in the real world.

The nights that followed played out the same way, and I felt guilty for wanting happiness while cancer consumed my mother from the inside out. I wasn't much of a son. I wasn't much of a student. I wasn't much of an athlete or entrepreneur, and if school taught me anything, it was that something needed to change.

Chapter 3

The car parks in front of the apartment building on Main Street, bedrooms bigger than city blocks, bathtubs made of diamonds, and it's mine. I live in the top floor and rent out the rest. The system scans my face and opens the door, letting me in, and letting my only neighbor out.

"Offer still stands." Gwen's a supermodel and the tenant below me.

"And what number would I be?"

"Eleven today, but we can pretend you're number one, baby." We do this dance every-so-often. She licks her lips and whispers some indecipherable seduction in my ear, making the hairs on my neck spike in her direction. She's a great dancer. "Sheets are clean, if that's what you're wondering." Her last attempt to trap me in her web. "We did it in the kitchen." She winks.

I give her the look, the one that says it's been fun but this is as far as it goes. The look she's used to getting from me, the look all women are used to getting from me now.

"Maybe next time, cowboy." She opens the door a little wider to send her late-night guest on his way. "Maybe next time."

Two sets of elevator doors open; one to her apartment, one to mine, and I climb the walls of the Emerald City in the embrace of television screens selling infinity like cheap door-to-door salesmen before spitting me onto the top of the world.

The apartment knows it's me, doors open, champagne on ice, coffees with unpronounceable names ready to shove themselves down my throat whether I want them or not, and I couldn't care less. It's midnight, and all I want is sleep.

Televisions light the control tower, my wizard room in the Emerald City, and everything blends, night and day, light and dark, until my life's a healthy shade of asphalt, collapsing into bed, waiting for the night's routine to start.

Perfume fills the room, liposuction, ads for wrinkle relief, take in, take out, rub on, rub off, over the sound of Gwen mixing her junk. She cries to someone somewhere, I don't know, and some nights I consider bridging the gap, but the needle goes in, the junk goes in, and she sleeps. Nights like these make me thankful no one remembers Oz. The Emerald City was a lie.

At one point I thought being alone would stop the emptiness. I shut out the world and buried myself in my apartment. It doesn't. The sun goes down, and I'm still caught in the never-ending spiral into non-existence.

Somewhere in the middle of the night, I wake with a night terror, no, not a night terror but rather a memory. In that split second, I remember more than I ever have about my past and as I grasp to control it, it fades from me, the TV screens humming their perfect world drown out my consciousness and slip me back to where I need to be. As much as I try to sleep, I don't. Time passes like sludge, gray and shapeless; it's night and then it's day, and the only thing that separates the two is the "fuck you" from my vintage alarm clock. It slaps my face, sends me off into reality again, screeching in the stillness like a banshee with two middle fingers in the sky, and in a few hours I'll be at the office again because I'm too much of a coward to admit I don't understand this dream anymore.

I sit on the edge of the bed after a night of whiskey and suicidal thoughts, and watch the morning advertisements insist their way into my head. "You could be beautiful," she says. "You could have everything you've ever wanted." It's always the same. I pull the blankets from my lap and walk toward the bathroom. "You could be happy."

The city's awake. Gwen's awake, mixing before her first caller arrives, and I'm standing in front of the mold while it tells me I look like shit. Again.

I had average looks when the city started. Some of my features were strong, others not so much, but I never needed major cosmetic surgery to fit in with the beautiful people. For that, I'm lucky. I can still fool the world with hair dye and make-up while my clients chase small fixes, then big fixes before they disappear altogether.

It sounds far-fetched, but it's true. People disappear all the time here. It used to shock me; I'd see them one day, wearing the smile I plastered on their faces, and the next it's like they never found the city. Where they go, I couldn't say, but if they're like me, they're looking for anywhere but here.

It doesn't matter in the end what I think; they'd stone me if they knew I thought life was better before we started all of this, but I don't spend time obsessing over it. I can't remember that life.

The mold flashes red, and Gwen knocks on my door, a whimper of misery trailing behind her. "Ya there, baby?"

"Give me a second, Gwen." I slap some gel in my hair, cover my face in make-up, and start the mold again. Still red. Not that I expected anything different this early in my morning routine, but I have an image to uphold. Mason Cosmetics runs this city, and I'm the face of Mason

Cosmetics. Just because I know Gwen personally, doesn't mean I'm willing to throw everything away.

From the other side of the door, she screeches, "Something happened last night, we need to talk."

I assume her first guy didn't show, and she's hurting. I hear it in the way she whispers my name behind the door, stroking her arms I'm sure. She's looking for purpose, and she's hoping I'm the ticket.

The screens pitch my slogans throughout the house, nothing I'm interested in hearing, but it drowns out the tapping on my door while I walk to the closet. The doors pop open when I get close, and the screens inside sound abnormal. There's usually a gentle echo as they spit the same message a fraction of a second apart. Today, it's one uniform sound.

One of the screens isn't working.

I grab a suit, clueless as to which buttons go where, how the belt buckles, where I left my watch because I'm stuck to the screen like deviants to porn, frantic, confused, scared. I can't break the eye contact. I don't know what happens when I break the eye contact. Is this how we disappear? Too many of us have fallen off the edge of the unknown, and maybe this is where it starts—with a secret.

After I'm good and ready, I give Gwen her due and open the door.

She breezes past me. "You worried me Jax, babe. Did you know the screens went down last night?"

"Down? All over the city?"

"Power went out, just our building, I think. My client started crying, I think I did too, but most of it's a haze now."

I shrugged. "Did you get paid?"

She leaned against the wall. "No, he ran out screaming. Can't believe you didn't hear him."

"And?" I can see she is stressed.

"I can't get some thoughts out of my head."

I ignore her. I ignore everything. I tune her out because there's a blank screen in my closet. We've never had a broken screen in the city. There's been talk about it, about what could happen if the power went out, if a screen broke or was stolen. If there was a reason to freak out, I'd certainly have found it. Still paranoia got the best of me over my equipment failure. I wanted to hide it. If anyone found out, I suspect there'd be mass hysteria.

There's an unspoken rule in Gospel: anyone who doesn't believe in its ideals and expectations is done away with, and part of those expectations is to never tamper with our free lifestyles. A city of Utopian proportions, furnished housing, furnished everything. Nothing comes from the outside world, and no one asks questions.

Gwen pushes off the wall and leans into me. "Jax, why are you so secretive? You don't need to be all prettied-up for me."

"I'm not that social."

"What's going on, Jax?"

"What do you mean?"

"I'm scared." She dances around me, "The same kind of scared as you."

I pretend to ignore her, packing my briefcase with bullshit, anything I can grab, but she'd know better than anyone, the look of fear. A lifetime of abuse will do that to anyone.

"What happened last night when the power went out?"

"How would I know, Gwen? I was asleep."

"I'm scared. I vaguely remember not trusting Gospel when the power went out. My shrink told me to be suspicious of people who doubt the message of Gospel."

I try to play it off like I don't understand, but I know more than anyone what her shrink's trying to do, and for some reason, I can't help but think my night terror was tied to the power outage. "Everything's fine, Gwen. I'm late for work. We'll talk another time."

She's resistant, of course, but I help her out the door with a nonchalant shove. The last thing I need is her gloating on top of her desperation if she finds out she's right.

She stands in front of her elevator, rubbing her arms, crying to someone, to me, and I drop my eyes in shame because this wasn't the life I promised her. This wasn't the life she deserved. I call her pathetic and annoying to satisfy my guilt, but it's a lie. She's one of those open books who make you feel at home, a hundred feet tall when you're really the size of a wad of gum, letting you believe her story is about you.

"Get some sleep, Gwen."

I don't have time to finish my morning routine; I look hideous and I know it. The car waits for me out front, the screen blows up in the darkness of early morning, and when I shut the door behind me, they consume all the air inside. I can't breathe. I can't think, and I'm stuck in that fog again, and the memory of the broken screen sits deep in the haze.

Chapter 4

My mother never told me how to kill myself. She taught me about being an adult, the freedoms and responsibilities, but she never told me how to shove a gun's barrel down my throat and pull the trigger.

Click.

The teachers told us graduation day would change everything. We'd stop being trailer trash and start a new life, big shots, onward, upward—bullshit dreams they used to push us through the system. I spent the day playing Russian roulette with a revolver because graduation day stole the last thing I had.

Click.

The doctors called it cancer. My mother called it an opportunity. "You'll be stronger without me, Dougy." Like I'd be stronger for visiting her once a year at the cemetery, flowers in hand, thrift-store suit half my size, talking about my new living arrangements in the trash heap outside Jimmy's smoke shack.

"Doug Mason," Principal Jenkins said over the mic. "Doug Mason, please approach the podium and accept your diploma." I sat in the computer lab outside the auditorium, counting the empty chamber clicks to my demise, listening to them cheer for someone who didn't exist while

Cybergirl2000 tried to act supportive through a series of emoticons.

Click.

We traded stories and pictures in a private chat room run by average losers like me, because in that cyber space, we could go anywhere, be anyone. We uploaded pictures of models and movie stars, claiming to look like them, and sometimes believing we did. I'd spend days at a time exploring that limitless world. No one knew my mom was dying, that my dad walked out, or that I lived in a one-acre trailer park with a hundred other people begging for purpose. We were the best possible versions of ourselves. We were infinite with infinite chances at happiness, sealed in cyber glamour.

"Doug Mason, please approach the podium and accept your diploma." Jenkins expected me to be there and smile my big-boy smile for the board members ready to cut his funding. My mother lay on an operating table, gutted and exposed like a fetal pig in biology class, and he expected me to stand behind the podium and give a speech about the light on my horizons.

"You there?" Bill McCoy—the school genius, weird, geeky, and awkward—opened the door to the computer lab and nudged his glasses closer to see if I was around. "Principal's looking for you."

Click

"I'm not going out there, Bill. Not today. Not tomorrow. Never again." Although I considered Bill a friend, he was the last person I wanted to talk to. The kids in school said he could read minds, and even though I didn't believe in that sort of thing, I knew what they were talking about. I didn't want him to see my pain. I set the gun down near the computer and listened for Cybergirl2000 to send another message. Maybe she'd help me escape.

"You're just going to walk away? There's 200 people out there waiting for you."

"They're not waiting for me. There's not a soul in that room who even knows who I am."

"All the more reason you should get out there. Maybe you'll get an award or a scholarship. Maybe they'll let you give a speech."

"When are you going to accept it, Bill? Stuff like that doesn't happen to nobodies like us. We're nothing, and every single person in that room knows it." Bill moved closer, ready to stare through my soul and find my darkest thoughts, when my phone buzzed in my pocket, a text from Ashton Cox, another nobody and my best friend, sitting in the auditorium. If anyone understands my life, it's Ashton.

Check this out. http://thefuture.com.

I broke eye contact with Bill and opened the link to the mayor's website and pressed play on the video. He promised big changes if he was re-elected, and from what I'd seen, he stood by his word.

"The future is here. We've waited so long for a chance to change the world, and today, technology and dreams come together to do just that. Gentlemen," he waved to the men standing near a curtain in the background, "Please reveal the screen."

The curtain dropped and a beautiful face started talking, so real you wanted to reach out and touch her.

"It may look like your average television. The televisions you have in every room, the televisions you've grown accustomed to, are a thing of the past. This is our future."

The woman on the screen spoke of perfection, striving toward a life with endless possibilities, working toward a world where sadness didn't exist, ugliness didn't exist, average didn't exist.

The last thing my father said was, "Do something with yourself." I never knew what he meant by that. It could have been some cryptic message from father to son, like those cheesy after-school specials I watched as a kid, warning me not to make the same mistakes he did. He could have been trying to tell me he believed in me and wanted to see me succeed. At the time, I was sure he wanted me to get lost so he could suck face with his new girlfriend in the taxi while they drove away. Whatever he meant, the words stuck with me.

He'd show up in his grubbed-up jumpsuit from the shop. "If you've fixed one car, you've fixed 'em all," he'd tell my mother when she asked about his day. We ate dinner in silence around the same chipped wooden table, miles apart in our own worlds.

"You happy, Jen?" He would twirl his spaghetti but never brought the fork to his mouth.

"I'm very happy." I was only six, and even I knew she lied. She hadn't been happy for years, always worried she wasn't good enough for him. Some days she'd watch sentimental sitcoms and cry when the actors kissed. I don't think I ever saw my father kiss my mother.

"I'm leaving, Jennifer," my father had said over dinner. We were silent, not because he shocked us with his confession, but because we'd expected it every time he walked through the door. My mother pulled the napkin from her lap and left the room. No fight, no argument, no emotion.

I had wanted to punch him in the gut when he left. I wanted to cuss him out with words I'd learned from him and his buddies, call him a bastard, call him a piece of shit, call him what he called me. I wanted to ask him what was so great out there in the world that he'd leave us for. When I opened my mouth, Cyndi Thompson knocked on the screen door. "Come on, Jimmy," she said with a finger in her mouth and a look on her face like she stared into the sun.

Cyndi had modeled for the local department store. Each change of season, we'd see her in the new catalog, always smiling, always loving life, always happy. I remember her skin, perfect like the leather on rich people's sofas, and I wanted to pinch her to know if it was real.

My father had stood from the table, gave me one of those *go-get-'em-slugger* punches to the shoulder, and kissed Cyndi on our doorstep. Her hair glowed in the sun, shimmering against her perfect skin, and they were happy. They were happier than my parents ever were together, and the only change was her.

They had hopped in the cab, arms wrapped around one another, and he'd given me one last wink as they pulled down the driveway. From that day on, I was sure of one thing—beauty brought happiness.

The woman on the screen never stopped. She talked from dawn until dusk about what we were capable of as individuals. What we should expect from ourselves.

"This is a motivational tool, and it is just the beginning of the changes to come." The mayor closed the curtain. "It can't be shut down. You can cater it to your needs, your dreams, and your expectations. It will help you reach perfection. It will set you apart from the people with no ambition. It will make you hungry for success. It wall make you focused. It will make you...."

Infinite.

Click.

Chapter 5

My mother bathed me in a claw-foot tub when I was a boy. When I'd wake with a fever, she'd put me in the water waist high and pour small handfuls on my head. Beads dripped over my face and neck, and the cool touch of her hand wiped them away. The thrill of hot and cold stopped my tears, the last time I remember feeling fully alive.

If you'd asked about my mother before today, I could have told you what's in my journal so far, and it isn't much, a year or so of our life together. Today, in a matter of hours it seems, I've remembered more details than I ever have. She died sometime when the sun was hot, and when I think of the blackened screen in my closet, it's the hypnotic black of her dress bouncing on the bus each Tuesday afternoon when she took me to her treatments; it's her obsidian hair, long enough to touch her thighs; it's the patches over her eyes.

I sit up, tired of tormenting half-images, and the car is parked outside the office. I don't remember stopping, and even worse, I don't remember driving. Headache's gone. Backache's gone, and nothing makes sense because I glance at my watch with a big fat 3:00 on its face, and it's trying to tell me I've forgotten the last nine hours of my life.

There's a line outside the front office doors and down the block. My nine o'clock appointment. My ten o'clock. My twelve and two and three looking like they've wilted from hours of sun. I check the clocks in the car, on my laptop, on my phone, all three o'clock. For the first time since I was a boy, I'm fully alive, and it all makes sense. I slept. It's been so many years, and I slept.

The emotion's caught in my head, and I'm grinning like an idiot, going about my day like nothing happened this morning. I pop out of the car, messy hair and buttons undone, make-up smeared across my face, the worst representation of perfection, toting my briefcase without a care in the world as the people walking past stop.

It doesn't take me long to piece together why they're staring, and I'm grinning like an idiot for a whole new reason, to smooth things over before they have a chance to react.

"One of those days, huh?" Tail between my legs, submissive, ready to do anything, even piss myself to stop them from asking questions. I cover my face with a folder, and they continue on their way. The crowds around the office grab me, tug me, try to pull the folder away from my face, and I relax, thinking things are back to normal, thinking they're drones once again drugged by the presence of the queen, when a bottle shatters at my feet. Dark wine beads on my pant legs and shoes, and the word "monster" drifts through the crowd.

Grace stands in the lobby, pitching our services like a champ, and I'm grateful, not because she's stuffing money down my pocket, but because she's a work-horse and won't notice my race toward the operating room. Once I'm inside, I'm safe.

When I push away from the mob, I'm a few steps from the operating room. Times like these make me wish I hadn't been so insistent on polished floors. A frantic pace and a few slips later, the doors slap closed behind me, and I spread out my mask and scrubs.

"Where were you?" Whenever I think I understand women, they surprise me. She never comes into the operating room, especially when there's a patient prepped on the table. "You're eight hours late." It's at least ten hours now, and I'm glad she's not counting.

"Got caught up." My head's down, hoping for mercy. I'm minding my business like a minnow passing a shark, thinking the ocean's not nearly as big as it seems, and even the smallest motions make ripples.

What's that law that says shit will happen no matter how much you plan? A screen rises out of the sink counter while I'm washing my hands, screeching big red warnings just as I'm trying to keep my face out of Grace's line of sight.

"That tells me nothing." I don't have to look at her to know she's standing with her weight on one leg, arms crossed, eyebrows arched, and I don't blame her.

Mrs. Jenkins sleeps on the table, prepped and disinfected with eyes half open and a nose twice the size of what she needs. It's my job to swoop in and tell her she was born with a deformity, that she'll never find those infinite chances at happiness unless she looks like the women on the screens, that she's worthless until she lets me save her. I keep my mouth shut, think of the screen in my closet, and do everything I can to avoid eye contact with Grace.

"Just feeling a little off today. Nothing to worry about."

"What happened to you, Jax? When did you lose touch with everything in your life? With me?"

"I'm sorry. You've been alone in the office all day, and I'm sure it's been nothing but chaos."

"I'm not talking about the office, Jax. Don't you think I care about what's going on in your life?"

What's going on in my life—the words hardly make sense anymore. I don't remember my past, and I'm not sure what my purpose is in the future. She's not talking about pasts, logistics, or purpose, though. She's talking about me.

She's been with me forever, at least it seems that way, and that's probably not far from the truth. She's seen my ups and downs. She's seen me as a saint, and now she wants to know about the monster. If it were anyone else, I'd spill my guts. Not her.

"I know." Scrubs go on, and while I'm trying to keep things organized in my head, chasing thoughts the size of boulders before they tumble through my skull, I forget to wear the mask. The table's below me, Mrs. Jenkins dreaming peacefully of a better life, and I'm tucking my chin to my chest like those old ladies who believe they'll tighten their sagging skin with a little exercise. I can't handle looking at Grace and the inevitable shit storm to follow.

"Talk to me, Jax."

My scalpel slides down Mrs. Jenkins' face, neat precise cuts around her nose. I'm focused. Hell, I may be fucked up, but I'm still a surgeon, and as a surgeon, I hate sloppy work.

My face drifts into the light.

"What have you done?" Grace covers her mouth with her hands, and when it registers in my head, it's me saying it again and again.

What-have-you-done—what-have-you-done. I'm caught.

I'm not a jumpy person, but when she mentions my face, the scalpel digs deep into Mrs. Jenkins' skin, and blood pours onto the table and floor.

"Son of a bitch!" I grab the gauze and press it into her face, and while I'm on damage control, Grace walks around the table to get a better look at me but only catching a glimpse from the side.

"You look terrible. Why would you leave the house looking like that?"

I ignore her question. Once I turn my face, she'll think I'm a piece of shit, just another Joe Nobody who couldn't cut it in the city, and attack like the rest of them.

"Just look at me," she says, and the words are full of comfort, like the Grace I met so many years ago. I turn and open my eyes, expecting castration or worse, but the operating lamp changes everything.

She makes the sound I expect, the horrible hiss she only uses when someone's hurt, and being ugly is worse than death in this city, but I stop listening when I see her skin.

"Your face," we say in unison, both confused by what we see. My face is hideous but hers is black. The scalpel falls to the floor when I push the table away from me. I back away to shine the light toward her and take a better look.

"What's wrong?" She can't understand why I'm disturbed, and I don't know if I'm delusional or not. Her hand reaches for me and each finger looks like it's made of a thick, black plastic.

"What's on your hand?"

"What are you talking about? My hand looks the same as it always does." She waves it in front of my face, and there's nothing. No freckles, no nail polish, no lines in the skin.

I hold it between my own; something she's waited for, before I became the mad man from Main Street, and it's plastic. I see her face in the light, and everything else fades away. Her eyes, her cheeks, her lips, none of them belong to the Grace I know. The plastic covers her face, deadening her movements like a doll on the store shelves.

"You're scaring me, Jax." She reaches for my arm, worried I've lost my mind, and let's face it, I probably have, but I can't stop staring into the plastic over her eyes.

"I have to go." There are too many abnormalities in Gospel today: the screen, the memories, Grace, and it means one of two things—I'm losing my mind or Gospel is crumbling. Either way, I need time to think.

"You just got here. Mrs. Jenkins is still bleeding!"

"I have to leave." I grab my bag and run into the parking lot. When I near my car, the troll and her child step in my way and stare.

"What do you want from me, huh? You want to fight me, take me down, beat my face in?" I jab my fists, parading my bloody scrubs in the street, swinging my arms like a fool.

They stare.

"Not good enough for you?" I move close to her face because I couldn't care less why she's there anymore. She's quiet, and so is the boy. "Of course not. You want to tell me how fucked up I am. Well, get in line because you have an entire city ahead of you."

I jump into the car, and they stare.

I'm sure I could find a way to explain why Grace looks the way she does, why my screen died, why I slept. There's an answer for everything, but it's not a matter of whether or not the solution exists. It's a matter of where.

I'm ready to walk back to the office, patch her up, tell her to moisturize, stretch, sleep, and head straight to my shrink's office afterwards with a question he must hear every day, "Hey, Doc, what pill can you give me today because I'm pretty sure I'm having a nervous fucking breakdown?"

I could blame it on something else, but it still comes down to the raving lunatic seeing plastic on his secretary's face. His name is Jax Mason. They say he had such a bright future. Now he's in a special ward in the state penitentiary.

The car finds my apartment again, a kaleidoscope of colors flashing on my suit when I open the door, cops parked around the entrance, shouting gibberish into mics, hearing gibberish on the other side, and blocking the doors to the building.

"What happened?" I approach Bill McCoy, the same kid from high school, the genius, the telepathist, and now the greatest detective we've ever seen, a weasel transformed into a wolf, sniffing out the people who grow lax in their commitment to Gospel. He's never wrong. They call him Wild Bill, and I suspect he'll tell me the truth whether I want to hear it or not.

"Hard to say. Looks like a trio of suicides." He's jotting notes on his tablet as a formality. We both know it was another suicide. It's only a matter of time before they realize infinite opportunity delivers limited happiness.

"Mind if I ask the names?"

"A banker named Arthur Hamish, a broker named Larry Newell, and a model—Gwen Something-or-Other."

Damnit, I shouldn't have asked, but hearing Gwen's name didn't surprise me. Her angst had that foreboding ring to it.

"You don't look too surprised. Did you know them?" Bill keeps jotting notes, glancing through me under the brim of his hat like he's ordering coffee.

"No, I didn't know them."

"The model lived next to you, and you didn't know her?"

"Nope, not really." In truth, I never gave her the chance. I had to be nonchalant about things with Bill. He couldn't read minds, but he had a sixth sense for fear, and he didn't get the name "Wild" from handling things with tact.

"Pretty little thing. Shame to waste such good looks."

Good looks. That's what it all comes down to. Good morning, Good Looks. Nice to meet you, Good Looks. Maybe we could hook up. Thanks for fucking me. Sorry you're dead, Good Looks.

"Okay if I go inside?" I know it is, and enter before he answers. He may be the police, but I run this city.

"You mind snapping some pictures of the body? It's just suicides, and my deputies are headed home. I'm not sure why I brought them for something so trivial. Everyone wants to catch a glimpse, I guess."

Three suicides are trivial? "Sure." It's probably a test, but if anyone owes them, it's me.

He looks up from his notes for the first time and hands me the camera. "Jeez, Jax. You look worse than the bodies. Better straighten up before anyone else sees you." His eyebrow piques in curiosity.

"I'll get this back to you tomorrow."

"And nothing too graphic, Jax, you know. We see enough of that down at the station."

When I was a kid, graphic meant something else. It's one of those words that changed over time. It used to mean gruesome, grotesque, gut-wrenching. Now it can mean anything as simple as a woman without mascara. I'm sure he meant the latter.

He speeds off, and I'm in Gwen's elevator surrounded by police tape, punching my fist into the steel door like I'm solving this poor girl's death by breaking my hand into a hundred pieces, screens in my ear telling me I've done everything right. It's tempting to ask myself what went wrong with her; everyone has problems, right? I'd be an idiot to think this had more to do with her personal life than the world I've created.

The elevator stops on her floor, chiming a pretty little tune called, "Bravo, Man, You've Gone and Killed Another One," and the door to her apartment's propped open with official police shit, like they gave a fuck about investigating her death.

I step through the proscenium arch, and there like an actress on the stage, she lies silent and still on her bed, the needle still hanging from her arm, black plastic over her face and breasts, like Grace before her. I don't have energy to battle with myself if it's real or not, and even if I did, would it change anything?

The bedroom's lined with my products, and my voice echoes from one screen to the next, "I'm Dr. Jax Mason. You've seen my face on your screens, on your molds, and wonder what my secret is. Stop wondering. At Mason Cosmetics, I can give you everything. Do you want fame? Riches? Sex? It all starts with a pretty face and perfect body. Join my team, and together we'll have infinity."

There's a note on her bed, and of course the cops don't think to mention it. I doubt they spent enough time in this room to find it. It's wrinkled, and not the kind of wrinkles from shoving it into your purse of pocket. The soft, warped wrinkles from tears.

"Sorry, Baby. I'm just no good at this kind of life. Thanks for the ride. Gwen"

The camera immortalizes her, one picture at a time, not for her family, not for her friends, not for me, but for an evidence file that'll never see the light of day. I take pictures of everything, even the graphic, despite Billy's wishes, because her death needs to be remembered as what it is, a cry for purpose.

I pull the sheet from the bed and drape it over her. "Thanks for everything, Good Looks. I'm sorry you ended this way. I won't let you go to waste. Sleep peacefully, Good Looks."

When I get to the other two sad saps, I see the same black plastic images I've seen all day. I see the same expressions, expressions of finality on their faces, as though they've discovered something I haven't. It also dawns on me that every one of the rooms is rather chilly, air conditioning running at full tilt. Did they do this?

Chapter 6

The smell of disinfectant made me nauseous.

"You didn't miss much." Ashton fiddled with his cell phone in the chair next to me.

"Jenkins wants me dead, I bet." I tapped my feet on the hospital floor, trying to take my mind off my mother's surgery.

"Nervous?"

"Wouldn't you be?"

"I can't say I had much of a chance to love my parents." Ashton spent his high school years in a foster home. His dad backed out as soon as Ashton could stand on his own, fourteen or so. His mom took off a few days later, said she never wanted a kid.

"Why is it taking so long? I swear I will kill him if he makes her suffer more than she already has."

"That your guy?" Ashton pointed to a doctor at the end of the hall scratching some notes on a chart.

"Yeah." My hands sweat through my jeans and left palm prints on the fabric.

"Go talk to him."

"I can't hear him tell me she's dead."

"You can't sit hear wondering either. Go talk to him. I'll be here if shit hits the fan."

I walked down the hall, the filthy trailer kid leaving footprints on the spotless floors. "Dr. Benson?"

"Just the boy I wanted to see." He handed the chart to a woman behind the counter and squeezed my shoulder the way my father use to do. "I have good news. We got it all."

"The cancer? But you said…."

"I know what I said. I have to cover my bases. We were able to remove all of the cancer."

I couldn't think of anything worth saying, so I hugged him, forgetting for a moment that brown shit and white lab coats don't mix.

"There is something I need to explain to you." He patted my back and pulled me away. "She lost her eyes in the process. The cancer was too thick. We had to remove them."

"She has a face with no eyes? Like a mummy?"

"It's not quite that drastic, but yes. There's some bruising and noticeable indentations where the eyes once were. We'll insert glass eyes to help preserve the structure of her face."

"She can't work if she can't see. How are we going to pay for this?"

"We've discussed some small cosmetic options with her that might make her look less disfigured."

"Will those help her see again? Will those make her whole again?" The question was rhetorical.

"No, but if we can restore her facial symmetry, she can likely find a job elsewhere."

"She works here. She's always worked here. I know she's just an orderly, but this hospital is her life. You guys can't give her some sort of discount? You can't cut her some slack and find her a new position here? You can't work a little overtime to make her look normal again?"

"I know it's hard, Doug."

"You don't know anything." I walked away and grabbed my jacket from the waiting room, Ashton tagging behind.

"You don't want to see her?" Dr. Benson waved his hand in the air like a hall monitor.

"No."

"Where are you going?" He followed us down the hall in his shining lab coat smudged with the pleas of a kid with no other options.

"I'm going to find a way to fix what you couldn't."

"You'll regret not being there for her, Doug. I see it every day."

"My mother has nothing." I stopped and turned toward Dr. Benson. "My father fucked her over, took everything away. She makes minimum wage, works a million hours a week so I can focus on school, and cries herself to sleep every single night because the world made her believe she wasn't good enough."

"Doug…." He tried to pull me into another hug.

"But she was beautiful. Maybe not the drop-dead gorgeous model type, but beautiful. No one could argue with that. She was a beautiful woman, and you took that away, her last chance for happiness, and now you're trying to tell me you understand how hard it is."

"How do you plan to fix this?"

"I'm going to see the mayor."

I didn't care what he had to say. The mayor was the only person who could fix the past by expanding the future, and I was going to be part of that expansion.

Chapter 7

I live alone, and aside from the awful sounds of the screens day and night, the house is empty. I've tried the modern tricks—buying plants, arranging my furniture to match my inner spirit—anything to convince myself I'm not a lonely miserable man, but most days, feng shui limps through my apartment—beaten, broken, and gagging on the anarchy.

The shower's on, filling the bathroom with steam, drowning the voices, blanketing the mold, leaving a hint of red light in its cloud while I stand in a white robe wondering where everything went wrong.

Gwen's death was nothing new. Sure, it felt new because I'd known her for so long, but people kill themselves every second in this city, and the ones who haven't wish they had the strength. They blow their money on boobs or drugs or prostitution because they want to feel like they matter in the master plan, and the master plan couldn't care less.

The robe's at my feet, and I step into the water's stream, trying to wash away what I've seen, taking my time to lather the soap in my hands because I'll likely never sleep again, terrorized with plastic stomachs, plastic hands, plastic faces.

The lather moves under my palms, touching my shoulders, and I cry for the first time since I was a boy because my hands move down my stomach, passing skin, passing ribs, before meeting the edge of what I can only assume to be solid black plastic, like all the others, and I don't know what to do.

I'm deep enough in this dream, or reality, or psychosis, to know that whatever's going on plans on getting worse before it gets better, and now I'm the sucker. The plastic's on my face, on my scalp, on my chest and hips and hands. I can't breathe under its weight.

I step out of the shower, soaped over and naked, dripping with helplessness in front of the mold while it scans the plastic scars, an executioner at my judgment, and it flashes red.

My hand's still sore from hitting the elevator doors, but that doesn't stop me from sending it through the face on the nearest screen. I'm like most men; I swore I'd never hit a woman, but it feels good watching the woman choke, gasping between spots of blood while the screen blacks out.

Blood follows me down the hall. The chick's still on all the other screens, but she's watching me now. She'll always remember the guy who punched her out and left her for dead. The closet doors pop open, and I've tried to erase the blackened screen from my mind, thinking if I stay in a state of avoidance, I'll wake up and this will be over.

It hasn't happened. I'm playing it cool the best I can, but I want to be near the screen, falling on my knees, worshiping that fallen god because no one else listens, seeking satisfaction like an addiction, hypnotic, magnetic, transcendent in a way I can't explain.

It's sitting in the back of the closet next to a box I haven't seen in years, and had you asked me yesterday morning, I'd have told you it doesn't exist, taped up, thrown under a stack of medical files. My name's on the side, done up in that fancy handwriting they taught me in elementary school.

I forgot how tough duct tape is and have to use my teeth to pry the lid off the box. My mother's patches sit on the top. They said they could cure her, give her life back, take away the pain, set her free. When I heard those words, I knew I wanted to be a doctor. I wanted to help people the way they were going to help us. Over time, right and wrong, black and white, blended together, and here I am, dying, miserable and disfigured like my mother.

I lie on my back, the closet doors open and closing on my hips because I'm confusing the sensors and rest in the comfort of the dead screen with my mother's patches over my eyes. "Take me with you."

Chapter 8

"I'm here to see the mayor." Screens talked all around me, trading visions and ideas for a better tomorrow, exploding in my system. Fancy drinks and snacks covered the counters in front of gorgeous secretaries typing away. I smoothed my hair a little to fit in.

"Do you have an appointment?" The receptionist tapped the keyboard with shimmering fingernails.

"No, I just need to see him."

"I'm sorry, the Mayor only sees people by appointment. Let me check his availability." She scanned the computer monitor, a goddess with light dancing over her face. "It looks like his next available appointment is in six months."

"He doesn't have an available time slot until after the election?"

"The mayor is a busy man. Changing the world isn't easy."

She resumed her position, typing away, and answered a Bluetooth piece in her ear. Ashton and I sat in the lobby, another waiting room, another dying room, limited, helpless, hopeless. I wouldn't see my mother until I could give her a solution.

"Let's go. My phone's almost dead." Ashton nudged my shoulder.

"You're worried about your phone? THIS..." I point around the room. "THIS is the future. THIS is going to change our lives, and you're worried about your fucking cell phone?"

"I like this place as much as you do, but she said the mayor won't see us."

"The answer is here. I'm not leaving."

"Then you're on your own. I'm eighteen, Doug. I'm free of my foster parents. I want to party and drink and black out in some alley just because I can. I can do whatever I want, and I sure as hell don't want to spend my entire day waiting for a meeting that isn't going to happen."

"Give me a minute to figure it out. Please." I stared at the office door. It didn't look like there was much security. I thought through a hundred scenarios were we could muscle our way in, but the door opened before I had a chance to do something stupid.

The mayor stepped out with a mob of people. His suit was perfect, his hair was perfect, his shoes, cufflinks, teeth, hands—all perfect. Infinite in his possibilities.

"Let's meet again next Tuesday." He patted the men on their backs and sent them away.

Before he had a chance to close his office door behind him, I wedged my foot in the crack. "Mr. Mayor? Can I please talk to you?"

"Sure, kid. Natasha will make you an appointment." He pointed to the girl I had already spoke with.

"I don't think Natasha can help me, Mr. Mayor. I need to speak with you today."

He looked me up and down—my clothes, oil and dirt smudged all over because I hadn't changed them since they told me my mother was dying.

"I have a few minutes before my next appointment. You talk while I get ready." He opened the door wider to let me in.

"Yes, sir." I waved Ashton over, and we stepped into his office, traveling to the future on plush carpet and the smell of oranges.

"You have eleven minutes." He looked at his diamond watch and organized some papers on his desk, screens chanting behind him, settling for nothing but perfection.

"My mother has cancer."

"I'm sorry to hear that, kid, but I'm not a doctor. Ten minutes."

"I know that, sir. And frankly, the doctors don't seem to be helping."

"Then what can I do for you?"

I didn't have an answer for him. I wanted to help my mother. I wanted to make her beautiful again, and to do that, I needed to be part of the future. More specifically, I needed to be a part of the mayor's future.

"I'd like a job." I tried to ignore the sweat on my palms smearing the grease over my jeans. Ashton smacked my arm with a *what-the-hell-is-wrong-with-you* look.

"You want to work for me?" The mayor laughed, hard enough to make one of the secretaries peek through the door and make sure everything was all right.

"Yes, sir. I believe in what you do, and I want to be part of it."

"You have balls, kid." He started organizing his papers again. "And I'm not saying that's a bad thing. I like my people to be determined, focused, ruthless even." He set the papers down and looked at my face. "You're a decent-looking kid, but you're going about life all wrong."

"What do you mean?"

"Look at you. You barge into my headquarters demanding time with me, and you couldn't even put on a fresh pair of socks. Your image is everything; you only have one shot in life, and your image is the gateway. You want to be part of my future, fix your image. Get your head on straight and offer me something."

"Like what? I don't have any money."

"I don't need your money, kid. I need you to give me a reason to invest in you, and until you have a solid answer for me, I can't keep you."

He called a secretary to remove us, and we were back in the past as quickly as we left, stuck in a waiting room from hell for the third time that day.

"What's the plan?" Ashton stopped messing with his phone and put it back in his pocket.

"I don't know yet."

We left the mayor's headquarters, rejoining a world with no purpose, a world ready to suck the air from our lungs.

"Whatever it is, I want in." Ashton watched the people on the streets, and I knew we thought the same thing. The past was disgusting. "Maybe we could be the mayor's drivers. I'm pretty good on my dad's old stick-shift. I bet I could drive those new cars the mayor's designing."

"If you settle for that, that's all you'll ever be. We need to think of something better."

"We could be his assistants."

"You're still settling."

"You're eighteen years old, Doug. You really think you'll just convince him to let you be the president and CEO of whatever he does in the future. Wake up."

"No, but I can walk through his door with a goal." I hopped off the curb and onto the nearest bus.

"Where are you going?"

"I need to see my mom."

The bus thumped over broken dreams, and I hopped from one connection to another until I made it to the hospital.

"Visiting hours are over, Doug. You know that." Judy, and old nurse who worked with my mother, stopped me on the way in.

"I won't wake her. I promise. I just need to see her."

She rolled her pen between her fingers, thinking it over. If she hadn't known me all my life, I doubt she'd make the exception, but she looked down the halls and waved me through when no one was watching.

My mother's room beeped and hissed with a dozen different machines singing her to sleep.

"I'm here." I pulled a chair close to her bed and held her hand. "You'll be proud of me, Mom."

Her heart pattered through the machine next to me.

"I'm going to college." I pinched her hand, hoping she might wake up without the nurse thinking I did it. "I know if you were awake right now, you'd be stunned. I know I said I'd never step foot on a college campus. They told me you were sick, and I couldn't leave you, but now I think I can make you better."

Another machine beeped. Maybe she listened.

"I'm going to be a doctor." I chose to leave the mayor out of it. My mother never liked him much. "A surgeon and I promise I'll fix you."

Judy knocked on the door and told me to get going. The doctors started their rounds, and she'd be in trouble if the found me.

"Thank you." I shook her hand and ran down the hall, the trailer trash kid high on the prospect of a better life.

Chapter 9

"You still got that camera, bud? I need it back at the station." The only thing worse than Bill McCoy at midnight, is Bill McCoy at daybreak.

"I said I'd get it back to you, Bill. Don't hound me." I expected to wake up with bruises on my sides from the closet doors, but lucky for me, my hips are made of plastic even at five in the morning.

"You sound awful. I wake you?"

I'm torn. Do I hide in here, wash the dried soap off me, dress, shave, and answer the door like nothing's wrong, or do I throw caution to the wind and cut his throat? It's nice to think about, but the truth is, this little weasel has the power to incite a riot against me. These people are wired like dynamite, and in my current naked state, I can't handle dynamite.

"Yeah, give me a second." The routine plays in reverse. Back in the shower, white robe slides on when I'm done, mold flashes red, and I open the door to hand the camera to the detective.

"You're not going to come out and talk to me?" He can't see my face behind the door, and I prefer to keep it that way.

"It's just been a rough night for me. Taking pictures of those bodies was a new experience."

"The model was hell of a looker, huh? You try anything with her? If my deputies hadn't of showed up, I'd have been all over that. Reminds me of that pretty little number down at your office." He grabs the camera, and I grab him, just enough to twist his finger until it cracks.

"Damnit, Jax." He's whimpering like the weasel he is. Blah, blah, blah. "I think you broke it. I paid you 90 grand for these hands, you bastard."

He paid 90 grand for compensation. Whether there's any science behind it or not, small hands send a clear message to the ladies. "Sorry, Bill. I'm sure it's just a sprain." For Grace's sake, I hope it's more.

"You have a first aid kit in there? I have three more stops after this before I can head back to the station."

I use the same strategy I've been trying all day and ignore him, but it's as useful as it was with Grace.

"I'm serious now, Jax. Open the door." Imagine that, Bill being serious about something. I have no illusions about what'll happen if he sees me or the broken screen, but I have a secret weapon. He has no idea how loyal I am to Grace, and if that means I have to kill a few people along the way, even someone I considered a friend for many years, so be it. I won't let her turn out like Gwen.

I shut the door in Billy's face long enough to close the closet, and while I pack the box of memories, I'm reminded more of my past. A baseball bat's propped against the farthest wall of the closet. A memory from my pee-wee days.

"I know you don't respect me, Jax, but I'm pretty good at my job. Smelling out cocksuckers who don't belong in the city, people who don't care for our way of life. They don't last long when I'm around, you know."

I grab the bat and close the closet because he's catching on. The door's unlocked, and it won't be long before Wild Bill figures that out. He's quiet, probably calling for backup because he has more brains than brawn, and I wait on the sofa in the living room, baseball bat at my side, bare feet, white robe, wet head.

Bill's clicking the door handle.

No it's not locked, you prick.

His plastic nose pops in first; sniffing me out, followed by a skinny guy pumped up from supplements, hand on his gun, still nursing his finger.

"You should get that looked at. I made sure it's broken." I slept with the broken screen, the silence, and now I remember my past better than ever. I caress the plastic through my robe, piecing the puzzle together, tummy tuck last fall, cheek implants eleven years ago, hair transplant the summer after college, Botox, waxing.

"What the hell are you doing, Jax? This your idea of a kamikaze mission?"

"I figured it out, Bill. It took me a while, but I'm not crazy."

"Figured what out? You think because you strutting naked under that robe, ditched your make-up and hair dye, that you're Nostradamus or something? You're cracking, Jax. You can't keep up, your products are slipping. You're losing clients, and you're on the fast track to the looney bin." He waves his broken finger at me. "And I'm going to let you destroy yourself, because as soon as that hottie in your office sees you're a joke, she'll find a nice home on my lap."

"She has a name." I tap the bat on the floor.

"Who cares? None of that matters here. You're either beautiful or you're not, and if you're not, you can pay to be or leave town."

"Do people really leave, Bill? You would know, wouldn't you?"

"What are you suggesting, Jax?"

"I think I'm being straight forward, don't you?"

"Careful what rocks you lift."

"What if I told you things are going to change?"

"You're pathetic, Jax, just like your mother, the faceless wonder."

I cock the bat above my head; he cringes because he thinks it's coming for him, and I smash the screen next to his face. Glass bits fall on his cheeks and hair, dotting his skin in blood. I smash the screen on the other side of him, and the pieces mist through the air again. I hit the screen behind him, and he's shaking, but as we progress, he's more afraid of the silence than my bat, and he runs.

I cherish the silence for a few seconds, memories flooding my head, before grabbing a pair of pants and running in the opposite direction. Little Billy will be back, and he won't be alone.

Chapter 10

"Your grades barely meet the required GPA, but I'm more concerned about your commitment to Westridge. It's customary to request information before you graduate. Most of our slots are already filled with students who made preparations months ago." The dean of admissions eyed me over the top of his glasses.

"I had to deal with a family issue." I had no intention of going into detail. He'd deny me for sure if he knew I made my decision the night before.

"Tell you what, give me a few days to look over your application again, and I'll be in touch."

Ashton stood in the hall with his application in hand. "How'd it go? Do we have a shot?"

"I don't know."

He nodded his head and stepped into the office after me. I wanted to believe he'd have better luck, but we were cut from the same cloth.

I left, went home; cupping my phone like it was a newborn baby, afraid to miss the most important call of my life. I flipped through the clothes in my closet; the mayor was right, shit for a shit-head, and if I let it happen, that's all I'd ever be.

I complained about my wardrobe, but it wasn't the real problem. I couldn't afford a new one, and that's what it came down to. Cold hard cash. I fished to the back of the closet and found the tuxedo my mom had bought me for the homecoming dance, mustard on the lapel because I never took the time to wash it.

I slipped it over my t-shirt and boxers, a little short on the sleeves and bottoms, but it was all I had, and suit or no suit, I wasn't going to miss the opportunity to tell the mayor about my efforts. I stood in the bathroom, wondering how the hell guys made their hair look nice, knowing I didn't have the products to do it anyway.

The closest thing I found was cooking-oil my mom used for Sunday breakfast. I slabbed it on and looked less like a business man and more like a grease monkey, but I wouldn't let it stop me.

My phone rang. "Well, Doug, looks like I have a place for you after all." The dean popped a can of soda in the background, kind of causal for a not-so-casual conversation.

"Thank you, sir. Can I ask what changed your mind?"

"Your buddy, the mayor, gave me a call. Said you had what it takes, and he'd make sure of it."

"But how did he know I applied?"

"That's a question for the mayor. All I can tell you is that you better meet with your advisor as soon as possible, or there won't be any classes left open."

The phone clicked, and I couldn't wait to run down to the mayor's office and start making plans. I grabbed my things and waded through the bus route to his office.

The same secretary met me at the front desk.

"Do you have an appointment?"

Seriously? We did this yesterday.

"No, I don't have an appointment, but the mayor wants to see me."

"The mayor doesn't want to see anyone without an appointment."

I stood in the lobby, a bigger loser than the day before because I wasn't just the kid from the trailer park. I was the kid from the trailer park in a goddamn tuxedo.

I stormed out, dragging my pride behind me, cussing out the paintings on the wall before the doorman let me out.

"There's mustard on your tux." The mayor sat outside the building, sipping some fancy drink and watching the valet park his car. "I always watch the guys. The new prototypes can be tricky to drive if you haven't done it."

"You called the school."

"Yes." He sipped more of the drink, leaving the ball in my court.

"Why?"

"I want you to owe me."

"What do you mean?"

"I see a lot of potential in you, Doug."

I smiled.

"I also see a lot of laziness. If you owe me, you'll work harder because you're not just working for yourself anymore. I'm investing in you, and I don't let my investments come up empty."

"What happens now?" I sat next to him and covered the mustard stain with my hand.

"You become a plastic surgeon. And not a shitty one either. You become someone who pays attention to detail. I want you obsessed. I want you focused. I want you to let go of everything in your past and chisel a whole new you. I want you to be…."

Infinite.

"Stick with me, kid. We'll turn the world on its head." He left the bench when the valet returned from the parking garage.

"Mr. Mayor?"

"Yeah, kid."

"What about Ashton?"

He glanced at his watch and sighed. "He'll be starting the same day you do." The doorman let him back into the building, and I sat there grinning while his drink bubbled on the bench next to me.

Chapter 11

I'm in the city streets, half naked, and have as many mixed feelings about the people passing by as they do about me. Some compliment my eyes or abs, so lost in their own cluelessness to see what's happening. Others cringe, and I grip the bat a little tighter because any day they'll stop cringing and start obliterating. I hope today's not that day.

Grace is at the office, filing paperwork, meeting with clients, prepping patients, and it's the most peaceful thought I've had in days, the normalcy of her by my side, building a dream in tandem like a well-oiled machine. I'd like to say we could pick up where we left off, maybe I'd stop being an asshole and tell her what she means to me, but dreams take hits just like the rest of us, and before we can unwind, we need to rebuild.

The office is a few blocks down the road, and while Johnny So-and-So stares through his gold plated sunglasses, doing his very least to hold back the disgusted look on his face, I remember why I never walk to work. Even his dog's back-peddling with his nose in the air. I used to like dogs.

The office is open, the usual crowd waits around the door, and I'm watching my back because each one of them is a spy looking to make a name for himself, half reporting to Billy, I'm sure, and now that I'm low-man on the totem pole, they're all looking to move up.

"Hey, bud, you definitely need to see the doc." A guy in line smacks my chest me as I try to step past him. "Just because you look like shit doesn't mean you can jump the line." Like I'm another nobody looking for a quickie before the work day starts. "Don't stand so close, dickhead," another says, holding his suit coat tight against his hips.

Dumb Fuck, I gave you those hips.

I can't complain though. It's refreshing, but I know it won't last. I lift the bat and push through the crowd like a bouncer in a club, and by the time they've figured out who I am, I've made it to the door, Grace's back turned toward me.

"Thank goodness you're on time," she says, still facing the front desk, organizing her day. We've been together long enough to develop that bizarre sixth sense that lets us know when the other's in the room. "After everything that happened yesterday, I thought you'd…. Well I don't know what I thought."

She can't tell everyone has stopped talking, screens blathering in her ears, all the suckers lined up against the waiting room wall, holding their breath because the monster's close enough to touch. They don't know whether to run, scream, or ask for my number.

"Grace." Most of our conversations start this way.

"It's weird. I have the strangest urge to drop work and go to the department store."

She turns and sees me. What do I say?

Hi, Grace. It's been a while. It's just a little blood.

Before I have a chance to decide, she's latched onto my arm, pulling me into the operating room.

"Excuse us," she says to the globs of clay in the waiting room.

"What is wrong with you?" She lets go of my arm.

"I think I can explain what happened yesterday."

"Explain?"

"I know you think I'm crazy, and believe me, I thought so too, but it's all making sense to me now. I'm remembering more every day, and I know it won't be long until I find the key to fix this."

She's still, like that split second before the storm hits and destroys your life. "You come in here like a mad man, no clothes, no product, blood dripping from who knows where, and you think you're just going to explain something, and everything will go back to normal? I'm not stupid, and I'm not sure I can keep doing this every day."

I didn't know there was an 'every day.' She's never done that before, threatened to throw in the towel. "It's the screens, Gracie."

"You're going crazy, Jax. It's nothing new; you've been acting strange for years. You don't talk to me. How many years have we been working side by side? And you still don't trust me? And now you want to dump some huge revelation on me? While you're standing here like you escaped from some prison? What do you expect from me?"

I have it all lined up in my head. I'm going to tell her about the screens, about the memories I have now, about Billy Boy and his mission to kill me, and she cries while walking back into the lobby.

Fuck.

I follow her through the flapping doors, muttering the words that don't make sense anymore, because I'm not sure how to convince her I haven't lost my mind. The suckers tuck themselves into every corner, scared to death of how I might infect them but selfish enough to hold their ground. They'd stand toe to toe with me for a nose job.

The bat's hanging at my side. Tap, tap, tap on the marble floor while I add things up. Gracie's hoping I'll leave, the suckers are hoping I'll stay and ditch the torn-up jeans for my operating gear, and the crowd outside's hope I'll stay in this fog long enough for them to taste my blood.

I never bothered to learn most of their names, and that makes it easy for me to throw the bat into the screen above their heads. Grace screams, and the suckers follow suit because it's real to them now.

"Just wait," I mouth to Gracie like it's a secret message. I want her to pay attention to the silence.

I pick the bat off the ground and send it through another screen. The suckers reach their *fuck this* levels and run for the door. It's about time. When they're gone, I watch Grace and Grace watches me, both afraid to move on this tight rope between despair and non-existence.

"Who are you?" She brushes the glass from her skin, no more tears, no more words before she opens the door and leaves, a blurred red dress and heels running for her life down the city block.

I don't know.

The old woman and her kid stand in the street, an odd satisfied smile stretching across their faces. The crowd, however, has a frightful look and absorb the space around the building while lights flicker in the distance.

Billy's back.

Chapter 12

Twenty-seven months didn't change much. I went to school during the day, six to eight hours cramming facts into my head. I spent four hours at the mini-mart, covering whatever shifts I could while some woman used her maternity leave and I cooked for eight hours each night at the Clucking Chicken.

Flour.

Water.

Flour.

Fry.

Again and again and again. The motions whirled in my head, and I heard waves. Average waves crashing on average rocks until they died on average shores. My arms moved like steel machines, prepping and packing and shipping, lining conveyer belts with engineered poultry into gaping American mouths. Shit eating shit. Diarrhea, indigestion, diabetes, and obesity pinned campaign buttons to their knit tops and ketchup stained jeans. Politics is a dirty sport.

People called us clerks, chicken fryers, bus boys. The names had nothing to do with our real job. We smiled at the customers, handed them their food with five-star service and pretended our identities mirrored theirs.

I smiled half the time. The rest I spent elbow deep in blood. Fat women with sixteen kids on their hips pounded the glass like battering rams when the fried chicken cooked for the full eighteen minutes. Some walked away with uncooked thighs and breasts at fifteen minutes. Some walked away with blood in their teeth.

Cybergirl2000 buzzed in my pocket all day long, and I had to refuse the itch because my 15-year-old boss would turn me in. The world's smallest amount of power had gone to her head, but I was safe near the fryers. She passed out at the sign of blood.

I taped a picture of the mayor's office above the fryer and pretended I was somewhere else. When the store closed, I pulled it down and kept it in my pocket for the walk home. I couldn't be without it, the dream of being anyone I wanted to be, of being gorgeous and rich.

Walking into a trailer park at night isn't all that different from walking into a cemetery. Most of the lights don't work, or they flicker between on and off because they refuse to die like the rest of us. Creepy sounds bounce between the trailer walls, guys growing pot in sheds or hoping cough drops on a Bunsen burner will be meth by morning.

Sometimes it was too much like a cemetery for my liking. I'd open the front door to our trailer and my mother would be curled up on the couch, silent and alone, before I had a chance to say a word. There weren't enough hours in the day, not if I wanted to be something better for us.

At least I didn't have to worry about homework. I'd step into my room and find a folder filled with completed assignments. Bill asked me to get him a date with his dream girl, an average girl with average dreams like me, and even though she left him after a few days, I fulfilled my end of the deal. He fulfilled his with math equations and essays about Edgar Allen Poe.

Some days I left before my mother woke, others I'd wake up early so she wouldn't feel inclined to make me breakfast. I wouldn't be able to live with myself if she burned her hand or worse.

"I'll make breakfast today, Mom. Just sit down and relax." I whipped eggs in an old plastic bowl.

"You don't need to do that, sweetheart. I'll find my way." She smiled.

"I'm going to fix you. I promised." The eggs slopped over the side as I poured them into the pan.

"I'm so proud that you decided to go to college, Doug. No one in our family has had that opportunity." She rocked in her chair, peaceful. "I'm even more proud of your dedication. Starting school is easy, but sticking with it takes guts. You've been at this for over two years, and you're still climbing the mountain."

"You keep me motivated, and so does the mayor." I hadn't mentioned the mayor before that day. I knew what she would say, and I didn't want to hear it.

"What does the mayor have to do with your schooling?"

"Not much." I stirred the eggs and avoided her.

"Douglas Alan Mason...."

"He promised me a job if I finished school."

"I see." She had the tone I expected. "And what does he do to motivate you?"

"Nothing, really. He pulled some strings to get me into a great school."

"And who is paying for this education?" Her rhetorical questions mounted.

"He's investing in me. He's making me a better person. Don't you want that?" I stopped watching the eggs.

"You need to be careful, Doug. The mayor is not an honest man."

"How can you say that? He's trying to help people. I asked him for help, and he gave me everything I asked for."

"The world doesn't give something for nothing."

"I'm doing this for us."

The eggs burned in the pan, and my mother rocked the day away in her chair, content to be blind, disfigured, and trailer-park bound. Ashton picked me up in his trashed Ford Focus, and it wasn't a moment too soon. I couldn't stand the thought of my mother losing her pride in me.

I hopped in. Bill sat in the back, loud music drowning our cares away.

"Let's ditch school today." Ashton turned the music louder and shook his head to the beat.

"I guess it wouldn't hurt. My assignments are already done." I looked at Bill and gave him a wink.

"I'm not going." Bill liked school. He'd have no life at all if we didn't shove it down his throat.

"Such a loser." Ashton shouted with the music. "Let's find a club and get high."

"That sounds a little too *in-your-face*. If we're going to skip, we need to make sure the mayor doesn't know about it." I turned the music down to bring Ashton back to reality.

"You can drop me off at the next street. I'll walk to school." Bill swung his bag over his shoulder.

"Why don't you meet with the mayor?" I turned the music off, and Ashton shot me a dirty look. "You're exactly the kind of guy he's looking for. You're smart and focused. Come with us next time we meet with him."

"I'm interested in psychology. I'm moving into my third year, and I'm not going to throw all of that away to join some vanity game."

"This is why you lost your chick." Ashton wanted to help in his own idiotic way.

"Suit yourself." I wasn't going to force him. If he didn't have the vision, if he didn't want the beauty and the fame, the beauty, the endless opportunities, then he was right. It was just a vanity game. I turned back to Ashton who shook his head to an imaginary beat.

"How's school going for you?" I asked to see his reaction.

"Oh, it's going great. Really great." He tried to keep shaking his head like he'd told the truth.

"And when was the last time you went?"

"I don't know." He stopped shaking.

"Yes you do." I grabbed his hand when he tried to reach for the radio.

"Last quarter, okay? What's the big deal?"

"What's the big deal? You have one shot with the mayor. Shit-heads like us only get one shot, and you're willing to throw it away for a few drinks and some ass. What the hell is wrong with you?"

"It must be real easy for you to look down on me. Not all of us have someone doing the work for us." He looked back at Bill who was more than ready to leave the car. "Some of us have to do it alone."

"I'm supporting my mother. Alone."

"Don't play that card again. She has nothing to do with your laziness."

"Don't use that word." I squeezed his hand harder.

"You guys can let me out now." Bill pushed on the back of my seat and slipped out when I opened the door.

"I'm done, too. Take the fucking car, big shot."

They left, and I drove Ashton's heap back to the trailer park, the cemetery of broken dreams. My mother was asleep in her chair, listening to the radio, and I spent the day staring out the window until a man in a perfect suit drove onto our lot.

He parked one car and stepped into another that pulled up behind him.

"Wait, you can't leave this here." I stumbled out the door and down the street after him, watching the prototype bump along the dirt road, the rest of the people in the trailer park watching me like I'd robbed a bank.

I turned around for a better look at the car he left in my driveway, a gold prototype. The door opened when I stepped close to the driver's side, and a voice from inside welcomed me. "Where would you like to go, Mr. Mason."

I looked around, expecting a knife to my back or worse for having something fancy in that shit-hole, and sat in the driver's seat, an envelope with my name taped to the dash and a folder on the passenger seat next to me.

"Open it." The car started and waited for me to read.

Doubling my investment. Don't let me down.

Behind the message was a check for ten grand, the most money I'd ever seen. I opened the folder to see every assignment Bill had completed for me. Mr. Mayor knew everything.

Chapter 13

"Hey, baby, where have you gone?" Billy sings in a sultry voice while he walks through the crowd. "You broke my heart in two." The people step aside, falling in line like soldiers now that their leader has arrived. "I don't know why you had to run." He tinkers with something outside the door. "But don't you worry, baby, this time I brought my gun."

A baseball bat versus a gun isn't much of a fight, and I'm content to leave the door closed between us. He taps on the door, a large faded screen, with a sarcastic smirk under his mustache because the weasel trapped the wolf.

"I've been waiting for this day, Jax. Did you know that?"

I'm not surprised.

"I've been building toward today, Jax. Do you want to know how I've been building toward today?"

It's bizarre while he watches me through the screen, one plastic man against another, sharks ready to fight on either side.

"You see, Jax, you don't understand what you preach. You don't understand what the rest of us go through to look like you. You wake up in the morning looking like a god, and the rest of us have to pay millions to taste what you taste. Who knows how old you are, but you always look young. We can't pull that off on our best days."

He doesn't know how much work I put into my image.

"You hate me for that?" I squeeze the bat like it's going to stop a bullet if he decides to pop one in my skull.

"I don't hate you for that." He snaps his gun. "I hate that you conned us into following you."

"You followed the Mayor just like the rest of us. When he took off, someone had to step up."

"That's so true. And you couldn't wait to step up, could you? How many lies did you have to tell to get the people to accept you? To get them to forget about the mayor and listen to your bullshit."

"You tell me. You were one of the first people on my doorstep."

"Do you think I regret how you've made me look? You're misunderstanding me. You made a skinny, miserable man into someone worth staring at."

"I still see a skinny, miserable man."

"That's where we differ. You built this enterprise on your own selfish desires. You had no vision. The people here were nothing but pawns in your big game. You never cared about us."

He makes a wide gesture over the crowd. "I care about these people, and they've been following me, one by one, while you walk around in a funk. I agree Mason Cosmetics has changed the world, but it's time for new management."

"You want to steal my hard work?"

"I want to improve your hard work, and I can't do that with you around."

He reaches for the door handle with his gun barrel focused on that little space between my eyes. He swings it open, expecting to find me in the usual chaos of screens preaching all the aspects of eternity, but it's quiet, the quiet that chased him out of my apartment, and he's paralyzed.

I suspect he's remembered a few things since the last time we met, and if he hasn't, this silence is working hard to fix that.

He may not know it yet, but we were friends when we were boys. We shared a classroom, chased girls, ate ice cream sandwiches outside of Rick's Tire Shop. I told him when my dad left, and he talked me out of it when I tried to run away.

It's written on his face; a little silence goes a long way.

"The woods by Napier's field," he says, gun pointed toward my head.

"You fell into a pit. Napier set up bear traps all over because he was convinced the bears destroyed his apple trees."

"He never saw a bear in his life, the old bastard. I sat in that pit for a whole day because there was no way for us to get home other than walking through his godforsaken woods."

"You broke your collar bone." No way I'm dropping the bat. I need to act first if I want to outrun a bullet.

"Still hurts most days." Still pointing the gun. Not very friendly.

"Your mom and dad took off on some campout, drunk as usual. Told you to stay with me and my mom."

He laughs and the gun waves back and forth. "Took them three days to remember I was at your house."

"I pulled you out of that hole, and my mom snuck you into the hospital to have her doctor friends patch you up so your pop wouldn't get hit with a huge medical bill."

"He beat me anyway. Told me I should have never come home."

We're in the silence, in the woods, in the hospital, in the house, hiding from his dad, in my office decades later, chests pumping, one gun, one bat. He lowers the gun, swinging it by his side because he can't decide whether to shoot me or let me go, and I take advantage of his indecision. Ten seconds from now, I may not have the chance.

I run into the hall and out the backdoor, thrilled no gunshots follow, forgetting the thousands of people piled outside the doors.

"Get him!" they chant like radicals, and I swing the bat to keep space between us, breaking hands and faces, blood dripping down my knuckles. I glance above their heads, plotting my escape route when a fist hits the side of my head.

Everything blurs, but I can't stop pushing. There are trees not too far behind the crowd; I can't decide if it's another memory or reality, and it doesn't matter. If I stay here, they'll kill me, but they won't enter the woods.

Call it evolution or human nature, once we adapt to a certain lifestyle, it's hard to go back to whatever was there before. They don't know how to survive in the woods. They don't even understand the concept of living without screens, cars, and money, and it terrifies them.

Nails drag along my skin in one last effort to hold me back, and I'm free, running to the woods before I black out.

Sunsets never last long, whether you're watching them or not. Water seeps into my pants, chills in my chest, and I wake in the trees outside the city, alone, shadows growing taller and darker as the mountains devour the sun. "Cowards. Pathetic cowards."

The crowds disappear in the lines of tree trunks, building a barrier between us, all except the old woman and her boy. They're on the edge of the road doing what they do best, watching me, and while I push and pull to get back on my feet, half dead, I don't mind so much.

Birds dip into the mud at my feet with no fear of who I am. Maybe being a monster is the same as being human. It's been a long time since I've been alone in the woods, and the sounds getting closer tell me I'm not the only monster here.

I can't go back to my house. They'll be waiting for me. If not the crowd from this afternoon, there will be someone new. This city's only concerned with what it sees; news travels fast.

The last bits of light fall behind the hill, and the old woman and her kid pack their chairs and blankets to return to the mountain, leaving me alone. Truly alone. At least I know they won't be after me in this darkness.

I've been living on adrenalin for hours, and my arms and legs won't let me forget. They shake and slosh through the mud, and while I gather my bearings, my mouth's filled with desert sand, dry and gritty from dehydration. I can't remember the last time I drank, or ate for that matter.

I'm not willing to hunt for water in these woods, and as dangerous as it may be, I need to ask for a favor. Ashton owns Flawless, the hottest night club in the city. I spent more time there than I did at home, and because we're both ruthless business men, we developed a partnership in spite of our failed friendship. You might even say we're still friends; we watch each other's backs, and that's as close to friendship as you can find around here.

He never opens the doors before midnight, and if I've been sitting in this sludge as long as I think I have, midnight isn't far off. It doesn't do me much good, knowing the time, when I can't tell the difference between right and left. Fires flicker on the mountain from the old woman and her posse of Jax Mason haters, but it's not enough to tell me where I am.

Everything looks different from the outside in. What I can see of the city lines up backwards, and it's not like I can take a casual midnight stroll to look at street names. I have to walk until I figure it out.

As I drift into the city, something overwhelms my thoughts. The hum of screens off every building, the constant repetitive drone of capturing beauty, of staying beautiful, of being beautiful, all encapsulated in the city of Gospel and the pitch delivered from pure beautiful, purloins my memory.

Sometimes left, sometimes right, guessing where I am doesn't matter because through the trees ahead, the club bounces. The ground changes from sloshy mud to concrete, and my knee bumps the edge of a dumpster. The music, Gospel's allowed music, is so loud; I doubt anyone notices me thumping around like an animal.

A spotlight wakes when I round the corner, and I jump into the closest darkness before the lines of people see me.

Shit.

Ashton never had spotlights before, and there's bile in my throat when I ask myself why he'd have them now.

I can't use the front door, but having been a VIP member all these years, I'm entitled to use the secret entrance in the back. He designed it for people like me, the highest clientele so we could come and go without hassle.

I enter the code, and the door opens. I'm surprised he hasn't changed it, but I don't have time to dwell on what that means. I need water and a place to hide while I figure out my next step.

"Jax!" one guy says when I step into the hall.

Shout a little louder, prick.

He's high out of his mind. Thankfully, everyone else is too.

I stand on the balcony over the dance floor. They're all morphing and blending to the music, and I can't recognize a single face. Plastic men. Plastic women. Snorting and drinking anything they touch, replicated, aimless, androgynous slugs hiding from birds and the sun and themselves.

"What are you doing here?" Ashton stands behind me.

"I just need water, and I'll go." I turn to face him, knowing whether I live or die depends on the outcome of this conversation. He raises his hand to adjust his hair, and I cover my stomach because if the roles reversed, I'd punch me in the gut.

"That's not why you're here."

"Maybe not." I try to wipe the dried blood from my skin.

"It's going to catch up to you, Jax. You can hide, you can beg, but you fucked up, and I can't change that."

"I didn't fuck up."

"Look at yourself. You're pathetic. You're walking around like some hotshot in your ripped jeans and bloody pecks, but you look like a clown."

"I just need to hang out here for a little while." I adjust my hair, trying to fit in.

"And do what? Kill the night for everyone? Cost me profits? Look, I'm sorry your life has gone to shit, but mine hasn't. I'm a great lookin' guy with a great lookin' nightclub. I'm gonna make sure it stays that way."

"Just a glass of water."

"I should kill you now for the way you look, but I won't because of our past partnership. Get out, Jax. Don't come back." He adjusts his suit and waves to someone in the corner.

A plastic bouncer grabs my arms and shows me the door I came in. His foot pushes me down the steps, and I'm back in the woods, terrified tomorrow will never come. The spotlight powers off.

Chapter 14

"There's no steering wheel because it drives itself." I sat in the school parking lot with a dozen beautiful girls asking questions about the prototype. Could it drive under water? Could it fly? Could it read my mind? They didn't care if I had an answer and neither did I. The interior was one big screen talking about the future, pushing air in and out of my lungs, and I was alive.

I cashed the check the next day. Two grand went toward a decent suit and some other clothes to help my image. The rest went toward my mother's medical bills. I learned a valuable lesson when I spent the last penny—ten grand doesn't go far in the real world, and when I thought it was back to square one, seven nights a week of wading through chicken blood and bagging groceries, the mayor sent another check.

Ashton dropped out of school, and I didn't hear much from him. Bill won research awards left and right, building his name in the psychology field and the name of his university. I focused on school and aced the classes on my own. I think Bill appreciated that arrangement as much as the mayor. More clothes, more nights on the town, more thousand-dollar haircuts, more debt paid off.

The faster the money came in, the faster I spent it. My mother didn't say much about the money. She hoped one day it would stop coming, and I'd be her sweet Dougy again, but I wasn't a kid anymore, and someone needed to take care of her. She smiled each time she heard my voice and spent time with her friends in the park to pass the time.

"Let's get out of here, Mom." I poured myself a bowl of cereal before another late night with new friends.

"We could get ice cream down on the corner. Or have Lily make us one of her favorite sandwiches."

"That's not what I mean. I'm making good money now, Mom. We should look into a new house."

"You mean leave the trailer park?"

"Of course. You deserve better than this, and frankly, so do I."

"But this is our home. We know the people, the people I grew up with, the people you grew up with. Are you ashamed to be here?"

"Just because they live near us doesn't mean we owe them anything. We're better than these people. My suit is worth more than they make in a year. We don't belong here anymore."

"You sound different, Doug."

"What?" The cereal tasted like shit.

"You're cold. I didn't raise a cold boy."

"I'm trying to do what's best for you, Mom. You want me to apologize for that? You want me to sit here and let you rot in that chair?"

She leaned back, rocking intermittently.

"I didn't mean that." I threw the spoon into the milk, splashes dot my leather jacket. "I just want you to be happy."

"You're changing, Douglas. I suggest you take time to look at yourself."

She grabbed her walking stick, walked to the bedroom, and shut the door behind her like she'd won the argument in one sentence, but I was a fourth-year medical student. I made great money, had no college debt, with a guarantee for an amazing job once I finished my residency. I didn't need to look at myself. I needed to keep going.

The milk dripped onto my jeans, and I cussed at the paper towels because they weren't doing a damn thing to help. When I finished scrubbing, I heard laughter, a bizarre sound in a trailer park.

I stepped into the living room and split the blinds to see who it was. It wouldn't be the first time some junky mistook our house for his.

Five or six punk kids, I couldn't tell, stood around my car pointing toward the driver's side. "Fuckers," I shouted when I threw the door open, arms up for a fist fight. I wouldn't let the same old shit happen anymore.

"Really? What are you gonna do?" The tall kid in the back grabbed his balls like I'd run screaming if I knew he had some.

Long scratches covered my car, and I had a strong suspicion they belonged to the knife in the other kid's hands.

"Back up." I moved closer, fists over my face.

"Pretty boy. What if you mess up your jacket?"

"Back up."

"There are five of us. You're nothin' but a scrawny loser always hangin' out with his mommy."

When he mentioned my mother, I snapped. If there hadn't been five of them, I may have ended up in jail, or worse, but they gave me a strong reality check when combined. Blood dripped into my eyes, and I threw punches at no one, flailing around like a fish out of water, and they kicked my head and arms and chest until the black in my head grew darker.

They laughed and walked away. I rolled around on the ground, holding my gut, the same trailer-trash kid with greasy jeans and sweat-stained shirts, covered in raw egg. I walked the walk and talked the talk of a big shot from the city, but nothing changed. We needed to leave the park.

Chapter 15

It's not as cold by the base of the mountain. It cuts the breeze, and while I wait for a miracle, I listen to the conversations of the people on the top of the hill, the people I've ignored for decades.

They talk about the day, tell stories about their kids, tell stories about me and the city, sing songs. The smell of onions and garlic falls down the mountainside while they cook their dinners. Real food, not the manufactured shit we eat to make our bodies look fake, chemically engineered plastic to fit all our plastic needs.

The conversations slow and laughter breaks loose. Who knew laughter was infectious? They're gasping and choking like they've all come down with an unknown disease, and I can't remember ever being that happy. Maybe they've had it right all this time, and the city's filled with hopeless suckers like me. Something tells me they're the only ones with the answers.

I hitch my pants a little higher, like it's going to prepare me for what's to come, and step onto the side of the mountain, the first dry ground I've felt since they forced me into this black hole. Hand after hand, foot after foot, I latch to the rocks, feeding on the sounds of happiness.

It won't take long for them to realize I'm scratching at their doorstep, a homeless cat ready to do anything for a scrap of kindness. I step onto one more rock and the push brings me above the edge of their civilization, putting my naked torso in plain sight. They stop singing. They stop laughing. They stop everything and stare at the monster from hell.

The adults look into my eyes while the kids stare at the plastic on my stomach and the *How ya doin'?* dumbass expression on my face. I keep quiet, and they do the same. We do what we can, stare each other down, species deciding whether we want to make the effort to communicate or say *fuck it*, and go for the kill. I'm having second thoughts about the latter option because they're not afraid of me.

The children approach me to get a better look at the results of countless bad decisions. They touch my hands, tracing the edges of the plastic with their fingers in amazement at my stupidity. The adults wait for an explanation. I consider telling them everything, but even I'm not dumb enough to buy it.

"There's an old woman who comes into the city every day at four o'clock." I'm hoping someone will chime in and tell me where she is. They don't. "I'm Jax Mason, the surgeon. She comes to my office. She brings a boy with black eyes."

No answer. They're weighing the pros and cons of letting me into their happy home.

A man in the back of the crowd lifts his arm and points to a hut down the road.

"Thank you," I run to the only hut with smoke coming from the chimney, the bat still attached to my hand.

I knock, standing on shaking knees like a kid waiting for dad to come home after a screw-up in school, not knowing whether to expect silence or a beating.

There's no answer, and I bang harder. I don't have the time to be a pussy.

The old woman swings the door open, a roaring fire burning behind her. Her shadow, larger than life, swallows me whole. What did I get myself into?

"You look like you could use a drink," she steps aside to let me in.

Chapter 16

The mayor asked about the car, and what was I supposed to say? They had guns? There were twenty of them and I couldn't take them all? I gave him the pathetic look I always did, no need for words because he already knew I wasn't good enough.

I spent the next ten months in the school gym, eating protein bars, mixing powders, benching, lifting, pressing, and clopping on a treadmill to nowhere. Flexing, stretching, burning, sweating, sculpting, until I was a god.

I'd known the mayor for fifteen years, and met with him half as many times. Sometimes I wondered what we were doing, if he was just stringing me along, but that couldn't be it. He spent hundreds of thousands of dollars on me, on my education, on my family. Anytime I needed something, he made sure I had it.

At the end of those fifteen years, he asked me to meet with him to discuss our relationship in the future. Fifteen years of hard work. Fifteen years of doubts and what-ifs. Fifteen years of dreams, and he finally made the call.

I wore my best suit, nothing like the tuxedo on my first day. I paid ten grand for a perfect haircut and shave, imported shoes and cologne, moisturizer, makeup, lip balm, all because I wanted him to know I was the best and he didn't make a mistake.

I stepped into his office, Natasha looking as gorgeous as ever, and said what I always say. "I'd like to see the mayor."

She smiled because she knew I deserved to be there. "Do you have an appointment?"

"Yes, miss, I do." A simple sentence, but it was enough to make me stand tall.

She fished through the computer list and found my name, Doug Mason. She escorted me to the door, and for the first time, I belonged.

The mayor waved me in and showed me to his conference room. I took a seat next to two other men. When I took the time to look them over, I knew I was in familiar company.

"Gentlemen, today is the day I share my vision with you." The mayor took his place on the other side of the table. "I'm sure you remember one another."

Ashton sat to my left and Bill to my right, both beefed up and dressed like kings, nothing like the sloppy kids I grew up with.

"You've all earned a place in my future. Bill has earned PhDs in psychology and neuroscience, in addition to a background in criminal justice. In my future, I need a smart, reliable police force, and Bill will see that is carried out." He pulled a roll of paper from a cabinet behind him. "Ashton's toured every club from Hong Kong to Paris to London to Los Angeles. He's eaten the best, drank the best, and will bring the best entertainment money can buy to us." He opened the map to our future and spread it on the table in front of us. "And Doug finishes his residency this year. Just as I suspected, he's turned out to be the finest plastic surgeon this world has ever seen. And together, we're going to set an irresistible standard."

We glanced over our shoulders, eyeing each other, secretly congratulating one another but too proud to form the words. It was nothing like our teachers said, but in that moment, we stopped being poor miserable white-trash shit-heads.

"Gentlemen, this is Gospel." He held the paper at both ends and pushed it toward us.

The blueprint covered the majority of the table, and from the look of it, the new city would be ten times bigger than anything we'd seen.

"Where are you building it?" I leaned closer to look at the parameters.

"Right here." The mayor held his arms out wide.

"There's already a city here." Ashton looked as confused as I was.

"Not for much longer. We'll build the new one right over this one."

"How can you do that? People live here. Their families live here, their kids." I pointed to the part of the blueprint covering my trailer park.

"I have connections." The mayor closed the paper, rolled it up, and put it back in the cabinet.

"And what about the people?" Bill chimed in, which surprised me. He wasn't a fan of people, so it must have been curiosity choking the cat.

"They either join us or move on."

"You can't just kick people off their property and out of their homes." My nerves laughing for me.

"We won't need to. We will buy them off, or they will buy in. They will buy into furnished living dwellings. We've developed the prototypes. Every unit has tomorrow's amenities, with a screen in every room, telling them about it twenty-four-seven. They'll be available for everyone at a price. And we have one last project to finish."

"Why the name Gospel?" Bill curious again.

"I want people to believe in one thing—perfection is happiness. And the only way to get there is through us. I want them to let go of everything, their insecurities and doubts, religion, family, memories. I want to revolutionize the way people see themselves until they believe in our gospel truth."

The three of us didn't have much to say. I loved the idea of the future, but not at the expense of losing my mother. No paycheck, new invention, or beautiful face could replace her, and if the mayor expected me to throw her off a bridge and walk with him, he could go fuck himself.

"Don't look so grim, boys. I'm not killing your new puppy; I'm making it better. I'd never ask you to part with your loved ones. They make up a great deal of who you are, and I can't have you walking around with missing pieces. I need a perfect team to build perfection." He reached into his pocket and pulled out his checkbook. "Which is why I'm offering each of you a check for ten million dollars to help your loved ones join our future. Buy them units, the rest will come with it—cars, clothes, screens, and food. Set them up, and let them enjoy Gospel. Give them a reason to believe in this with us."

He wrote each of our names and handed us the checks. Bill and Ashton couldn't help but smile, but I had a bitter pill to swallow, a mother who wanted nothing to do with the mayor's future. The mayor stared me down over the table, knowing I had reservations.

"Ten million dollars sets her up for life, Doug. Ten

million dollars gives her the best medical care, the best supplements, the best future possible. You'll be my right hand in this new city. You'll never worry again."

I traced the writing on the check and sat in his office with the weight of ten million impossible decisions on my shoulders.

Chapter 17

She sits me down at a table with a tall glass of water and a single shot of homemade liquor while she takes a seat on the other side, staring the way she always does, judging.

"What'd they do to you?" She throws her feet up on the table and leans back in the chair. Scare tactics 101, and it's working.

"Nothing yet." I drink the water and follow it with the liquor shot that packs a serious punch. The burn spreads through my nose and throat and fills my eyes with tears.

"You look like shit." She hands me a damp dish towel to wipe my face.

"I'm not sure why I'm here."

"Yes, you are." She doesn't hesitate. "You're here because you want answers, and you think I got 'em."

"I guess you're right." Another sip of liquor burns my throat.

"Guessin's a dangerous game. It's like gambling. You're bettin' all you got on someone else because you don't know what the hell's goin' on. No idea you're changin' the world." She's talking less about gambling and more about me.

For once, I understand. "When did things change?"

"You should remember by now."

"I remember major events, but the details blur."

"Gospel started forty years ago, just a shiny little city no one'd ever heard of, spewing nonsense about infinity. You were the president, founder, editor-in-chief, and master general of spewing. You laid it on so thick, people couldn't wait to fall in your sludge."

Things trickled in. Without the hum of the screens, more and more came back. "That's sounds about right."

"I am right. I was there, boy. I watched you con people out of house and home with your dreams and give them nothing in return."

"You have no problem saying it like it is."

"I popped out of the womb that way. No sense in holding things back. Just causes confusion."

My throat acclimates to the steady burn when I down another shot, and out of the corner of my eye, I notice the black-eyed boy sleeping near the fire.

"Xavier's mom was one of those people." She points to a picture near the boy's bed, a woman I remember operating on five or six years ago.

"Boob job. I remember."

"He doesn't. She left him on my doorstep because she'd found a place where she could live forever. She never came home, and he's been with me ever since."

I drink glass after glass of the liquor, hoping she'll stop staring at me, waiting for a response I don't have.

"You can drink all you want, but it won't undo what you've done."

"Why do you watch me every day?"

"Well, look at you, growin' a pair of balls." She slides her feet off the table. "I watch you because your mother asked me to."

"What do you mean by that?"

"I worked with her at the hospital before she passed away. Kindest person and proudest mom I'd ever seen. I'm not too proud to admit I was sick to death with her bragging about her son, the big-to-do college student studying to be a doctor."

"She never mentioned you."

"Maybe she did, and you were just too busy to hear it. When she started getting' sick, I saw less and less of her, but when she'd come in for shifts here and there, she'd talk about you and how you'd changed. How you weren't the boy she raised. How you'd forgotten everything she'd taught you."

She's right, again.

"She knew she didn't have much time left, and eventually you'd be left to your own devices. She asked me to keep an eye on you and make sure you didn't destroy yourself. Looks like I did a lousy job."

The blood and dirt on my fingers leave prints on her glasses. "What do I do now?"

"Where's your woman?"

"What woman?"

"Don't play stupid, Douglas. That sweet lady who dances around you in the office. She's just about gone. Where is she?"

The sweat in my palms fogs the glasses. I'd rather not ask any more questions. "What are you saying?"

"You've noticed by now. Some people are here one day and gone the next."

"Grace is going to disappear?"

"Soon."

"What does that mean?" I smash the cup to the table harder than I want to, and it wakes the boy. He sits up and rubs his eyes. When he realizes it's me at his dining room table, he runs to the woman and hides.

He raises his hand and makes a hand gesture.

She does likewise and I realize they are talking in sign.

"Is he deaf?"

"Duh. Why do you think he has no problem pushing his way through all that noise in that place you call

Gospel?" She continues signing, but verbalizes for me, "Don't you worry about anything, sweetie. He won't be here long. Why don't you go on outside with the other kids while I talk to Dr. Mason."

He walks a large circle around the room to avoid getting close to me and slips out the front door with a slam.

She pours another drink and sits a little closer to me. "You wanna know what happens when those poor people disappear?"

"Yes." I'm one hell of a liar.

"I don't suspect that's true, but I know you love that assistant of yours, so we'll go." She stands to throw a simple shawl over her shoulders, and pops two old sandals on her feet. Before we leave she grabs two ear pieces and places them in each ear.

"What are those?"

"A type of noise dampener. You really are brainwashed, aren't you?" She hands me a pair. "Shove these in those brain holes of yours."

In a moment of clarity, it all comes together. "The screens?" I do as she instructed and put in an ear aid. I can still hear her, but all the ambient noise is deadened.

"Bravo. Didn't it ever strike you as odd that everywhere you go a screen there?"

My closet, the one sanctuary for me in all of Gospel—the broken screen, the reason I'm here, and the reason I know she is right. "There's no reason Gospel needs to brainwash its citizens. We are perfect. Who would want to leave that?"

She grins. "Near perfect and only for a brief time." She hustles me out the door. "Let's go."

"Go where?" I grab the baseball bat just in case.

"You won't need that, hun. You can't bring down a whole city with a piece of wood. It's gonna take heart, love, and just about everything you've got."

She opens the hut door, and we walk side by side with her people. They speak to me now, wishing me luck, shaking my hand, offering me food and water for the journey.

"Where are we going, Annabelle?"

"I sure do like the sound of that better than 'old woman.' That shit was getting old."

She winks, and I forget we're in crisis.

"The department store," we exit the crowd, "They all eventually head to the department store, and because of that little power outage we provided, a whole lot more of them are heading there than usual."

Chapter 18

The prototype drove in circles around the trailer park, and I stared at the check in the back seat, too selfish to tear it up and stay with her, too dependent to leave the park and never look back. A coward either way.

"Park in the driveway, please." I folded the check and kept it in my pocket when I stepped into the trailer.

"Mom?" The lights were off in the middle of the afternoon. Radio off. Television off. I checked the kitchen and bathroom; it wasn't a big trailer, and the bedroom was the only place left.

I cracked the door enough to see her bed, in the same position I left her that morning. The check didn't mean much at that point, and I ran to her side.

"Wake up, Mom. Wake up." I nudged her shoulders, and she rolled over and grabbed my hands. "You scared me half to death. Why are you still sleeping?"

"I didn't realize I was. I closed my eyes for a minute after you left."

"I've been gone for hours." I felt her head for a temperature, and handed her some cool water to help her perk up.

She sat up in the bed with her wounded eyes in plain sight. I handed her the patches.

"I don't need them, sweetie. I'm not ashamed of the way I look."

I kissed her eyes and held her hands. "I promised to fix you, and I will. Very soon."

"What brings you home so early?"

"I need to talk to you."

"You're making me leave my home." If she had eyes, she'd have seen right through me.

"I wish you'd stop making it sound like I'm abusing you. Let me do this for you. Let me take care of you. Let me spoil you. Let me love you the way you've always loved me. Let me give you what you need. You can mingle with better people, people dress nice and can afford to have their carpets cleaned every once and awhile." I pulled the check from my pocket.

"There are enough shallow people in this world, Douglas. I won't be adding to it."

"The mayor gave me a job. I'll be his head of plastic surgery in a few months, and he gave us some money to get settled in a new place."

"And how did the mayor get that money?"

"He's not a thief, Mom. He's trying to help people, giving them the best possible opportunities."

"Where will we be going? If we're above the people around here, we'll have to travel pretty far to be with peers who match our status."

"We won't be going far. The mayor is building a city nearby."

"Where nearby?" She pulled her hands away from mine. I couldn't understand how she always knew what was in my head.

"I'll take you there when they start building."

She turned on her side and went back to bed, her way of telling me I screwed up.

"You don't need to worry about anything. I'll take care of you."

"And who will take care of you?" She pulled the blanket up to her chin. "I'm tired, Dougy. Let's talk about this another time."

The car started when I stepped out the door, and I cashed the check from my phone before I let my mother's words talk me out of it. She didn't know what was good for her.

The days after that meant nothing. They were waiting days. Waiting for the workers to build the city. Waiting for the mayor to tell us his whole master plan. Waiting to finish my residency and start my own practice. Waiting to make the world beautiful, my mother beautiful.

Waiting for me to be a trillionaire and my mother to see that it wasn't a bad place to be.

The phone rang from time to time, adding distraction to the waiting, but some distractions had a way of making me forget everything.

"What happened?" I held the phone away from my face so the doctor couldn't hear my voice shake.

"She collapsed in the grocery store. We think the cancer has been back for a while, and she didn't mention it."

I don't know why I didn't see it. I'm a doctor, and I couldn't see my mother relapsing. The exhaustion, the headaches, the forgetfulness. It'd been so many years; maybe I thought we'd won the fight. "How bad is it?"

"We're running tests now. It's still too soon to tell just how far the cancer has spread."

"Be straight with me, Jon. You're a doctor. I'm a doctor. You don't need a hundred tests to know what your gut tells you."

"It doesn't look good, Doug. The cancer has obviously spread, and due to the sensitive area it manifested in last time, there is a good chance it has returned in that area and the surrounding areas."

"What are you trying to say?"

“There is a possibility it could have spread to her brain.”

I was starting to hate possibilities.

Chapter 19

She makes it look easy while we climb down the mountain. "What's wrong with you, boy? Those plastic feet weren't made for hikin'?" She trickles through the rocks on muscle memory.

"I'm not sure if this is the right time to say this, but I think I'm drunk."

"You're kidding. From what?"

I wish I was kidding. "I don't know if I've ever had liquor that strong."

"Liquor? That's the watered-down stuff I use to brush my teeth. You're worse off than I thought." She swipes a few stones out of my way so I don't slip. "Don't expect me to carry you. My heart's bad enough. If you fall, you're on your own."

"Pretty sure I'm floating, not falling."

"You're definitely drunk. Here, take my arm." She reaches for me, and I can't tell left from right. I slip, she slips, and before we know it, we're halfway down the mountain, laughing, asses covered in mud.

"You'll be the death of me. I always knew it." She wipes the mud from her face and throws it at mine.

"Maybe we could wait here for just a little while." I hang my head between my knees, laughing. "I feel like I'm in college again."

"So, you were always a lightweight, huh?"

I roll my eyes, and other than the song of a few lonely crickets, it's quiet. "Can you tell me more about my mother?"

"She loved you more than anything. Anyone with eyes could see that. She was strong, and not the kind of strong I consider myself to be. Everyone she touched, she touched with tenderness. She stayed strong for everyone around her even when the pain was miserable. She lived for the people around her, but I suspect you already knew that."

"Did she ever mention my father?"

"Not really. He stopped by the hospital once and hardly said a word. I figured he must have been a jerk, else she'd have bragged our ears off like she did about you."

"I was hoping you might know where he is. If he's still alive."

"You're kidding right?"

"Why do you say that?"

She huffed, tilted her head and asked, "You are aware that I knew your mother when I started as a candy striper, and she was with housekeeping?"

"So."

"Just think about that." She changed the subject back to my question. "Anyway, losing a parent's hard, especially when it's the parent's choice."

"Part of me wishes he'd show up at my doorstep just so I could slam the door in his face."

"Closure comes from the inside. Had that man come back into your life it would have done no good for anyone. He'd open his can of worms all over again, and you'd have been right back where you started. You have to forgive and forget or he'll always have control."

I wanted to come home with some beautiful girl on my arm, and have him slug my arm in congratulations, but I realized it had nothing to do with the girl. It was about his blessing, a blessing I never received.

"You looked like him before all the perfection cream and operations." She pinches my cheeks and they mold like putty around her fingers.

"I'm not sure what to think about that."

"Good things. You were handsome like your father, and you got to keep the best part of him."

"What's that?"

"Your mother."

"I wish every day the cancer took me instead."

"Cancer?"

"She died of cancer."

"Oh, honey."

"What aren't you saying?" I grabbed her by the sleeve and pulled her closer to me.

"I thought you knew."

"You thought I knew about my mother dying from something OTHER than cancer? You couldn't be more wrong."

"She had cancer, no one can debate that, but she didn't die from it. The mayor needed you to concentrate. He'd perfected the cream, and he needed your full attention."

"He killed her? Why would he do that?"

"Why did he do everything he did?"

I knew the answer because it was the same force that drove me, but it didn't mean he was a murderer. "He was greedy and powerful, I'll give you that. But he couldn't get away with murder. Someone would have stopped him, or tried to stop him."

"You're looking at her." She flicked my hand away from her shirt.

"I still don't believe you. I knew the mayor for a long time and would even consider him a friend. He did more for me than anyone ever has."

"And why do you think that is?"

"He saw value in me."

"He saw profit in you."

"I was part of his plan, Annabelle."

"And your mother wasn't."

I clenched my jaw, swallowing pride and truth and words I'd regret later.

"I was there when they injected the first batch of cream into her. Didn't work like they'd hoped, Doug. I was there when they did it the second and third times. I was there when the machines screamed on her behalf, and I was there when they did nothing."

"Why didn't you stop them?"

"I was just a teenager, I hid in the shadows, or I would have been another of their experiments. Sometimes forces are too strong to overcome."

"Wait, are you saying when my mother died, you were a young girl?"

"Yes."

"What happened?"

From the bottom of her belly, she threatened to wake the dead with her laugh. "That's just it Doug, nothing happened," she shook her head, "you've been so disenchanted with Gospel for such a long time, I truly thought you knew."

"I was part of his plan. He never intended to let me go." I stare off into the trees, thinking over what she's said, suffocating under that familiar emptiness, that familiar static, and tears of hate drip down my skin.

"Nancy McCoy tried to save her, too."

"Bill's sister?"

"She was one of the nurses. They cut her open and tried more experiments on her. When they saw me, I ran and they didn't catch me. With anyone who would listen, we fled and started a safe place on the mountain."

I must have been the only one who had no idea what was going on, the biggest sucker of them all. "I must be more drunk than I thought because it looks a band of people are all heading to the cosmetic department store at once."

"You'd be right."

"Why?"

She stands, wipes the mud off her pants, and offers me her hand to help me up. "You're better off seeing it for yourself."

The club passes, the dumpster passes, the trees pass, and I forget I'm drunk. I forget Wild Bill, and his armed assassins. I forget my mother, the boy with black eyes, Grace, and everything else when I see the people on the road. "They're all patients of mine."

"You sound surprised."

I study them. "The ones with the most surgeries. They're what I call the...."

"Mannequins? You'd be right again."

"Why are they marching?"

"Some people spend so much time trying to stand out, to rise above what's considered average; they forget everyone else is trying to do the same. Turns out, being perfect's a lot like being average when there's enough people in the circle," Her eyes widen, "but that's not the real problem."

"Then what is?" I touch the plastic on my stomach while they march in single file toward the department store. "The department store. Why there?"

"Come on," she says and tugs my arm toward the road.

"I can't go out there."

"They don't care." She points to the plastic assembly lines.

"They're still people. I'm not welcome in the city. It only takes one of them piping up to send word to the police, and I'm dead."

"They're gone, hun. You could blow off a bomb in their faces, and they wouldn't flinch."

"Why?"

"Expiration therapy." She stops and turns me, holding my hands to lessen the blow of bad news. "Perfection has a shelf life, and these Gospelites have reached theirs."

"Says who?"

She motions to the screens. "They tell you."

"You said that you caused the power outage. Are you responsible for this?"

"I don't know, Doug. We thought they would revolt, but whoever is running your town, did something to the programming. It would appear they are making wholesale changes to the people here."

"What do you mean?"

"A lot of people want this lifestyle, but there's only room for so many. If you run out of money for cream and surgeries, what do you think your worth is?"

"You still haven't told me why they are heading to the department store."

"It's time to fix this."

There's angry mobs in my head and dogs after my throat, but Annabelle's eyes tell me everything's going to be okay. I haven't been a trusting man in a long time, but I step from the curb onto the city streets and wait for a knife in my chest.

Chapter 20

Sometimes life screws you and makes you run to the ones you love. Sometimes it makes you let go of everything and leave town. Sometimes it makes you obsess over whatever still makes sense.

I stood in line at the mayor's "Introduction to Gospel" event with boxes of every sentimental thing I owned. Ashton and Bill stood behind me; they didn't own much, but we believed in the mayor. We believed in his ideals, in his direction, in ourselves, and no one could tell us otherwise.

"You've heard about this day." The mayor took his place behind the podium. "You've planned for this day. You've weighed the pros and cons, and if you're standing with me here, you've seen the merits." He glanced at the hundreds of wealthy people he'd brought into his reality.

"There comes a time when the human race butts heads with change. Before each world war, we debated with change, trying to find a way to keep things the way they were. Before the industrial revolution. Before the introduction of medical technologies. People said the machines would suck out our souls. They said we'd get sick from the various emissions. They said we'd never perfect them. We have.

"The human system was designed to adapt to change, to make the best of it, stiffen its upper lip and move on, and I'm not here to introduce a new change. I'm here to give you the opportunity to be part of a revolution, a revolution against loneliness, emptiness, isolation. A revolution against poverty. A revolution against laziness. A revolution against tradition, against religion, against societal expectation. A revolution inspired by YOU, the individual, and your inevitable success."

The people murmured in excitement, the way millionaires often do, against a backdrop of thousands in front of the city dump, toting clothing, books, photo albums, and anything they could carry, those the mayor knew hadn't the funds to make Gospel real. The mayor promised furnished housing to join his future. The first step to joining his future: destroy the past.

Interesting that he held that press conference at the dump, because within a week of all of us living there, we found our cleansing in dumping all our items from our past in that dump. It became a place where we could part ways in peace and enter his future free from guilt.

My mother's voice echoed in my memory, "You've lost yourself, Doug, if you think he's leading you to a better future. You're completely lost."

It was probably for the best that she'd passed, although my heart ached. The doctors had changed her medications on a weekly basis. Everything made her sick. Between those and her chemotherapy, she hardly had the strength to stand. She spent most days hurling into the toilet. She sat through treatments, one pain always stronger than the last, drugs that made her better, made her worse, made her better, made her worse, made her worse, made her worse until there was no more worse to be had.

She would have given me a guilt trip with, "How can you throw your life into the dump? Don't these things mean anything to you?" She would have flipped through old college photos, books, stuff around the house.

As I came to rest with my decision to dump my treasures I whispered to her presence, "It's not a big deal, Mom. It's just junk. I'll always get more of it." Torn jeans, baseball cleats, pictures of my dad, trophies, birthday cards. I wasn't throwing them away. I was trading them for a better life. For my future. She would have been upset, demanded I keep everything to remind me of my nothing life. She wouldn't have known how important I'd become. I had become the architect of the mayor's vision. With his cosmetic company's special cream, and my ability to mold it into anyone's desired image, we were going to revolutionize beauty and the meaning of 'forever.' I, of all people in Gospel, needed to dispatch my past. The three of us, Ashton, Bill, and me, set the example by being the first tenants of Gospel, and those two were my first patients.

It was such a success that the dump began to fill to the brim with memories, and the mayor paid us graciously because we'd brought the people there. We advertised for months, and millionaires and people who'd saved everything came to fill our quota. Soon, we had all that Gospel could hold, and more and more construction went up around us. We had created the future, beautiful, seething, dreaming, infinite reality.

Chapter 21

"You can stop cringing. If you want to avoid drawing attention, you need to stop looking like an idiot." Annabelle's losing her charm.

"Is this what you see every day?" I point to the mannequins.

"More or less. Usually not it this number, but always in this death march."

"Why didn't you say anything?"

"Have you had any luck getting people to believe you?"

She's in between them, in front of them, behind them; they're gone, they aren't paying attention to us. I'm not strong enough to push or pull them from their positions. I'm in a river, things rushing past and I can't control any of it. Maybe they're strong, maybe I'm weak, or maybe it's both.

"Hello?" I say to one of the bodies. She doesn't answer, and I didn't expect her to. It's one of those things you need to see for yourself.

"Sobers you right up, doesn't it?" Annabelle stands next to me while the lines march past us. "Brace yourself. It gets worse." She glances toward the department store, big mechanical doors swallowing them alive, screens screaming. "We're here."

"How long have they been marching here?"

"Since you convinced them that lookin' good was better than being human."

The automatic doors open and close between the gaps in the lines, and we slip inside undetected. It's weird to think of it that way now. A year ago, I would have walked into the store like everyone one else, looking for the latest products, ready to sell a kidney to look younger than I did the day before. I wouldn't have noticed anyone around me; I haven't noticed anyone around me in decades. They've been marching, and I was marching too.

The store's the same inside. I expected to see a factory, pumping mannequins in and out on conveyor belts, but it's the same marble floors, elegant light fixtures and counter tops. The same products. The same services and the plastic people file here and there like nothing's changed.

"They all end up here." Annabelle points to the cosmetics counter. Some people pay for full make-overs, some people buy products for home use, and everyone receives trial samples whether they want them or not. Of course, they do.

The mannequins behind the counters apply sample products to mannequins in the lines, targeting what little bits of human remain.

"This is as much as I've seen." She sits with elbows on the counter. The plastic workers cover the people in powders and creams. The little bits of skin or fabric, a belt buckle, a freckle, natural hair color, elbows, knees, eyelids disappear and the products seals them in a plastic shell. "They suit up and take off toward that stairwell."

"What's down there?"

"Couldn't say. I've never been willin' to find out."

"I'll go alone."

"I kinda like you, Doug. Now that you have your head out of your ass." She stands up straight. "Don't go doing something stupid. Your momma would curse me in her grave if I let you kill yourself now."

"We're not going to be able to fix this if we don't know what THIS is."

"You really think you can fix this?"

"I started it. I better be able to stop it. I'm remembering more every second."

"I'm glad to hear you say that, boy, 'cause I'm getting' too old waiting for you to figure this shit out." She smiles, the same smile my mother gave me when I made her proud, and although she cusses like a sailor, she reminds me of my mom.

The mannequins who've finished their bath in products march toward the stairwell, and we march with them. I hang behind a little so Annabelle doesn't notice how much I resemble the mannequins. Another surgery and I'd be gone. Who'd save me?

"You don't need to hide from me," she says. "I've seen the real you from the start."

"I'm not hiding, I guess." I walk next to the single-file lines of has-beens and let them lead the way to a destination I'm terrified to find. In my head, we carry on all the conversations we've missed over the years. *How's your family? What are your children's names? What are your hopes and dreams?* I make up the answers as I go. "I just don't know if I'm the right person to do this."

She pulls me aside. "I'm not gonna sugar coat this, because I'm thinking you've had enough of that in your life. This is gonna be the hardest thing you've ever done. Once you accept that, you can move forward. Fear and doubt ain't worth a damn." She nudges me back into the lines.

The stairwell grows closer. The front of the line's already reached the first steps, and one by one they drop off the edge of the world, marching down the stairs toward oblivion or worse.

I'm next.

"There's light." I lean forward to look down the stairs. "Lots of light."

"That doesn't sound too bad." Annabelle closes in behind me, and we both stop talking while the stairs shimmer in flickering red light.

"It's fire." I grab the railing for balance.

"I'm guessing it has nothing to do with great balls."

Chapter 22

"It's as we thought." Jon stood in the corner of the room with my mother's chart.

"It spread to her brain?" Part of me asked for clarification and the rest of me asked to help wrap my head around the implications.

"I'm afraid so."

"What do we do now? Can I see her test results?"

"I don't think it would do you much good. We're in a scary situation."

"What do you mean?" I grabbed the chart from his hands. "Sorry, but this will help me visualize."

"The cancer's in her brain, entwined pretty thick in some places."

"You're saying you can't operate." I flipped through the papers without making eye contact. There was no way in hell I planned on listening further.

"I'm not saying that. I'm saying that it's complicated."

"Spit it out, Jon."

"The operation is very risky."

"But...."

"But it has been successful in a few cases. That being said, it has been unsuccessful in most cases."

"It could kill her?"

"Yes." He took his chart back and closed it.

"What are the other options?" My toes tapped on the floor, and I was in the same spot I was seventeen years before.

"There are no more options. She'll die without the surgery, and it's likely she'll die with it."

"That's it? What about experimental stuff?"

"There's nothing left, Doug. It's too advanced."

"You're just going to sit back, collect your check, and give up on her? You're a doctor, you piece of shit. You never give up on a patient."

He put a hand on my shoulder, the straw that broke the fucking camel's back, and I sobbed all over the floor.

"I'm sorry, Doug. Truly. I love her too."

"How much time does she have?" I couldn't care less about my suit at that point and wiped the tears and snot dripping from my face.

"Without surgery, a few days. Maybe a week. If she has the surgery, it's harder to say, but the end result will likely be the same."

I put my hand over his, the same helpless teenager while the mayor buzzed on and off in my jacket pocket. "What do I do, Jon?"

"I'd talk to her when she wakes up. I'll call you as soon as she does. From the sound of it, you have a lot of business to attend to." He pointed to the phone in my pocket. "No sense in waiting around here."

I couldn't move, not with her slipping away.

"I promise I'll call you as soon as she wakes." Jon patted me on the back one more time and went about his business at the hospital.

The mayor put me in charge of construction while he worked on his newest project, but it wasn't much responsibility. The workers knew the mayor accepted nothing but the best, and in an effort to save everyone's time, they made sure he got what he wanted.

I paid attention to my new abode and office. I wanted to make sure both were easily accessible for my mother because I wasn't going to sit back and let her die. She'd see the new unit and love it. She'd recognize my success and cheer me on. She'd be happy, even if she didn't admit it at the time.

"Do you guys mind if I check out the operating room?" I walked through the new office, screens chatting already, workers adding finishing touches, floors shined enough to see my reflection, state-of-the-art equipment and computers, phones ringing off the hook as soon as they were plugged in, the smell of money in the air.

The operating room doors swung behind me, glimmering tools stacked on the counters, and the surgical table bathed under the light of a 200 watt sun, the paradise where I'd make people perfect, where I'd make my mother perfect.

"You look pleased." The mayor stepped through the doors behind me.

"Very. Thank you."

"I have something I want to show you. Follow me." He walked me to his new command center, the largest building in the city.

"Is this your new project?" I leaned over his shoulder while he opened files on the computer.

"Once the programmers finish the final codes, we'll be set for business." He clicked a button to rotate a blank face on the screen.

"What is it?"

"A mold. We'll make one for men and one for women. We'll find the best of the best, the specimen closest to perfection in each of the sexes, and have both model for the system.

"I don't understand."

"I thought you'd have caught onto this whole ordeal by now. We're building perfection, right? Making it possible for people to exceed their highest expectation.

We're taking the mousy wallflower and giving her the life of a supermodel with surgery and technology."

"And this mold helps them get there?"

"This mold keeps them there. You can't expect these people to know what perfection is, so we need to keep them on their toes. This mold is their North Star."

"How does it work?" I leaned closer to watch the tutorial.

"Simply put, they match their features with that of the mold. Any time something is off, even a single hair out of place, the mold will flash red, letting the user know they're slipping. If they're new to Gospel, it will give them a goal." He stood in front of the camera and the computer scanned his face. The mold flashed green.

"Green means you're perfect?" My heart sped enough that I had to step back to keep the mayor from hearing.

"Give it a try." He stood from the chair and let me sit down.

The computer looked me over, judging me, labeling my future. It took less than a second for the screen to flash red.

"Tie's crooked." The mayor adjusted it until it matched the outline on the monitor and ran the scan again.

Still red.

"You'll get there, kid. I'll finish modeling for the program later this week. Once we've found a female specimen, it will be ready for mass production."

"It seems so simple."

"That's because you're a natural, Doug. I knew it from the start, but I needed you to know it too. Now that we're on the same page, there's one last thing I'd like to see you change."

"What's that?"

"Your name." He closed the program and leaned against the desk.

"What's wrong with my name?"

"It does nothing for your image. Doug, Douglas, Dougy. They all convey a small town boy with two left feet."

"I never thought of it that way."

"You're new from the bottom up, Doug. You've made sure of that. You're not the dopey kid from the trailer park now, and your image needs to represent the new man you are today."

"What do you suggest?" I leaned closer to him, drooling over his words.

"Jax Mason, the future of mankind."

Sweat in my palm, sweat on my forehead, sweat on my lips at the taste of the words on my tongue. "Jax Mason."

"Jax Mason."

"Jax Mason."

"Jax Mason."

"The future of mankind."

Chapter 23

"You go ahead," I tell the mannequins marching past me.

"Surprised to see you still have a sense of humor after all of this." Annabelle sits with me at the top of the stairs.

"Where do you think they are headed?"

"I don't' know but just so you know, nobody comes out from what we have observed."

"I'm scared. Not afraid to admit it."

"Who wouldn't be?" She puts her arm around my shoulders.

"I'm not afraid of dying. I'm scared to know how deep this goes."

"Does it matter?"

"Yeah, it does matter. I need to know if the there is any good to any of this."

She turns to the men and women marching into the red light. "Doesn't that look good to you?"

"I suppose not." I turn and an indigestible question nags at me. "The real question is do I really want to save them? Will everything wind up back where it was? You know people. We always say we're going to change, and we do, I admit, but it doesn't last."

"You think you're just fightin' for these people?"
She closes her eyes. "Honey, you're fightin' for the future.
You're fightin' for kids like Xavier, givin' them a place to go
to school, givin' them opportunities, teachin' them what
matters in the world. More than we can on that mountain.
You got a lot of people countin' on you, boy."

"So, the architect of this place is your savior now?"

"Trust me, you aren't the architect, you were the
pawn."

"And what if I fail?"

"Let's cross that bridge when we come to it, eh?"

She takes my hand, her vein riddled old-lady hand
clutches mine with fierce determination, and pulls me until
we align with the marching lines, and we move down the
steps with the crowd, dropping six inches at a time to our
demise. Red on my face, on my chest, like a disco dance
hall, bodies in my face, nameless, ageless, androgynous,
ignorant bricks of plastic.

I don't notice the heat until Annabelle wipes her
brow, a big streak of dirt across her skin, probably seconds
away from telling me she's done with this bullshit and
wants a divorce. She gives me a little grin once she notices
me watching, pretending to be in love.

My sweat mixes with the dried blood on my skin,
and it's a mess, a zombie from the deep. No wonder

everyone's running away from me. Annabelle stays close behind me, at least she's not scared, and we touch down on the basement level of the department store.

The light's bright, but not direct, and when I follow around the bend, the hall drops off into barrier of fire.

"Holy shit, these people are going to just walk into that?"

"It appears so."

"Why?"

"They are spent, I guess."

"So why not just lie down and die?"

She shrugs.

"You wait here," I say to Annabelle.

"Like hell." She grabs my arm with fingernails.

"I'm just going to look and come right back. You don't need to kill yourself tagging along." She pulls back because she's hurt, the sidekick who didn't know she was a sidekick, and even though that's not what I meant when I said it, if it keeps her safe, I'll run with it. "I kinda like you now, too, since you stopped being the ominous bitch outside my office."

She smiles and I let go. The hall's hotter than my skin can handle, and I pull designers tops off the wall to shove in my face, blocking the debilitating smell in the air.

The bodies march over the threshold and fall into what I assume to be a vat of fire. There's no hesitation, like they're buying a burger and fries from Joe Nobody's Burger Hut. No one stops them. Hell, no one even notices when they slip away, and the fire glows every time another sucker falls to the bottom.

I lean closer, hoping to catch a glimpse of their end. Hair singes on my arms, and Annabelle coughs in the hall behind me, gagging on the poison, weakening in the bombardment of screens.

"Here." I run to her side and tie a shirt over her nose and mouth. "Let's get out of here."

I hold her hands and try to help her up the stairs, but she can't breathe. The more I pull, the heavier she becomes, and the weight's enough to pull us both to the bottom.

"Over there." I point to a door at the other end of the hall, hoping things will be better on the other side. Annabelle falls limp in my arms. Maybe she's dead. I pull her through the mannequin lines, "Move, you worthless fucks."

The door's locked. Of course it is. I rest Annabelle against the wall while I cover the door in desperate, blood-red smudges from my shoulder, thinking I can muscle my way through the lock. I can't. I couldn't lift a feather if I had to, and I can't figure out why I've felt so weak.

There's another door at the end of the hall, and I throw Annabelle over my shoulders. She's stopped breathing. The smell of burning plastic's not so bad on this side, and the door's unlocked. It's nice to catch a break, even if we die in the end.

I lay Annabelle against the wall again while I look for a light in the room. I'm fumbling in the darkness like an idiot bat, that seems to be my M.O. these last few days, and while I bump into mops and buckets, I feel better knowing we're in a janitorial closet and not a trash compactor.

I can't find the light, but when I shut the door, there's enough seeping under the door to know what I'm doing. I pull the shirts off Annabelle's face. "Hey, old girl. Wake up." I tap her cheeks and shake her arms.

They taught us CPR when I was a cub scout, and to be honest, it was a waste of time. No eight-year-old boy was going to sit still long enough to learn how to do it right. It didn't really sink in until I started medical school. I could give CPR in my sleep.

I lay Annabelle on the floor and push out a pattern on her chest. She wakes up faster than I expected with a hungover look. I wish I had a camera. I help her sit up while she acclimates to the darkness.

"Where are we?"

"Storage closet. Nothing to worry about."

"Why are there no screens?"

I hadn't noticed, but she's right. It's quiet, and I think I'd like to live here forever. "We can't stay here long. Do you think you can stand?"

"You're one hell of an idealist, Doug." She complains while she swings her arms over my shoulders and holds on tight. My legs tremble, still weak from who knows what, and I gather her into my arms before rushing to my feet. While I switch her this way and that, I see shadows coming from two directions.

The light coming from the main door shines across the floor, and now that my eyes can see, there's a small line of light on the other side of the room, shadows moving on the other side. "I think there's another way out."

We scoot across the floor to be closer to the light, little helpless bugs ready to ZAP for one last thrill. "It's another door," I bend low to look through the gap over the threshold.

"What do you see?" Annabelle focuses on her breathing between conversations.

"It's hard to tell. Looks like they're processing and packaging. New products most likely."

"Packaging what?"

"Appears to be cream."

"Screens?"

She brings it up again, and I feel stupid. Maybe it's because I've been around them so long. Maybe it's because she hasn't. "None that I see." Either way, there's a reason.

"We can't go out that way, Doug."

Yeah, no screens is odd. Are they us? Are they creating us? They'd probably not let us walk right on through. We're trapped rats.

"That's probably worse than the furnaces."

"Oh, no." I leave the door and sit against the wall with Annabelle.

"Do I want to ask what you saw?"

"The cream is coming from conveyer belts that start at the far wall."

"I'm not following."

"The furnace is on the other side of that wall."

"Shit. You think they're melting them down?"

"Repurposing them. And from the looks of it, using them to make the new product lines."

"We can't go out that way."

We're sitting ducks. I don't know what to tell her, and I'm sure she feels the same, but it doesn't matter because a voice over the store's loud speaker drowns the silence.

LOOKS LIKE LITTLE DOUGY MASON DOESN'T KNOW WHEN TO QUIT.

I forgot about Wild Bill, which was ridiculous because I knew he'd never forget about me.

Chapter 24

The highs and lows never balanced. I never reached the state of contentment all the inspirational speakers talked about. I had good days, days filled with Gospel, advances in cosmetology, in nutrition, in plastics, and I struggled to focus on anything else. The rest of the days turned to shit because my mother's surgery date arrived, and I had to make the hardest decision of my life.

"There's a chance." I sat at my mother's bedside and held her hands between my own, silent goodbyes because we both knew I was lying.

"Doctors always say that because they want you to die happy." She rubbed my fingers, too frail to do much else.

"Are you happy?" I opened the door I spent years shutting. I wanted her to speak her mind before she lost the chance forever.

"I'm happy for many reasons."

"Like what?"

"I'm happy you're my son. You're everything I could have ever wanted in a boy."

"But you hate what I'm part of."

"Someday you'll understand true beauty. It's not something you can manufacture. It's not something you can create or manipulate. It's buried deep down inside and if we cultivate it, it grows. I don't care for your current mindset, no, but I understand. You're distracted by the glamour and the money. None of that lessens my love for you and the happiness you bring me."

"I wish you were proud of me."

"I've never been more proud."

"How can you say that?" I stood from the bed and paced. "You hate the way I look. You hate what I do for a living. What's left? You might as well say, 'Fuck you, Dougy.' And be done with it."

"Is that all you think you are?"

"I know that's all I am! Take that away, and I'm nothing."

"My sweet Douglas." She held her arms out, inviting me to sit beside her again. "This is who you are." She put a hand over my chest. "This is what you are. This is what makes you Doug Mason. And I love Doug Mason with all my heart."

She rubbed her fingers over my face, temples, and forehead, making one last memory.

"You have to fight. I don't care if it hurts. I don't care if you're tired. You have to fight this. You have to be stronger than this." I cried on her fingers, and she wiped the tears down my skin. "Please, don't leave me alone."

"You won't get rid of me that easy. I'm a mother. Even when I'm dead, I'll still have one eye on you."

I smiled a little; I knew she'd see to it. "You're going to love the new house in the city. I promise you, Mom. You'll wake up from this surgery, and everything will finally be the way it's supposed to. I'll make you beautiful. I'll help you live again, and it will still be us against the world."

"I look forward to it."

Four nurses bumped through the door with more machines and carts. "Okay, Mrs. Mason. Let's get you prepped for surgery." They folded the arms of her bed, added new concoctions to her IV, and wheeled her away.

I wandered the halls, too nervous to sit, too determined to prove I wasn't that trailer trash kid anymore, tapping my toes in the waiting room. Those hours blurred in my head. The hallways looked the same. The people looked the same, and everyone who spoke, talked in an indecipherable tongue.

"Sir?" A woman waved her hands in front of my face. "Sir, you have to keep the line moving. Corn or peas?"

I looked at the tray in my hand and the people lined behind me. "Where am I?"

"Hospital cafeteria." She ladled corn onto my tray. "I think you should sit down. You don't look so good."

She untied her apron and walked around the counter. "Here, let me take the tray. There's a seat over here." She set me up at a table by the exit, probably thinking I needed to puke or run or both.

"Thank you." I wiped the sweat on my hands with a napkin.

"Surgery, huh?"

"Pardon?"

"Someone you know is in surgery. I see the face all the time. The waiting face."

"My mother." I pushed the tray away. I couldn't bare the sight of food.

"I'm sorry." She moved the tray further away and spilled the drink onto the floor. She scrambled to sop it up with the few napkins we had, and there was something endearing in the way she moved, clumsy, awkward. "My name is Gracie."

"Doug."

When she met me with silence, I thought she hated the name, until I looked across the table to see her fidgeting with her fingers. I'd know a nervous tick better than anyone.

"You okay?" I tapped on the table to get her attention.

"Me? Yes, I'm fine."

"You don't look it." The tables turned and I was the one comforting her.

"I don't do this often."

"Sit?"

"Speak to men. Or people really."

"You work in a cafeteria. How do you not speak to people?"

"You'd be surprised what you can do with hand gestures."

I studied her mousy brown hair, nails chewed to the skin, chubby arms and neck, and my mind reeled with possibilities. I could make her beautiful.

"So, what do you do, Doug? That's quite the suit." She still fiddled with her fingers until I looked over the table. "I'm so sorry. That was rude. You don't need to tell me."

"Don't apologize. I'm a surgeon."

"Surgeons around here don't look like you. You must be part of the new city."

"Why do you say that? You've never seen someone like me?"

"You're suit is worth more than my house." She smiled, crooked teeth but pleasant. I could do so much for her.

"Have you been to the city?"

"Do I look like I belong there?" She waved her arms over her clothes covered in food stains.

"You could change that."

"How? Sell my kidneys? Only the richies can survive there, and besides, people would faint if an ugly duckling like me waltzed in."

For the first time since I met the mayor, I could help someone for the right reasons. No sex, no money, no obligations. I could give her a life she only dreamed of. I could take away all of that insecurity and doubt. I could change the way she saw the world.

"Why don't you let me show you around sometime? You might like it."

"You're serious? Why would you do that for me?"

I looked at the tray of food. "I want to return the favor."

Chapter 25

YOU KNOW WHAT I THINK'S FUNNY, DOUG.

The room's smaller now. There's one too many people.

I FIND IT FUNNY THAT YOU STILL THINK YOU RUN THIS CITY.

"We need to find a way out of here," I take Annabelle by the arm.

"Who is this joker?"

"He's very real, Annabelle. He won't hesitate to kill me because I know what's going on. I was lucky to get away once."

"Then we better be on our way." She wipes her face and stands next to me.

YOU THINK THE PEOPLE HERE REPORT TO YOU. THAT YOU CAN TRUST THEM.

"Do you trust me, Annabelle?" I put my hand over the door knob leading to the factory room.

She hesitates a little; we've known each other for less than 24 hours, and now I'm asking her to put her life in my hands. "Yes," she says, and it must be an answer for my mother because I know she's scared to death.

We push through the door, conveyer belts chugging all around us, carrying ashes from the furnace, and thanks to the robotic ideology this city feeds on, the workers do their job and keep working.

LOOK AT YOU, DOUG. COVERED IN BLOOD. NAKED, AND NOT IN A FUN WAY.

It's bad enough to know he's here, but now he can see me walking aimlessly through this never-ending room with no windows or doors like a zoo attraction.

"You have a plan here, Doug?" Annabelle's winded, following me the best she can.

"We need to find a way out. He'll kill us both."

"We've gone through this whole room and there's no way out other than those conveyer belts. You're not dumb enough to go climbing onto one of them."

The look on my face is enough to tell her I'm thinking otherwise.

"It'll kill you."

"We're in this, Annabelle! We have two options. We dive onto that conveyer belt hoping we survive, or wait here and let Bill kill us both. I'm leaving, whether you come or not, because no one out there is going to save Grace."

She's quiet, weighing options with time we don't have. "Okay."

She steps closer to me while I watch the belt closest to us, just above my head. "It's moving fast."

"Yeah, but look around. It's probably the slowest one in this place."

The weakness in my legs worries me. What happens if I grab onto this belt and find it's in my arms, too? All those years in the gym mean nothing now.

I jump to touch the nearest pipe speeding past. "Really fast. We have to do this together; otherwise I'll be on the other side of the room before I can pull you up."

"We have to jump together? Honey, I haven't jumped since I was a little girl, and I don't intend on starting now."

"I can't exactly fly, Annabelle."

"You got all those muscles, and you're telling me you can't carry us both?"

I don't want to discuss it now, especially when I'm trying to pump myself up before we plunge to our deaths. "I haven't said anything, but I'm not feeling as strong as I used to."

"Meaning?"

"There's a weakness in me I can't explain. Not exhaustion; I've worked through that before. Not hunger. A weakness that doesn't go away." I rub my legs a little, like it's helping.

Someone flips the switch in the storage room next to us, Wild Bill and his vanity junkies on a mission to add me to the furnace inventory.

"Yes or no?" I extend my hand toward Annabelle, one last chance before I jump.

"If you drop me, whether your mother's memory's in the picture or not, I'll kill you."

That's my girl. She wraps her arms around my chest. "Wrap one of your legs too."

It's awkward, but she wraps around me anyway. Her grip's pretty strong for an old gal, and I take a deep breath before I jump and hope my hand touches a metal pipe and not the chain pulling the conveyer belt.

We barely leave the ground.

"Shit." I check the room one more time for something we could stand on.

"They're here." Annabelle taps my chest, and the storage room doors open and fill with a hundred soldiers carrying guns, tasers, and dogs. I call them soldiers because that's what they've always been to me. I'm seeing them for what they really are—robots.

"Get close and hold on as tight as you can." I give myself a running start, hoping it will help, and Annabelle presses against my chest, dried blood and sweat smudging her cheeks like a porcelain doll wearing blush.

We leave the ground, surreal in all of this chaos, when Bill steps through the robots and pulls his gun, the barrel pointed right at my head.

The fingers on my right hand touch the pipe enough to wrap around, and we speed through the air with the remains of our neighbors.

"I can't hold both of us much longer. Climb up and grab the pipe"

"Okay." Annabelle squirms over my body and grabs hold of the pipe. She's a tough broad, thank goodness.

The sound of Bill's gun takes over the silence. One shot. Two shots. Three shots. Lonely shots because he's too power hungry to ask for help from his squadron. They're his scare tactic and that's it. He wants to take me down alone.

He tries again, but we're moving too fast, and the gun drops to his side. Annabelle exhales in my ear, and for a moment, it's peaceful, hovering over the rest of the room, lured into a false sense of security before we notice the pitch-black tunnel.

Black everywhere through patches of hot and cold air, and it's hard to tell how fast we're moving, light fading behind us, Billy nothing more than a focal point on some bizarre work of art.

"I'm glad to finally know the real you," Annabelle says into the black.

"We'll be fine."

Machinery clicks when we pass a certain point, the bar we hold onto is a picker and it opens as though it should be dropping something. A person, mannequin, whatever you call them, sounds as though it plunges into a bath below us, then the one behind us does the same thing. It triggers mist in the air, a thick chemical bath.

"It burns." Annabelle squirms in my arms.

"Try to hold your breath." I don't want her passing out again. I can't hold her if she's dead weight.

The mist stops, and the fans start, sealing chemicals to our skin. Light grows in the far end of the tunnel, and despite all the clichés, I'd prefer to move away from the light. I'll take chemicals over light any day.

The light takes over, and we're in another factory room, mannequins counting, shipping, packaging, dividing the ashes onto different conveyer belts. Our picker belt is headed toward a smaller entrance than we will fit. "We need to switch belts or get off this one, I think this one is going back the way we came, and is used to pick up people for termination."

She stammers. "Um, I think off is better than not knowing where our next stop is."

"I think the worst is behind us, Annabelle, I think those belts go to some sort of delivery room."

"And you think that's a good thing?"

"If Bill is back there trying to confirm we are dead, yeah, maybe it is."

Before I can stop her, she reaches out and grabs the bar of another conveyer and is whisked away to my right. I do the same, but my belt takes me left, headed toward a separate tunnel.

"Sing!" I try to watch which direction each tunnel goes.

"What?"

"Just keep singing. Maybe we can keep track of each other."

She rubs her neck and starts a song. "Hush, little baby. Don't say a word. Mommy's gonna buy you a mocking bird."

"Louder!"

"And if that mocking bird don't sing, Mommy's gonna buy you diamond ring."

"And if that diamond ring turns brass, Papa's gonna buy you a looking glass." I sing with her, shouting as loud as I can. The tunnel turns black, and her voice muffles through the walls. Machinery moves around me, and I wonder if I'm hearing her voice or imagining it in my head.

I keep singing. "If that looking glass gets broke, Papa's gonna buy you a billy goat."

When the tunnel ends, I'm in a third factory room filled with vats of product, and I can't hear Annabelle's song. She speeds down from the highest tunnel, gagging on the chemical fumes swirling about this place. We wiz around, sometimes far, sometimes close, but I can't grab hold of her.

I can't jump to the floor. It won't do her any good if I'm dead, but maybe I can jump onto her conveyer belt. Who knew Parkour would come in handy after all these years? I hope I'm strong enough to hold on when I get there.

I don't have time to debate whether I'll make it or not. We're together, and that may not happen again. I jump to the belt below me, only a small drop, but it's not the right belt.

"Annabelle!" I tried to get her attention without falling off the belt. She's still gagging on chemical fumes. "Annabelle, stay awake. Move toward my voice."

She moves a little down the belt, but stops before she's made any real progress. I jump to another belt, and follow it with my eyes, and it leads to Annabelle. I run over the powder to be by her side.

"I'm here. I'm here. Can you talk?"

No response.

I've always had a problem with tunnel vision, and it's here again. I cradle her face in my hands, trying to open her eyes and make her coherent, when the belt disappears and we fall into a vat of black.

I'LL ADMIT IT, DOUG. I WANTED TO BE THE ONE WHO PUT THE BULLET IN YOUR HEAD, BUT I'VE HAD A CHANGE OF HEART.

I don't know if he's eulogizing my death, or if he knows I'm still alive.

Annabelle sinks in the black sludge. Treading water and treading sludge are two different things, and the more I kick and paddle toward her, the more I slip underneath the surface.

I THINK IT WOULD BE MORE REWARDING TO WATCH YOU KILL YOURSELF.

I'm not ready to die. Who's going to save Grace? Who's going to save Annabelle? Who's going to save ME? My arms and legs turn to putty, blending with the mixture, and I don't know where they stop and the black vortex starts. Annabelle's unconscious, dragging me down, and it's hard to ignore that we're dying.

DON'T STRESS SO MUCH, DOUG. I'VE MADE ARRANGEMENTS. EVERY ASPECT OF YOUR LIFE

WILL BE TAKEN CARE OF AFTER YOU'RE GONE. I ASSIGNED MY BEST MEN TO MAKE SURE OF THAT.

The junk's up to my neck, like it wasn't hard enough to breathe before.

OH, AND DON'T WORRY ABOUT YOUR GIRL. I'LL TAKE CARE OF HER PERSONALLY.

"You bastard! I'll kill you. I swear, I'll kill you." My body's on fire and it must be the same experience mother's feel when their children are in danger. "You think some little pile of shit is going to stop me? You're wrong about everything, Bill! I'm hunting YOU!" I'm careful to not speak loud enough to churn above the noise of conveyors. I'm better off if he doesn't know if I'm dead or alive.

I'll find you one way or another, and your puppets won't stop me.

His voice booms over the intercom: THAT'S THE BEAUTY OF IT. ALTOUGH I DIDN'T REALIZE ITS BEAUTY WHEN I FOUND OUT.

Fuck you and your riddles.

Annabelle's head slips into the black.

As though he needed to purge his soul, or show his power, he gives a soliloquy that draws my attention more than all of Annabelle's history lessons. YOU SEE, THE MAYOR HAD A PLAN, AND EVERYONE IN HIS PLAN

PLAYED A PART. UNFORTUNATELY, EVERYONE ELSE IN HIS PLAN WAS EXPENDABLE. FINITE.

Adrenalin slaps me awake, and I pull her through the sludge until her face touches the air again. I tread hard and strong, and it's enough to move us little by little toward the edge of the vat. I grab the side and pull us close, thinking we can lean over the side and fall out.

There's nothing to grab. I lift Annabelle out of the sludge, but I have no leverage to toss her over the side, and we slide down the wall together.

The intercom sounds again, and I ignore it to lift Annabelle over my head and throw her over the side. The black junk is thick and sticky enough to slow her fall, and I jump out after her. The intercom stops, and I carry Annabelle out the nearest door and into the woods where little Billy has been too afraid to follow. As we approach, the boy points behind.

Under the shine of TV screens, I see Billy with a look of horror on his face.

Yeah, I made it. I salute him and walk farther into the woods.

He stands at the edge of the woods with his posse. "You're going to die, Doug. I made sure of it, and according to your programming, it shouldn't take too long."

"I already know about the screens, Bill, but of course I'm sure you figured out that I already knew?" I set Annabelle down.

He chuckled, and it had one-uppance dripping from each echo. "The mold."

"It's just there for guidance. It has no control over us."

"That's what the mayor wanted you to think. He wanted you to believe in this vanity game to fill his pocket, but we're nothing but lab rats, buying his products, building his masses. The screens keep you from reminiscing, but the cream, Dougy, the cream is intoxicating, alluring, addicting."

"The mayor wouldn't have wanted this, Bill."

"What? Of course he did. He didn't get a conscience until he fell prey to the same thing you did—your memories."

"What happened to the Mayor?" I shouted.

"He outlived his usefulness."

"What did you do to him?"

"What I'd like to do with you."

"And that solved everything?"

"Well, it solved my predicament. He had us all programmed to buy any and every product, pay for every surgery, the clothes, the cars, the accessories until we reached the perfect green screen, but once we reach that screen, we're no longer financially viable. At that point, we're programmed to check out and recycle ourselves. Then new people start the process all over. Everyone except the mayor, of course. He made himself exempt. He planned on living off of us for all of his life, and that didn't sit well with me."

"Killing him doesn't seem to have made much difference." I pointed to the black sludge all over me.

"I have all of the access codes. It's proven very helpful. My men and I are free and clear, and now your money, and the money of all the other suckers, pours into our pockets. And the beautiful part is that whenever an annoying little bug like you hovers around, we just have to wait it out, and the system will take care of it. We may be an army, but we spend most of our time eating Chinese food and watching people burn."

Chapter 26

My teachers used to tell me patience was a virtue. I never understood what they meant. Patience changed the strong into sitting ducks, stuck in the ditch while life ebbed away. It took away opportunity, ambition, and the future.

"If you don't mind me asking, who are you waiting for?" Gracie sat across from me in the oncology waiting room.

My teachers failed to mention no one wants to be patient alone. She made small talk with a stranger, and I sifted through a hundred thoughts between each word, memories of my childhood, my mother, Gospel, the mayor, the way Gracie looked in the fluorescent light, the simple way she folded her hands over her knees, endearing me to her every move. "My mother."

I spent a lifetime proving I was tough, that I could run with the big boys and carry my own weight, but it's hard to stay tethered when the last leg of my dock grew weaker under the scalpel.

"My brother had cancer a few years back." For the first time, she looked me in the eye. "He pulled through it."

The doctor stepped out of the side doors and whispered something to the nurses behind the desk. He saw me at the end of the hall and rubbed the back of his head to comfort himself. In my mind, I stopped time. I stopped it a thousand fucking times, but he walked toward me anyway.

"We did everything we could, Doug."

"You bastard." I clocked him across the jaw and sent him to the floor. Grace pulled me away, probably afraid I'd kill him, and I couldn't blame her. I was afraid too. "I'm a doctor, too. Don't feed me that bullshit line. I want you to say it."

He picked himself off the floor. "We couldn't save her."

"Say it, Jon."

"She's gone, Doug."

"Say it!" I panted like a dog, and Grace rubbed my back in comfort.

"She's dead. Your mother is dead."

All the patience in the world couldn't change that moment. Time couldn't change it. Jon couldn't change it. Grace couldn't, and neither could I. The universe didn't give a shit.

I wept.

Long, hard, slow, silent, and I wept. No memory could dull the pain. No laughter. No smile. I let go of everything and sobbed into Jon's shoulder, holding his arms around me because I couldn't admit she'd left me completely alone.

"I'm so sorry, Doug." Jon held me close until I was ready to let go. It may have been hours or minutes. I only remember the inside of my car during the drive home. Grace sang me a song, something sweet like a lullaby, and I died on the seat next to her.

"Do you want me to help you inside?" Grace held my hand and pointed to my penthouse in the city.

"No, thank you. I'm sorry you had to see all of this."

"Don't be." She gathered her things and opened the car door. "Can you point me to the highway? I've never been this far north."

"You're not walking home."

"It shouldn't be far to the bus station."

"You're not riding a bus home. My car will take you. Just tell it your address."

"I couldn't do that."

"I'm not asking. It'll drop you off and find its way back here."

"Thank you." Her skin shimmered in the reflection of the screen, like snow under Christmas lights, peaceful and still against the shapeless sky.

"Just returning another favor." I kissed her hand and left the car.

Chapter 27

"Say something, Annabelle." I set her against a tree stump and wipe the black slime from her face. "I need you to say something if you can hear me." Her body slumps whenever I let it go. "I need you to wake up!" I shake her against the tree. She slumps. "Wake up!" I slap her face. "Damnit, Annabelle! Get your head out of your ass. You're losing sight. You think this is about you now, like you need some sort of special treatment. Get over it. Xavier needs you, you selfish bitch. You expect me to save him if you can't even spend the time of day!"

Her hands move.

"Annabelle, can you hear me? Move your hands again if you can."

Her head leans back against the tree. She pulls her hands to her thighs and mumbles under her breath.

I can't understand her through the sludge and claw it off her lips. "Say it again."

"Water."

There's a puddle a few feet away. I splash the water over her face to clear the sludge and help her lean over to drink from my hand. She sucks down five or six handfuls before she opens her eyes and looks at me. "Your mother owes me big time."

I smile. After everything, she still has spunk. "Come on. We can't stay here. Bill's stayed out of the woods so far, but I wouldn't write him off. His men might be under the spell of the screen, hell, he might still have some latent spell on him, but he'll find someone to come in here."

"We can clean up back at my place." She props a hand on the nearest tree to keep her balance.

"I'll help you get there, but I can't stay."

"You're not even gonna shower before you go running back out there?"

"I know Bill, more than taking Grace from me; he'd rather have her repurposed. I can't help but think she'll be on her way anytime, and I need to stop her."

"Fair enough, but what about Bill?"

"Let's forget about him."

"Forget? What the hell happened while I was out?"

"I don't have much time. I need to get to find Grace and get to the police station. It may have to be in that order."

"Bill is at the police station. He's the police chief. There's a flaw in your plan."

"The mayor programmed us all to strive for perfect looks. We're all on a timeline, and mine's almost up. I need to stop the program and save Gracie before I'm diving into the fire with her. That program is with Bill, and that means it's in his care."

"That's one hell of an idea for an old gal to understand. I feel like this might be the last time I see you."

"Glad to know you believe in me." I wink at her.

"You know I don't mean it that way, but things have a way of moving fast in times like this. A lot can happen on your way there. An awful lot."

We walk side by side through the woods, following the trails we walked before and reach the trail up to her village. "I promise I'll find you again."

She steps onto the trail. "If you don't, little Billy will be the least of your worries."

I walk with her long enough to hand her to the other people in the village. "Get some rest. I don't know what'll happen after this." I kiss her cheek and run.

I follow the tree line to Grace's house, the labored breathing and weakness commonplace, the rest of the world moving in slow motion because my mind races, sights and sounds muted by the rasp of lungs struggling to keep me moving.

When I met Annabelle and the others, I wasn't a monster, and until now, staring into the city streets while the sun rises behind me, I believed it. The people wake early, shopping, stretching, jogging, filling the streets until there's no safe path to Grace, and I'm another soulless sucker.

Without my baseball bat, I have no choice but to make a run for it and hope the other suckers are too high to notice me.

I step away from the trees, expecting a blow to my skull. Joggers pass and flash a smile toward me. Lawyers and businessmen clog the streets with their fancy cars. Models, actors, and musicians start their days, and I'm left untouched in the eye of the storm.

I try to act nonchalant, but I've forgotten that part of me. It's awkward walking up to Joe Schmoe to chew the fat knowing he tried to kill me the day before. I wave and notice the black sludge still on my skin.

I'm one of them again, covered in their products, covered in their remains, blending in like a chameleon. I approach Grace's house with one eye on the target and the other on patrol.

Screens line her house and look me over like everyone else.

Please be home.

Less of a prayer and more of a dying wish because I'm weaker by the minute. A mat welcomes me, and I knock on her front door.

I scared the shit out of her last time we were together. I'm trying to avoid that again, and maybe this sludge will help. No answer.

"It's Jax. Say one word, and I'll go. Let me know you're okay."

The screens ignore everything I have to say. I'd ask them to give her a message, but they'd snub me that. It's not what I wanted to do when I came here, but I hunch over and smash my shoulder into her door. Nothing happens, and I hit it again until I feel the wood crack inside. One more hit and I'm in.

Grace isn't.

No one's in the house, the nausea returns, and the familiar hiss of angry mobs presses against the back of my neck.

"You don't have to do this." I hold my hands up in surrender. There are too many of them to outrun, especially in my current physical condition. I will do anything to save Grace, and if they think I've given up, I might have a chance.

Maria Ronner and Gage Greenwood tie my hands behind my back. Little Ken Menzies dips his hand in red ink and uses his index finger to draw an X on by bare stomach. He's been one of my patients since he was born— cleft pallet, extra fingers and toes—you name it, he had it.

He's ten or so now, and he's beautiful. His plastic hands swirl in the paint while his plastic face watches in anticipation.

Kelly McLaughlin and Heather Huntsman gag and blindfold me. I smell their perfume as they move around me, perfect hygiene, perfect breasts and legs while they sentence me to death for abandoning their beliefs.

We've seen each other on the surface, and that's all it's ever been. I don't know their dreams, their hopes, if they have any. I don't know their loves and losses. I don't know their ambitions. I don't know them at all.

A black car pulls up, and they shove me inside. Screens all around, sucking out the heart I've discovered in my chest, erasing everything in my head. They hold me down, force me to consume their ideas, and wait for the parasites to take hold, and so do I, but while they talk around me, I feel the same.

I remember my mother, my father, my childhood home. I remember Annabelle and Grace. They think I'm another member of society who's snapped, but they don't know about the television in my closet. A crack in an otherwise perfect glass casket.

They chatter about products and procedures, not a single human thought amongst them, thinking I'm lost in some out-of-body experience under my blindfold, and maybe I am, because while they hold a knife close to my throat to keep me still, I fiddle with the door handle to find a way out.

"You gonna just jump out of a moving car?" I recognize the voice. It's Ashton.

"You told them where I was?"

"As soon as I shut the door."

That's how the screens work. When you're out of their reach, you bloom. When they can see you, you haven't got a shot at survival. "You won't keep me here."

"You know better than anyone we don't need to keep anyone here. Gospel is the future."

"We were wrong." I fight to keep his hands away from my throat as he pins my head against the seat to shut me up. "It's crumbling, Ashton. This whole life is a lie."

He pushes the knife deeper to my neck, and cool blood drips along my skin when I kick the back of his head. My tied hands pull the car door handle, and we both fall to the ground and skip on the road like stones.

I can't see much with the blindfold over my eyes, but I must have kicked hard enough to stun him. He'd be all over me. Or maybe he's dead. I pull my blindfold off, see blood dripping from my arms and legs and chest, and chew at the knots in the ropes on my hands, pieces of the fiber sticking in my lips and gums like thistles, but they won't loosen.

I untie my feet, and look for Ashton. He's gone. Mannequins bump me in passing, and I think how any one of them could be him, or worse, Grace.

Chapter 28

"Jen was a role model if I ever saw one." Judy, one of the nurses from the hospital and my mother's dearest friend spoke behind the podium at her funeral. "She worked hard, told the truth, and made you feel like a million bucks. She'd give her right arm to help you, and I don't think many people can claim to be as selfless as she was. She was absolutely unique, and I'll never forget how she touched my life. She was taken before her time, and I think I can speak for everyone here when I say she will be dearly missed."

Women dabbed their eyes with tissues and fresh eyeliner. Men shifted in their seats so no one would see them choking back tears, and I was a thousand miles away.

"And now Doug Mason would like to say a few words." The minister waved me to the microphone, like a wingman guiding a plane into its gate.

I adjusted my suit and tie before standing behind the podium. "My mother was one of a kind." I expected to fall apart at the service, break down in front of everyone, lose control, punch someone, but I struggled to feel any of those things. "I didn't know a lot of great parents growing up. Most of them found something better to do than raise their kids. My mother made sure I had everything I needed and most of what I wanted. She put me first, always, and I'm happy to see she touched so many lives other than my own."

I threw a single rose onto her casket. "She battled a monster for too long. Always silent suffering because she didn't want to burden us. Every day worse than the last, filled with pain, and now we can find relief knowing she's peaceful."

The people made their lines through the church, saying hello, saying goodbye, begging for a do-over. I recognized some of the faces, but most of them were strangers. They shared their stories of my mother and how she saved them when they were at their worst, patients in the hospital who needed a friendly ear to talk to, to give them hope.

Grace stood close to me when they lowered the casket into the dirt, a beam of support, but I didn't need support. I didn't need anything at that point. I should have left the suckers in the dust and started a new life.

"Things will get better. They always do." Grace rubbed my shoulder.

"I know." I'd make them better than they'd ever been. If that meant ditching everyone in the process, I'd do it.

"I know I've only known you a few days, but you seem distant. Disconnected."

"What do you think about plastic surgery?" I ogled her tiny breasts and love handles.

"It's fine, I guess. For people who are into that sort of thing."

"Are you one of those people?" I stroked her cheek, desperate to fill the mammoth hole in my life.

"I wasn't." She paused under my fingertips. "But that doesn't mean I can't be now."

"Would you let me make you beautiful? My first patient in the new city? We could change the world together. Set the standard. Make the whole world envious."

"I think I'd like that."

"Let's start tomorrow. We can make a plan and have you gorgeous by next year. Every other woman in this town will be begging to trade places with you."

"That doesn't sound too bad." She giggled like a schoolgirl, and I knew everything would be okay.

Chapter 29

"I leave you alone for less than an hour, and you go screwin' everything up." Annabelle's shadow hovers over me.

"What are you doing here?" I struggle to my feet, covered in dust from the road.

"Savin' your ass." She brushes off my broken motivation.

"Well, you don't have to. I think it's over."

"There's still time, kid."

"Is there really? She could be anywhere. You saw it out there. Thousands of them lined up; every one of them ready to sell their lives for a bottle of cream. Their time is running out, one by one, and I can't stop it."

"That's it, then, huh? We've come this far and just give up on your lady love. On all of them because it looks like it might be a little difficult." She cocks her head.

"You learned that from my mother."

"What's that?"

"That tone that makes me do whatever the hell you say."

"Oh, honey, every mother past, present, and future, has that tone. It's part of our survival guide. Otherwise, all you lazy kids would sit at home on your asses forever."

"You're a mother?"

She slides her foot along the ground, thinking up memories or futures, I don't know which. "That was a long time ago."

Memories. And they're not good.

"Alex would have made me a grandmother by now." She looks at the bracelet on her wrist, a dozen little charms dangling down below. "He wasn't as smart as you, Doug. He didn't have the same opportunities, but he had your determination. He'd go to the ends of the earth and back for something he loved. In many ways, you remind me of him."

"What happened?" Normally I'd regret asking something so personal, but we're beyond pleasantries now.

"He was born with a heart defect. There weren't many surgeons like you in our parts when he was a boy, and even if there were, they wouldn't have been able to save him. It's just one of those life tragedies we're dealt, and we'll never understand why." She looks out the door and down the street at the mannequins. "This is yours."

I understand why my mother chose Annabelle to look out for me. No one else would care the way she does. She's a perfect mix of tough love and wisdom, unlike anyone I'd met, unique. No one would push me as hard as she does. The sun rises behind her like a sign that victory might have a chance.

I gather myself, not just my thoughts, but my nerves, because I only know one outcome. I won't give up, and that's the best that I can do. "Let's get to the police station."

Annabelle half smiles, the kind that says she's proud of me for finally making a decision and she's scared to death to be a part of it.

"I don't know what to expect when we get there." I pant while we power step on the sidewalks. My endurance isn't what it used to be, and Annabelle tags behind me.

"Marching into the lion's den has always been a guessing game, I think."

"This isn't the time, I know, but I miss my prototype."

We march along with the mannequins, keeping a close watch for Grace while we approach the police station. Bill's probably waiting for us, and I'm not sure whether to walk through the front doors and fight to try to outsmart them.

"You wait here and be the lookout. I'm going to sneak around back." I point to a bush and help Annabelle hide behind it. "If anything happens, run."

"Easier said than done."

I crawl through the bushes on my stomach, reopening old wounds, and hope to get close enough to see something inside. If I know Bill, he has the place lined with traps, but it's a risk I need to take.

Screens cover the outside of the building, making it almost impossible to hear and distinguish any other sounds, and the closer I get, the more difficult it is to see through their advertisements to the rooms inside.

I glance back toward Annabelle, and she gives me the sign to move forward, and I sprint while I can toward the back side of the building. Every door is locked, and cameras follow me back and forth while I pace.

The cameras zero in on my face, and my hindsight does what it always does and tells me I've made another big mistake. I can't run until I know more about what's going on. The screens slow down a bit, and I have enough time to catch a glimpse of the computers inside the station.

Dozens of screens filled with names. Some names red, but mostly green. I assume they match the status on the molds, and my heart sinks when I recognize all of the people on the list. People I grew up with, people I operated on, people I lied to. The names scroll by the thousands until I see Grace's name flashing in bright green. I can't make out the time listed next to her, but it can't be long.

I run from the building and signal Annabelle to follow. I don't have time to break into the system and fight whoever might be inside. We need to find Grace, and we can't waste another second.

"What did you see?" Annabelle huffs behind me.

"Grace is about to burn."

We step onto the city streets, burying the fear of the mobs, and we hunt for Grace in the lines. Faces, faces, faces, man, woman, man, woman, faces, faces, faces, and not a single feature to go by. Some have bare patches of skin, others have fabric showing, but without the whole picture, it's like guessing a puzzle from a single piece.

We walk up and down the streets, sometimes the same street three and four and five times over because we're never sure if we've passed her up. The more we pass, the more they blend together.

"Grace!" I study the lines for miles hoping to see any head turn my way. "Grace!" I wait, and they march.

"What if I break the screens all over the city? That would get their attention, right?" I make my hands into fists, wondering when I dropped the bat.

"You don't have time for that." Annabelle huffs behind me, trying her best to keep with my frantic pace. "That poor girl is in this line somewhere. There's no telling how much time we have left."

"So, we just sit here and watch them march into hell?"

"We're missing something. Maybe it's something big, or maybe it's something small, but either way, we've been looking at this wrong."

"What do you mean?" I don't want to, but I stop searching to hear what she has to say.

"These people have lost their humanity. Maybe we need to stop trying to find a way to remind them who they are, and start reminding them who they were."

I'm confused, and she knows it.

"Before Gospel," she says, and I think of the broken screen, the box in my closet, my mother's patches, and if I hadn't found them, I may not remember anything about my past.

"Maybe all they need is a nudge in the right direction, and that humanity will filter on through afterward."

Grace has no reminders of her past. I forced her to let go of personal things because she was meant for something greater. I've been in her unit a thousand times; it's empty, just like the rest of them.

Annabelle sits on the bench near the road. This quest sucks everything out of her and asks for more, and if I don't think fast, I might lose her too.

I think through everything I can remember about my life as a boy, about the ways people preserved their memories, where they kept them, when they did away with them. I remember chests and suitcases, photo albums, and when I visualize all of those items, I know where we need to go.

Chapter 30

"Has anyone seen the mayor? It's been three days." I stormed through the waiting room to his office. Natasha knew to keep her mouth shut. I opened the door and everything was the same as it was a few days ago when I'd met with him. My glass of water had dust in it.

"Natasha, I need you to get ahold of Ashton and Bill and find out where the hell he is. Gospel opens in three days, and I don't need to tell you how important it is that he be there."

"Yes, Dr. Mason." She tapped away on the phone.

"Why are the screens so quiet?" I looked around the room at the two dozen boxes screaming in my face.

"They're at the same level they always are, doctor."

"Make them louder. I want the people coming in here to be overwhelmed with the experience from start to finish."

"Yes, Dr. Mason."

I threw my bag over my shoulder, ready to get things underway at my own office.

"Mr. Cox is not answering his phone, and Dr. McCoy is in the parking lot with his men."

"His men? When did acquire 'men'?"

"As far as I know, sir, he's had them for months."

Natasha returned to her phone, trying to reach Ashton. It'd take her at least ten times to make it through. I watched for Bill through the window.

Dozens of men dressed in black uniforms marched in unison through the parking lot, practicing drills, guns on their right hips, clubs on their lift, hailing Bill as Chief.

"What's going on out here?" I stepped out of the mayor's backdoor.

"Halt!" Bill stopped his men. "What can we do for you, Doug?"

"What is all this?"

"This?" He pointed to his boys. "This is our militia."

"I'm seeing that. Why does Gospel need a militia?"

"To make sure we maintain proper order."

"And what do you mean by that?" I set my bag on the ground and walked through the men to get a better look.

"Not everyone understands our vision. Some might even go as far as trying to destroy it. I've taken it upon myself to make sure that doesn't happen."

"Right." I pulled a club from one of the soldiers and tapped it on my hand. "I assume you know what you're doing. You're the brain of this operation."

"Glad you see it that way." He waved his arm and the men marched, drowning me under the sound of boots hitting concrete.

My car pulled around the corner and scooped me up. Phones rang off the hook at the office, and I had to be there to answer questions. It was nice to enjoy a few minutes alone with the screens before the chaos picked up again.

When the car stopped, I couldn't believe the turnout. People smothered the city streets in sleeping bags and tents, waiting for my practice to open, waiting for Mason Cosmetics to change their lives, waiting to be beautiful and all that comes along with that.

I stepped through the back, and Gracie met me with caring eyes.

"Where have you been? I thought we were meeting over an hour ago. You had me worried."

"I haven't been able to find the mayor. The last I saw of him, he was overseeing the final touches on the department store, but it doesn't look like he's been home or to his office. His car's still parked in the store lot."

"How are you going to open Gospel by yourself?"

"I'm hoping it doesn't come down to that, but I can't count on Ashton or Bill. Ashton's probably high or drunk in some club, clueless as to what day it is, and Bill is so blinded with all this militia stuff that I can't see him doing much to help."

"He scares me." She squirmed in her dress.

"Bill?"

"I can't explain it, but he knows what I'm thinking."

"Gracie, he does not know what you're thinking."

"I would be the first person to believe you. I'm not superstitious at all, and if he was just guessing my likes and dislikes, it'd be one thing, but he knows things no one could ever know, like when I'm going to move my left hand or right, wave my arms, speak."

I didn't want to bring any more attention to it, but I knew what she meant. He knew things no one could know. As a kid he finished most people's sentences, even the people he'd just met. Over the years, he developed a bizarre sixth sense.

I chose to leave it at that. She didn't need to know about his PhD's in psychology and neuroscience.

The screens talked around us, filling my silence, and people pounded on the glass.

"Hopefully the building holds up for three more days." I tried to make light of the situation, but it was like the zombie apocalypse everyone used to talk about.

They turned into animals in the streets. Eating whatever they could find, herding closer to save their place in line, ready to slit each other's throats at the slightest move, and all I saw was money, money, money.

"You scared?" I turned her toward me.

"A little."

"That's because you haven't transitioned into this kind of life. Let's start now. You're no longer Gracie, the shy wallflower from nowhere. You're Grace, the elegant goddess from Gospel."

"And who are you? You can't keep being Dougy Mason."

"Jax. Dr. Jax Mason, the best cosmetic surgeon who ever lived."

My phone buzzed in my pocket, and for the first time in three days I was relieved. The mayor's office number popped up.

"Where the hell have you been?"

"Sorry, Dr. Mason. I haven't found him yet." Natasha again.

"Then why call?"

"Bill and his men searched the department store and the rest of the city. They checked the airlines, trains, buses, and the mayor is officially gone."

"He left town?"

"No, he disappeared, and Bill seems to be certain he's not coming back."

"This isn't happening." I leaned over the reception desk.

"We still have three days to figure things out for the opening, but there is one pressing matter."

"Do I want to hear this right now?"

"The mayor was supposed to model for the mold this afternoon. The programming company has called a few times to confirm, and I've lied. Said he'd be right over."

"Fuck. That thing was his baby. I can't just pick someone off the street to take his place."

"The appointment's in two hours."

I had two hours to change history. Without the mold, Gospel wouldn't function. People would grow sloppy, set their own standards, make exceptions for money and energy and health. They'd never be flawless.

"Should I cancel, Dr. Mason?"

The screens hounded me, pulling pieces out of me and shaking them up before putting them back in place. The zombies bellowed through the glass, savages, hounds, their paychecks waiting for products and services. Grace stood at the counter, beautiful under the glow like she always was, and I changed history.

"No, don't cancel. Tell them the model will be there on time."

Chapter 31

The yard sits on the outskirts of the city, and when we round the corner, I'm sure we missed it. The whole block is overgrown in weeds, each lot of land indecipherable from the next, locked together in the vines of what seems like half a century. Cracking pavement, worn houses condemned, broken "for sale" signs in the front of every yard.

I recognize the houses. Kids I went to school with called them home. Some lived with their aunts and uncles, some their grandparents, others all alone. I didn't see it that way at the time; I considered their parents to be beautiful and successful, dedicating their lives to the future. They weren't beautiful; they were absent. Who knows what happened to the kids.

"There's a gate over here." Annabelle points from deep inside the bushes. "It's got one hell of a lock on it."

"A lock?" I stumble into the bushes behind her. Thorns tear my naked skin. She's standing next to a chain-link fence ten feet high with a rusted lock and chains around the entry way. Why the fuck can't anything be simple? "I don't remember a lock. I walked by here after the mayor's event, and there wasn't a lock." The rust on the metal says a hell of a lot about how long it's been there, and how long I've been absent. "It wasn't supposed to be like this."

"Sometimes life has a way of changin' things around on us. What starts out as something pleasurable and simple turns into an addiction, and it blends so seamlessly, you don't see it happening." She grabs hold of the links to catch her breath. "What's your plan?"

"I doubt I can break through it, but I can climb over and find a way for you to get in after me."

"I can't climb a ten foot fence, Doug."

"We'll find a way!" When I finish the sentence, I know yelling wasn't the best method of delivery. It's silent until I dig my feet into the links and they clank below me. Annabelle waits at the bottom, staring up at me like I'm all she has in the world, and I remember how much easier it used to be climbing fences. My feet are too big for the holes, and my legs tremble with every thrust upward.

I round the top, finding my footing, and stare into her eyes on the way back down, thinking I'll have do this on my own, when I see a split in the fence where someone had cut their way in.

"Over there!" I wave my arm and Annabelle moves toward the opening. "Just wait there and I'll help you in."

I jump to the ground, and my knees buckle beneath me. Hands on the ground, knees on the ground, losing more blood over this, desperate to know what's happened to my body in the last twenty-four hours.

"You okay?" she says through the fence.

"I can't breathe. I don't know what's happening, but everything's getting harder." Saliva drips from my mouth, the last of the water inside my body. I might as well be locked away in a retirement home. I'd fit right in—weak, listless, and delusional.

"Maybe the plastic is weighing you down."

"I never noticed it before. I can't imagine that much has changed."

"I'll need you to hold the fence open if you want me to join you."

I find the strength to stand and walk to her. The hole in the fence is smaller than it seemed from the top of the fence—kids from outside Gospel. I pull at both sides, and Annabelle pushes through on her stomach.

"What are we looking for specifically?" She stands and brushes the dirt off her chest.

"Anything that might remind them, something personal. If we can find the items they threw away, it might work."

"I hope you have a plan B."

I look over the hill at acres of ashes. "What did they do?"

"They burned everything once all the people cleared out. It's been a soggy mess for a long time now."

"But everything's gone. What are we supposed to do now?"

"Sometimes life…"

"Don't you say another fucking word. You knew I was coming here, and you never said a thing. You talk constantly and you never told me there's no hope left!"

"I wasn't sure what you were looking for."

"We're not going to save her, Annabelle. I can't think of anything else."

She stares over the rolling hills of waste. "Maybe there are still bits and pieces that survived." We're sitting ducks again. The shit storm never ends, and I think we walked right into the spider's web, but sometimes knowing you're stuck gives you innovation. "Let's spread out and cover as much ground as we can."

"And what if we can't find anything?"

"We can't keep thinking that way. Let's just look in this general area, then move onto the next." She covers one side of the entry way, and I take the other. Most of the stuff is destroyed, bits and pieces we'd never be able to put back together, much like life. There are pop cans and beer bottles where people slept to get away from the new and improved Gospel message.

We walk farther and the view changes. The fire barely touched a small circle of items, but they're covered in soot. Cradles and children's stuffed animals, old and moldy, still visibly worn around the necks where the kids held them at night. Night lights, knit blankets, rocking chairs, paintings hung of refrigerator doors, video tapes, religious items, and I remember repeating the mayor's ideals to the citizens of the city, do away with the crutch of family and religion. Across the way, Annabelle wipes tears from her eyes.

I pull a photo album from the debris. Each picture destroyed by heat and exposure, erased the way we intended, sent into oblivion with the rest of us. Whenever I think I've found something we can bring to the department store, it's worthless.

I meet with Annabelle after hours of searching, and we say nothing because that's all that's left to say, acknowledging our failure. Even if we could identify the people in the lines by their markings, we'd never find their stuff in here, and we're playing with borrowed time.

"What for?" I throw another photo album in the dirt.

"Excuse me?" Annabelle wipes the sweat from her eyes with a handkerchief.

"What's the point of going back to the department store? We have nothing to help them, and the trips back and forth are likely to kill both of us. We're better off staying here."

She has nothing to say. Either she agrees with me or thinks I'm pathetic. We sit on an old bed together, and she holds my hand between hers.

"What's that over there?" I point to a patch of land hidden in shrubs.

"I don't see anything."

"It's yellow. I know that yellow." I plow through the debris toward the yellow that drove my father away, the yellow that drove my mother to the hospital, the yellow of a city cab.

"Why are you running?" She doesn't understand, and I don't have time to explain. Instead I strip the branches off the shrubs so she can see for herself.

"It's a car!" I wave my arms and point toward it. I haven't seen a car with a combustion engine in decades. Ugly things.

She walks toward me, and I hop in the driver's seat. Mold everywhere, but no keys. As a kid I saw a movie where a guy started a car with a paper clip and gum wrapper. I'm not that guy.

"Looks old, Doug."

"It doesn't matter. No keys."

"They all look old."

"So?"

"An old car that's been sitting here for who-knows-how-long is never going to start, keys or no keys."

"You're saying we can't use any of them?"

"I'm not saying that. I'm just making sure you have realistic expectations. They look like they've been here a while."

"And if they haven't been sitting, we might be able to get one running?"

"In theory."

"Well, look at this place. There's cars all around the perimeter, and that sure as hell didn't happen in one day. They've been dumping stuff here for who knows how long. Maybe recently."

"Maybe."

I hop from car to car, and they all have the same answer, 'Fuck you, Doug.'

"There's a cab over there." Annabelle points to a bush not far away. Another piece of shit, no doubt.

I settle into the driver's seat again, another disgusting interior, and I remember that some cabbies kept their keys tucked on top of the visor. I flip it down, and for once since we started this, something works in our favor. The key drops into my hand, and I push it into the ignition.

"Think it'll start?" Annabelle joins me by the window.

"To be honest, I don't know. I never owned a car before the prototype."

"Maybe I better be the one to try."

I slide to the side and let Annabelle take over the driver's seat. She twists the key and listens. The engine gurgles and quits. Annabelle pushes the pedal on the floor, twists the keys again, and slumps into the seat when it responds the same.

"What's wrong?" I don't want to accept that this might be the end.

"I don't think it's going to work, and I don't have the tools to fix it."

She mentions fixing cars, and I think of my father.

Chapter 32

"Everything off." A photography assistant held her arm out to grab my boxer briefs.

"Is that really necessary?" I held my hands over my manly bits and handed her the briefs. As much as I wanted to act the way I looked, I didn't have the confidence to back it up.

"You said you're a model, right? What's the big deal?"

"Nothing. I just didn't know it was this kind of job."

"Don't worry so much about it." She threw my briefs on the chair. "I won't be looking, and since the mayor has modeled for the majority of the program, you won't have to do much." She took a seat behind a computer screen and fired up the body scanner.

The computer probe scanned my face, my chest, my manly bits, and I didn't feel much better. When the initial scan finished, a less than specific image of me appeared on the wall.

"How long does this usually take?"

"You really have no idea what we're doing? This is the final scan. We put everything together today, and when and where we need your scans is yet to be determined. Could take hours. Maybe days."

"Days?" I crossed my legs a little.

"We're about to head into a long stretch of photography and digital data collection. Do you need anything before we start? Water? A snack?" She stared at the screen and waved her hand over the top.

"Water would be good." I thought she'd continue waving and point me in the right direction, but with the push of a button, a group of men and women entered the room, some carrying water, some carrying makeup, and some carrying razors.

"Your water." The gal behind the computer typed away again. "The rest of them are here to make last minute adjustments."

"What are you planning on doing with those?" I covered myself with one hand and pointed toward the razors with the other.

"Precision grooming." One of the women approached me and lubed my body with something citrusy. Had the circumstances been different, I could have enjoyed it.

"Just be careful."

She etched the razor over my pecs and abs. "You'll have to move your hand, and I'll get the rest."

"You sure you know what you're doing? I mean, you do this for a living? Shaving junk?"

"Don't worry so much. I haven't had an incident in a while." She winked, and it made everything worse.

The razor lady finished her business and the computer lady barked commands one after another. "To the left, Mr...." She hesitated and peeked over the computer screen. "I'm sorry; I didn't catch your name."

"Mason. Jax Mason."

"Right. Now turn to the center."

I blended into the wall, one image at a time, surrendering whatever made me unique. They scanned every inch of me. Some images took hours. Others took seconds, and by the end of it, a vibrant image shown on the screen.

"How'd it go?" Grace walked out with me.

"Good, I think. I'd rather not talk about it though." I doubt she'd have wanted to hear about the lube and razors anyway.

"You look tired. The grand opening of the clinic is today." She touched my hand. "Are you going to be up for it?"

"I don't have much of a choice. It's my clinic."

"I can help, if you'd like."

"Really? That would be great. It would only be for today, and if at any time you hate it and want to leave, you're free to."

"I doubt I'll hate it. I like being with you." She was the first to bridge that gap, and I wanted nothing more than to reciprocate, but with everything moving and bending and dying around me, I didn't have the energy.

"We better get going then. I'd like to change and finish any last minute adjustments to the operating room."

We sat in the prototype, watching the first batch of ads for Mason Cosmetics run on the screens, and the static choked me for the first time, a disconnection, like I was floating and falling and empty all at the same time.

Grace mouthed words of concern, a mime in my circus: no sound, no color. Black and white static, and I couldn't shake it.

"Are you feeling alright? You've gone completely white. Maybe you should eat something." She handed me an apple from her purse.

"I can't." Maybe it was motion sickness. Maybe I was dying. I collapsed on the seat next to her trying to figure it out, helpless to the static in my head.

Astronauts popped into my thoughts, exploring the endlessness of the cosmos, strapped to rockets to guide them home when they'd finished. They sputtered here and there, camera flashes aglow in the darkness, taking leaps for mankind, capturing a world out of reach, until they stopped sputtering, stagnant men in white suits floating into the distance.

They dislodged the rockets, unplugged the tubes, and waited in the abyss. No sound, no panic, and they ignored the oxygen gages on their tanks. Dying in static, losing air, losing life, nothing to keep them grounded while they floated into absence.

They were underwater. Blue and green waves thrashed over their suits, and water hits my face.

"You passed out." Grace set down a glass cup, pulled me upright, and wiped the water from my eyes, like a mother, like a lover, like a friend.

"I'm feeling better."

"What happened?"

"Just a weird feeling. It's gone now. Come on…" I opened the car door. "Let's open the clinic."

"You can't be serious. You just lost consciousness."

"Look out there." I pointed to the thousands of people filling the streets outside my office. "They're here for me. For us. We can help them. We can give them the happiness they're looking for, and we can make a shit ton of money doing it. I have no intention of passing that up." I said it like I meant it, but I didn't. I wanted to be a million miles away.

We changed our clothes, started the molds, slabbed makeup and hair cream all over us, sprayed cologne and perfume, colored contact lenses, lip balm, lip stick, high heels, ironed suit, tight skirt, lotion, rub on, rub off.

The system opened the doors. Every face I knew, young and old, walked through the front door. Battering rams, each one of them, trampling me down like roadkill on the road to happiness. No please, no thank you. Money, money, money.

Grace stood at one end of the room, and I stood at the other, two lovers torn apart by greed and vanity, handing pamphlets to savages and their progeny.

Five o'clock struck and the system shut the front doors. The savages fled to their new dwelling, terrified someone might see their ugliness before they had the opportunity to get it fixed, and the streets stood empty, except for a young woman holding a sign condemning Gospel and a smirk plastered across her face better than any surgery I could give someone.

Chapter 33

My dad told me to keep it clean. "Always keep the motor clean, inside and out. It'll save you a lot of heartache." He'd sit me down and make me sandblast parts for hours. I couldn't tell you the name of a single one of them, and to be honest, I didn't care. I didn't want to learn a thing from the man who treated my mother like shit.

While I'm staring under the hood of the cab, I hear his voice in my head, laughing at me, criticizing me, mocking me—his way of teaching me something new. I remember his words like they happened yesterday, but the car parts don't look familiar in the slightest. I unplug everything I can; careful to remember how and where they went together, wiping my fingers over every inch to shift the sludge.

"Here." Annabelle hands me her handkerchief, and it's black in a matter of seconds. "What if it's out of gas?" She leans under the hood with me.

I hadn't thought of that. I can hardly remember filling a car with gas, but if that's the case with this one, we're screwed. Modern cars don't use gasoline. I choose not to answer Annabelle and continue wiping the engine.

"Wanna try it again?" I stand and wipe the sweat dripping from my nose.

"Sure." She hops back in the seat again and looks like she was born to do it, like she'd been a cabbie all her life, and maybe she had. I never asked about her past.

The engine chokes when she twists the key. She does it again and again and again. I assume there's method to her madness because each time she twists the key, the car breathes a little better.

"Come on," she says while she stares out the front window. "You stupid piece of shit, come on!" I haven't heard her get worked up. She's had an annoying way of staying calm in every situation so far.

She shouts again and the car roars in return. "Yes!" I say and jump into the passenger seat.

"Let's not waste any time. This thing may never start again." She pulls it into gear, and we drive over the debris toward the front gate. While we bump and lurch this way and that, I hang out the window to scoop as many items as I can. We're not going back empty handed, and there is plenty of room in the car to take a little of everything.

By the time we reach the front gates, I have the car stuffed to the ceiling, sit down next to Annabelle, and savor the feeling of a manual car. I'm lost in memories of trips to the ice cream shop after long days of swimming, no screens fucking it up, when Annabelle chimes in over my thoughts.

"We're not alone."

Bill's standing on the other side of the gate with his posse of idiots. It's time for the showdown. They raise their guns. I wasn't much of a fighter as a kid, and I'm not any better now, but life's made it pretty clear I can't continue being that same man.

"I thought they just sat around and waited for people to die."

"We must be doing something right."

"Drive through them." I roll up the windows and reach for the steering wheel. "Slouch down and just worry about pushing the pedals. I'll steer."

"What about the gate?"

"Drive through it."

"It might kill the car. That engine isn't going to like being slammed by a fence post."

"Then let's not hit the post in the middle. Hit it in the center of one of the gates where it's all chain link."

She looks at me and winks like she's excited about the prospect of doing something dangerous. I get the feeling it's been years since she's done anything fun on that mountain. Bill raises his hand, ready to tell the boys when to open fire. Anabelle revs the engine.

She pushes a pedal to the floor, and the car's tires spin in the dirt to pick up speed. We bounce like pinballs on the inside, bumping heads and shoulders and elbows on the glass before we hit the fence head on, and the chain around the posts snaps like a rubber band.

Billy's first bullet shatters the windshield. I'm used to glass shattering on me at this point. A dozen bullets follow. The engine pants under the hood.

"Faster!" I aim the car toward Billy.

He runs like the coward he is. Most of his men follow, but some tough it out and collapse under the impact of the car.

Annabelle launches the car off the curb and into the street like she'd done this all her life. We come to a gentle stop not far from Grace's house.

"I think you might be a little too comfortable in the driver's seat."

She smiles and sits up while we speed down the street. "I drove a city bus for a year after I left the hospital. Not much I haven't seen, but this was a new adventure."

I roll the windows down to feel the wind, glancing back, watching Bill and his boys hopping into cars of their own, savoring this single second of peace. We won't get lucky like that again. This is the end.

Annabelle looks down the street, chasing memories I can't follow.

"Gospel changed your life," I say because I know it did for me.

"You may not remember, but this was a normal town. People of all incomes had jobs and families. Things changed, and before we could catch our breath, it was gone. Life was gone. Those of us left behind, or refused to join, didn't know how to start over."

I could tell her how sorry I am; adding insult to injury, but it doesn't change things. Too little too late. We stare down the road together, wishing we could run toward the horizon and never look back, when Annabelle shouts.

"Shit." She slams on the brakes and runs to the boy with black eyes. He's on the curb, crying for the only family he has left, and she picks him up to kiss his tears away.

I follow behind, an intruder in their perfect space. "I don't want to cut this short, but we don't have the time to stay here."

"He's coming with us."

"What if they kill him?" I have to be realistic. She's too caught up in emotion to process the danger.

"I'm not leaving him here alone."

Against my will, I let him tag along, and it adds another life to preserve under my watch. With my failing body, I may not be able to keep them all safe. Can I withstand losing another life on my watch? I don't have much of a track record.

We pile into the car and Xavier sits between us, holding the edge of Annabelle's shirt while we drive, silence overtaking the front seat, innocence on the left and the grim reaper on the right.

She signs and he laughes.

I take it all in. "What did you say?"

"That you're okay but funny looking."

I'm smacked back to reality where I'm a human lego. He loosens his grip on her, but still keeps a steady eye on me. While he watches me, I watch the road behind us. Car lights flash in the distance.

"Faster, Annabelle."

Chapter 34

Food lost its taste. I'd wake at night ravenous, plundering my penthouse like one of the savages in the office. Nothing filled me. Nothing quenched the thirst. Nothing stopped the guilt of losing my mother, letting her die with my broken promises in her heart.

The screens kept me awake, *fuck you* on the tip of my tongue every sleepless night. In and out of the office, time blending together, days blending, months blending.

At first I thought the worst part of my day was stepping into the office. When I looked closer, I knew it started much sooner than that. I'd shower in the morning, trying to wash the filth away, and when I'd step out of the stall, an awful reminder stared me down.

He had boyish good looks, thick black hair, smooth skin trapped inside the shell of a murderer. A man stared through me, older but certainly not wiser, and condemned me for everything I'd done to my mother, to Grace, to the people of the city. He laughed. He called me names. He blamed me for everything.

He was right.

Even when the mirror filled with steam, he was right. Most mornings I'd let him win. I'd let him throw his punches, and I'd crawl away into hiding the way I always did, the shithead from nowhere who killed his mother.

Blood filled my fists. I tore him off the wall and stepped on his head until it broke into a hundred helpless pieces under my feet. It helped at the time.

"Take all of the mirrors down." I stormed through the office and yelled at Grace.

"Why?"

"Stop asking questions, and do it." I pushed her toward the women's bathroom. "I'll get the ones out here."

"What am I doing with them once I've taken them down?"

"Trash them."

"You paid a lot of money for these." She hesitated in the bathroom doorway.

"You're not listening, Grace. Trash them, and get me Bill on the phone. This needs to happen everywhere."

One by one, she tossed broken pieces of glass into the dumpster while I saw to the influx of clients.

"That's the last of them, Jax. In here anyway, and Bill's waiting on line one."

I ignored the woman spitting her problems all over my suit and hopped behind the desk to talk with Bill. "I need a favor."

"You've never seemed like the kind of guy who asks for favors."

"I need you to get rid of all the mirrors in the city."

"That sounds like a big job."

"Use your militia."

"That's not really the purpose of the militia, Doug."

"It's Jax." I itched my hands, tiny hives forming when I saw my reflection in the computer screen. The same murderer staring back.

"Today."

"That's ridiculous. What's this all about? Are you having some sort of mid-life crisis?"

"You're committed to Gospel, right?" I had to get through to him in a way he'd accept.

"Of course."

"And the ideals of the mayor."

"Yes."

"So am I. And I want to add to those ideals."

"What's your plan?"

"If we remove the mirrors, we further remove the past. People won't need to be reminded of their failures, of their lousy looks, of anything. They can focus on Gospel, like we originally intended."

"I don't know if it's going to be that simple."

"Why not?" My hand itched more. "They'll have their molds. That's all they need. They only need to know where they're going. Where they've been doesn't matter. It didn't make them happy the first time around, and it's not going to make them happy now. We can all relate to that."

A long pause lingered on the other side of the phone. "When you put it like that…."

"You'll do it?" I itched some more.

"I think I can make it happen. The militia has tripled in size."

"Good. Do it as soon as possible, and let me know when you've finished."

The hives spread.

Chapter 35

"I know it doesn't mean much now, but I'm sorry," I say to no one in particular, hoping Xavier might look my way. He reacts the way I'd expect, tightening his grip on Annabelle and burying his face in her sleeve. I let myself forget I'm still a monster.

Annabelle drives the cab, and the breeze dumps through the windows onto my face, cleansing me of fears and insecurities, a type of peace I'm not sure I've ever felt before. My body and mind refresh, and more importantly, my motivation grows behind the fear of being too late for Grace, too late for all of them, and I close my eyes to refocus.

"We're here."

I keep my eyes closed. As long as they're closed, I can say I'm dreaming. That I didn't fuck everything up. That I'm not going to lose Annabelle and Grace. That everything will be all right. As long as they're closed, I don't have to be the hero. I'm not strong enough to be the hero. I'm Doug Mason, the shithead from nowhere.

"You coming?" Annabelle stands in the street with the car door open, her words ringing through my head.

This is the moment that makes or breaks a man.

She's right. "Maybe Xavier should wait here. They're not after him; they're after you. He won't be able to keep up in there and might wind up hurt or worse."

She scoops the boy into her arms and kisses him on the neck before hiding him in the back of the cab while we pile memories in our arms and walk toward the door.

"There's always a chance this won't work." Annabelle looks through the glass doors at the marching mannequin lines. "What'll we do after that?"

"Anything we can."

"I'm your conscience, Doug. Your mother trusted me to watch over you. I need to know you'll be okay if anything happens to me."

"Why are you talking like this?"

"Because we need to know where we stand."

"We're standing at the front doors of the department store. We're standing before the battle of our lives. Isn't that enough?"

"I'm dying, Doug."

"What?"

"I've had a dozen surgeries in the last ten years. My heart won't survive the stress of saving the world. I need to know you'll be alright if I don't make it."

It doesn't matter how much I've been through, death never feels normal. Sometimes I'm reminded of death when a pin pricks me. Annabelle hit me with a train moving at full speed. How the fuck am I supposed to do this without her? She plays it off like it's simple, but it's not simple. It's ridiculous and heartless and selfish, and she made damn sure of it. She took everything away in one gulp of air.

I shut my mouth and walk through the doors because words won't fix a goddamn thing. The marching footsteps drown out our silence, and I dig through the box of memories. Bullshit. Bullshit. Bullshit. I wave items in front of every face that passes. They march, and I switch items, waiting for any sign of life. They march, and I switch items. They march, and I switch items. Annabelle switches. I switch. They march, and Bill parks in front of the doors.

"Please," I say to the woman headed toward me, "You must have some idea who this belongs to. Please, tell me."

She marches toward the staircase in the corner.

"Wake up! This is your life!" I hold up a photo album filled with barely recognizable faces. "This is who you are. You've been brainwashed into believing you need to be someone else. That there was something wrong with you, and physical changes could make you better. It's all been a lie. I know this because I developed this lie. I lied to you and your families, and I'm asking you now to follow me one last time. Walk out with me. Leave this place behind and let me take you to the lives you deserve. The lives I underestimated. This won't make you happy."

They march.

Annabelle sits on the other side, waving stuffed animals and sheet music in front of each plastic face, when I notice a small patch of blue from Grace's favorite dress.

"Stop!" I run through the lines, dodging and bending through the plastic bodies like a contortionist, and when I reach for her, Bill digs his knife into my thigh. The black sludge didn't last long enough.

"I can't let you do that, Dougy." His posse moves through the rest of the crowd. I can't see Annabelle through the chaos.

"You know I'm right."

"Whether you're right or wrong doesn't matter. This is business. You've managed to slow down your time on the program, and I'm here to make sure it gets moving at full speed again."

"I'll die for her."

"I sure hope you mean that. Otherwise, this wouldn't be much fun, and I promised my boys some fun."

Screens cheer for him in the background. The mannequins march at their leisure, stepping over my blood on the floor, tracking it through the building, etching a map of my misery, and his boys hunt for Annabelle.

He stoops to my level and sticks his finger in my knife wound. "I'll kill you, don't worry about that, but it's not a matter of killing you. I'm going to use you as an example for anyone else who might be thinking about ditching Gospel."

He's talking, and I'm weighing options. I can't outrun him. I can't beat him in a fist fight, and while I'm stuck here, cut open like a steak, I don't have the option to outsmart him. He pulls his finger away from my leg, and fuck, it hurts as much as when he shoved it in. He lifts his hand to his face, smelling my blood like a fucking weasel dressed as a wolf, knowing damn well he's never tasted blood in his life. While he's trying to mess with my head, I focus on his height. I've forgotten throughout all of this, but I'm twice his size.

My left hand latches to his throat like a wild dog, and I lift him high enough that he can't reach the knife on the ground or the gun pushed into the top of his boot. He's a heavy son-of-a-bitch, one of those stalky people just as thin but twice as dense. It's a test of who can last longer, and I hope to God it's me.

He's above me squirming and writhing for air while I'm below squirming and writhing for the strength to put him in the fucking ground, and fate takes its sweet time deciding who'll be victorious.

"I'll be back." I drop him to the ground once he's limp, pathetic, and unconscious, and I crawl through the mannequins, hoping the posse's preoccupied. I search for Annabelle's shoes and Grace's dress, and lose my train of thought in the sea of marching black.

White flashes in the corner of my eye, and Anabelle's on her chest scooting toward me, giving a signal to stay quiet because they're hot on her trail. She points to the store's front doors and we crawl together.

While we crawl, a familiar blue moves past my cheek. Annabelle grabs my arm when she sees I'm hooked.

"We'll come back for her." Annabelle keeps her head low.

"I can't leave her." I reach for her dress and rub the fabric between my fingers, smelling the last trace of her perfume. "It's you. Grace, listen to me. I'm here. I was wrong about everything. I'm here to take you home."

She pushes me closer to the stairs with every step. "No, stop please." She pushes and pushes, and I can't slow her down at all. Her plastic feet hit me in the chest over and over, left right, left right, left right, and I reach up to hold her waist. "I love you, Grace."

She marches.

"We need to get out of here." Annabelle pulls me to the ground before anyone can see me. "You're gonna bleed out."

I let go of Grace and crawl toward the doors, and the sun beats down on my skin once we're outside the shade of human bodies. We rise and hustle to the cab.

"What the hell did I think was going to happen?" I hang into the cab window while Annabelle tends to Xavier. "I was going to walk up to her, tell her I love her, and all this bullshit was just going to go away? So fucking clueless."

"Keep your voice down. You want them to cut your other leg open?" She wipes sweat from Xavier's face before tending to my leg. "Besides, there's still some time." She wraps a tourniquet around my upper thigh. "They are marching steady but slow, and that's the biggest line of repurposing I've ever seen. You probably have an hour."

"Is that supposed to be a comfort to me?" I'm yelling, and if I'm being honest, I'm glad. I can't think when she tries to be wise and comforting. Every word she says at this point pisses me off.

"There is a difference between comfort and self-preservation." She finishes wrapping my leg with whatever clean rags she can gather in the cab.

"You've been hiding on a mountain for God knows how long, and you want to tell me about staying calm in the face of adversity? You're oblivious, Annabelle. Completely oblivious. Maybe you should leave, so I can figure this out myself."

She grabs the door to the cab, and at first I think she's crying tears of anger and is on her way to punch me in the face, but she lifts her other hand to hold her chest while her head dips into the steering wheel.

"Help her." Xavier gives a deaf plea from his lips, a guttural voice I fully understand. It's a cry for help to save the only mother he's ever known.

"Wake up, Annabelle." I rush to open the cab door and touch her face. "You're okay. Just wake up, and we'll work this all out." I hold her face in my palms, and she's limp. "Annabelle?"

Xavier tugs on her blouse, his cheeks raining tears down upon Annabelle. The moment hits me in the chest like a silver bullet.

"Annabelle!" I pull her onto my lap and cradle her like a child. "You are not leaving us now! You have to fight! Too many of us still need you." I'm trying my best to stay strong for Xavier, but I know it's over. "I still need you," I say and cry over her fading face.

Xavier pulls away and sits in the back seat of the cab, as far from me as he can be. I'm now the man who's taken away both of his mothers. There's nothing I can say or do to make that up to him.

He already knows the answer, and I lay her down in the front seat while I pace along the street, shrieking indecipherable words to no one. "I can't do this alone." I rest my head on the glass of the side windshield. "I'm not a hero." I pull up, filled with anger, and hurt, and disgust in everything I am. "Is that what you wanted to hear, Gospel? I am not your hero. I'm the same, worthless, white trash shithead. I'm pathetic. And lucky for me, with all I've done, I'll probably live forever. Halle-fucking-lujah."

With the last words, I smash the mirror with my plastic fist and watch the pieces fall onto the concrete. Xavier cries in the back of the cab, but I can't hear him because there's something on the glass I've not seen in years.

I hunch lower to look at the pieces, and in each one, there is a face staring back, a black plastic face looking just as shocked as I am. I move to the left; it follows. I move to the right; it follows. I claw my plastic fingers down my plastic face, and it follows. It's me.

Breathe, Jax. I whisper, still watching the face from the corner of my eyes, and the image changes. The plastic fades little by little off the face. I see eyes, a nose, teeth, a hairline, and when I feel my own face, the plastic's gone.

Xavier stares in shock and scrambles to exit the car and run away because I look like I'm a part of some dark magic.

He stands behind the rear bumper.

I bend to pick up the pieces of the glass, and the face staring back is human, a beautiful human with wrinkles in the corners of its eyes, lines over its brow, and salt and pepper hair.

"I'm old." I cry and laugh and sigh all at the same time because I don't know what it means, but I may as well be flying. "I'm an old man." Xavier steps away from the car and smiles through tears when he sees all of my plastic fade. He comes close and pulls the sagging skin on my elbow. He signs something that I understand. "Old" He points to Annabelle and back at me, joins his hands.

"Yeah, we are the same." I never thought I'd be happy to hear those words, and I snatch Xavier under his arms and throw him into the air, giddy. I don't think I've ever been giddy, not even as a boy. We might win this thing after all. Xavier smiles because the monster's gone. I wipe his tears away.

When I set him down, I can't catch my breath. It makes sense now. I'm an old man. That's what she meant about being a candy striper. Annabelle was younger than I am. I can't do the things I did while I was on supplements and tonic, working out at the gym hours a day, undergoing surgeries non-stop, and applying the cream.

When the moment slows down in my head, I'm slapped back down to reality and reach down to grab as many pieces of mirror as I can hold. I motion to Xavier and hold some of the pieces outstretched. I try to get him to understand I can't do this by myself, and I keep him safe out here. He looks at Annabelle in the cab and back at me before reaching his hands out to grab the glass.

We smile; part in victory, part in fear, and we both kiss Annabelle on the cheek before covering her with a blanket. We turn to the department store. Time to act.

Chapter 36

Bill's men removed all the mirrors from Gospel, and I ordered new construction to fill all the empty spaces with more screens.

"Is everything all right, Dr. Mason?" An expectant mother sat in my consulting room.

"What?" I flipped through her chart and couldn't remember her name. I couldn't remember a lot of things, and I was thankful.

"I just asked you if I should stop surgeries while I'm pregnant."

"Oh." I added some notes to her file. "That would best, I think." What was I saying? Why was she pregnant? Gospel wasn't supposed to have families. We weren't set up for that.

"You shouldn't be pregnant."

"Sorry, I was pregnant when I got here."

"I'll need to consult the commission to find out what to do; in the meantime, you'll have to take some time off from your beauty treatments, Okay?"

She looked horrified as I shoveled her out and brought another patient in, smiling when I felt nothing at all, learning to enjoy the static in my head.

"That's the last of them." Grace closed the computer program and packed her bag under the desk. "I was wondering if you wanted to spend some time together. You know, outside of work."

She talked, and I heard static. "I think it would be best if we maintained a professional relationship."

The hives on my hands and arms disappeared, and I embraced the emptiness.

"You haven't been yourself lately." She finished packing her bag and moved to the door, beautiful because I made her that way.

"I think I've been this man all along, and I never had the opportunity to show it."

"I can't believe that's true. I've known you for a while, and you're not the same."

"Did you ever think I don't want to be that person anymore? You've been selfish enough to take advantage of my services, impose on my life, and now you want to take it a step further and claim that you know me? You don't know anything about me. You don't know what I've been through, and you don't know what I'm going through now."

"If that's anyone's fault, it's yours." She set her bag down.

"What?" I thought about cutting her off and sending her out the door, but the screens chattered, and I felt nothing.

"You've kept me at an arms-length since we met; only pulling me close when you screwed up and needed comfort."

"I won't be needing anything from you anymore." I stared at the screens, content.

"I may not know a lot about you, but I know one thing—you are not well, Doug. You're not well at all."

"My name isn't Doug. It's Jax Mason. I run this city, and I'll keep running it, with or without you."

<h1 style="text-align:center">Chapter 37</h1>

Reflections have trouble lying. They're terrible poker players, patient listeners, and the worst critics we'll ever face, and we did away with them. We became nobodies and were happy to do so to be part of the crowd, part of the perfect smiles, part of the happiness and possibilities.

I scribble on a piece of paper, hoping Xavier can read: We're looking for a blue floral dress. Little yellow flowers. Xavier crawls next to me through the front doors and by his actions understands. He's relentless, and I'm grateful, because I don't have the energy to be relentless alongside him. I focus on my breathing and hope my legs can last long enough to find her.

He grunts and points to a patch not far from us, and he's right. It's Grace.

I nod. She's standing in the process line. So many, they can't go quickly.

I scribble again: Don't lose track of her.

Xavier runs ahead to hold onto her, his head far below the surface of the crowd, and falls under the pressure of marching limbs. He stumbles, but I can't risk taking my eyes off Grace, and I crawl faster to pick him up while watching her approach the stairway to Dante's Inferno.

He jumps to his feet and runs through the bodies again, sliding underneath their flailing arms on shoes with no tread. He grabs hold of Grace, and I join them.

I stand because Bill doesn't matter anymore. I face her, and even though she's doing her best to march through me, I'm smiling. It's almost over. I pull the largest piece of mirror from my pocket and hold it close in front of her face. I've missed her. It's been less than a day, and I feel like I haven't seen her in months, already forgetting the details of her features.

Seconds seem like hours and minutes seem like days until I realize nothing's changing. She's still marching.

I look down at the mirror and realize it's too dark to see a damn thing. No old man face to reassure me that my plan is working.

There's not enough light in the store for them to see their reflections.

Xavier is a step ahead of me and points to the dim lights with his head shaking. I can't believe he's telling me it's not going to work. Not after all of this. Not after being so close. He shrugs his shoulders. He wants to save them as badly as I do, and I can see that in his face.

"Why can't anything work?" I take Xavier outside, maybe a light source is in the cab. Xavier sits with the body of Annabelle, and I find nothing in the glove box.

Annabelle's sacrifice is going to be for nothing because we've lost.

As I'm talking in my head, maybe I'm talking out loud, I can't keep track of anything anymore, I do know I'm not the only one talking. An old man mocks me from the corner of my eye. I turn and connect with the man, and all of my memories snap into my head. I remember all the gaps. I remember who I was, who I am, and who I want to be.

"Too dark in there, huh?"

"Yeah."

He hands me his cell phone, something long since outlawed in Gospel. Our screens communicate all we need to know. "Use the flashlight on my phone."

We weave through bodies, agile and fast, because we've learned how they move, and the staircase taps under our feet while we run into the inferno, chasing a life we left behind.

I can't make out which one is Grace, flashlight or not, they look all the same. I start to shine on the clothing but pass for a better solution. I'm going to stand at the mouth of the furnace and wait. Xavier stands across from me, and we pull the mirrors from our pockets. The first body pushes toward me, and I can't slow it down long enough to keep the glass steady and the light on it. It takes another step and plummets into the lava at the bottom of the furnace.

"No." I look into the fire and watch him melt, and another body falls off the edge. I curse the furnace. "You can't have anymore." I stand directly in front of the next body and hold the mirror and flashlight in front of its face.

The body pushes hard against me, and my shoes slip closer to the opening of the furnace. "I'm not going anywhere," I say to the body. "You can push all you want, but I'll die before I let you fall into that pit. Wake up, damnit. Wake up."

It keeps pushing, and the fire burns the edges of my clothes, singeing the hair on my arms and legs. "Fight!" I shout it for them and for me, digging my shoes into the ledge between the department store floor and the flames soon to be my demise, begging anyone who will listen for the strength to hold on longer than the plastic people in front of me.

"Please," I say and hold the mirror to its face, pushing with everything I have against its torso to slow the pace, "I need you to look into this mirror. Really look at it. And tell me what you see."

They march. "Tell me what you see!" I slap my hand across its face, back and forth and back and forth while the mirror shard cuts my other hand.

The plastic over its eyes melts down its face, and I think it's because we're so close to the fire, but under the mask, the eyes of the woman I love stare through me. "Grace. Keep looking!"

The plastic melts, her face revealed, aged and wrinkled, making me lose my grip against the threshold. "Gracie, I need to look at me. Look at me, sweetheart."

Her eyes grow wide and she gulps the air like she has been without it for decades. "Doug," she says and falls limp into my arms as soon as the plastic breaks its hold. Together we pull away from the inferno.

"What's happening?" She struggles to speak.

"You're safe now." I lift her to see the reality of our current lives. Plastic nobodies marching to their deaths, and for the first time, she can see it with me. She looks through the store, shocked at the differences, and screams when she sees Xavier trying to save the bodies marching into the fire.

"What have we done?" She looks at me, and I don't need to answer; she understands the lies we've lived. She holds my hand and looks onto the marching lines. "Where are they going?"

"To them, they're marching to happiness, and they're leaving everything behind to do it; to Gospel, they are replenishing the cream."

Grace's hands cover mine, age spots cover hers, and she's frail in my arms. All of the plastic surgeries faded away, all of the genetically-engineered supplements, all of the products, all of the unreal, and I look into the eyes of an old woman who never wanted to be part of this life.

"I'm so sorry, Grace." As much as I try to stay strong for them all, I scream into her hands. We've wasted so many years.

"Sorry for what?" She looks as innocent as ever.

"I stole your life. You'll never get this time back."

"Doug, I never cared about the products. I never cared about the surgeries, the molds. I cared about you, and that gave me a reason to live."

"I need your help." I hold her closer. "All of these people are here because of me. Each one has a past, and I need you to help me bring them back to life. I can't do it alone."

She rubs lumps of arthritis in her hands and wrists, likely in pain like me and watches the lines. "Tell me what to do."

I smile and kiss her for the first time in forty-five years. "Take these." I hand her all the pieces of mirror from my pockets. "Hold them close to their faces, make sure the flashlight reflects their image, and never give up. I have to run back to the car to find more light sources." She hears the last sentence, and I know she's terrified to lose me again. "I promise I'll be right back." She kisses me again, and I run.

My legs move faster than before. I'm hopeful. I haven't felt hope since Gospel started, since I started spreading a truth that couldn't have been more wrong. The cab's sitting in front of the building in the hot afternoon sun, Annabelle's body withering under the blanket. It takes all of my willpower to rifle through her belongings. I find a lighter, then another in her pocket. "Sorry, Annabelle, I know you'd want me to have these. I cover her back up and sprint toward the front doors.

Plastic arms throw me to the ground when I approach the store again. I don't know why I thought I'd get lucky again. Billy's posse ties me up, this time with bodies bigger than mine. "Couldn't take me down yourself, huh Billy? Once a weasel, always a weasel."

"Awfully smug for a man about to die." Bill works his way through the robots, gliding on his own slime, polishing the side of his gun.

"Smugness and confidence are two different things."

"I suppose everyone's entitled to die in the state of mind they see fit."

"It won't matter if you kill me." He cocks his head.

"Talk to me, Dougy." He pats me on one cheek and presses the gun into the other. "You're not being very clear."

"I've already won."

"You and I must have different definitions of winning, because all I see is a man who screwed up everything. One little tug of my finger and you're gone for good."

"The catalyst's already lit. I'm disposable now."

Billy runs to the store doors while his robots keep me stationary. "You." He glances back and points to one of his men. "Get inside and stop her."

"Won't make a difference."

Come on, punk. Bite.

I sneak my hand into the pocket of my slacks and fiddle with the mirror pieces.

"Shut your fucking mouth, Mason. You never should have been able to open it in the first place. I should have been the mayor's replacement." He walks closer to make the threat seem bigger.

"You see, whether you stop me, or Grace, or the boy, or all of us, who's going to stop them?"

Bill stares through the open doors at the dozens of people already transformed, running through the store with little bits of mirror, changing the world, taking back everything that was taken from them, and never looking back. "All of you, inside." He orders the rest of the men to leave except the big guy holding me in place.

"One dozen becomes two. Two becomes four. Four becomes four hundred." I fiddle with the pieces again.

"What are you doing?" He rushes thinking I have a gun. "Think you're going to pull a fast one on me? I do this shit every day. I've seen it all." He grabs my hand and pulls it from the pocket, one piece of mirror inside. "Let me see it." He opens my fist, unaware of how it works and takes the mirror to inspect it.

"Tell me what you see."

"You little shit; it's just a piece of glass."

"It's a mirror." I know he hasn't seen one since that day either.

"So?" His eyes make contact with the one's staring back, and the plastic melts from his eyes. "What's happening, Doug?"

"Purpose." I push the mirror closer to his face. "Keep looking."

Plastic from his forehead droops down his skin before slipping away to reveal the real Bill McCoy. He's an old man, just like me, and for the first time, he sees the world the way it is. One, two, three, four mannequins pass, and I can hear his wheels turning. "Everyone's plastic."

"Because of us."

"I don't understand."

"We took away their identities. We convinced them that they'd be happier as someone else. They'd be happier fitting into the crowd."

"It can't be real. How could something like this happen?"

"I doesn't matter how it happened. We know how to fix it now." The big guy holding me back loosens his grip, and I approach a faded long lost friend, Bill. "Will you help us?" I hold his face in my hands, looking for the boy who ran in the woods with me, the boy who called me brother, the boy whose life I saved.

Bill glances at the big guy and then back at me, connecting with memories while he scans my face.

"How do I know I can trust you?"

"You don't, I guess."

"You're not known for telling the truth, Dougy boy." He pulls away, and waves the big guy over—Joey, Johnny, Jimmy, whatever his name is. "You've never been good at telling the truth."

"Where's your sister, Bill? Do you know what happened to her?"

I shift the mirror to catch his reflection again, and more plastic melts.

"My sister? My sister?" He struggles with the memory. Bill steps closer and the big guy gives my neck a squeeze under his bicep.

"You had a sister, Bill. Her name was Nancy."

"Don't ever say that name again." His eyes strike gold. That memory has taken hold.

"Why? Is that because you can't remember, or you don't want to remember?"

"Shut up."

"Why?" I cup another piece of glass in my hand, hoping the big guy might take a glance at it and see his reflection. "She and my mother were experiments before this stuff worked." If they wanted me dead, I'd already have a bullet in my head.

"That's not true."

The big guy looks at my hand and jerks my neck when he sees his reflection, at first holding tight, but the longer he stares the less he's worried about my neck.

"You idiot, why are you letting go of him?" Bill rushes the big guy and smacks his face.

"Looks like you've lost another one." I hand the piece of mirror to the big guy and pull his arm off my neck.

"Nancy was sick; they tried to save her so she could join us."

My laugh is pathetic, pathetic for him. "Your sister died so we could live like immortals. Her pain, along with my mother's was for our benefit."

"Bullshit. The mayor said she refused to be a part of Gospel, and is probably still living in another town, or up there on the mountain."

"I wish that were true, Bill. But it's not. Death is not sacred here, never has been. You of all people know that. They killed our loved ones."

Plastic melts off his arms and chest.

"She chose to reject Gospel. She chose to start that band of rejects on the mountain, and she chose to cut me out of her life."

"No, she caught the chemists working on my mother and they made a guinea pig out of her. My mother was patient zero; your sister was the next victim."

"No, no, no! She made her choice." He mumbles, an old man with sagging skin watching the marching masses pass by us. "She's probably still there. On the mountain, I mean. We could go see her right now." Plastic melts.

"Go look then. Ask if anyone has seen her in forty-five years."

"Forty-five years?"

"How old do you think you are?"

He picks up a shard of mirror and looks into it again. "But we've only been in Gospel for a little while."

"Really? Look at yourself."

"But I'd remember."

"We live in a city with screens that sublimely control our lives. We have no calendars, no birthdays, nothing to celebrate the past. Hell, you know that, you run it now."

"I just keep the programs running; push the shelf life button when it turns red." He takes a seat on a step. "Forty-five years?"

"I'm sorry."

The last bit of plastic flows to his feet, tears stream down his face. "They killed Nancy, and I've been a part of it?"

"She wouldn't have held it against you. She would have been here had she not seen what they did to my mother."

He touches his skin for the first time, the skin of a man, not the skin of a machine, a robot, a mannequin, a nobody. "I don't know how much I can do, but I'll help."

"Thank you."

"The people in that department store need our help." I point to the doors.

He hugs my torso despite the sweat and blood, a genuine hug, a simple apology, something I'd forgotten.

"We need to help Grace inside. They need more mirrors and good lighting." We struggle to our feet, pushing and nudging each other, an old man helping an old man, and together we approach the doors.

Grace stands in the lines, using her sweet voice to bring people to their senses, and plastic melts over the clean department store floors. Xavier still stands at the edge of the inferno to save the ones closest to destruction. He's tired, arms growing limp. I run to his side, and the overhead lights come on and the fire dies. I motion to the door and nudge him to help in the outer room. I bow in thanks and he runs up the stairway.

The bodies pile toward me, and I hold mirrors in both hands, "Look, look, look." The plastic melts, and it's Bert Lesley. "I don't have time to answer questions, Bert. Please, take this and hold it in front of every plastic body you see. Help me save them."

Bert finds his bearings and leaves with his piece of mirror. I melt the next body coming toward me, and the next and the next and the next. Soon the gaps in the line are much larger because they are saving each other.

Not sure where Bill found more mirror, but he joins me, passing out mirror pieces to every person saved, breaking them smaller and smaller to reach as many bodies as we can. No words, no explanations, we move from person to person until the room fills with color and faces while the black disappears.

"Where do we go from here?" John asks.

I look around the room of living, breathing people. Grace, Xavier, and dozens of others move into the streets with pieces of mirrors, transforming the world, enforcing a chain reaction. I look around the department at all the cream, enough product to cover the planet. Aware that other Gospels probably exist out there. "Bill, do you ship this stuff out?"

He sighs. "Two places."

"Is this the only processing plant?"

"I don't know."

"Well, we need to make sure that the other two locations don't get supplies."

He leads me into another room, a warehouse with boxes and boxes, high to the rafters, of cream, cream processed from humans we once called friends.

"These need to be destroyed."

Bill nods. "I'll take care of it."

"The central program, the screens, everything that is Gospel, needs to go."

I leave Bill to his task and go out front to dazed Gospelites; people are just discovering they are people. I direct the people who've been saved. I should have done this long ago, been the leader they needed. The people congregate around my like winding DNA.

The room fills with familiar faces, or at least I think I recognize them. It's been so many years since I've seen most of them.

Bill runs, as fast as an old person can, out of the warehouse and into the hallway. "Time to go, this place is going up in flames." He turns to all the people freed from the slavery of perfection. "Go to your penthouses and get what's worth keeping and leave. Gospel has no rudder."

I whisper, "Is the program still running?"

"I'll take care of it."

"You remember when the mayor made us get rid of everything?"

"Yeah."

Looks like we are circling back around to the same thing."

Bill smiles. "Yeah, guess we are, except, none of this shit means anything to me."

"Me neither."

"Everyone, get out of here, this place is going to be engulfed in a minute." Bill's the real leader. He's a natural and everyone heeds his warning.

Smoke billows through the crack in the door and Bill nods to the exit. "That means us too."

As we leave, I turn to see the flames flail through the room like tentacles of serpent.

Outside, Grace is waiting with Xavier. "Um, I think you have a monster on your hands, Bill."

The flames shoot into the main room, and Bill sighs. "It's getting too big,"

I pull Grace and Xavier back, short of breath and panicked. "Fuck. Destroy one monster, create another. Let's just get as far away as we can."

I pick up Xavier, and rest him on my shoulders "Let's go, Grace. We're going to run as fast as we can." I turn one last time to make sure all the people in the store are gone. Bill has left for the program shutoff, and there are still masses of Gospelites who live in plastic coverings, unaware that they will soon be aware. The rest of them are probably waiting for me to make things right, and right is pure destruction of perfection.

Every person who has been released, I warn. "The flames are growing, and there's no knowing when they'll stop. We are not set up for a disaster like this. We need to think fast on our feet. Grace and I will be moving west. I know I've steered you wrong before, but I hope you'll join us. We're stronger as a group. If you see anyone who hasn't been released from the plastic, convert them the same we you were converted."

Behind us, the flames eat away at the walls of the department store.

"We have to act fast," Grace says to anyone who doesn't know where to go. "Stay with us. Stay strong. Keep one another safe. We have no idea what might happen"

A Gospel "Special Guest" bus cuts past the burning building, rushing toward us. It pulls up alongside Grace and the tinted window slides open. Ashton grins. "Bill says programs off, how about we gather as many people as we can. I suspect the department store is going to ignite the rest of the high rises." A flow of people pile into the bus.

"Take everyone west, just on the outskirts of the high rises. Come back and get more. "We'll be walking."

"Are you sure, I have room."

"Trust me, you won't as you drive."

We moved west, and dozens joined us. Dozens turn to hundreds, hundreds to thousands, thousands as far as the eye can see. Ashton picked up fifty at a time. Chances were we'd be on foot the rest of the way.

Chapter 38

Gospel started as a city offering infinite opportunities to anyone who could afford it. It didn't take long for it to consume the world, built *by* the best, built *for* the best, and once the best arrived, everyone else followed. Black people, white people, Jews, Buddhists, Catholics, factory workers, bus drivers, fathers, husbands, uncles, wives—they gave up everything, some even their children, for a new identity, hoping we could change them into someone else. We did.

We offered a service unlike any other, permanent cures for insecurity and doubt, a sense of community, a truth never proven wrong. We hunted the world for perfect human specimens and designed the silhouettes in their images. The woman—breasts neither too large nor too small, long legs, tanned, crystal eyes, shining hair, full lips, thin waist, firm butt, porcelain skin. The man—chiseled chest, strong chin, thick hair, solid arms, abs, straight white teeth, perfect skin, deep voice. I was that man many years ago.

He's dead now.

Chapter 39

We pass the remnants of dumping grounds of our past, walking through it like ants on a farm, carrying any bits of our former lives we can hold, searching for a safe place to avoid the flames, but it won't be in Gospel. The flames consume every street and we can't stop it. Bill has turned off all water, and ordered the fire department to stand down. We move west, finding destinations only miles away that we haven't ventured to in forty-five years. We never left the screens; they tethered us to our existence in Gospel.

"I need to rest, Doug." Grace collapses to her knees on a trail to somewhere.

"We can't stop moving, Gracie. The flames are right behind us."

"I can't."

I put Xavier down. "Are you okay to walk on your own?" He nods his head, forced to be stronger than a child should need to be. "I want you to hold onto my pocket at all times, and if you need me, yell as loud as you can." He nods his head again, thankfully understanding my lips and gestures, and I pull Grace into my arms and hold her close to my chest while we keep moving west.

"You're taking us to the woods, Jax," Bill says from behind me. "Fire and trees don't mix."

"That's not where we're going." I say it as quietly as I can to avoid the others hearing. I don't need a riot. I've seen enough riots for one lifetime.

"I don't understand."

"We're going to the mountain."

Bill stops in his tracks. "With the tribes?"

"Yes."

"They'll kill us, though, won't they?"

"No, they won't. Turns out they've been keeping a helpful eye on us all along. They'll help us."

"How do you know that?"

"Because they already have." I nod toward the Xavier, and Bill stays quiet.

We reach the woods of the mountain, and we sift through the trees. "We're almost there, everyone. I know you're tired and hungry and scared, but I think we'll be safe."

No birds singing, no bugs chirping. Everyone's had the good sense to get out of here while the going's good. The clan behind me follow suit and maintain the silence. They've lost the energy to converse about the future, until we reach the bottom of the mountain.

"I know what you're thinking, but I've seen for myself that they're willing to help us. They're willing to set aside our differences. Some of them are even willing to die for us. Don't be afraid." I find my footing, step after step on the mountain, turn and smile at the sight of thousands of faces climbing below me. Xavier leads the way, showing the rest of us the safest way to the top, and soon we're stepping over the ledge.

The mountain people stare back at us, and for once, there's no difference between us, no barriers, no plastic, people staring at people.

"We've been waiting for you," a man stands next to one of the huts. "We've made accommodations, but we didn't expect this many of you."

"We're grateful for any help you can offer." I reach out to shake his hand, worlds colliding, peace breeding, lives blending, and the crowds fill every inch of the small village to watch the city burn.

"The fire won't touch us here," I sit Grace on the edge of the mountain.

I haven't the slightest idea what the fire can do. She holds my hands, and Xavier sits on my lap while we drink water.

"What happens now?" The city burns to ash around us, destroyed to the ends of the earth, and there's nothing left.

"Start over, I guess." I hold them both closer to me. "Be happy."

"I vaguely remember you saying that once before."
She winks. "Want to hear something funny?"

"What's that?"

"I was happy before all of this."

The people around us chime in, "We were happy, too."

Bill echoes, "I was skinny and awkward. Didn't have a date until I was 19. Couldn't connect with my parents or teachers, and was ashamed of whom I was, but when I went to school, I felt complete. I could accept my other faults, knowing I had a strength. I couldn't remember it until today, but I was happy, too."

Another man stands. "I was a plumber. My wife was never happy with that. She was never happy with my weight or hair loss, and she left me for someone else. For the longest time, I blamed myself. Told myself if I only looked better, I would have had a better job, that she would have stayed with me. I know now that none of that is true."

A woman admitted, "I wanted a child, and couldn't have one. I would have done anything for a child, and I thought the only way to impress a man was with big breasts and long legs. Well, I had the breasts and legs, and all the wrong men came running. I know now that I'm beautiful; however I look on the outside."

Ashton cuts through the murmuring, "I tried to fill a void. I drank, did drugs, had sex, spent money, whatever I could to help make up for everything I didn't have growing up. I thought I needed to be accepted, I needed to fit in. I didn't want to feel alone anymore, but it turns out, everything I worked for was surface deep."

The crowd soaks in the realization that we had everything backwards.

"I'm Doug Mason." I hand Xavier to Grace and stood on the edge of the mountain. "I'm an old man, and in all my years, I've learned one thing. I don't need to be beautiful to be respected. I don't need to be beautiful to find love. I don't need to be beautiful to have success. I let the world convince me I needed to be something I wasn't. I have strengths and weaknesses, and it's okay to accept them both. I'm an old, gray, caring, white trash shithead, and I'm happy."

The fire consumes the stars. Hours fill with silence and what ifs, and when the flames die at the base of the hill, laughter lights the night, shrouding the end of the world in a layer of possibilities.

BIO

Stephanie Vichinsky studied creative writing at Eastern Washington University. Her writing focuses on the universality of human nature, the good, the bad, and everything in between. She grew up in the Pacific Northwest, sledding, swimming, hiking, and biking in a place where there truly are four seasons. She owns a dog training company in Idaho with her Husband, Julius, and her daughter, Leah.

randall 'Jay' andrews lives in Southern California and runs JaCol Publishing and R.A. Editing Services after a 25 year writing career in Los Angeles. All of his work, as well as that of all the authors at JaCol Publishing, can be found at www.jacolpublishing.com